Marshal South Rides Again

His Anza-Borrego Novels

Marshal South's author photo that appeared on the cover of
Flame of Terrible Valley

Praise For *Marshal South Rides Again: His Anza-Borrego Novels*

It is an easy read, a fun read, and a book you will not be able to put down. You will feel the desert heat, the suspense, and excitement in two novels that were overlooked for decades, until now. Buy and read this great treasure of western literature.

—Don Bendell, author of number one best-selling western *Strongheart* with over 3,000,000 copies of his 26 books in print.

Marshal South was as compelling a man as his writings, and his books were every bit as good as the best works of Zane Grey. Timeless prose and storylines, glowing descriptions and characters—readers would be hard-pressed to find a Western on the bookshelves today that are any better.

—Steven Law, best-selling author of *Yuma Gold* and president of ReadWest Foundation

Marshal South is a terrific storyteller; his books are filled with tense situations, intriguing mystery and prose that'll keep you turning the pages. Western action not to be missed.

—Steve Myall, *Western Fiction Review*

Major kudos to Sunbelt for giving Marshal South his due place as a major American literary voice, shoulder to shoulder with American Western greats such as Zane Grey and Louis l'Amour, and sharing another piece of the old American Desert West…with a whole new generation of readers.

—Ruth Nolan, Professor of creative writing, College of the Desert, and editor of *No Place for a Puritan: the literature of California's deserts*

Marshal South knows how to rivet your attention right from the first page with foreboding, exciting scenes. That skill evidences itself nowhere better than in these two novels…Robbery Range in particular gives us the very finest work of this unjustly forgotten author whose own life makes a fine tale in itself.

—Fred Woodworth, *Mystery & Adventure Series Review*

Marshal South Rides Again

His Anza-Borrego Novels

Edited and with a foreword by
Diana Lindsay

Sunbelt Publications
San Diego, California

Marshal South Rides Again: His Anza-Borrego Novels

Sunbelt Publications, Inc.
Copyright © 2013 by Rider South
All rights reserved. First edition 2013

Edited by Diana Lindsay
Cover and book design by Leah Cooper
Project management by Deborah Young
Printed in the United States of America

Sunbelt Publications, Inc.
P.O. Box 191126
San Diego, CA 92159-1126
(619) 258-4911, fax: (619) 258-4916
www.sunbeltbooks.com

17 16 15 14 13   5 4 3 2 1

Library of Congress Cataloging-in-Publication Data

South, Marshal.
 [Novels. Selections]
 Marshal South rides again : his Anza-Borrego novels. , First edition
    pages cm
 ISBN 978-0-932653-12-3 (alk. paper)
 1. Anza-Borrego Desert (Calif.)--Fiction. I. South, Marshal Flame of terrible valley. II. South, Marshal Robbery range. III. Title.
 PS3569.O75A6 2013
 813'.54--dc23
                        2013013867

Credits:
Front and Back Cover: Original book covers designed by John Long, Ltd. (London) and World's Work Ltd. (Surrey)

Map Page 9: Lowell Lindsay, digitized by Ben Pease, from *Marshal South and the Ghost Mountain Chronicles: An Experiment in Priitive Living* (San Diego: Sunbelt Publications, 2005)

Interior Photos and Illustrations: See photo credit on page 309.

To Lucile Iverson South ...

She helped Marshal South live again through her interview with
Rider South for the introduction to *Marshal South and the
Ghost Mountain Chronicles: An Experiment in Primitive Living.*

Lucile began dancing professionally at age 16. She was the beloved wife of Rider South, Marshal South's oldest son. Rider said this about Lucile who lived until she was 100 years old: "I am very proud of her. Even though she never finished high school, she taught at San Diego State University for 20 years."

Lucile Iverson South, author of
**Dancing Thru Life on Toes
of Gold**

CONTENTS

CONTENTS (CONT.)

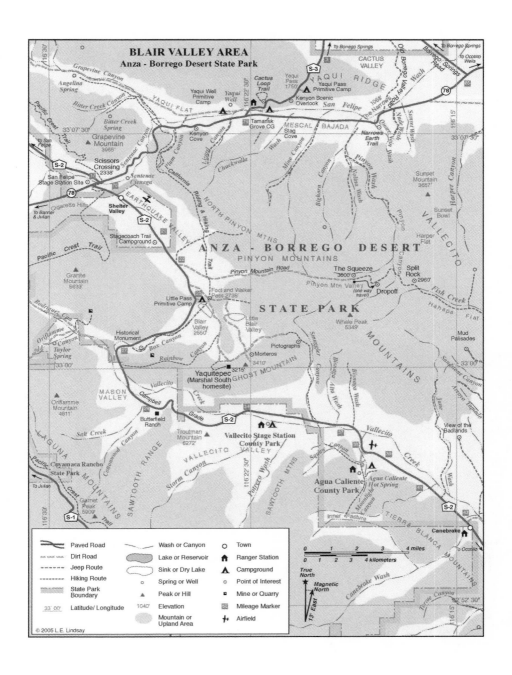

BLAIR VALLEY AREA
Anza - Borrego Desert State Park

CACTUS VALLEY

To Borrego Springs
To Borrego Springs
To Ocotillo Wells

YAQUI RIDGE

S-3

Grapevine Canyon

Angelina Spring

Bitter Creek Canyon

YAQUI FLAT

Yaqui Well Primitive Camp

Yaqui Well

Cactus Loop Trail

Yaqui Pass 1750'

Yaqui Pass Primitive Camp

Kenyon Scenic Overlook

Stag Cove

San Felipe

MESCAL BAJADA

78

Pacific Crest Trail

Bitter Creek Spring

Grapevine Mountain 3955'

Kenyon Cove

Tamarisk Grove CG

Wash

Mine Canyon

Narrows Earth Trail

To San Felipe

33°07'30"

Plum Canyon

Ligal Canyon

Chuckwalla

Bighorn Canyon

Pinyon Wash

Nolina Wash

Narrows

Quartz Vein Wash

Nude Wash

Sunset Wash

Pinyon Wash

Harper Canyon

Sunset Mountain 3657'

33°07'30"

S-2

San Felipe Stage Station Site

78

Scissors Crossing 2338'

Sentenac Canyon

California Riding & Hiking Trail

NORTH PINYON MTNS

Sentenac Cienega

Sunset Bowl

VALLECITO

Cigarette Hills

To Banner & Julian

Shelter Valley

EARTHQUAKE VALLEY

S-2

Harper Flat

Stagecoach Trail Campground

ANZA - BORREGO DESERT

PINYON MOUNTAINS

Pacific Crest Trail

Granite Mountain 5633'

Pinyon Mountain Road

The Squeeze 3600'

Split Rock 2960'

Foot and Walker Pass 2735'

Pinyon Mtn Valley (one way travel)

Dropoff

Fish Creek

STATE PARK

Hanspa Flat

Little Pass Primitive Camp

MOUNTAINS

Mud Palisades

Rodriguez Cyn

Oriflamme Canyon

Taylor Spring

Historical Monument

Blair Valley 2550'

Little Blair Valley

Whale Peak 5349'

Box Canyon

Rainbow Canyon

Pictographs

Morteros

Sandstone Canyon

33°00'

33°00'

Oriflamme Mountain 4811'

MASON VALLEY

Vallecito Creek

Campbell Grade

3215'

3410'

Yaquitepec (Marshal South homesite)

GHOST MOUNTAIN

Smuggler Canyon

Arroyo Tapiado

LAGUNA

Butterfield Ranch

Troutman Mountain 6272'

Salt Creek

Cottonwood Canyon

VALLECITO

Storm Canyon

S-2

Vallecito Stage Station County Park

VALLEY

Borrego Ato Wash

Bisnaga Wash

Vallecito

Vallecito Creek

View of the Badlands

Cuyamaca Rancho State Park

MOUNTAINS

Pacific Crest Trail

SAWTOOTH RANGE

Sawtooth MTNS

Palpayo Wash

Squaw Canyon

Agua Caliente County Park

Agua Caliente Hot Spring

Moonlight Canyon

Wash

To Julian

Garnet Peak 5909'

S-1

TIERRA BLANCA

Inner Pasture

S-2

Canebrake

MOUNTAINS

To Ocotillo

32°52'30"

Canebrake Wash

Coyote Canyon

≈ Paved Road		Wash or Canyon	○	Town
Dirt Road		Lake or Reservoir	♠	Ranger Station
Jeep Route		Sink or Dry Lake	▲	Campground
Hiking Route	○	Spring or Well	⊙	Point of Interest
State Park Boundary	▲	Peak or Hill	▣	Mine or Quarry
33°00' Latitude/Longitude	1040'	Elevation	⌗	Mileage Marker
		Mountain or Upland Area	✛	Airfield

0   1   2   3   4 miles
0   1   2   3   4 kilometers

True North
Magnetic North
13° East

© 2005 L.E. Lindsay

Marshal South as the "hero" model for his western novels

FOREWORD

By Diana Lindsay

The enigmatic Marshal South of the Anza-Borrego desert region remains a controversial character to this day, and perhaps that is what makes him so interesting.

He was a prolific writer of poetry and prose beginning while still a teenager in Adelaide, South Australia, and continuing until he died at the age of 59 in 1948. He wrote more than 90 poems; about 30 newspaper articles, essays, and stories; 97 *Desert Magazine* articles; 54 other magazine articles and stories; 12 books; and 8 booklets, plays, and greeting cards. He was also a talented artist who painted, made pottery, and designed jewelry.

His earlier life as a writer, debater, militia organizer/supporter, and adventurer was overshadowed by his controversial lifestyle and his experiment in primitive living during the 1930s and 1940s that were featured in his *Desert Magazine* articles written between 1939 and 1948. The fact that he was the poet laureate of Oceanside and was considered being named the poet laureate of the United States is virtually unknown as is the fact that he was the founder and president of the Oceanside chapter of the American Defense League. When the local chapter became amalgamated with the San Diego chapter, he became the organization's national

representative. He even met with Theodore Roosevelt in San Diego to discuss the policies and objectives of that organization and also foreign threats to the San Diego area.

It is the latter years that have colored his history. Images of his family living on a waterless mountaintop leave a lasting impression. He and his wife Tanya had moved to Ghost Mountain following the Great Depression as an alternative to joining a bread line. They had chosen a life of "freedom" from all societal obligations and most material possessions, living in isolation, practicing nudism, and professing a return to nature and spiritualism.

Marshal South thrived in this environment. Many of his desert writings inspired a generation of readers to learn more about what the desert has to offer—peace, solitude, health, inspiration, mystery and lore. He was passionate about the desert, and like his publisher Randall Henderson who reflected about the "Two Deserts" in his famous November 1937 editorial in the first edition of *Desert Magazine*, South advocated discovering the *real* desert which is spellbinding.

The South Family at Yaquitepec, 1946

He wrote, "*If you love it, it will hold you and draw you as will no other land on earth.*" And, if you see only danger and a wasteland, "*you will fly from it and never wish to see its face again.*" He advocated leaving civilization behind to find the real meaning of life through simple living and by becoming one with nature. He took inspiration for his writings from things he observed around him and shared with others in his published works. Typical of these nature/inspiring works is the following poem entitled "Giant Cacti" printed below:

Giant Cacti

Against the skyline rim or in the sand,
They loom, these sentinels of a lonely land,
Guarding from dawn to dusk the waste untrod,
Where broods the Silence and the Peace of God.

Here in this desert land of sun and sky,
Beyond man's grasp of greed the hours drift by,
Marked only by the wheeling buzzard's flight,
And by lone coyote wails at dawn and night.

Starlight and noon and dark—the seasons pass,
Soft as the shadows through thin desert grass.
No fevered "Progress" here, no turning wheel;
No roar of crowds or clang of steel on steel.

Only the desert peace, and in the shade
Of mesquite or of greasewood, sherds, once made
By Indian potters, o'er whose hopes and fears —
And graves—the sands have rolled a thousand years.

Giant, towering, desert cacti; when the roar
Of cities and their crowds shall be no more,
Still will their wasteland breed, with arms upthrust,
Keep lonely vigil when mankind is dust.

It shocked readers of *Desert Magazine* when the divorce occurred, as there was no real indication of problems within the family that was detected by readers in the monthly articles. Two years after the divorce, Marshal South died and was buried in an unmarked grave in the Julian cemetery. After a fire destroyed cemetery records some years later, even the location of his grave was lost until recently.

South also contributed to his own cloudy story. He had concealed his earlier life which was only slowly uncovered after Tanya's passing in 1997. He had stated he was born in London, England, but in fact

Roy Bennett Richards, aka Marshal South, drew this self-portrait while living in Adelaide, South Australia

he was born in South Australia as Roy Bennett Richards. He adopted the pen name of Marshal South when he began writing in the United States, and kept that pseudonym for his own name and for all of his writings after 1912. He was encouraged to select a pen name for his writings because his mother was concerned that his father in Australia would find them. Annie Richards had left her husband and had taken the two boys to America.

South chose this pen name probably because he was from South Australia and because he was fascinated by the American West and military preparedness, whether it was fear of the "Yellow Peril"—a phobia common in his early youth in Australia, or concern about impending involvement in World War I for the United States.

During his teen years in Adelaide he wrote stories about the American West. In 1905 he wrote a short story entitled "A Dangerous Tale" with a Texas setting. In that same year he also wrote another short story entitled "The Second Gun: The Story of a Great Revenge." He was interested in how the country was protected in the American West which would have led him to think about the role of U.S. Marshals. The fact that he chose to spell his first name as a "marshal" vs. the common name Marshall is another indication of his thinking. He may also have liked the double meaning of "marshal" as in ushering or leading in ceremoniously. He may have viewed himself as taking a lead in being an author of western fiction.

South also became familiar with the American Southwest and Mexico when he began exploring those areas soon after he arrived in the United States sometime after September 1907. Those early trips provided the background he needed for some of his later novels in which the action takes place along border towns just south of the international border with the United States. His fascination with guns and national defense led to his organizing the Oceanside Rifle Club which became part of the National Rifle Association a few years later. He also organized a local militia and became its "captain" and founded a monthly magazine entitled *Defense* "devoted to the encouragement of public interest in matters of National Defense." His poetry also reflected his concerns about war and defense of the country, earning him the title of "the warrior poet."

In 1916 South moved to Arizona and served with the Transportation Division of the Army Quartermaster Corps. Some photographs of South, taken while living in Arizona at that time, show him in western attire, sometimes riding a horse or holding a gun, obviously enjoying his image as being part of the western frontier. However, he did not begin writing in earnest about the American West until after he had married Tanya Lehrer in 1923. He began concentrating on the publication of his novels when he was already living on Ghost Mountain.

His first novel, *Child of Fire*, originally appeared in a five-part series in *Ranch Romances* in 1928. It was later published in 1935, simultaneously with *Flame of Terrible Valley* by London publisher John Long, Ltd., who had this to say about South's first

South riding his horse in Arizona

two novels: *"Flame of Terrible Valley* and *Child of Fire*...are strong stuff, but in the best senses, that of excitement, colour and originality. There is, in our opinion, no doubt that Marshal South is to be classed as one of the finest Western storytellers of today."

By 1936, he had four western novels published by this publisher: the two listed above plus *Juanita of the Border Country* and *Gunsight*. Like *Child of Fire*, *Gunsight* was also previously published. It appeared in a six-part serial in *Rangeland Love Story Magazine* in 1930-31.

The cover jacket for *Juanita of the Border Country* included high praise for his first two novels. The *East Anglican Times* reported that "Marshal South is an American who is capable of producing vivid fiction, and these examples of his creative ability will win appreciation. They are distinguished by resourceful inventiveness and power of expression...." The *Bristol Evening Post* stated: "Marshal South should speedily rise to the fore as one of the most original and interesting writers of Western stories," and the *Dundee Courier* said, "Mr. South is

South portrait painted by Thomas Crocker

a newcomer to Western fiction, but he is likely to create a permanent place for himself in the affection of the public."

Other books would follow, with all of them following a basic formula, differing only in the setting and the characters. There was always a treasure, a damsel in distress, a hero with sterling qualities that prevailed over the villains and won the heart of the damsel, and all the books were cliffhangers. To his London audience he promoted himself as an American western novelist with "a drop of Red Indian blood in his veins."

Whether he actually had "Indian blood in his veins" is unknown. His grandfather Thomas Richards was from Wisconsin and it is possible he could have had an Indian ancestor. On the other hand, it could just have been marketing hype to help the books sell. Marshal did have a history of embellishing his credentials for his audience, having claimed that he served in the British Army and that Tanya was a graduate of Columbia University, neither of which was true.

Rider South, Marshal South's oldest child who was born in 1934, stated in *Marshal South and the Ghost Mountain Chronicles* (San Diego: Sunbelt Publications, 2005) that his father had written his western novels before any children were born to this family. His novels were originally rejected when submitted for publication, but with the beginning of World War II and interest in Americans, they found a British audience. Marshal South worked with the Charles Lavelle Literary Agency to place his books.

Additional novels were published in the 1940s, including *Robbery Range, Tiburon: Isle of the Sharks, The Gold of the Gods,* and *The Curse of the Sightless Fish. Robbery Range* was published in 1943 by World's Work Limited in Kingswood, Surrey, Great Britain.

Speaking about the sales of his father's books, Rider South said, "His books sold well because he had a wonderful way of describing the Southwest. His characters were alive and vibrant. His stories of adventure were fascinating and held the reader's attention until the last page. Before he had married Mother he had traveled in Arizona, New Mexico, and Mexico, which gave him the background material for his stories."

Rider also explained that as the years went on both Marshal and Tanya changed their views and became more environmentally conscious. Their stories became more philosophical. "Mother mentioned God more often in her poetry. While Father still had the talent for writing the Wild West stories, he didn't care to write them anymore," he explained.

When Marshal South met Tanya, she was active with the Rosicrucian Fellowship in Oceanside. She was deeply religious and became a major influence in directing Marshal's thoughts toward the spiritual realm.

Four of South's novels remain unpublished manuscripts. Two of those were children's books. A third was based on life at Yaquitepec, his Ghost Mountain home, and the last was a religious tract.

It is very rare to come across a copy of one of Marshal South's published novels. They are collector's items and command a high price. Two of those novels are of special interest to those who visit the Anza-Borrego desert region: *Flame of Terrible Valley* and *Robbery Range*.

The setting for these novels are areas that Marshal South regularly visited while he lived on Ghost Mountain in Blair Valley: Julian, Banner, Earthquake (Shelter) Valley, Pinyon and Vallecito mountains, Little Blair Valley, Blair Valley, Smuggler Canyon, Box Canyon, Rodriguez Canyon, Mason Valley, Rainbow Canyon, Vallecito Valley, the Vallecito Stage Station, Agua Caliente Hot Springs, Vallecito Badlands, and Carrizo Gorge. The descriptions of some of the landmarks of the area will be familiar to the reader. They are described in Marshal's terms before County Highway S-2 was designated and later paved. He wrote of a time period of which he was very familiar, when the first cars and jalopies (flivvers) were on the road and transportation by horse was often a preferred choice for the backcountry.

Some adventurous readers may enjoy exploring the trails and the byways along the Highway S-2 corridor to speculate on Marshal's place names to compare with today's geographic counterparts. South wrote details of local topography that provide clues to actual locations. Descriptions of surrounding desert plants also help to identify possible geographical locations.

In *Flame of Terrible Valley*, the Vallecito Stage Station is described as "a sinister, crumbling ruin, which is said to be haunted." The story, according to the publisher's promotion "deals with the dogged vengeance of a Chinese Tong and the quest for stolen gold." The inspiration for this story came from two sources. One of which was Tanya's experience of camping at the old stage station ruins in the 1920s when she felt the presence of ghostly apparitions and told Marshal that she did not want to camp there anymore. Marshal was also aware of stories from his neighbor to the north in Earthquake Valley, Stewart Hathaway, who had purchased the old Las Arena Ranch, originally owned by Edward R. Burns. It was rumored that Burns was involved in smuggling Chinese into the United States from Mexico. Burns also mysteriously died on the ranch. Chinese jade was found on the premises after his death. The fascination with the possibility of Chinese smugglers being part of the area history played a role in his two novels published here.

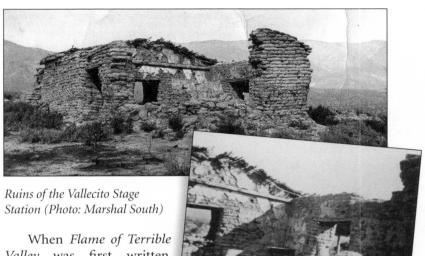

Ruins of the Vallecito Stage Station (Photo: Marshal South)

When *Flame of Terrible Valley* was first written in the 1930s, derogatory phrases used for the Chinese ("Chink," "Chinaman," "Yellow Devil," or "Oriental") and Mexicans ("Greaser," "Dago," or "Mex") were being used in

(Photo: Used with permission, California State Parks)

some quarters. These phrases have not been changed in this reprinting as they reflect the usage of that day and of the characters that Marshal South wished to portray. Also words no longer in common usage, such as "electric torch" or "torch" for a flashlight or "flivver" for an old car or jalopy have also been retained.

In *Robbery Range* the historic Wahrenbrock's Book House on Broadway in downtown San Diego was the inspiration for the beginning of this story. South as an avid reader would have been very familiar with this landmark San Diego bookstore. The early legends surrounding the Vallecito Stage Station were weaved into the story and inspired a reference to the "Lost Woman of Carrizo" which was probably based on Vallecito's "Lady in White." Some of the local homesteads, cattle ranches, and cattlemen of the area were used as models for characters he described.

This later novel written some 12 years after *Flame of Terrible Valley* and after living on Ghost Mountain for about 10 years reflects more of Marshal's thoughts about the desert's mysteries and his spiritual beliefs than the previous book. By then he had been highly influenced by Tanya who studied astrology, believed in the supernatural, and followed the teaching of the Rosicrucians. Desert solitude and silence became vehicles that led to questioning the meaning of life and death and of the existence of reincarnation and other-worldly possibilities.

South also had time to reflect about the area's early history. From the top of Ghost Mountain, where the South family made their home, the route followed by the Butterfield Overland Stage along the Southern Emigrant Trail is clearly visible. It is easy to contemplate what those early days may have been like as stages stopped at Vallecito, worked their way through Box Canyon, and crossed Blair Valley and the Foot and Walker Pass before entering Earthquake and San Felipe valleys. South's fascination with the Butterfield and the many legends associated with Vallecito Stage Station inspired him to write the following poem, printed in *Desert Magazine* in November 1947. The poem not only reflects South's poetic artistry but also sets the stage for the novels that follow:

The Tracks of the Overland Stage

There's a valley I know in the wastelands,
    Where, down through the greasewood and sage,
Like a dim, ghostly thread from the years that have fled
    Stretch the tracks of the Overland Stage.
Lone, ghostly and dim in the starlight;
    Grey, desolate and pale in the dawn,
Blurred by heat-waves at noon — still o'er mesa and dune
    Wind the tracks of the wheels that have gone.
Old coaches whose wheels long have mouldered,
    Old stage-teams whose hoofs long are dust;
Still, faint and age-greyed, wind the old wheel-ruts made
    By tires long since crumbled to rust.
And down where the silence lies deepest —
    Like a lone, crumbling bead on a thread —
In the mesquite-grown sands the old stage-station stands,
    Hushed with memories — and ghosts of the dead.
The desert rays wake not its brooding.
    But oft 'neath the star-powered sky,
Round the walls on dark nights there move dim, ghostly lights,
    As once more the old stages sweep by.
And again, across dune, wash and mesa,
    As the dead years turn back on their page,
Pass the dim, racing teams from a ghost-world of dreams,
    Down the tracks of the Overland Stage.

Tracks of the Butterfield Overland Stage, San Felipe Valley
(Photo: Diana Lindsay)

This new printing of the two books is made possible through the Marshal South estate via his eldest son, Rider South. It is Rider's wish that readers rediscover his father's writing talent and that they have fun reading these western cliffhangers. Rider is proud of his father's talent as a poet, writer, and artist. He loved his father and felt the public was overly harsh in its criticism and judgment of Marshal South. Marshal South's choices in life need to be separated from his talent as a poet and writer.

For more information on Marshal South's earlier life, daily life on Ghost Mountain, and to read all of his articles printed in *Desert Magazine*, see *Marshal South and the Ghost Mountain Chronicles: An Experiment in Primitive Living* (San Diego: Sunbelt Publications, 2005).

The task of republishing the two novels in this book was made easier by the assistance of Fred Woodworth, the publisher and editor of *The Mystery & Adventure Series Review* in Tucson, Arizona. Woodworth took the time to scan each page of the original books and provided copies to me for this publication. Lowell Lindsay provided editorial insights.

Yucca and Cacti.   *Linoleum blockprint by Marshal South.*

FLAME of TERRIBLE VALLEY

by

MARSHAL SOUTH

Originally published in 1935:
John Long, Limited
34, 35 & 36 Paternoster Row
London, E.C.4

Printed in Great Britain:
Anchor Press
Tiptree, Essex

FLAME OF TERRIBLE VALLEY

MARSHAL SOUTH

MARSHAL SOUTH

Author of "CHILD OF FIRE"
(Uniform with this volume)

BOTH FIRST
PUBLICATIONS

First
Publication

FLAME
OF
TERRIBLE
VALLEY

3'6
NET

REDUCED TO
1'6

C.4

CHAPTER ONE

The White Terror

Jim Brandon stopped with a startled jerk and faced round in his tracks. The thing was still following him—over his shoulder, as he had glanced back, he had seen it again. And this time it had been much closer.

Brandon was no craven—in all his twenty-eight years of life he had never been accused of cowardice—but as he stood there in the gloom of the thickening dusk and strained his eyes back into the shadows that cloaked the lonely desert trail over which his plodding footsteps had carried him, he was conscious of something that was uncomfortably like terror.

The spectral silent shape that for the past mile had trailed him through the shadows of the creosote bushes was uncanny. Each time that he had glanced back he had caught a fleeting glimpse of it—yet each time when he had halted and stared into the darkness of the back trail it was gone. Yet he was certain that he was not mistaken; the flash glimpses that he had had of it were sufficient to convince him that his eyes were playing him no tricks. The thing—whatever it was—was ghostly white. It moved without sound of footfall.

Brandon strained his ears, listening. But no sound came to him through the thickening night. The silence of the desert was absolute. And once more—as it had done so many times already—the queer, pale shape that followed him had melted and vanished again into the blotting obscurity of the mesquites and creosotes that bordered the sandy road.

In spite of himself, Brandon felt shaken and unnerved. Had it been daylight—had it been any other section of California—had he had a horse under him even—he would have laughed at the strange fear which, since the coming of evening, had begun to lay hold upon him—a fear which had reached a climax with the discovery of the pale, persistent shape that was dogging his footsteps. At any other time or place he would have dismissed his apprehensions without a second thought.

But now, however, he felt far from sure of his nerve. The toilsome tramp through the foothills and the waterless misery of his all-day plodding through the sand of the seemingly interminable trail that led up the valley had sapped his physical endurance to the point of exhaustion. His feet, swollen and blistered from the torture of walking in high-heeled boots, gave him misery with each step, and his body still ached dully from the bruises he had sustained that morning when his pony had fallen, crashing into the canyon.

Added to all this was the agony of a burning thirst. Jim Brandon was near the point of physical collapse, and it did not help his thin remnant of resistance to remember that this desolate desert valley under the black shadow of the towering Laguna Mountains had a sinister reputation. Wild tales were told about it. Many of the old-timers who knew its history avoided it, and the few surviving Indians of the region, dwelling now on reservations high up in the mountains that bordered the valley to the westward, steadfastly refused to descend into it.

Swaying unsteadily on his weary feet, and peering uneasily into the bulking gloom of the shadows from which the white sandy ribbon of the trail emerged wanly, Brandon cursed himself for a fool. Why, he asked himself, hadn't he gone on direct to Yuma?—that was where he'd been headed for until the tales of that old fool Seth Ross in Jacumba had fired his curiosity.

Once back in Arizona he'd have got a job easily enough. Why had he been idiot enough to abandon a certainty for the slim chance that this one-horse Truman outfit, towards which he was headed, might need a cow-hand? They probably didn't, anyhow—even that old liar Ross had warned him as much. And now, just for a fool curiosity—just for a fool romantic notion—he had lost his horse and everything that he had in the world. And it began to look mighty like he might also lose....

With a savage mustering of his remaining will-power, Brandon thrust this last grim thought from him and, turning resolutely, plodded painfully on. The whole valley couldn't be deserted surely, he told himself. True, he had passed no sign of habitation since he had been following this trail up the wash, but it stood to reason he must come to something soon—some ranch or some shack. People must live here somewhere—or else why this road? California had settled a lot everywhere since the days when the old Butterfield stage route had first traced out this desolate desert trail. There must be houses or ranches somewhere.

The Truman outfit couldn't be so far off now. And there was the old Vallecitos stage station that Ross had told him about—that must be close now. If only he could get somewhere—if only his six-shooter were in his belt now instead of in a San Diego pawnshop. If only he could get to some place before that damned white steer—or whatever it was—caught up with him! If only...

Brandon stumbled on desperately, his heart pounding. He couldn't fool himself. He knew well enough that it wasn't a steer that was following him. He hadn't seen any sign of cattle all day—and no steer could move so stealthily through the shadows and vanish so swiftly whenever he glimpsed it. No, it wasn't a steer! And yet....

Brandon involuntarily quickened his pace, driving his aching limbs frantically. What was that yarn about the Ghost Rider that old Ross had told him?...That was another lie...it must be...the ghostly White Horse and the phantom rider that haunted the vicinity of the old stage station!...A man would be crazy to believe that!...Still...

The grip of a great fear was closing relentlessly on Brandon. He was running now, weaving and staggering drunkenly through the cumbering sand of the trail that dragged at his boots and hampered his every step. Creosote bushes whipped against his face as he reeled past them; mesquite branches slashed at him thornily, tearing at his clothes and hands. He ran headlong. His breath was coming in great gasps. His knees shook under him. A cold sweat seemed to burst suddenly from his every pore. It was coming—the thing behind him was coming! It was galloping after him—with each step he took it was gaining on him! Without looking, he could feel it coming—could sense its sudden whirlwind approach. He plunged on madly.

His head spun dizzily. The pale sandy ribbon of the trail seemed to go black before him. All the uncanny, crushing oppression which had come upon him with the first lengthening shadows of the valley rushed back upon him tenfold. He knew suddenly that he was afraid—horribly afraid. A gun—a six-shooter!...If only he had a six-shooter!

In spite of himself—forced by a dread impulse against which he struggled vainly—he glanced over his shoulder. God!...a hoarse, choking cry broke from his lips. The Ghost Rider!...The White Horse!...It was there!...There almost upon him!...It was rearing over him! In the gloom he caught one flash of a pair of glaring, flame-lit eyes, red and terrible...heard all at once the thunder of beating hoofs, a dreadful cry...

Sick with terror he swerved blindly aside from the trail and plunged frantically into the bordering tangle of shadowy bushes. As he did so his feet struck suddenly against a low ridge of piled stones. He stumbled and fell sprawling into a long shallow depression, in the sand in which something pale gleamed wanly.

And as he fell the great white shape at his heels leaped upon him, crushing him, beating him into the sandy earth.

Many are the tales surrounding the old Butterfield stage
(from South frieze on the wall of the old Julian library)

∽

CHAPTER 2

Flame

For the fleeting fraction of a second, as he went down with a crashing thud, half-blinded in a sudden tempest of whirling sand and gravel, Brandon's senses blurred. The fall and the hurtling impact of the thing that had leaped upon him had driven the last remaining gasp of breath from his lungs. His eyes spun in a sudden blinding whirlwind of shooting sparks; the blood roared in his head; his ears were filled with a dreadful snarling and, as in the blind automatic instinct of self-preservation he flung up an arm to protect his face, he was conscious of stabbing pain; of the dreadful fangs of something tearing and slashing at him—something that was snarling and roaring in its efforts to reach his throat.

An instant only the hideous tempest beat upon him. Out of black chaos a voice cried suddenly from close at hand. A light flamed. Dimly, as he fought madly against the snarling horror that pinned him down, Brandon was aware of another shape, that struggled in the sudden light-glow about him—a figure that dragged and panted and cried out in frantic commands.

And then—sudden as it had launched itself—the white terror leaped back and away.

Shaken and gasping Brandon tottered to his feet. Half-blinded in the beam of a small electric-torch that was turned full upon his face, he found himself confronting the shadow-hazy figure of a girl. And by her side, red-jawed, glowing-eyed and terrible, stood the most gigantic white hound he had ever seen.

"Who are you? What are you doing here?" The girl's voice was crisp and clear and searching as the light in her hand. She swept the torch-ray over him deliberately. Dazed as he was, he seemed to feel the sharp hostility in her shadow-masked eyes.

For a moment, still breathless, Brandon made no reply. He struggled out of the shallow trench into which he had fallen and shook his head and face clear of the clinging particles of twigs and gravel that had been hurled upon him. Though shaken and panting, he was conscious of a vast relief that eclipsed, for the instant, his amazement at the girl's sudden appearance.

The marrow-freezing horror of fear was gone from him. He had missed death by a fraction, he realized, but the dreadful fangs that had driven into his arm and torn furiously in their efforts to reach his throat had not been those of any ghost-beast. The slavering jaws and huge gleaming teeth of the great white dog before him were real enough. Their very reality and physical menace seemed to give him a new flood of strength and courage-in spite of his exhaustion.

The girl repeated her question sharply. For the first time Brandon was aware that behind her, half hidden in the shadows, a saddled horse stood waiting—obviously where she had left it when she had sprung to drag off the dog.

"My name's Brandon, miss—Jim Brandon. I was headed for…."

The girl cut him short with an angry exclamation:

"I don't care about that. What I want to know is what you were doing digging here in these graves? What were you looking for?" She swept the light beam across the ground at his feet with an imperative, questioning gesture.

Brandon jerked back, startled. In the flooding radiance of the torch he realized suddenly that it was indeed a grave into which he had fallen; an old grave that, plainly enough, had been recently opened— splintered grey-white fragments, half concealed in the gravelly earth, showed gruesomely here and there on its bottom. The piled rocks which had originally covered the mound had been flung aside by the diggers. It was these scattered stones, Brandon saw now, that had tripped him and caused him to fall headlong into the grave. The realization gave him a chilling shock that for the instant robbed him of speech.

"What were you digging for?" the girl demanded again angrily. There was a hard, metallic click in her voice. She swept the light in a swift arc over the ground just beyond. A startled exclamation broke from her:

"All of them!—so you opened all four of them? What for? Quick now—and don't lie to me!"

Brandon found his tongue with an effort:

"You're mistaken, miss. Your hound took after me and I tripped and fell in there. I didn't know till this minute what I'd fallen into."

His eyes followed the path of the light. With an unpleasant shock he realized that there was more than one grave. Spaced at short intervals from the first were three others. They were evidently all old graves—and all of them had been opened.

The girl stamped her foot. Her temper was mounting:

"Don't try to spring those bedtime stories on me, stranger! You're lying! You're the second four-flusher that's blown into these parts within two days, and I'm about fed up. If you can't talk up straight, I've a notion to...."

She left the words unfinished, but touched the hound beside her with a meaning gesture. The great beast tensed and gathered himself. His eyes flamed over Brandon hungrily.

"All right, then—set your dog on me!" Brandon flared in exasperation.

In spite of his weakness and the fact that he could scarcely force speech through his thirst-parched throat, he was conscious of a sudden fierce resentment. The tone and bearing of this unknown girl, with her suspicion and accusations, maddened him. He couldn't see her clearly. Her outline in the shadows behind the glow of the torch told him only that she was slim and not much over five feet tall. She was bareheaded, and as nearly as he could make out she was dressed in a shirt, boots, and a short riding-skirt. And, even though he could not distinguish her features clearly, the sharp ring of her voice told him that she was quite capable of carrying out her unspoken threat and setting her monster hound at him.

Brandon was conscious of a surge of fury. He squared himself. "Set your dog on to me if it'll do you any good," he repeated defiantly. "I guess you just don't want to believe anything. I've been hoofing it through this blasted wilderness since an hour after sun-up this morning. I'm fed up too!"

He thrust forward a step, reckless of the deep, coughing snarl of the menacing hound. "Look at me!" he challenged savagely. "Do I look like I've been amusing myself robbing graves?"

The girl moved the light a fraction, so that the beam beat full on his face. For at least a half-minute she studied him without speaking. Though no model for a collar advertisement, Jim Brandon was far from bad-looking.

Tall and lean and resilient, and with an athletic strength that spoke from every line of him despite his weariness, his keen, clean-shaven face, sun-mellowed and graved in self-reliant lines by the suns and winds of the open range, was by no means unattractive.

The seasoned blue eyes were clear and level-looking, and the crisp crop of dark-brown hair, brought into view by the fact that his battered

Stetson had been knocked off in the struggle, did nothing to spoil the picture.

The girl studied him deliberately. She lowered her torch suddenly.

"Maybe you aren't lying," she admitted a trifle grudgingly. "I guess you're half-dead from thirst. Where'd you come from? And where's your horse?"

"I headed down here from Jacumba, miss," Brandon answered, his anger cooling with the realization that at least the edge of dangerous hostility had passed from the girl's tone. "I tried to take a short cut through the hills."

"Through the gorge?" the girl demanded sharply, suspicion flashing back again into her voice. "That trail's impassable."

"It is now," Brandon admitted; "at least it is in one place. The ledge round the shoulder above that deep canyon crumbled and went out under me. That's where I lost my horse. He went over into the canyon—and I all but went with him. I reckon it's a good two-hundred-foot fall there."

"Three hundred," the girl corrected coolly." "I guess you were born lucky, cowboy—that's if you're telling me the truth. You walked from there here today—in those boots?"

"Yes, miss."

A half-audible exclamation escaped the girl—whether of sympathy or disbelief Brandon could not determine. But the light swung away from him as she stepped swiftly back towards her horse and began to untie something from her saddle. The big white hound growled and lurched towards Brandon.

"Midnight! Behave!" There was sharp authority in the tone as the girl checked the dog's threatening move. She came forward and handed Brandon a small canteen.

"Here's water," she said. "Go easy now—no more than a mouthful to start with."

The water was warm, but Brandon gulped it gratefully. He needed no warning, however. A scant swallow and he forced himself to lower the vessel from his lips.

"That's right"—the girl's voice was a trifle more friendly—"I guess you're no tenderfoot, anyhow."

She took the canteen from his hands. "You were real thirsty, right enough," she admitted. "I'll give you some more pretty soon. And maybe you are telling me the truth. Midnight did slip away from me awhile. He went on ahead. I guess he'd scented you.

It's lucky I caught up with him when I did. You'd have been hash by this time if I hadn't."

Her fingers were busy replacing the stopper of the canteen. Closer— and with his nerves and eyes steadied a little by the swallow of water, Brandon could see the outlines of her face more clearly. He wondered who she was. That she was still suspicious of him he sensed plainly enough. He sensed also that it was not only himself—it was something also in connection with the opened graves beside him that had roused her suspicion and hostility.

Who was she? Her face was exasperatingly veiled by the dimness behind the torch-glow. He wished he could see it clearly. In spite of his exhaustion he felt the surge of a burning curiosity—a curiosity that all at once flashed a sudden thought to his mind. Could she be....

The half-formed question was answered almost before it had leaped to his brain. A sudden twist of the girl's wrist as she fumbled at the canteen with both hands flung the beam of the little pocket torch full on her face. Brandon took an involuntary step back, his suspicion startlingly verified.

The face, that for an instant had flashed up before him in all its details, was that of a young girl of not over twenty; a face the like of which an inspired painter of magazine covers might create once in a lifetime; a face dazzling almost in its delicate molding, clean, golden-tinted outdoor beauty and deep-blue eyes—and about it like a halo, flashing back the light like a glowing mist of glorious red-gold fire was a great clustering bob of tumbled, waving curls. Brandon caught his breath in a gasp. It was Flame—Flame Truman—the girl from the Truman ranch, towards which he was headed; the girl whose face and wonderful red hair old Seth Ross had described to him so minutely— the girl, tales of whom, more even than the old prospector's yarns, had been the urge which had drawn him aside into this grim, wild country.

It was Flame—Flame of Terrible Valley!

↬

CHAPTER 3

Mystery

But Brandon was given little time for astonishment. The beam of light which had fallen on the girl's face as she replaced the canteen stopper passed in an instant and left her features again veiled in shadows.

"You haven't told me yet where you were going?" The question came abruptly, but the girl's voice had lost much of its raw harshness. As she swept the light over him again Brandon realized that, busied for the moment as she had been, his involuntary start of surprise at recognition had passed her by unnoticed.

"I was headed for your ranch, Miss Flame"—flustered as he was at discovery of her identity, Brandon unconsciously used the girl's first name, a name that had somehow rung in his head incessantly since he had first heard it from the lips of old Ross—"I was headed up there. I thought that maybe—"

"How do you get that!"—sharp as the crack of a whip the girl cut him short. "How do you get that stuff?" she demanded. "I've never seen you before in my life! How do you know who I am?"

"I—I met an old timer named Seth Ross in Jacumba, miss"— Brandon was staggered a little by the sudden fury of suspicion in her voice—"he told me about you, an' I recognized you just now when the light flashed on your face. Ross said your uncle had a cow ranch up here aways in a little side valley to the west of this one, right up at the foot of the mountains—Terrible Valley, I guess they call it. I'm hunting a job, and I thought maybe your uncle might need a good cowhand."

"Oh, so that's it!" Vast relief was in the girl's tone—a relief that was shadowed by annoyance. "So it was old Ross who started you down here. That's about what he would do! He's got no more sense!...It's too bad, but you're out of luck. We don't need any hands—outfit's too small. We do all our work ourselves. And besides..."

She broke off, as though checking something that had almost slipped her tongue. "Let's see how bad you're hurt," she said abruptly. "Did Midnight chew you much?"

"Only my arm, miss—and that don't amount to anything. He didn't have time."

"Let's see it."

Obediently Brandon extended his right arm for her inspection. She ran the light over it.

"I guess you were born lucky all right," she said in relief. "He's ripped your shirt up pretty bad, but he missed your arm mostly. There's only a few tooth marks, and they're not dangerous. I'm glad it's no worse. Midnight's a queer dog—he's almost human—and I guess he suspected you were...."

Again she checked herself sharply as though once more her tongue had almost betrayed her. She handed Brandon the canteen. "You can have another swallow or so now—I guess you've got sense enough not to drink too much. It's too bad that you came all the way down here on a fool's errand. Now you've lost your horse and got chewed up into the bargain—and it might have been much worse. Old Ross ought to have warned you. He must have been crazy to give you the idea that we needed help. He knows better."

She flashed the light away from him to the row of opened graves, and, as though on a sudden impulse, stepped quickly towards them, followed instantly by the big white hound. Moving swiftly from one to the other she paused a moment by each and inspected it carefully by the searching rays of the torch.

Brandon gulped a mouthful of water and, canteen in hand, followed her, his weariness displaced for the moment by an overmastering sensation of excitement and mystery. Prepared as he had been by the voluble description of the girl's striking—almost unearthly—beauty which old Seth Ross had poured into his ears, the actuality had stunned him. He still felt a bit dazed by the memory of that flash glimpse he had caught. He was suddenly not at all sorry that he had come—notwithstanding the loss of his pony and the punishment of Midnight's fangs. It was worth it all, even for a glimpse.

And there was more. Brandon sensed mystery. A sense of something strange and grim was suddenly upon him. As strongly and unmistakably as the grimness of the valley had pressed upon him he now felt this new and closer thing. He realized that the girl was laboring under a strain—a feverish anxiety which the easier friendliness that had followed upon her first suspicions of him could not wholly conceal. The opened graves were obviously the cause of her uneasiness. It suddenly flashed on Brandon that Seth Ross had told him something of those graves. But there had been nothing in his story to connect them with the Trumans of Terrible Valley.

The girl was already standing beside the farthest open trench when Brandon reached her side. Her excitement and uneasiness had increased. The light of her torch, streaming down into the long sandy pit, revealed in startling distinctness the crumbling human fragments that lay on the bottom of it. But it was evident that it was not this that was responsible for her nervousness.

"There was a gang of them," she said, half to herself, flashing the torch about on the trampled earth on the edge of the pit. "And it must have been done some time today—I went by here yesterday and they hadn't been dug into then. Say!"—she wheeled suddenly on Brandon—"did anyone—any car—pass you today while you were walking?"

Brandon shook his head. "No, miss—not a living soul."

The girl darted out into the sandy road. Her light searched the ground. She gave a cry:

"But they *did* come by car. They must have come from the other direction—down from Mason Valley. And they went back the same way. Here's where they backed their car round." She pointed to the crushed sand and broken bushes on the side of the road where the backing tracks of a big motor-car were plainly visible.

"I reckon it was a bunch of city folks down here hunting souvenirs," Brandon suggested, studying the marks. "By the look of the tire tracks they—"

"Souvenirs!"—the girl's interruption was scornful—"who'd want souvenirs from here?"

"Some folks have queer notions," Brandon persisted. "These are the graves of the Morgan gang, aren't they?—the bunch that murdered Captain O'Hara, way back in 'fifty-nine, and got wiped out themselves the next day trying to hold up the stage?"

The light came up on his face again with a startled jerk. "You must have wasted a lot of time gabbing with Seth Ross," the girl said dryly. "Yes, this is where the Morgan outfit was buried—where they fell. What's that got to do with souvenirs?"

"Some folks like to collect skulls an' things," Brandon answered. "They've got queer ideas, and—"

"Then it's a pity they took all this trouble and then left all the skulls behind 'em after all!" the girl interrupted sharply. "Everyone of 'em is still there—what's left of them! Look for yourself! No, the gang that dug in here wasn't looking for that sort of souvenir. I'll bet they were looking for…." Her teeth clicked shut abruptly over her unfinished words.

"Looking for what?" Brandon demanded.

"Nothing !" the girl snapped shortly.

She turned abruptly, switched off the light, and began to walk swiftly back towards her horse.

"Come on!" she called over her shoulder. "I've got to get back home. I'm late now."

Aware that again, by his incautious question, he had trodden upon dangerous ground and aroused the flare of the girl's temper and mistrust, Brandon followed her. He found her fumbling with nervous haste at the saddle of her horse.

"Here!" she said, thrusting a stirrup leather into his hand. "Quick! Alter 'em to your length, and let's get out of here."

"But I'm not going to take your horse!" Brandon stared at her astonished. "I'm not that…."

"Don't waste time!" the girl snapped angrily, breaking in upon his amazed stammer. "Fix those stirrups and shut up. I can't leave you here, and we won't make any time if you walk; besides, you're too footsore. I'll take you along with me and leave you at old Gus Weidner's shack— I've got to pass there on the way home. Monte can carry double that far. Gus is away in Julian today, but he'll be back tomorrow. He won't mind you staying there tonight—I'll leave a note for him. But you're going to ride in front—I'm not fool enough to let you sit behind me. Here! Give me that canteen—I'll tie that while you're fixing those stirrups!"

Brandon dragged at the leathers in silence. He was beginning to realize that Ross had spoken truly when he had said that Flame Truman had a gunpowder temper. But there was more than temper and distrust behind her mood now. There was something else weighing upon her—something which he could not fathom. Brandon judged it was a deadly fear of something—fear mixed with rage. But if it was fear it did nothing to improve her irritable mistrust of him.

The girl finished tying the thong of the canteen and darted away. Her torch flashed up an instant and then snapped off again as she snatched up Brandon's Stetson from the ground. She raced back and jammed it on his head from behind with an ungentle hand:

"There's your hat! Now let's be moving!"

Brandon finished with the second leather. In silence and a bit stiff from sore and aching muscles he swung himself into the saddle. Scarcely had he touched it than, with catlike agility and scorning aid, the girl was up behind him.

"Just give Monty his head," she said crisply, "he knows the trail. Come on, Midnight!"

She gave a low, short whistle. With the huge white hound flitting ahead like a pale shadow, they swung away into the darkness.

Riding the trails of the Anza-Borrego desert (Used with permission of California State Parks)

CHAPTER 4

A Trail of Shadows

For a mile they rode in silence, the stillness of the desert night broken only by the sand-muffled thud of the horse's hoofs and the ghostly rustle of a thin cold wind that had begun to gust down from the blackness of the western mountains. Flame spoke suddenly:

"There's springs to the left here, up near the foot of those hills. You weren't so far from water after all—if you'd only known it."

Brandon made no answer. Close upon the heels of his amazement over the happenings of the last few minutes a feeling of depression had settled upon him.

In spite of the easing of his thirst his fatigue had begun to reassert itself, and, in addition, he felt keenly the hostility of the girl behind him. Her persistent lack of confidence in him was chilling. Moreover, he was busy with a host of vague theories and conjectures as he struggled vainly to establish some thread of connection between the old graves of the half-forgotten desperados back there in the desert and the girl who rode behind him. That there *was* a connection somewhere he had begun to feel certain, no matter how preposterous the thing might seem. But what was it?

He revolved all the facts in his mind as he remembered them from Seth Ross's rambling yarn about the murder of Captain Terrence O'Hara, discoverer and first owner of the now lost and almost legendary Lucky Ledge mine, and the spectacular attempt of his murderers, a day later, to hold up the Butterfield stage. An attempted hold-up which had resulted disastrously for the Morgan gang, every member of which had been slain owing to quick shooting on the part of the stage guard and passengers.

But what had the killing of Captain O'Hara and this frustrated hold-up of the late 'fifties to do with Flame Truman? Almost seventy years had passed since then! The thing was absurd.

And yet, from the girl's own actions, he felt convinced that there was a link somewhere. Who were the Trumans, anyhow? he asked himself. Even Seth Ross, it appeared, hadn't known very much about them; no one seemed to know much about them. Old Abe Truman and his niece, according to report, had come from no one knew where three years ago, and had bought the Terrible Valley ranch, a run-down property which had long stood abandoned. They had stocked the place and improved it, according to Ross's account, but had kept pretty much to themselves.

"A likeable kind o' feller, old Abe Truman is," Ross had said, "for all that he's so powerful close-mouthed about hisself. He's an old hand at the cattle business, plain enough. But the girl! There ain't another like her in all California, I reckon. Prettier'n a picture an' gentle as a cooin' dove if you tread careful an' don't cross her. But when she gets mad she goes off like dynamite an' acts as amiable as a basketful o' rattlesnakes."

Such had been Ross's description—and it had been quite enough to fire Brandon's naturally adventurous nature with a burning curiosity. Now, as the horse beneath him followed the windings of the lonely road up the silent valley, Brandon admitted to himself that the description was accurate. Flame's clear, clean beauty had dazzled him. The touch of her hand, where it rested upon him as she steadied herself as they rode, thrilled him oddly. Somehow, strangely, powerfully, he felt drawn to her.

But stronger than every other feeling was the sense of her bitter hostility. It chilled him. There was a hidden reason for it, he felt sure. He recalled that the girl, in her first anger, had declared him to be the "second four-flusher within two days." He wondered who the first had been—and what he had done.

Somehow, of a sudden, it seemed to Brandon that all the romantic glamour which had lured him down into this desolate region had evaporated. More than ever now he seemed to feel the grim menace of this lone, dead desert pressing upon him. He had blundered headlong, he realized, into a mystery—and it was plain that the girl resented his presence. She had not had the heart to leave him afoot on the road, but she was anxious to be rid of him. The realization galled him. Jim Brandon was the last man in the world to elbow in where he was not wanted. He determined to drop off at the first chance. He could back-track to the main highway and reach Yuma somehow. He had had enough of this ghostly desolation already.

The trail up the wash seemed interminable. The chill of the desert night was setting in; the air was growing cold. The blaze of the stars as the darkness deepened seemed only to render blacker the grim bulk of the sierras that towered above them in jagged outline to the west; the shadows of the creosote bushes seemed denser; the mesquites, looming up darkly from the pale sand of the wash, appeared menacing and fantastic. Away off, along the summits of the mountains, the stars were slowly blotting out behind gathering masses of cloud; there was an intermittent flicker of lightning above the distant peaks.

The wind had increased. Already it was swirling and scooting down from the higher slopes, whistling through the wiry-leaved bushes in sudden mournful, chilly gusts that caught up the sand raised by the horse's plodding hoofs and flung it pattering against the cactus and dry-leaved yuccas which grew thickly among the shadowy ranks of the tall creosote bushes lining the road. The wide sandy wash had become a black sea of heaving shadows through which the pale ribbon of the trail, blurred by the wind-tossed tops of the waving bushes, seemed to twist and writhe in phantom uncertainty. And ahead, loping silently like a white wraith through the shadows, the spectral shape of the great hound led the way onward.

The trail swung presently to the right, and struck suddenly into the shadows of a gloomy/tangle of tall mesquites. The wind came down the valley in clearer sweep. Brandon's senses caught the soughing rustle of tules and the damp breath of water. Underfoot Monty's hoofs beat all at once upon a crackling crust of alkali. To the right, upon a little hillock close beside the track, gleamed something sharply white, the shape of which proclaimed it unmistakably a gravestone. As they emerged from the fringe of mesquites a hulking adobe building with blackly gaping doors and windows loomed up suddenly before them on the right of the trail.

"The old Butterfield stage station," Flame said briefly. "This is Vallecitos."

Brandon reined in the horse. "I guess I'll stop here, miss," he said.

"What!" The girl checked his movement to dismount with a sharp hand and sharper voice. "What's the idea?" she demanded. "There's no one here. This place has been deserted for years and years—don't you know that?"

"Yes, miss, but there's water hereabouts, I guess. I'll camp here tonight and back-track in the morning. There's no sense in me going farther—with no chance of a job."

"That's alright too," the girl admitted, "but you can't camp here. It's not so awful much farther up to Gus's mining claim now. You can camp in his shack. And maybe, when Gus gets back tomorrow, he can take you at least part of the way back. He's got spare horses and he'd do that. He knows me well enough. I'll leave a note for him."

"I reckon I can start just as well from here," Brandon said stubbornly. "I'm kinda used to taking care of myself, and I don't aim to be—"

"*Dammit!* Sit still—and let's get moving!" There was venom, this time in the way the girl checked Brandon's movement. He felt something round and hard jabbed suddenly into his back. "Just you try and get off, and I'll blow the daylights out of you!" she stormed. "'Monty! Get a move on!" She struck the horse with her heel so sharply that it leaped forward with a bound that almost unseated both of them. The dark bulk of the old adobe building fell back into the darkness behind them as they sped up the trail.

Of a sudden, with an unexpectedness that was startling, the girl burst out laughing. She clung to Brandon for support and choked with explosive mirth.

"I'm sorry," she sputtered presently, when she could gain her voice, "I didn't mean to get mad and stick a gun in your ribs. But you're so dam stubborn. If I wouldn't leave you on the road, it's likely I'd leave you to camp at the old stage station—it would have been real nice of me, I'm sure. You've heard so much from Ross—didn't he tell you anything about that place?"

"Yes, miss. But I thought that maybe—"

"Well, you've got another think coming," the girl cut in. "The story about that old 'dobe is no lie—whatever else is. That old station's haunted. It's not healthy to camp there. Gee! But you made me mad for a minute. It's a wonder I didn't plug you. I'm half Irish and I've got red hair. You ought to have more sense than to be obstinate with anyone that's got a make-up like that."

Her volcanic outburst seemed to have steadied her nerves. Brandon sensed a change in her. In great measure her icy antagonism was suddenly gone. For the moment the tension of hostility vanished. Brandon's spirits rose a little. He ventured a question:

"So you reckon it's true, the yarn about Captain O'Hara still riding his big white horse around the old station, miss?"

"I don't know if it's Captain O'Hara or not," the girl answered soberly; "there's more than one opinion as to who it actually is. But Captain O'Hara was riding a white horse that day when the Morgan outfit ambushed and shot him. And it *is* a white horse that haunts the station—I've seen it myself. I wouldn't camp in the front room of that old building for anything. I tell you it isn't healthy to sleep there. Whenever anyone does…ugh!…." She broke off with a little shiver.

Brandon felt a little startled. He was gripped suddenly with an eerie conviction that Flame was utterly sincere. He risked another question:

Flame's answer gave him a queer, uncanny chill.

"Whenever anyone does sleep there they wake up scared to death, and find the white horse rearing over them," she said grimly. "That front room used to be the bar in the old days. The horse comes right in through the doorway."

"It doesn't sound hardly possible," Brandon protested.

"No, it doesn't," the girl admitted. "But there's lots of 'impossible' things that are more than possible in a place like this. This whole valley's haunted, I think—haunted by the spirits of the dead. Lots of queer things happened here in the days when the Butterfield stage was running—gunfights and murders and hold-ups. The valley's dotted with graves, lost and hidden among the mesquites most of 'em. Terrible Valley, where we live, to the west of here, got its name from the way the Indians used to murder every white man that strayed in there. But it's no more terrible than this main valley, I guess. If you're sensitive you can feel things in the air here. It crushes you."

A faint, involuntary shiver ran through her, and she lapsed into silence. As though unconsciously, her hands, resting against Brandon for support, tightened a little.

The pressure, slight as it was, sent a queer thrill through Brandon's veins. This was a new Flame that he had just glimpsed in the girl's sudden change of mood. For an instant the mask of will-power and self-reliance had slipped aside. There had been revealed to him a girl more than a little lonely and crushed by the grimness and solitude of her environment; a lonely spirit craving companionship—a girl who was infinitely tender and human despite her fighting spirit. And he did not tell her that she was not alone in her secret dread of the valley. The omen of it hung over him also.

Following the flitting white shape of the loping hound, Monty swung aside presently into a side trail that led off to the left. They crossed the bed of the wash, threading once more through a whispering sea of low, wind-waved tules, and squelching in muddy earth a moment as the track led across the seepage from the springs.

The road led up into the hills. The sandy dreariness of the wash gave place slowly to the grimmer desolation of barren rocks, piled in knolls and ridges and ghostly in the shadows, with a scattering of the towering dead flower-stalks of Spanish bayonet.

In spite of the fact that the girl had said the shack of Gus Weidner was not far off, it seemed to Brandon that they were a long time reaching it. The trail appeared to wind endlessly among the rocky hillocks and gullies. Glancing back a moment as they crested the summit of a long barren ridge, Brandon was surprised to find how far they had already risen. The black gloom of the wash lay far below them, a vast lake of shadow that, in the distance—somewhere, he judged, beyond the old stage station—was broken by a tiny flare of flickering light.

The glowing light-bead held Brandon's glance an instant. It looked like a distant camp fire—or perhaps it was a lighted window. A camp, or some homesteader's shack, he concluded. But he wondered that he had not noticed it when passing the stage station. It was seemingly not far from that. If it had been in existence when they had passed it must have been screened from sight in a hollow somewhere. He wondered if Flame had noticed it.

But before he could draw her attention to it, the girl uttered an exclamation that brought Brandon's eyes back sharply to the trail in front. In the darkness at the foot of the slope, less than two hundred yards ahead of them, a lighted window glowed sharply.

As they cantered down towards it he saw the shadowy shapes of trees and the dark outlines of a shack.

"You're in luck!" Flame exclaimed with satisfaction. "This is Gus's place—and he's home. I guess he didn't go to Julian after all. Now I can explain things to him myself, and I won't have to leave you there with just a note." She whistled sharply. "Gus! Ho, Gus!" she called.

The door swung open as Brandon reined the horse in before the little shack. A lean, slightly stooped figure, holding a rifle, appeared in silhouette upon the threshold. There was a sudden exclamation of astonishment.

"Why!…'Evenin', Miss Flame. You kinda startled me." The rifle disappeared. The old man shuffled forward.

"I thought you were in Julian, Gus," Flame said. "Uncle told me you'd be away today."

"That's what I told him yesterday mornin', Miss Flame, but come noon yesterday I put a shot in the tunnel an' uncovered some likely-lookin' rock. Reckon I'll stay now a coupla days till I see how it's comin'. Where you headin' for this hour o' night?"

Flame explained the situation briefly. Old Gus's deep-set, steely eyes ran over Brandon—a deliberate, appraising scrutiny that seemed to satisfy him.

"You couldn't have brought him to no better place," he declared heartily. "Come right on in. There's coffee on the stove an' th' finest pot o' beans you ever seen. I just brought up a fresh bucket o' water from th' spring—you'll prob'ly 'preciate that. An' I reckon I can fix you up all right with a bunk, pardner. Come on in. An', Miss Flame, you better have a cup o' coffee too, afore you start home. It won't take but a minute."

CHAPTER 5

"Hoss Thieves an' Chinamen"

In Gus's tiny cabin, lit by the glow of a flickering oil lamp and warmed by the almost stifling heat of a wood-crammed cook stove, Brandon got his second good look at Flame. As he quenched the fag-ends of his thirst with spring water, and hungrily attacked the steaming plate of beans that had been set before him, his eyes followed her, fascinated.

A trifle to his surprise, though greatly to his satisfaction, she had accepted old Gus Weidner's offer of the coffee. It would probably be the last time that he would ever see Flame, Brandon reflected dismally, and he wanted at least to see all he could of her.

Somehow, in the last mile or two of their ride, since she had dropped for a space the hard, almost savage mask of speech and action and given him a glimpse of her real self, his heart had gone out to her with a queer sense of tenderness—something different, deeper and more gripping than the luring glamour of curiosity with which her strange name and Ross's description had first filled him.

Brandon was conscious now of a curious, uncomfortable feeling; he was aware suddenly that he was sad and dejected. Mysteriously, in as short a time as he had known her, this girl with the clear blue eyes and hair of golden flame had gripped his heart as no other girl had ever done. And he would probably never see her again. She had made it plain that she wished to get rid of him. Life seemed to Brandon suddenly unutterably bleak and lonely.

And, studying the girl as she sat by the little board table waiting while old Gus rustled the coffee, it seemed to Brandon that, for all her will-power and self-reliance, Flame at that moment was more than a little lonely—and scared—herself. The conviction came to him that it was for this reason that she had accepted the offer of the coffee before going on.

There was a sense of strain and fear about her which she did her best to conceal. Her eyes were restless, and her face was drawn with anxiety. He noticed that two buttons of her khaki shirt were open—and an instant later he realized why. The cloth of the shirt bulged suspiciously beneath her left armpit. It was there that she wore her gun in a shoulder holster. It was not by any accident that those two buttons were left unfastened. And it had not been lost upon him that, in her explanations to Gus, Flame had carefully avoided making any mention whatever of the opened graves.

Old Gus was moving pots about on the stove, and shoving more wood into its already overheated firebox. He paused a moment to glance over his shoulder with an abrupt remark.

"You might tell your uncle he better keep an eye on that Mex you got workin' for you, Miss Flame. That hombre ain't no good."

Flame sprang to her feet.

"Did he go past here?" she exclaimed excitedly. "Did you see him? He's not working for us. He's a horse thief! He's stolen Wings, the thoroughbred!"

"The hell you say!" A chunk of firewood still in his hand, Gus straightened round in open-mouthed consternation.

"But he did!" Flame cried breathlessly, her uneasiness for the moment forgotten. "That's where I've been today—way down to Davidsons at Smoky Springs looking for him."

"Well, I'll be damned! If only I'd a knowed it!" Gus was still struggling with his astonishment. "How come, Miss Flame, that he got a hold o' the hoss?"

"That Mexican four-flusher turned up at the ranch last night," Flame explained heatedly. "He said he was walking to Julian and he'd tried to save time by using the old trail—you know, the old washed-out one that runs past our place and cuts through to Banner. He said he'd somehow lost his way back in the hills and had been all day without water. We fixed him up and gave him a meal and a bed in the barn. Daybreak this morning he was gone—and Wings too. The trail's stony around our place, you know, and we couldn't be sure of the tracks—we didn't know which way he'd gone. So uncle went up the old Banner road and I came down this way. And you say you saw him?"

Gus nodded. "I had th' cuss right under my hand," he said regretfully, "an' I let him go—not knowin' anythin' was wrong. Y'see, it was this way: Just a bit after daybreak I seen a feller come gallopin' over the rise, comin' down th' trail from your way. I could tell it weren't you nor your uncle, but I rec'nized that little bay thoroughbred o' yourn by his action. I suspicioned somethin' was wrong, so I run inta th' shack an' got the thirty-thirty an' slipped out an' hid behind that big cottonwood where the trail crosses th' crick between them two short lines o' fence.

"Well, in a minute or so, here comes this feller a tearin', an' I seen then that he was a Mexican, so I steps out an' hollered an' throwed down on him with th' rifle. He stopped pronto all right—almost atop o' me. 'Where yuh goin' with that hoss?' I says.

"Well, sir, Miss Flame, that Greaser was a cool hand. He jest grinned—which didn't help his looks much, account o' that old scar that runs clear across his cheek-an' reaches in his pocket an' pulls out a letter. 'I get job Truman ranch yesterday,' he says. '*Señorita* send me with this an' say to hurry. You think I steal *caballo*—no?' An' he grins some more.

"Well, Misss Flame, I squinted at th' envelope an' I rec'nized your writin' all right. An' when I seen that it was addressed t' young Ted Davidson, well I nach'rally thot—"

Flame's amazed exclamation cut him short. "Why—the dirty thief!" she exploded angrily. "I wrote that letter in the kitchen last night—while he was eating his supper at the other end of the room. I got through before he finished, and I sealed it and stuck it up on the shelf, behind the clock. I was going to get Tom Hadden to take it down to Davidson's next time he went past our way. Then I went out of the room for a minute—that sneaking coyote must have taken it then. This morning, in the excitement, I forgot all about it and didn't notice it was gone…It was a letter uncle wanted me to write to Ted Davidson about some cattle he was going to buy."

There was a trace of confusion in her voice as she added this last bit of unnecessary information. Glancing at her, Brandon sensed that her embarrassment and the sudden rush of color to her cheeks was due to something else besides anger.

"Oh, o' course I don't know what was in it!" old Gus hastened to assure her. "But I knowed th' letter was genuine enough, an' th' hombre's yarn sounded square an' honest. Nach'rally, bein' a born fool, I let him go."

Flame clenched her hands and stamped her foot in impotent vexation. "Oh, if you'd only known!…But it wasn't your fault, Gus, that you let him by. Anyone would have been fooled by a bluff like that. I wonder where he went. It wasn't long after daybreak that I lit out after him. He couldn't have had much of a start."

"You didn't come this road, did you, Miss Flame? I never seen you go past."

"No," the girl said bitterly. "Like a fool, I didn't come past here. I was sure you weren't home, anyhow, so I turned off just behind the rise and took that old cut-off trail that strikes across the west end of your horse pasture. I was so dead certain that he'd got a good start and that he'd naturally go in the direction of Smoky Springs, that I thought my only chance was to get in ahead of him somehow. That short cut saves a lot of distance."

"It do, but it's hell t' travel. I reckon you had a rough trip." There was a glint of honest admiration in the old man's eyes.

"I sure did! You'll notice I didn't come back that way," Flame said dryly. "But after all, I lost him somewhere. He didn't go past Smoky Springs at all. Old man Davidson and Ted were away in Brawley, and there was only Ma Davidson and old Joe at the ranch. But they were both certain that no one had gone past. The trail goes right by their house, you know. No one could have got by without their knowing it."

"That's plumb peculiar," ruminated Gus. "Th' Greaser musta doubled back towards Mason Valley or somewheres."

"I guess he must have," Flame agreed wearily. "Anyway, there wasn't a thing I could do at Smoky Springs. Ma Davidson said she'd send old Joe right off to notify Bill Watson, the deputy, and that she'd have old man Davidson and Ted come up here to help us search as soon as they get home, which'll be either tonight or tomorrow. So I came back. I wasted a lot of time searching side canyons on the way, but I'd told uncle that maybe I'd stay at Davidson's tonight, so I took my time. I knew he wouldn't be worrying if it got late and I didn't come back. But there wasn't a trace of that Mexican anywhere—he's just vanished. I guess, though, the officers will pick him up somewhere. I've given his description—scar and all—and Wings is too conspicuous a horse for anyone to hide out long." Her voice held a forced note of hopefulness.

Old Gus shook his head.

"I dunno," he said dubiously. "I hate t' spile your hopes, Miss Flame, but I reckon your chances o' seein' Wings again is slim. I'll tell you why. When I seen that Greaser this mornin' I kinda thought his face looked familiar. But I couldn't place it. But a coupla hours after he'd gone by it come back to me in a flash. That Mex is Pedro Martinez—that's why I started in to warn you agen him."

"Who?" Flame eyed the old man inquiringly.

"No, you wouldn't ha' heard o' him, o' course—seein' as you ain't lived in these parts more'n three years. But he's one bad egg. He's one o' Slant Galloway's men—an', moreover, he comes o' a bad stock. His grandfather used t' be hoss wrangler at the old stage station down here—he was workin' there the time the Morgans tried t' hold up th' stage. He never had no flatterin' reputation, so I've heared tell."

Flame's eyes widened with a sudden, startled look. But she shook her head. "I've never heard of Slant Galloway either."

"You would have, if you'd lived across th' Border any." Gus shrugged and shoved the chunk of wood he had been holding into the stove. "Galloway's a high light in th' gamblin' an' smugglin' society down in Baja California. He's a no-good crook. He was Jake Templeton's main lootenant in th' Chink smugglin' business years ago. You've heard o' Jack Templeton maybe?—he was th' smugglin' kind they used t' call 'Red Beard', account o' his face bein' smothered in a brush o' red whiskers. I never had th' luck t' see Jake myself, but I've heared a plenty. He had to skip out fer parts unknown about nine years ago, account o' th' Chinese secret societies gettin' sore at him fer somethin' he done."

As he talked the old man had been fumbling in a rough little wall-cupboard, producing three chipped and ancient cups and saucers—his cherished "company china"—which he set out on the table. The sudden whitening of Flame's face at his words passed him unnoticed.

But Brandon was startled. All at once the girl had gone pale as death. The momentary excitement which had held her as she spoke of the horse thief was wiped out utterly. All her previous uneasiness and fear, which for the moment she had apparently forgotten, seemed to have returned upon her—and with tenfold intensity. Her lips had gone white. Her hand, resting against the table, clutched the edge of the rough boards for support.

Gus was punching a hole in the top of a can of condensed milk.

"An' that's why, since I rec'nized that Dago what stole Wings, I kinda think you ain't got much chance o' gettin' th' hoss back, Miss Flame. He'll be across th' border into Mexico afore th' officers even get started."

He reached for the coffeepot. "I hope this here coffee ain't too strong fer you, Miss Flame?" he said as he started to fill her cup.

The girl shook her head. Watching her face, his eyes held with a strange, compelling fascination, it seemed to Brandon that the action was automatic—that she had not really heard the question. She had subsided in her seat once more, but her eyes were full of the vacant light of some inner fear. The fingers of her hand that lay upon the table were twisting nervously.

"It's kinda queer, too, that Pedro Martinez is roamin' round these parts again," Gus ruminated garrulously as he methodically filled each cup with the boiling, coal-black, molasses-thick coffee. "Mebbe he's got a hunch where the O'Hara gold is cached. Might be. From what I've heard there was always a suspicion that his grandfather and Si Slade, who used t' be station tender at that time, knowed more'n they told about th' murder o' Cap'n O'Hara. But if they did, no one ever found out nothin', because they was both killed theirselves in a gamblin' row th' day after th' Morgans was wiped out.

"So there ai'nt no knowin' where that cache o' gold or th' mine is. Lots o' people has looked for it. I've heared rumours that even Jack Templeton hisself come up once from Lower California an' tried t' find it. But I reckon that's jest a yarn—I never met no one that actually seen him up here. But if he was he never found nothin'. Th' gold won't never be discovered, I reckon. But th' ghost o' th' old Cap'n gets uneasy over it every once in a while. Th' last month he's been ridin' round th' old station pretty regular. I seen him three different times—ridin' through th' mesquites at night—plain as I see you settin' here."

He set the coffeepot back on the stove and stooped to get more firewood.

Opposite each other across the rough little table made from the sides of packing cases, Brandon and Flame sat silent. Brandon drank his coffee and finished the last of his beans. Absorbed as he was in watching the face of the girl before him, he had not paid particular attention to Gus's remarks. They did not seem to him especially important, and most of the facts concerning the lost O'Hara mine he had heard before from the lips of Seth Ross. But what gripped and startled him was the change that had come over Flame; the way in which—utterly unnoticed by old Gus—her agitation had seemed to increase with every word.

White as a sheet she sat now, staring at Brandon with unseeing eyes and mechanically sipping at her steaming coffee—apparently utterly unconscious of the fact that her hand was shaking so violently that she could hardly hold the cup to her lips. Outside, the wind, tearing in sudden gusts down the creek, snored through the cottonwoods. There was the sound of old Gus grubbing around in the wood box. The fire-door of the stove clanged. Midnight, his huge length stretched out on the warm floor, lifted his head and whined uneasily.

"All right, dawg," said Gus tolerantly, stooping to pat the big brute's head, "I got somethin' for you too. There's a beef bone here you can have."

He opened a wire-screened box that hung on the wall and felt about in its interior. "Reckon I'll have t' buy Midnight offen you, Miss Flame, an' keep him here t' pertect me if traffic on this road keeps up like t'day," he said jokingly, "hoss-thieves passin' in th' mornin' an' a ottermobile load o' Chinamen in th' afternoon."

There was a sudden crash. Brandon jumped. Meat-bone in hand, Gus wheeled round, startled. Midnight was on his feet, bristling—the cup of coffee had slipped from Flame's finger and shivered to pieces on the floor. The girl had risen from her chair. She was standing with clenched hands, the spilled coffee widening in a dark stain over the rough floorboards at her feet.

"W-why, Miss Flame!…"

"I—I'm sorry—the coffee burned me!" the girl gasped, cutting short the old man's surprised stammer. She stooped and made a pretence of collecting the shattered fragments of the cup. "W-what was that you said about Chinamen?" she asked faintly.

"Them?…Oh, that didn't amount to nothin'." The old man's startled surprise subsided. "Just a car crammed full o' Chinks that went by here late this afternoon…some more smugglin', I guess, from th' look o' their car. It was a big one with a extry reserve tank o' petrol on behind. They was headed up your way—mebbe they think they kin dodge th' officers by travelin' that old road t' Banner that goes by your place. Or mebbe they got a system o' scatterin' into th' canyons and crossin' th' mountains on foot.

"Tom Hadden told me that when he come through from Banner last week he seen a lone Chink sneakin' around in a gully this side o' your place a ways. Tain't none o' our business, anyhow, I reckon. Lemme give you some more coffee, Miss Flame. You're white as a sheet. You got burnt pretty bad, I reckon. I got another chiney cup up here, an' I'll kinda cool it off for you this time." He reached towards his cupboard.

"No—no, I've had plenty!" the girl gasped. She drew her breath sharply. Brandon could see that she was fighting hard to control herself. "I've got to go now. I—I shouldn't have stayed at all. I'm late, and…"

She caught her breath again and pushed her chair aside. "Thanks for the coffee, Gus—and I'll see you tomorrow. Good night, Mr. Brandon. Come on, Midnight!" She started hastily towards the door.

"Hold on—hold on jest a minute!…I gotta give you a spec' men o' that new rock from th' tunnel…I want your uncle t' see it! Hold on a minute. I got a piece all ready. It's settin' out back!"

Old Gus blundered away. There was the sound of the back door opening and banging windily shut as he went out.

Brandon snatched the opportunity afforded by the old man's absence. He touched the girl's arm:

"Miss Flame," he blurted impulsively, "I—I don't want to butt in or anything, and it's none of my business, of course. But there's something wrong—I can see that with half an eye—and I'd sure like to help you if I can. You hadn't ought to go home alone like this—worried an' upset like you're feeling. You better let me go up with you tonight. I can come back here first thing in the morning, and…."

He broke off hurriedly, checked both by the sound of Gus's returning footsteps and by the quick leap of suspicious hostility in the girl's eyes—a flash of distrust that, of a sudden, died and was succeeded by something very like gratitude.

"Here's th' specimen...an' it's a dandy! Ef you hold it up t' th' light...."

Flame snatched the bit of rock from the old man's fingers and thrust it into her shirt pocket, cutting short his explanations. "Gus," she said hurriedly, "I've changed my mind. I'm going to take Mr. Brandon up to the ranch with me tonight. He'll be able to help us hunt for Wings for a day or so. Can you lend him a horse to ride up on?"

"Sure! Sure!" Obviously astonished but evidently used to Flame's sudden changes of plan, the old man nodded vigorously. "There's th' buckskin in th' corral out back—o' course he's th' poorest o' th' three. Ef you'd set an' wait 'bout half an hour I'll walk up t' th' pasture an' get one o' th' others. The white an' th' pinto's up there. Either o' them would be better'n—"

"The buckskin's all right," Flame interrupted hastily, moving towards the door. "We'll help you saddle him—I guess we'll have to borrow your spare saddle too, Gus."

She pushed open the door, stepped out into the windy darkness and darted away into the shadows, Midnight and Brandon at her heels, and the slightly astonished Gus bringing up the rear.

"Let's hurry!" the girl cried breathlessly, "it's cold, and I'm tired! Let's hurry! I've got to get home!"

But as he followed her to the gloom-shrouded little corral beneath the cottonwood trees, Brandon knew that it was neither cold nor weariness that was responsible for her suddenly chattering teeth and for the trembling nervousness that had laid hold of her.

CHAPTER 6

The Tong Strikes

To Brandon it seemed that the few moments needed to saddle the little buckskin horse passed in a blurred scramble of frantic haste. Almost before he knew it, the little shack and the breathless Gus were behind them, and he found himself galloping madly into the night at the heels of this strange girl whose goading, unnamed fear had suddenly become his own.

For, in spite of himself, and why he could not have told, Brandon was conscious of the crushing, chilling fear of some unknown, deadly peril; a fear so real and poignant that, for the first time, it seemed to have banished the last traces of his fatigue. His nerves were tingling with a strange, uncanny sense of impending disaster. The night seemed darker; the raw, gusting wind, swooping down upon them as their hard-pressed horses clattered round the winding turns of the rough mountain trail, had a grimmer and more ominous snarl to it.

The night *was* darker. Glancing up, Brandon saw that the cloud rampart along the summits of the sierras was spreading—a ragged scud was driving eastward and forming a swiftly thickening canopy overhead. Already half the starts were blotted out and the black shadows of the mountains into which the galloping girl and the pale, loping hound ahead were leading him were stygian and impenetrable. It came to Brandon chillingly that he was unarmed. He had been on the point of asking Gus for the loan of a gun before he left the shack, but he had checked himself. In face of the fact that Flame had been careful to conceal her fears from Gus, the request would have seemed queer and suspicious.

The trail writhed and twisted maddeningly as they pushed into the hills. A straight line could have covered the distance in a fraction of the time, Brandon realized. But apparently anything like a straight trail that horses could travel was out of the question in this rocky country.

They rode without speaking, in a silence broken only by the clattering hoofs of the galloping horses and the snarling whistle of the wind. Indeed, even had Flame been in the mood to speak, speech, except in shouts, would have been out of the question, for, as Brandon soon discovered, Gus's little buckskin pony was no match for Monty. It was only constant urging that kept him laboring in the wake of the speeding horse in front.

At length, rounding the steep shoulder of a hill, Flame reined to a halt. As he forged up alongside her and checked his panting mount, Brandon saw that ahead the country fell away into a lake of inky darkness that was evidently a little hill-walled valley. In the distance, on the valley floor, a glowing point of light shone up through the blackness.

"That's the ranch." Flame's voice was breathless with mingled dread and hope as she pointed. "Someone's there. Uncle must be home. Or… or…."

Her words died in her throat. She jerked her horse back with a sudden involuntary cry of terror. "Look!" she gasped "Look! Oh, my God! We're too late!…."

But Brandon had not needed her choking cry nor the sudden clutch of her hand upon his arm. He had already seen—and the thing that had happened had brought him erect in his saddle with a galvanic jerk.

The light in the valley had gone! Of a sudden, before his eyes, it had winked out with startling abruptness. But, as it vanished, the black darkness that blotted it was pricked with a half-dozen scattered and momentary flashes, sudden and transitory as the snapping gleams of monster fireflies. Faintly to his ears in a lull of the wind, came the unmistakable *crack!…crack!* of distant shots.

"They've killed him!…Oh, God, they've killed him!" The cry broke from the girl in a strangling, half-articulate sob. From a split second of stunned horror she woke suddenly to furious action. As though fired with a gust of blind fury she leaned forward and struck spurs to her horse. Before Brandon could lift a finger to prevent her she had shot away, and, at breakneck speed, was tearing madly down the trail into the valley.

Brandon whirled in pursuit, his startled surprise blotted in sudden apprehension as he realized the girl's mad purpose. What had happened in the valley below them he could only guess—but he needed no guess as to what would surely come to pass if Flame's furious, grief-blinded charge could not be halted. His blood went suddenly cold. He hurtled down the steep trail at breakneck speed, urging the winded buckskin with merciless desperation.

And somehow, lifted almost it seemed to Brandon by the sheer force of his own frenzy, his tired, gasping little pony achieved the impossible. At the foot of the long slope his stretching muzzle reached Monty's flank—passed it. As the two horses raced neck and neck across the clattering stones of the wash, Brandon reached out and clutched the girl's bridle-reins with an iron grip.

"Flame, you're mad! Where are you going?" Above the smashing beat of the hoofs and the rush of the wind his voice was a shout. He dragged both horses to a sliding halt, side by side.

"Let go those reins! Let me go!" The girl beat at him with her fist and struggled furiously to break his grip of the leathers. "Let me go!" she cried hysterically. "Let me go this minute, or I'll—"

"No you won't!" With a lightning-like movement Brandon released his own bridle-reins and pinioned both her hands in his. "You won't do anything of the sort!" he said sternly. "Listen, Flame. I don't know just what's happened down there, but I do know that I'm not going to let you ride down like this and be murdered. I'm going to stop you—if I have to fight you and your dog both."

The girl gasped. As though the harsh determination in his voice had startled her and broken the spell of blind madness she seemed of a sudden to go limp. He felt the steel-spring tension of her muscles relax. She drew a sharp breath.

"I—I guess you're right," she stammered huskily. "I was crazy to act that way. But I must go—I must go on and find out what's happened. Maybe he's still alive—maybe they've got him prisoner. Don't you see! I must go—I *must*! We're wasting time! If you won't come, I... Oh, God!..." Her voice broke in a pitiful sob.

"I'd come with you to hell, girl," Brandon said impulsively. "I stopped you so you wouldn't commit suicide, that's all—you couldn't have done any good to anyone, heading in like you were."

He released her hands. "Who are they, anyhow?" he demanded. "What are we up against?"

"The Tong—it's the Tong!" Her voice came in a chattering gasp.

"The Tong?" For a moment the significance of the word was lost on him.

"Yes—yes!" the girl panted. "The Yellow Dragon Tong from San Francisco. For nine years they've...."

Realization broke suddenly upon Brandon. "You mean those Chinks that Gus said he saw this afternoon?" he cut in sharply. "You mean they were—"

"They were Tong gunmen!" she choked breathlessly. "Oh, I did hope that Gus was right—that they were just smugglers. But they aren't—they're the Tong. Oh, hurry! For God's sake, hurry!…If they've taken him alive they'll…."

She twisted her hands in an agony of horror and did not finish the sentence. But there was no need. Brandon jerked upright in his saddle, tensed with purpose.

"I reckon we'll hurry," he said, his voice of a sudden hard with grim understanding. "How far's the house from here?"

"About a mile—straight down this trail."

Brandon listened an instant, straining his ears. No sound came to him from the blackness in front save the gusting moan of the rising wind. The pall of darkness was unbroken.

"Come on then," he said. "You better let me go ahead—I've scouted before. Go easy now—if they see us first we won't have a chance. And there's only your gun between the two of us. Where's the dog?"

"He's gone on in front somewhere."

"That's bad—he's too plain to see. If they spot him they'll be on the lookout. But we can't help it now. Come on!"

He touched his panting horse and moved off into the darkness, the girl following obediently at his heels.

As swiftly as he dared Brandon led the way forward. The trail was stony and the hoofs of the horses beat upon it with a clatter that was dangerously loud in spite of the muffling rush of the wind. Brandon's every sense was strained into the night ahead. Only too well he realized the foolhardy thing they were doing in venturing thus blindly into what was probably a nest of waiting gunmen. But there seemed no other course. The girl was right; they could not retreat before they had at least attempted to discover what had occurred. Apart from old Gus Weidner, there was no chance of securing help. And, even if they were, to waste the precious time necessary to ride back and get him, his presence would not materially alter the hopeless odds against them. No, there was nothing for it but to go forward and find out for themselves what had happened. And if it should turn out—as the girl seemed to fear—that Abe Truman had been taken prisoner….

Brandon snapped off his speculations on this point abruptly, conscious that some of the chilling horror that had filled Flame had transferred itself to him also. Vaguely all the disconnected scraps and hints that had been accumulating in his mind began to arrange themselves, fitting together in a sort of mosaic. The pattern of it seemed hopelessly tangled as yet, but he was beginning to have a glimmering suspicion. He found himself all at once hoping fervently that Abe Truman had not been taken alive.

Eyes and ears keyed to the limit, Brandon picked his way ahead. The windy blackness seemed to mock him; there was something vast and uncanny in its apparent emptiness. Almost he began to doubt his senses—to doubt that the lighted window and those ominous gun flashes had ever been anything other than imagination. Why was there now no gleam of light anywhere? Where had the attackers gone?

The soughing whip of wind-tossed branches and a blacker mass of shadow looming up suddenly at his left told Brandon that he was skirting a dense clump of large mesquite trees. Flame urged her horse up beside his.

"The house is just beyond this clump," she whispered. "It's on bare, open ground, right at the edge of the canyon. This is the last shelter. We'd better tie our horses here."

Without waiting for his answer she swung silently from her saddle and led her mount cautiously into the denser obscurity.

Brandon followed her example. There was wisdom in the girl's suggestion. If the ground about the house was bare of cover, then their only chance was to make their way stealthily forward on foot.

Silently, working by the sense of touch alone, they tied their horses to stout branches of the swaying trees. The blackness in the mesquite clump was impenetrable and almost everywhere the waving branches were too low to walk under. Except for the wiry whistle of the wind and the scrape and thresh of the trees there was nothing to be heard.

Brandon reached out and found the girl.

"How wide's this clump?" he whispered.

"Not so very—only a few yards"—her lips were pressed close to his ear—"and the house is about thirty yards beyond the edge of it. This way." She faced him in the right direction with her hands.

"Come on, then," he whispered. "Keep close behind me."

He dropped on his hands and knees and crept swiftly forward under the thorny tangle. It was black here—black as the inside of a coal mine—and, in spite of the wind above, it seemed strangely silent. Suddenly, and without warning, out of the darkness at his side something cold and damp reached out and thrust against Brandon's cheek. As he jerked back, stifling a startled cry, a great dim shape of white materialized silently from the gloom, sniffed at him with tolerant acceptance and slipped past towards Flame. With a throb of unspeakable relief Brandon realized that it was Midnight. But his hand, brushing over the huge white form as it passed, told him that the dog's hair was bristling.

Brandon resumed his crawling advance through the low trailing branches. From the stealthy movements behind him he could tell that both Flame and the dog were following him closely; he caught the sound of the girl's guarded whispers and Midnight's gusty snuffing. This sudden reappearance of the big hound puzzled Brandon; he did not know what interpretation to place upon it. But the dog's bristling tenseness was ominous.

Above the soughing whistle of the trees a new sound came all at once to Brandon's ears—the creak and slam of an unlatched door swinging backwards and forwards in the wind. He found himself suddenly at the outer fringe of the mesquites. The wind gusted savagely down and whipped the thorny branches against his face. Straight ahead of him, looming up blackly in the gloom of the night, he saw the house.

In the belt of inky shadow beneath the outer trees Brandon crouched listening, Flame and the quivering dog at his side. The rushing gusts of the wind and the beat of the branches seemed to fill the night with a lifeless emptiness. Rayless and desolate, the dim bulk of the ranch house hulked before them. The unfastened door creaked and banged mournfully with a hollow, empty sound. The place seemed utterly deserted.

"They've gone," Brandon whispered. "Wait here. I'll make sure."

"Not that way!"—the girl checked him as he moved—"keep away to the right and go round the corral. That'll be safer. Come!"

Before he could stop her she had slipped from the cover of the trees, and, pistol in hand, was leading the way.

He followed her swiftly. Together, the big dog slinking warily beside them, they picked their steps stealthily across a bare, stony space. The shadowy, uneven posts of a small corral loomed suddenly out of the dark. Brandon stumbled all at once and fell sprawling upon something large and hairy. His hand struck in a little puddle of sticky wetness—a puddle that was still faintly warm. He heard the dry scrape of leathers. Flame uttered a faint, gasping cry:

"My God! It's Wings—and dead!"

"How do you know?" Brandon's hands were already traveling in swift exploration over the prone body of the still saddled horse.

"By the saddle," the girl whispered. "This is the saddle that Mexican stole this morning. Besides, I know Wings by the feel of him—by the feel of his head and mane. How did he get here—outside the corral like this? And why?…Wait!" She darted towards the dimly outlined fence and vanished.

Brandon sprang after her. But almost before he had realized where she had gone the girl reappeared, slipping out like a shadow from between the rails of the gate.

"They've killed uncle's horse too!" she whispered breathlessly; "the one he rode today. It was the only other one we kept here besides

Monty and Wings. And now it's lying dead there in the corral. They must have killed the horses first—to make sure that he'd have no chance to escape."

Brandon caught her arm.

"You stay here!" he commanded in a tense whisper. "I'm going across to the house. Give me your flashlight."

"I won't!" Despite her fear-chattering teeth there was stubborn defiance in the girl's voice. "I'm going with you. There's no one there now. And if there is…."

She left the words unfinished. "Come on!" she breathed suddenly.

With a swift movement she wrenched herself free of his grasp and, with Midnight at her heels, darted recklessly through the windy shadows towards the dark loom of the house.

South's pencil sketch of a cabin

CHAPTER 7

The House of Silence

Brandon's heart missed a beat. The dread fear of what the girl's fool-hardy action might bring upon her swept all thought of caution from his mind as he dashed in pursuit. There was no telling who—or what—was lying in that darkened building. He must get ahead of her.

A savage gust of wind hurtled down out of the night and swept whistling round the house. As Brandon reached the steps of the little porch, about one jump ahead of Flame and the dog, the unlatched door banged violently, then swung slowly open again on its groaning hinges. As they halted, breathless and peering, straining their eyes into the shadows, the doorway in front loomed black and silent.

"Give me the light!" Brandon whispered hoarsely.

The girl thrust the little electric-torch into his hand and followed him as he stepped cautiously across the creaking, weather-dry boards of the porch. Before the black yawn of the open door they stood an instant, listening. In the darkness Brandon felt Flame's quivering hand against his; his fingers closed over it instinctively. His own heart was pounding with a violence that seemed to strangle his breathing. He did not know what those black shadows hid. Without warning, at any instant, the darkness might vomit fire and death. And even if the inky gloom hid no living being, of a certainty it must hide....

But the house was empty. The first flooding gleam of the little torch told Brandon that. One glance around the interior of the windswept kitchen, into which he found himself peering, was sufficient to tell him that his fears of an ambush were groundless.

The attackers had gone. Open doors of connecting rooms gaped at him blackly. The house concealed no one living—and a swift round of the rooms revealed no dreadful spectacle of death. Abe Truman and those who had swooped down upon him out of the night had vanished utterly.

And—except in the kitchen—there was little trace to tell of tragedy. The ranch-house was small. Besides the long, narrow kitchen, which occupied one end of the building and ran clear from front to back, the old frame structure contained only three other rooms—a living-room, that stretched from the kitchen along the entire remaining front of the house, and two bedrooms; one of which—plainly enough Abe Truman's from the array of boots and chaps—was reached by a door in the far corner of the living-room, while the other could be entered only from the kitchen.

None of these rooms, as the limited rays of the little torch revealed their interiors to the eyes of Brandon and the girl, appeared to have been much disturbed. In the bedroom that opened from the kitchen— the bedroom that was obviously Flame's—the window had apparently been opened and shut hastily. The curtain was torn from it, and many of the photographs and trinkets that had stood upon the top of the heavy chest of drawers immediately beneath it had been scattered and upset. A large photograph in a bent silver frame lay face downward in a sparkle of glass slivers upon the floor, with a heel-mark plainly enough visible on its pasteboard back. But these were the only signs of disorder. Mechanically, as Brandon flashed the light over the big bed and into all the corners, Flame stooped and picked up the fallen picture. She glanced at it and clutched it tightly against her skirt.

"They've gone!" Brandon said, satisfied that this last room was empty. "There's no one here—not in the house, anyway."

As though his words had broken the tension of silent, wide-eyed horror which, since she had stepped across the threshold of the house, had held her like a spell, Flame found her voice in a stricken gasp:

"Oh, God! They've got him!" she moaned. "They've taken him away alive! And they'll...they'll...." Her words choked shudderingly.

"Bear up, girl! We don't know anything yet!" Brandon caught her arm with a steadying grip of sympathy. "We can't tell yet what's happened. Wasn't there anyone living here beside you and your uncle—no help? No one at all?"

Flame shook her head. "Just the two of us. We didn't dare to have anyone else here because—because...." Her dry voice checked falteringly.

Brandon stepped back into the kitchen where already Midnight, his hair bristling, was snuffing up and down in tense excitement. Here the signs of violence were visible enough, for it was here, evidently, that Abe Truman had been sitting when the attack had fallen. A crumpled old Stetson hat—with which, obviously, he had dashed out the light—lay on the table beside the overturned oil lamp and the remains of an unfinished supper. His chair was lying upset near the table, and by the iron cook stove, which was cold and stood drearily in a drying puddle of ash-greyed water, lay an empty bucket, the contents of which had plainly been used to hastily drown the glow of the fire. It was clear enough that Abe Truman—with some instant warning of his peril—had sought protection in darkness—whether vainly or not it was impossible to tell.

But it was upon the kitchen that the guns of the attackers had been focused. Bullet marks were visible here and there in the woodwork. A heavy can standing on a shelf had a ragged hole in it from which a stream of sugar had cascaded down and formed a white mound upon the floor. A stone crock in the far corner lay in fragments; there were three bullet holes in the boards of the back door; and, through the two lower panes of the little side window—smashed plainly enough by shots—the wind swirled and whistled shrilly.

The violence of the windstorm was mounting. Roaring eddies of air rushed in through the open doorway with a fury that threatened to lift the kitchen roof. Brandon sprang to close the wildly slamming door. But just as his fingers touched the handle a sudden savage gust tore it from his grasp and almost instantly whirled the door back upon him full force. The smashing impact dashed the little electric-torch from his hand and sent it hurtling across the kitchen floor. The light snapped out.

Brandon dragged the door shut and fastened it. In the hushed, pitchy darkness that filled the interior of the kitchen he heard plainly the thin whine of the wind skirling in through the broken window-panes and the rustling sound of Flame's hand fumbling frantically along a shelf. An instant later there came the rattle of a match-box. A match spurted in the girl's fingers.

Brandon leaped across the floor and caught up the flashlight from where it had landed beneath the table. An exclamation escaped him:

"It's dead! Bulb smashed, I guess!"

"There's a big flashlight in the gun cupboard," Flame said breathlessly. "We'll get that!"

The match in her hand shriveled and went out. She struck a fresh one, led the way swiftly back into Abe Truman's room and jerked open the door of a high cupboard. She gave a startled cry.

"It's gone! And the spare revolver and all the cartridges!" She flung the door wide and peered into a narrow compartment that ran up at one end of the shelves. "And the rifles are gone too!" she gasped. "They took the flashlight and every gun and cartridge in the place! They must have known just where to look!"

The flickering match flared and died, leaving them again in utter darkness. Flame had left the matchbox on the kitchen table, Brandon remembered. He fumbled in his shirt pocket, found one of his own matches and struck it hastily. The inky shadows that pressed upon them seemed of a sudden charged with new peril. The few seconds that had elapsed since they had first entered the dark house had passed in a fevered whirl.

With something of a shock Brandon realized that the relief of finding the place empty had for the instant made him forget his own weaponless condition; and it was little wonder, as they had run hastily from room to room dreading each instant what they might find lying there, that Flame had not thought of the extra arms before. Now, with this sinister discovery that all the guns had been removed, the realization of his own defenselessness rushed back upon Brandon tenfold. He was conscious of a sudden apprehensive chill. His eyes swept about him in frantic search for something that might serve as a weapon. But he could see nothing of any use.

"There's a lantern in the kitchen!" Flame said, with sudden remembrance. "We'll have to light that!"

Together they hurried back. In the last flare of the expiring match the girl snatched an oil lantern from a shelf. Brandon lit it hurriedly. By the spurt of the new match and the spreading glow of light which grew as he snapped the lantern-glass back into place, he saw that the silver-framed photograph which Flame had picked up in her bedroom lay now on the table next to the lamp, evidently where she had placed it when she had first reached for the matches. It was face up this time. His first glimpse told Brandon that it was the picture of a wedding group. There was something about it that seemed to grip his eye startlingly, but in the passing glance of the instant he could not tell just what it was.

There was no room in his mind just then for unconnected details—the whereabouts of the missing man held his whole thought. The stealthy assassins had struck and fled—that much was evident. The body of their victim was not in the house. Unless the girl was right and Abe Truman had been captured, it was probable that his corpse lay outside.

On the impulse of the thought Brandon sprang to the back door and flung it open. A furious gust of wind and Flame's warning cry, as she realized his intention, checked him on the threshold as the light board door swung outward.

"Take care!" the girl cried, "I'll bring the light! The side of the canyon slid in last year in the big storm. The drop's right close to the doorstep. You'll go over the edge and break your neck if you're not careful!"

She was at his side in an instant. As the dim radiance of the wind-flickered lantern in her hand cut the night's gusty dark Brandon saw with a start that she had spoken the literal truth. Little more than three feet from the back doorstep the ground seemed to drop away into space. The edge of the recent slide was still raw and sharp on the stony earth. Wind tore up out of the black void, and mingled with its rushing note was the beating scrape and slap of tossing branches in the canyon depths.

"It's deep right here," Flame said. "The flood water cut under and caused a regular landslide. We've been going to move the house."

Brandon took the lantern. Together, swiftly and cautiously, they examined the edge of the bank. The cave-in of the canyon lip was irregular, Brandon discovered. Its nearest approach to the house was almost directly opposite the back door of the kitchen.

On either side of the doorway, at a short distance, the area of firm ground widened rapidly. But neither on these wider benches nor on the lip of the abrupt slide itself could his eyes discover any trace of struggle or footprints. The ground was far too hard and stony to receive definite impressions, and any slight marks would have been blotted out almost instantly by the swirling wind. Unless the body of Abe Truman lay here somewhere there was little hope, by lantern light, of gaining any clue to his disappearance.

But there was no body. Buffeted by the wind, stumbling their way in the wan circle of light flung by the dim, gust-flickered lantern, Brandon and Flame searched the outskirts of the house with feverish swiftness. Hastily, and with Midnight, still tense and bristling, snuffing and circling the ground around them, they examined the vicinity of the corral and the two dead horses and explored the mesquite clump where, tails to wind, their tethered mounts hunched bleakly where they had left them among the trees. As a last hope Brandon scouted along the edge of the canyon, and finding a place that seemed a little less steep climbed down into the depths with the lantern, while Flame crouched waiting above. Making his way back along the rough, bush-grown bed of the canyon he examined the foot of the steep, caved-in bank. A tangle of old torn-up roots and a sprinkling of later growth bushes scattered the steep face of the slide and partly screened the foot of it, but again the hard earth and the dim light defied his eyes. He could see no signs and there was no trace of human presence either living or dead.

Baffled, and out of breath from the strenuous return up the side of the canyon, Brandon led the way back to the house. The futility of further search for the vanished man was evident. In the dark the task was hopeless. It would need daylight to decide whether Abe Truman had been murdered or spirited away a prisoner. For the moment, Brandon realized, the safety of the girl and prompt action to set pursuit upon the trail of the gunmen were the two things that were vital.

Prompt action!—but what? Brandon found his thought checked abruptly. There was mystery to this grim happening. It hinged upon something which he did not know—something at which he could only vaguely guess. Flame's stubborn reticence and efforts at concealment of facts told him that there was much more to the tragedy than appeared on the surface. The girl held the key to the mystery. The action to be taken depended upon her.

Brandon tugged at the door and held it open against the beat of the wind so that Flame could enter. The girl seemed utterly crushed and unnerved. As she stumbled across the threshold she stopped short with a sharp, breathless question:

"Where's Midnight?"

Brandon shot a glance round. For the first time he noticed that the great white hound was no longer with them. He raised the lantern and peered an instant. "He's not here," he said. "He's slipped away somewhere. I guess he'll come back."

He followed the girl into the kitchen and shut the door. As he set the lantern upon the littered table the big, silver-framed photograph of the wedding group once more caught his eye. Out of it, of a sudden, a face seemed to stare up at him—the face of the bride. With an exclamation of astonishment he wheeled on Flame:

"You?"—he cried, pointing to the picture—"is—is that *you*?"

Flame shook her head wearily:

"No," she said. "You might know it isn't me by the old style clothes they're all wearing."

Brandon's eyes flashed back to the photo and returned to the girl's face in amazement.

"Then, if it isn't you, it's—?"

Flame nodded:

"She was my mother," she said softly. "She's dead now. She was Mollie O'Hara—the last of the O'Haras. That picture was taken the day she married Jake Templeton in San Francisco—twenty-one years ago."

Brandon took an involuntary step back, startled by the sudden realization that his dimly formed suspicions had been correct. "Then you"—he gasped—you are—"

Flame's drooping shoulders squared. Her weary eyes lit for an instant with a flash of reckless defiance:

"Yes!" she snapped. "Now you know it! I'm Mollie Templeton—daughter of Jake Templeton, the worst scoundrel on the west coast."

Oil of South with his two burros painted by Thomas Crocker

CHAPTER 8

The Skein Unwinds

For a moment Brandon felt staggered, not so much by the girl's confession of her real name—which already he had dimly suspected—as by the clue her statement had given him. Impulsively, reading easily enough the defiant humiliation in the tired, white face, he reached forward and caught her hand:

"That doesn't make any difference, Flame—who you are or who your father is. I want to help you—and him. If you think he's been taken prisoner—"

The flash of gratitude in the girl's eyes changed abruptly to a harder light. She clenched her fists...

"My *father*?" she cried angrily. "Him?—help *him*?...It isn't *him* they've taken! That's the horror of it!"

"Not your father?" Brandon released the girl's hand in amazement. "Not your father? Then—then whom?" He stared at her in bewilderment.

"It's Amos they've got!" Flame said chokingly. "Amos! Jake's twin brother!"

Brandon shook his head helplessly: "I don't understand."

Flame took a step towards the table and laid her finger on the photograph.

"There's not much to explain," she said in a low, tired voice. "There were two Templetons—Jake and Amos. They were twins and looked almost exactly alike. That's the reason Jake always wore a beard and Amos went clean-shaven—so folks could tell them apart. This is my father—here." She pointed. "And this one is Amos."

Brandon's eyes followed her finger in astonishment. Except for the nattily trimmed Vandyke beard and moustache which the bridegroom wore, the resemblance between the two men was startling.

"Jake looks pretty good there," Flame went on. In the reaction of terror and grief her reticence seemed to have broken down utterly; but there was a threat of hysteria in her dull, level voice. "He was a gambler in San Francisco then—a regular dandy they say.

Afterwards—when he was in the smuggling business—he let himself go and used to be proud of the ragged mass of beard that covered his face. They called him Red-beard, you know." Her voice was low and oddly mechanical. But there was no hiding the hard, bitter note in it.

"And Amos?..." Brandon's question was tense. For a moment the truth of the mystery as it slowly dawned on him banished all else from his mind.

"Amos was the finest man in the world!" Flame said with sudden vigor. "He was just as fine and straight as Jake was rotten and crooked. He had a cattle ranch in New Mexico. He came to 'Frisco for Jake's wedding. And three years later—when mother died—he came again and got me and took me out to his ranch. He wasn't married—he never has married. But he's taken care of me ever since I was two years old. Most of the schooling I've ever had he's given me. He'd had a good education and he taught me himself. He's sure been good."

"But your father?" Brandon said. "How about—"

"*Him*?" Flame interrupted with sharp scorn. "He deserted mother a year after I was born. He used to beat her. He left her sick and starving in San Francisco. Amos didn't know for a long time. When he found out, he sent money. But it was too late then. Mother died. Jake? He didn't care. He'd only married mother in the hope that he'd find out the secret. "

"You mean the secret of the old O'Hara mine?" Brandon said. "Did your mother know it?"

The girl's white face and dry, burning eyes held him. Her low, steady speech, each word of which brushed back the dark shadows of mystery that had baffled him, made him forget the scene around. For the moment he was oblivious to the yell of the wind roaring round the house—oblivious to the shadowy, lantern-lit kitchen and to the grim tragedy which had just taken place. For a space, gripped by the girl's words, even the menacing shadow of peril which might well be hanging over themselves was blotted from his mind.

"Did your mother know the secret?" he repeated.

Flame shook her head.

"No," she said, "but there were some that thought she did. Captain Terrence O'Hara had a brother—Patrick—in San Francisco, according to what I've heard. And the rumor is that Captain Terrence, just a few days before he was killed, made a will stating that in case anything happened to him the Lucky Ledge was to go to this brother Patrick and his descendants.

"Years afterwards the lawyer in San Diego who drew up that will was discovered to have been a crook. It was proved that he'd had secret dealings with the Morgan gang. He's supposed to have given the Morgans the tip about the will. He knew that when the Captain sent the will up to his attorneys in San Francisco there would be a map of the location of the mine attached to it. He knew, too, that the Captain intended to send a shipment of gold at the same time. And he knew about what day the shipment was to be made. He gave the gang the tip. That's why Captain O'Hara was ambushed and killed.

"But the Morgans were killed themselves the next day. Neither the papers nor the gold were ever found. Some folks believed that Captain O'Hara had sent them earlier and by another way, and that they'd reached the attorneys in San Francisco safe, like he'd intended."

"And Jake Templeton thought your mother had that plan?"

Flame nodded. "She was the last of the O'Haras. She was the daughter of Rodney O'Hara—Patrick's only son. The O'Haras haven't been lucky. The old folks—Patrick and his wife—were dead. Rodney and his wife died within a year of each other. My mother was left alone in the world at eighteen, and she married Jake Templeton when she was twenty. She was the last of the line. All the family papers came into her possession, including a box of documents that had originally come from Captain Terrence's lawyers.

That's what Jake was after. When he'd gone through all the papers and found out that there was no secret—that mother knew nothing—he deserted her. He's a devil! He's responsible for my mother's death. And...and now this!..." She clenched her hands.

"You mean that Jake has...," Brandon began.

"Yes, yes!" Flame cried fiercely. "It's *him* they're after! It's his fault. He's drawn the Tong on us again. Oh, God!...Nine years—nine years of hiding and fear and loneliness and terror!...And then...then this!"

Her voice broke chokingly. Once more Brandon's hand went out to hers in a pitying grip. The touch seemed to give her courage. She pulled herself together with an effort.

"Yes, yes! It was Jake," she went on bitterly, answering the question in his eyes. "After he deserted mother he went to Lower California and began to smuggle Chinese into this country. His daring and craftiness made him successful for a long time. But he went too far at last. He murdered a cargo of Chinamen one night and threw their bodies overboard so that the Government officers who were in pursuit of his boat wouldn't find them on board as evidence against him. The officers let him go—they couldn't prove anything on him—but the Yellow Dragon Tong—the most powerful Chinese society in San Francisco—swore vengeance on Jake and every living member of his blood.

"Jake bolted from Lower California. He came to us. He'd shaved his beard and disguised himself. He stayed with Amos only one day, and then slipped away. Agents of the Tong were on his trail. Afterwards we realized that his coming to us had been a black scheme to save his own skin by diverting their vengeance on to his brother.

"The Tong gunmen believed Amos was Jake. They came to our New Mexico ranch one night—two of them. Uncle woke up just in the nick of time and shot them both or we'd have been murdered in our sleep. The sheriff thought it was just an attempted robbery. But uncle knew better—and he knew Chinese persistence. He sold the ranch for a song, and the minute the money was paid we took the first train out of New Mexico. I was only a kid then—just over eleven—but I can remember it like it was yesterday. We changed our names, and we've been trailed and hunted ever since. There's no protection against a terror that trails you like they did—no use appealing for police protection. Every shadow and dark corner is a peril. The only safety was to hide.

"I guess Jake's trick worked. He got away apparently. But we've had an awful time. For the first four years we were hunted like rats. We moved from state to state—changing our names—hiding out. We had a dozen close calls of being murdered."

"And in the end you came back here—close to the very district Jake used to operate in?" Brandon said in amazement.

"It was the last chance," Flame answered huskily. "For two years before we came here things seemed to have quieted down a little—we hoped we'd given the Tong the slip. But our money was almost gone, and we knew we couldn't keep on moving much longer.

So while we still had a little money left uncle suggested that we come down here. He figured that the very daring of moving right back in the thick of things might save us for a while. They wouldn't be expecting such a trick.

"And besides, he'd studied up all the old papers and the rumors about the Lucky Ledge and the lost gold shipment. He figured we might have a chance to find either the one or the other. We decided to take the risk. The plan worked, partly, too. We've been hidden here safe for three years. But we've never found the gold or the mine. We searched everywhere for the secret. Everywhere except in the right place—in the graves of the Morgan gang."

Brandon started. The full truth burst on him at last. But it was not in the fashion that he had expected.

"You think that the gold was…That someone dug into those graves for—"

"I think Jake is back," Flame answered tensely. "I think he's taken heart over the way things seem to have blown over—he probably wasn't hunted at all after he set the pursuit on us—and he's got a new tip somewhere and come back after the hidden map and the gold. The instant I set eyes on those opened graves I suspected it—that's why I thought you were a crook.

"What Gus told us makes me all the more certain that it was Jake who opened them. That Pedro Martinez must have come up from Mexico with Jake, and he's been prowling around here spying. He stole Wings so as to hurry back to Jake with news. Jake can't be so far away from here because Wings must have come back of his own accord. And Wings must have come after uncle had got back and gone into the house. Uncle would have unsaddled him and put him in the corral if he'd known he was here."

Brandon started. With a flash of recollection he remembered the fire he had seen far back in the dark near the stage station. He voiced his suspicion in swift words.

Flame nodded in agreement. "Yes, that was probably Jake's camp," she said wearily. "I wish you had told me. But it wouldn't have made any difference. The Tong was ahead of us then, anyway. They must have got wind of Jake's return and trailed him. But, as usual, he's managed to switch them on to an innocent man. And now…."

She broke off abruptly, her hands clenching and unclenching nervously as she stood staring with hard, unseeing eyes into the flickering shadows. In the tense pause that for a moment seemed to hush the dim interior of the lantern-lit kitchen, the roar of the outer wind came with louder fury. The old ranch-house shook in the charging gusts that swirled around it. Flurries of flying gravel rattled like buckshot upon the tinder-dry siding.

Brandon pulled himself together, breaking with a jerk the instant of spellbound inaction in which the girl's suddenly ended words had left him. The mystery had cleared, he realized. The tangled skein had all at once unwound and now lay plain before him. And with the realization there came instantly a warning sense of peril. Almost fiercely he gripped the girl's arm.

"Quick," he cried hoarsely, "let's get out of here! They'll come back—they'll come back for *you*!" Deadly fear for the girl's safety was suddenly upon him. This ruthless Oriental vengeance which had clung so persistently to its purpose would not now stop short of completion—it would not be satisfied with but one victim. With a stunning realization of danger—imminent danger—he whirled the girl towards the front door and snatched for the light.

But with a sudden tigerish fury, and before his reaching fingers could close on the lantern handle, Flame swung him aside and jerked herself free. With a flare—as though his words and action had been electric sparks to powder—her mood of crushed despair had changed in a twinkling to one of blind, defiant rage. She snatched up her pistol from where she had laid it on the table.

"Run!" she gasped furiously. "Me? Bolt now like a frightened rabbit—me? Nothing doing! I've had enough of running—we've run for nine years. Now I'm going to fight! Fight!—do you hear me? Fight!"

Her face was flushed. Her eyes sparkled dangerously. The outburst was hysterical, Brandon realized that. And, startled as he was by the abruptness of it, he felt of a sudden easier. The crisis had passed. Despite her blind burst of unreason the girl's nerves had steadied. Her dull half-coma of despair had vanished. Her self-reliance had come back. He knew now that he no longer need dread her weak collapse.

"Listen, Flame!" Brandon laid a steadying hand on the girl's shoulder. "Pull yourself together. We've got to get out of here and back to Gus's place while the getting's good. There's not a second to lose. We've got to get action. The quicker the alarm is turned in the better chance there is of heading those devils oft. We can't do a thing by ourselves –you know that. It was madness to stay here this long. For all we know they're not far off. And if they come back…."

Flame stamped her foot. "God!" she breathed between her tight-clenched teeth. "If only some of the yellow devils *would* come back! If only I could get a shot at them, I'd…."

She stopped short. A sound had come all at once from outside the house—a sound that was not caused by the wind. An instant later, as he stood tensed in a sudden frozen immobility, the noise came again to Brandon's ears—a padding shuffling as of something soft and heavy moving over dry boards.

Flame's face cleared. She caught her breath in relief.

"It's Midnight come back!" she cried. Impulsively, before Brandon could make a movement to check her, she had sprung to the rear door and flung it open.

But it was not Midnight. Even as he uttered his shout of caution and darted after the girl, Brandon saw a crouching, shadowy figure straighten up suddenly from the gusty blackness outside the door. A lean yellow hand shot forward into the light, snatched Flame's pistol from her unready grasp and sent it hurtling out into the darkness.

And almost at the same instant the front door of the kitchen whirled open with a bang. As he leaped blindly to the girl's aid, Brandon heard from behind the running thud of shoeless feet racing towards him across the boarded floor.

South's pottery sold well in Julian (Photo: Marshal South)

CHAPTER 9

Trapped

There was no time to think—Brandon acted by instinct only. In that whirlwind flash as he hurled himself forward upon Flame's assailant, he was conscious of nothing save the dread realization that the gang had returned—that the girl and he were hopelessly trapped. In a reckless fury of despair, careless of the leveled pistol which belched fire almost in his face, he whirled the girl aside and flung himself barehanded upon the lean—faced Chinese gunman who sprang through the doorway to meet him.

And, for the instant, the sheer insanity of his headlong rush saved him. Startled a little by the lightning-like savagery of it, the gunman's shot went wild. Before he could fire again the full weight of Brandon's leaping body crashed into him like an avalanche.

Knocked breathless by the impact, the Chinaman toppled backwards in the open doorway, with Brandon, unable to check himself, sprawling on top of him. Locked together, clutching and heaving, they rolled from the kitchen doorstep to the narrow ledge of stony ground beyond.

It had all happened so suddenly, Brandon's movements had been blindly automatic. But the impact with the hard ground as they struck it seemed to clear his mind to a flash warning of new danger. The precipitous drop of the canyon edge lay just beyond the doorstep he remembered; he realized that they must be on the very lip of it. With a desperate, instinctive effort to avoid it he heaved sideways, thrusting and pounding at the straining, writhing form that gripped him.

But even as he rolled over, panting and struggling in a desperate effort to prevent his furiously fighting antagonist from bringing his pistol into action, Brandon suddenly felt his feet kick out into empty space.

He felt the hard earth crumple under the thrust of his striking heels. A roaring gust of wind swept up out of the depths, driving the flying sand grains into his face. Undermost, pinned down momentarily by the weight of the cursing, clawing man on top of him, Brandon heaved frantically to squirm back from the brink. With his main strength centered on a herculean struggle to pin useless his opponent's pistol hand, he realized that the next roll would carry them both into the depths.

But of a sudden, as he heaved and battered in a mad effort to writhe clear, some heavy body, catapulting from the darkness, hurled itself upon the man above him with a snarling roar. Crushed breathless and flung sideways by the violent impact, Brandon's grip loosened. His right hand struck with a jar against the edge of the doorstep, and with a sudden instinct of preservation his fingers locked round the rough board with a vice-like grip. The next instant the weight upon him lifted. With a wrench and a jerk the struggling body of his antagonist tore free.

For one whirlwind flash Brandon had a dim glimpse of a huge white shape and a fighting human form swirling together in the darkness. Then, with a plunge, the lashing, clawing mass vanished abruptly into thin air. From below, blurred in the rush of the wind, came suddenly the crash of breaking bushes and a frantic spatter of pistol shots that snuffed out in a strangling scream and a dreadful, dwindling snarling.

Panting and shaken, Brandon scrambled to his feet. The realization that Midnight's timely attack had saved him was eclipsed in the instant rush of his dread fear for Flame. Even as he gained his footing, aware half consciously that beyond the corner of the house the posts of the corral were of a sudden shimmering ghostly white from the glow of distant motor-car headlights, a pistol-shot crashed somewhere in the lantern-lit kitchen—a shot that was drowned in a girl's terrified cry and the pounding trample of feet. In the dim light as he hurled himself headlong into the room, Brandon had a glimpse of Flame crushed back across the cold stove and fighting frantically in the clutches of a squat and powerful Chinaman. Both her hands were locked desperately about the gunman's heavy automatic. Plainly enough she had managed somehow to escape the shot, and with every ounce of her strength she was struggling now to hold from her the still smoking muzzle of the deadly weapon.

Brandon crossed the floor in a bound. The first glimpse as he plunged through the door had told him that the solitary gunman who grappled with Flame had no companions. The realization brought him a sudden flare of hope that gave new strength to his muscles as he flung himself upon the girl's assailant.

Swift as he had sprung, however, his rush was not quick enough. With a guttural exclamation of fury that was more like a bestial snarl than a human cry, the Chinaman whirled to meet him. Tearing his pistol with a jerk from the girl's hampering grasp, the heavy-set man leaped aside with an agility that was startling. His gun belched fire in two merging detonations.

But neither of the shots found their mark. Quick as the gunman had moved, Flame, released from his pinioning clutch, had moved quicker. With a lightning-like snatch the girl had caught up the empty water-bucket from the floor and hurled it. The light, galvanized pail crashed squarely into the Chinaman's face, spoiling his aim. The heavy bullets flew wild. And the next instant, as the half-dazed gunman instinctively flung up his arm, the smashing blow of Brandon's fist, intended for his jaw, struck full force upon his pistol hand instead, hurling the heavy automatic from his grasp and sending it flying through the kitchen window in a shower of splintering glass.

Quick as thought Brandon struck again. But his advantage was but momentary. Like a flash the squat-bodied man recovered himself. With the snakelike move of an expert Oriental wrestler he sidestepped and leaped forward. Tripped adroitly by an unfamiliar trick, and flung headlong by his own momentum, Brandon crashed heavily to the floor. With a jerk that seemed almost to snap the muscles, his arms were twisted violently behind his back. Half stunned by the fall he found himself sprawling face downward upon the floorboards, pinned suddenly helpless by the merciless lock-hold and the crushing weight of the muscular man who knelt triumphantly upon him. He felt the swift movement as his victorious opponent snatched out a knife.

But in the same instant, even as he realized that death was upon him, Brandon heard the clang of metal and the dull thud of a crushing blow. As though from an electric shock the man kneeling upon him stiffened, and as suddenly wilted forward in a relaxed heap. With a violent heave Brandon tore himself free of the loosening grip and rolled clear. He scrambled dizzily to his feet to find Flame bending in tense, tigerish watchfulness over the inert form of his stunned adversary. In her hands, poised aloft in instant readiness for another blow, was the heavy, cast-iron stove door which she had jerked from its hinge pins and used with deadly effect.

"Quick!" With no instant either for gratitude or for a second glance at his stricken opponent, Brandon snatched the girl's crude weapon from her hands and, catching her arm, swept her towards the rear exit. There was no moment to lose, he realized. Subconsciously, even through the whirlwind daze of those last frenzied seconds, the gleam of the approaching motor-car lights—flashing and vanishing fitfully through the gustily banging front door—had registered upon his brain. Even above the rush of the wind the churning throb of a suddenly stopped motor had penetrated to his ears. The realization that the lights had of a sudden been switched off galvanized him to frantic haste.

But, even as he clutched the girl and raced her towards the back door, there came a trampling stamp of feet on the front porch and a sharp, reassuring English shout—a shout that jerked Brandon to an abrupt halt. These newcomers were not Chinese, he realized: they were Americans. As he spun round in amazed relief at this unexpected arrival of help, the dull lantern rays were paled suddenly by dazzling beams of light. Through the door, a high-power rifle in his hands and his weather-tanned, bushy-browed face clearly outlined in the glare of the electric torches carried by his close-crowding companions, came a hatless, toughly built man of about fifty.

Flame leaped towards him with a glad cry:

"Oh, thank God! Thank God! I thought that you…."

Her voice froze. She recoiled as from a blow, her eyes of a sudden traveling dazedly from the seamed face to the leather jacket, rough corduroy pants, and high miner's boots of the man before her. She shrank back—staring—terror-stricken.

"*Jake!*" she gasped fearfully. "My God! It's not Amos! It's *Jake!*"

South's pencil sketch entitled "pear tree"

⁐

CHAPTER 10

Jake Templeton

It had happened so swiftly. Checked for the moment by the sudden hope of rescue born of that reassuring English shout—a hope that had been confirmed by Flame's first thankful cry of relief—Brandon had been thrown completely off his guard. Before he could recover—before the full significance of the situation had dawned on him—the newcomers, four in number and all heavily armed, had crowded into the room and surrounded them. Even as Flame's startled gasp of recognition woke Brandon to a realization of who these new arrivals were, one of the four stepped swiftly past him and shut the back door. Escape was cut off.

Jake shouldered forward, a grin of malicious enjoyment on his seamed face as he noted the girl's sudden terror.

"Correct, kid—It's me!" he said thickly, the unmistakable blur of liquor in his voice. "You've growed some since I see you last, ain't you, eh? But what's all this—what you been playin' round at here?"

He halted, his narrowing eyes sweeping the kitchen at a glance and focusing sharply on the prone figure of the Chinaman. "What yuh got here?" he demanded. "Been a fight-uh?"

He strode over to the already feebly stirring gunman and peered down at him. A startled oath escaped him:

"Hell! It's a Chink!" he exploded. "An' by God, it's...Hey, Slant!" He beckoned excitedly. "Come take a look at this bird! Ain't this Yee Fong—the Chink that runs that little eatin' house in Ensenada?"

The man addressed, a tall, flashily-attired individual, approached and turned the beam of his electric torch full upon the face at his feet.

"Yeh—that's him right enough!" he said in astonishment. "It's Yee Fong. An' I reckon that means...?"

"Hell! It means that this varmint recognized me down there an' trailed us here!" Jake straightened up with sudden fury. "Th' dirty yellow skunk's in th' pay of the Tong. He was aimin' to bump me off—that's what!"

His jaw stiffened savagely. He wheeled abruptly on the girl. "What's been happenin', kid?" he demanded. "How come this Chink here?"

Flame drew back, her lips tightening. But the fear in her face seemed of a sudden to have given place to scorn and loathing. "Why ask?" she said coolly. "You know more about it than I do. It's your favorite trick to save your own skin by switching your enemies on to us." Her eyes flashed dangerously.

Jake's face darkened. "None o' that, kid!" he snarled. "Don't try to run none o' that high-hat stuff on me. You're my brat an' you be damn' careful and remember that or I'll whale hell outa you. What happened here? Spit it out!"

Flame drew her breath sharply. It seemed to Brandon that her face went suddenly steely hard. But her voice came quietly:

"You can see just what happened. This man"—she pointed to the reviving gunman—"sneaked up here and tried to murder us. That's all. You got here just at the finish."

"Yuh mean to say there was only this one Chink?" Jake demanded incredulously. His eyes swept round, taking in the evidence left by flying bullets.

Flame nodded, her eyes following the suspicious glance.

"We had some shooting," she said coolly, "before the guns went through the window in the fight. But there was just this one man."

Jake's relief vented itself in an explosive guffaw.

"Shootin'? I'll say yuh had some shootin'—an' damn poor shootin' too, on both sides, looks like." His eyes again took in the bullet holes about the kitchen. "Haw, haw! Some fight, eh, Slant? Chink comes here lookin' t' bump me off an' he runs inta my brat an' her willie-boy an' they chase each other round th' room shootin' holes in th' woodwork till finally they have t' fight it out with their mitts—durin' which process they both loses their guns. Haw haw! Some fight—some fight."

His thick, liquor-sodden voice was charged with an unnatural jocularity which sprang, Brandon surmised, from a vast relief that had been inspired by Flame's skillful and deliberate lie. It was plain that Jake had had no suspicion that the Tong gunmen were trailing him—he apparently knew nothing whatever of the motor-car load of them that had come up the valley. And now, under the illusion that Yee Fong had been his only peril, the fear which he had displayed at first sight of the Chinaman had utterly vanished.

Brandon's mind worked swiftly. This sudden appearance of Jake boded no good. Flame's account of her ruffianly parent and the very real terror which sight of him had inspired in her were more than sufficient to convince Brandon that no good was to be expected from either Jake or his gang. The promptness with which the gang had surrounded them and blocked all channels of escape pointed to a deliberate and preconceived plan. They had come evidently on some definite purpose, and their coming, Brandon realized, had brought not rescue but new peril.

And, for the moment, Brandon sensed only too clearly that the girl and he were helpless. Surrounded as they were by a quartet of well-armed, watchful ruffians, whose faces were clue enough to their characters, any move to escape would be madness. There was nothing for it but to await developments. He could do nothing yet but stand by helplessly.

But more than by the realization of the futility of any action on his part Brandon was held by amazement at Flame. The girl's coolness and skillful lying had startled him—and he had construed more than one meaning glance, which she had managed to flash in his direction, as a plain intimation to hold his own tongue. The purpose of the girl's subterfuge puzzled him. That Flame realized quite as well as he that the two Chinamen who had attacked them were but advance scouts of the main gang he did not doubt. Why, then, was she so deliberately concealing the truth? Was it possible that some scheme of revenge had flashed into her mind? Was it possible that, utterly indifferent now to her own safety, she was hoping to delay Jake and entrap him in the same fate that he had drawn upon her uncle?

And, as this explanation of the girl's purpose dawned upon him, Brandon was filled suddenly with a wild hope that the scheme would succeed. Something of Flame's hatred of this villainous, unnatural parent of hers had entered into him also. The studied, contemptuous way in which Jake had ignored him, the sneering insults in the ruffian's speech and, above all, his deliberate attitude of brutality towards Flame, filled Brandon with an insane fury that blotted all else. He was suddenly thankful for the easy manner in which Jake had fallen for the deception. And he found himself hoping fervently that none of the gang would awake to the fact—plainly revealed by the splintered wood—that most of the shots, with the exception of those through the back door, had come from outside the house.

But if Jake had been hoodwinked to a large degree his suspicions were by no means quieted. His burst of relieved jocularity ended in an abrupt snap-back to his natural manner of watchful, overbearing brutality. He kicked the dazed and writhing Chinaman savagely with his heavy boot.

"Hey, Rufe!" he barked, with a jerk of his head to one of the others, "this damned yellowskin's wakin' up. Get that coil o' line off the wall there an' knot him up. Make a good job of it, so's th' skunk'll stay put till I get time to attend t' him."

A short, hard-faced man with one eye and a gnawed, tobacco-stained yellow moustache reached down the light rope from its peg and shambled forward to the task. Jake wheeled on Flame:

"Where's Amos?" he demanded.

"Amos went after the deputy sheriff this morning when we found that this bright friend of yours had stolen our horse," Flame answered with a gesture towards the scar-faced Mexican who now lounged watchfully beside the back door. "I'm expecting Amos and several others back any minute. They'll be glad to see you."

Jake snarled. "None o' your damned lip! If Amos ain't here, what th' hell's them two horses doin' tied in th' mesquite clump?"

"One of those horses belongs to me," Flame answered crisply, "the other is Mr. Brandon's."

"Meanin' this jasper here, eh!"—Jake gave Brandon an insolent stare. "Then what in hell'd yuh tie 'em in th' mesquites for—saddled? Why didn't you put 'em in th' corral?"

"If you had eyes sharp enough to see the two live horses in the mesquites when you drove up maybe you saw the two dead ones at the corral too," Flame retorted. "My friend and I had been out all day hunting that horse thief." Again she jerked a thumb at the leering Mexican. "We got back here real late this evening and found our missing horse lying dead by the corral. The one inside the rails had been killed also. We didn't want to track up the ground any more before the deputy had a chance to examine it.

That's why we tied our horses to the trees. And naturally we left the saddles on—after we'd discovered those two dead animals we didn't know what was likely to happen. Now, is there anything else you'd like to know?"

"A hell of a lot!" Jake's tone was menacing. "Who killed them horses?"

"You can tell me that perhaps," Flame said dryly. "Maybe it was this same gentleman who came here to try to kill Amos—in mistake for you."

"Huh!" Jake scowled. His eyes roved about the room. "An' yuh mean t' say this Chink was waitin' for you in th' house when you got here?"

"No. He was outside somewhere. He waited till we'd got the lamp and the fire alight. Then he started shooting through the window."

"Huh! An' you soused a bucket o' water on th' fire an' knocked out th' lamp, eh? How come this here lantern lit?"

"I lit it afterwards," Flame answered coolly, "after he'd rushed into the house and attacked Mr. Brandon."

"Huh! That ain't your hat," Jake's stubby forefinger indicated the Stetson on the table.

"No, it's an old one of Amos's that I wore today. I knocked the lamp out with it."

"Huh!" Jake grunted. He gave a dubious shrug, but it was plain enough that much of his suspicion had been allayed. His hard, blood-shot eyes fastened suddenly on the girl with a new purpose.

"I reckon that there's a lot that's phony in your yarn, kid," he said—"you're probably lyin'. But I reckon it don't make so much damn' difference, seein' as we've got th' Chink where he can't do no more mischief. So we'll just forget th' details that don't matter an' get down to business right away. Where's Amos got that gold cached?"

"What gold—what do you mean?" Flame demanded, startled.

Jake grinned thickly.

"You're kinda dumb, ain't yuh, kid?" he said with a flash of malevolent sarcasm. "O' course you ain't never heard of no gold—never heard tell o' no such thing a-tall. Haw! Haw! I reckon I gotta explain t' yuh, careful and polite, eh? All right! Yuh see, dearie, it's like this. Yer dear father an' Mister Slant Galloway an' these other two gents have made a long trip up to these parts lookin' for a mislaid sack o' nuggets an' some papers which was once th' property of an old geezer called O'Hara, and which now, by marriage, rightfully belongs to' me—your lovin' dad. Actin' upon a tip supplied by Mister Pedro Martinez, we makes this trip at considerable expense and does some diggin' inta th' graves o' th' Morgan boys. And we finds"—he paused, taking in with shrewd satisfaction the suddenly tense expression on Flame's face—"we finds *that th' gold ain't there.*"

Flame's unconcealed start of surprise was something for which Jake had evidently been watching. It seemed to confirm his suspicions. His face twisted in an evil grin of satisfaction. "Naturally we was plumb disappointed at not findin' th' gold," he went on, his thick voice heavy with a malicious enjoyment, "but a bit later, while we are settin' around in camp feelin' down in th' mouth, Pedro here, who had been doin' a little nosin' about th' valley on his own account, ambles up on a nice-lookin' hoss an' with th' information that he has run inta a outfit which, knowin' somethin' of the circumstances, he opines is my affectionate relatives.

"He brings a letter along too, fer proof. An' that—together with what he tells me—gives me th' notion that he's probably correct in his guess. Not bein' altogether a fool, therefore, I naturally hops on to th' explanation of what's happened—nice brother Amos an' his little pet gal has give the Tong th' slip an' has got here an' done some diggin' ahead o' me. So I decided t' pay a little social call an' claim my property—or what there is left of it.

"So here we are, dearie. An' I reckon it's a reg'lar surprise t' you—in spite o' th' fact that th' hoss Pedro took broke away this evenin' an' so got back here before us. Now, Miss Innocence, I reckon I've about satisfied your curiosity, so now it's your turn to speak a piece. Yap up now I—where's th' gold hid? I reckon there's a plenty somewheres. Yuh musta found th' Lucky Ledge as well as th' cache o' nuggets."

Flame recoiled, stark dismay in her face.

"You—you think—you think that?...Oh, but you're crazy!" she gasped. "We haven't got the gold! We never could find it! We thought...."

Jake cut her short with a savage, impatient gesture.

"That's enough o' that stuff I" he growled. "Cut th' play-actin', kid, an' come across with th' truth, pronto. Talk up, now!" His jaw thrust forward threateningly; he took a half step towards her, his fist clenching.

"But I tell you we haven't got it! We haven't got it, I tell you! We haven't...." Flame's voice broke in frantic helplessness. Bewildered and alive all at once to her peril, she recoiled in sudden terror from Jake's lurching movement.

With a quick stride Brandon stepped in front of the girl and thrust her behind him with a sheltering arm.

"You're mistaken, Mr. Templeton"—Brandon confronted the glowering bully—"your daughter knows nothing of that gold. And if anyone has dug it up, it certainly wasn't her uncle. It won't do any good to bully her. She doesn't know. Probably someone found it years ago."

His voice was steady. Though his brain was whirling with an overwhelming urge to hurl himself bare-handed upon the brute before him and smash with his fists that leering face that seemed to swim at him through a swirling red mist, Brandon held himself and forced his speech to a carefully studied mildness. He realized his peril. He knew well enough that Jake and his pals would welcome the slightest excuse for putting an end to his existence; even as he had moved he had seen the guns of the other three leap from their holsters and cover him. Dread for the girl forced him to caution. Alive he might find some chance to help her. To recklessly throwaway his life would be to leave her utterly at the mercy of a quartet of scoundrels whom he well knew would stop at nothing.

But his action and words came near to bringing about the very thing that he feared. Taken aback for an instant, Jake recovered himself with a burst of lurid fury.

"Damn you!" he roared. "Who in hell asked fer you to come buttin' in? Shut your jaw, damn yuh!—you—!" He swung the muzzle of his rifle up savagely.

But even as Brandon's muscles tensed and Flame, with a sharp cry of terror, sprang forward recklessly, Jake's manner changed. He lowered the rifle with a jerk, the blind rage in his face supplanted of a sudden by an expression of calculating cruelty. He eyed Brandon through narrowed lids.

"You're a smooth-tongued kinda bird, ain't yuh?" he said sneeringly. "An' I reckon you an' my little red-head's plumb fond of each other, eh? You'd hate t' see anythin' happen t' her, wouldn't yuh? Well"—he grinned evilly—"it's up t' you. Make her blat out where that gold is hid or you'll see a plenty."

"But I tell you there's no gold—the girl doesn't know anything about it!" Brandon exclaimed desperately. "Can't you see by her face that she's telling you the truth? She doesn't know."

"Yeh?" Jake sneered. "I'm green-lookin', ain't I? Listen, hombre!— th' kid an' her uncle mighta fooled you but they ain't foolin' me. I been keepin' a little track on things, even if I have been hid out. Th' last time I heard anythin' about Amos was four years ago. Him an' this kid was in Denver then—flat broke an' starvin' t' death. They was in rags—both of 'em—huntin' any odd jobs they could find fer enough money t' buy beans—they was plumb out. Now, all of a sudden I runs on to 'em here, all as nice an' prosperous as you please—all safe an' hid out an' ownin' a cattle ranch. Where'n hell did th' money come from? Mean t' tell me Amos earned it swingin' a pick whilst th' brat here scrubbed floors? Hell!—what yer think I am—soft-headed?"

"That's not true!" Flame cried vehemently, amazement and consternation mingled in her voice. "Whoever told you that lied. We were hard up in Denver—yes. But that was because we were trying to hold on to every cent we had, knowing we might need it for an emergency. Amos still had a little money left. And we came here and spent it to buy this place—it was our last hope. This was an abandoned ranch and Amos got it for next to nothing. And we've scraped and saved and…."

Jake silenced her with a furious movement.

"Listen, kid!" he said, his voice suddenly low and deadly—"forget your lyin'. We come here t' get that gold—an' we're goin' t' get it! I'll give you about thirty seconds. First I'm goin' t' attend t' this Chink"— he kicked the prone figure of the bound, but now fully conscious Chinaman savagely—"an' if you ain't ready to tell the truth by the time we've bumped him off we'll bump off this willie-boy of yours too, and then start in on you. Don't kid yerself that bein' my brat's goin' to save you any. We'll *make* you talk, an' damn' quick—you ain't the first stubborn heifer we've handled. Now get th' hell over there, both o' you, an' think it over. An' if you think I'm bluffin' just watch me an' you'll learn different."

With a sudden furious shove that was a startling indication of tremendous strength, he hurled Brandon and the girl aside and jerked round viciously towards the trussed Chinaman. "Hey, Slant!" he roared. "Bring that coil o' balin' wire off that nail yonder an' come help me upend this yaller polecat. We're goin' t' have a neckin' party."

Recovering his balance on the instant from the savage thrust that had sent them both staggering back, Brandon clutched the reeling girl and saved her from falling. More harshly than anything else that vicious shove, with its startling revelation of Jake's brute strength, seemed to force home to him the dreadful helplessness of their plight. For a moment his brain seemed to go numb; the blind urge of reckless fury and the sober voice of reason were alike blotted in a wave of awful fear. The fate of the girl at his side was sealed, he realized—nothing that he could do or that she could say would save her now.

No pleas or entreaties would save her from the brutality of this quartet of devils who were convinced that she was concealing the truth from them. And even if, in the end, they might be forced to believe that she knew nothing about the gold—what then? What mercy could she expect from the disappointed rage of these three callous scoundrels, and from this fiendish parent who plainly enough regarded his relationship to her only as an added license for brutality. They would vent their fury upon her. They would....

Brandon's senses reeled before the dread visions of horror that rushed up in his mind. He felt suddenly sick. The disordered kitchen, its yellow, flickering lantern light dimmed now in the harsh, constantly shifting glare of the three powerful electric torches, seemed to go round before his eyes. As through a blurred nightmare he saw Jake and Slant Galloway and the short man who had been called Rufe heaving together about the form of the writhing Chinaman. Already a long length of doubled baling wire had been flung up across an overhead beam, and one of its ends twisted tightly about the helpless man's neck.

Hauling and lifting, Jake and the two others were raising him from the floor—through the dulling roar of the outer wind their panting oaths and the terrified victim's strangled, choking screams for mercy seemed to beat on Brandon's brain like some ghastly tumult from the depths of hell.

But it was a moment only that the surge of dizzy weakness held Brandon in its grip. With a rush, wakened by the feel of Flame's terrified clutch on his arm, both reason and courage swept back to him—and with them a wild gleam of hope. He and Flame were close to the back door, he realized suddenly. Jake's furious, humiliating shove had done for them something which it would have been fatal to have attempted themselves. Staggering back from its unexpected violence they had brought up within a pace of the rear exit, and the lounging form of the scar-faced Pedro Martinez who guarded it.

The back door!—they were almost within arm's reach of it! The realization lit Brandon's heart with a savage flare of joy that was repayment enough for the humiliation he had forced himself to swallow. The back door!—the canyon behind it!—the black darkness of the night. There was yet a mad, bare chance that the girl might gain safety. If only the man guarding the door could be...!

Alight suddenly with a desperate hope Brandon's glance darted warily about, weighing chances. The back door against which Martinez stood opened outwards, he remembered. It was a roughly made affair of light, up-and-down boards. It had sagged a little out of shape and so made a pinch fit with the door-frame that was tight enough to keep it closed under ordinary conditions, and on this account, perhaps, it had been fitted with nothing but a flimsy strap-iron latch. To open the door would be no problem. But Martinez was a different matter. The Mexican was leaning against the door-frame. In his left hand, its beam focused upon the milling group in the center of the room, he held a heavy, miner's flash-light. And in his right, ready for action, was an ugly Colt's forty-four.

But, watchful as the Mexican was, it was plain enough to Brandon's swift glance that for the moment the edge was gone from his alertness. The ghastly little drama in which the others were engaged held most of his interest. The strangling screams of the helpless Chinaman had ceased. A quick look in that direction told Brandon that by dint of lifting and hauling, Jake and the other two had dragged the stubborn-sliding wire across the beam and secured its end to a hook in the wall. Swung well clear of the floor the victim hung now writhing and twisting, his face blackening swiftly.

The purpose of the fiendish trio was all but complete.

Even as Brandon glanced, Jake sprang back flushed and panting from his exertion, his seamed face alight with a flare of devilish triumph as he jerked his rifle to his shoulder. "Come on, boys!" he roared. "Fill th'—full o' lead! Give him...."

The crash of his rifle as he pulled trigger drowned his own shout and woke thunderous response as, following his lead, the heavy six-gun of the others leaped into instant action. The room seemed to heave and reel in the swirl of deafening detonations. For an instant the awful writhing shape dangling from the beam was blurred in an eddying cloud of choking yellow vapor.

Brandon at that moment, however, had neither eyes nor thought for the ghastly bedlam about him. In that split second, as the guns flared, he had realized his chance. The dreadful target swaying from the beam had drawn the fire of Martinez's pistol also—and almost at the same instant that the heavy Colt belched flame Brandon leaped. His hand clamped about the smoking gun and with the fury and the strength of desperation he whirled the startled Mexican aside, at the same time kicking back savagely at the door behind with a violence that tore the frail latch from its fastening. The door whirled open with a bang and a roaring inrush of wind. "Run!" Brandon shouted to the girl. "Run! Hide!"

Flame leaped for the opening. But even as she sprang and he heaved back the furiously fighting Mexican as a shield to shelter her movement, Brandon realized in chill despair that the ruse had failed. Almost before the girl had moved—before even the noise and the crash of the opening door had brought Jake and the short man charging towards the struggle—Slant Galloway had seen what was happening and with a panther-like leap had crossed the floor at a bound, caught the escaping girl at the very threshold of the door and dragged her back.

And almost at the same instant, before Brandon could either leap aside or wrench free the gun from Martinez's vice-like grip, Jake and his companion hurled themselves upon him. For a moment, as with a sudden burst of superhuman strength he forced his cursing antagonist around in front of him as a barrier against which the other two dared not use their guns, Brandon held his own. But a split second later, as he swerved sideways to escape a savage swing of the short man's pistol, Jake's fist shot out in a terrific lunge which, though it missed his face, caught him fairly in the shoulder.

Wrenched free of his grip and hurled across the floor as from the smashing blow of a steam hammer, Brandon whirled through the open door behind him, crashed heavily down the outer step and, unable to check himself, staggered backwards over the lip of the canyon behind. Clutching frantically at thin air, and with the terrified screams of the struggling girl still ringing in his ears, he shot downward into a black gulf of roaring wind and breaking bushes.

∾

CHAPTER 11

"The Gold!—Where is it?"

Checked by the warning yell of Martinez, as the three men surged through the back door in pursuit of the vanishing figure, Jake lurched cautiously to the edge of the drop and peered down at the windy, bush-sprinkled blackness into which the torches of his two companions stabbed shafts of light.

"*Mira*!—there he lies!—there against that bush at the bottom!" the Mexican cried, pointing. "The accursed swine has broken his neck!"

"We'll make damned sure of him, anyway!" Jake snarled. He jerked his rifle to his shoulder and aimed deliberately.

In the focused glare of the two torches the motionless form, sprawled face-downward at the foot of the steep slope, was plain enough. It offered an easy target, and as Jake fired viciously three times the sharp, spasmodic jerks of head and body as the high-powered projectiles tore through them was visible proof that none of the shots had missed. Under the impact of the bullets the body slid down a few inches further and lay still and lifeless beneath the tossing branches of the mesquite bush at the bottom of the slope.

"That settles that part of it!" Jake growled triumphantly as he lowered his smoking rifle. "Come on, boys, we'll tend to th' rest o' this business!"

He wheeled about and stamped savagely back into the kitchen where Flame, white-faced and hysterical, was still fighting impotently against Galloway's pinioning grip. As Rufe and Martinez entered and dragged the door once more shut against the wind, Jake's arm shot out and clutched the girl by the shoulder.

"Now you—brat!" he roared, wrenching her from Galloway's arms and shaking her with brutal savagery. "Your willie-boy's got his!—an' yours is comin' t' you—right now! Damn you! Where th' hell is that gold?"

With a frenzied twist, nerved by a sudden burst of hysterical strength, Flame tore herself free and sprang back, her eyes blazing.

"You devil!" she choked. "You've killed him!...you've murdered him!...You fiend! You!...you!..." her voice strangled in an inarticulate, gasping sob of grief and fury. With a lightning-like movement, snatching up from the floor the heavy cast-iron door that she had wrenched free from the stove in the struggle with the Chinaman, she darted aside from the savage reach of Jake's lunging arm and hurled the weighty slab of metal full at his face.

But the missile did not reach its target. Jake glimpsed its coming and ducked. The flying chunk of blackened iron which, had it struck full would certainly have brained him, grazed along his head and crashed with a dull clang into the wall boards. With a roaring oath of pain and anger he leaped forward, striking viciously at the girl with his clubbed rifle. Flame dodged and sprang madly for the front door.

Luck was against the girl, however. Swerving to avoid the suspended body of the dead Chinaman, her flying feet stumbled over the empty water-pail. She fell heavily, and though, winged by fear, she was up in a flash, the split-second of delay had snatched away her slender chance. Slant Galloway had reached the door ahead of her. Escape was blocked.

Panting, dodging by a hair's-breadth another furious swing of Jake's rifle-butt, Flame swerved towards the closed door of the living-room. Wrenching it open just in time to escape from the clutching hands of Rufe she plunged into the darkness beyond. She had acted on impulse—without plan. But as she reeled into the black gloom of the unlighted room, a ray of hope leaped to her mind. Gasping, crashing blindly against chairs and tables, she darted towards the further window—conscious from the cursing yells and pounding of feet that Rufe and Jake were scarce a leap behind her.

But again Fate mocked her. The window defied the wrench of her frantic fingers as she flung herself against it. The catch was jammed—and she had no time to unloose it—Jake and Rufe were upon her. With a half-articulate cry of despair, Flame spun round. In the glare of Rufe's electric torch which had suddenly cut the darkness, the doorway of Amos's room yawned blackly before her. She reached it in a bound, and darting through slammed the door behind her and shot the bolt.

In the sudden inky blackness of the little room, she stood gasping as the door groaned under the sudden impact of the cursing men who had flung themselves against it. She was trapped now—and hopelessly—she realized. The only window in the little room was high in the wall—and because the roof of a small lean-to shed just below it on the outside of the house made it easy of access, Amos, as a precaution to safeguard his guns and valuables, had fixed a piece of heavy woven-wire fence across the opening. Amos had secured the thick wire in place with his characteristic thoroughness. To smash an opening big enough to climb through would have been a job of many minutes—even with tools. Bare-handed, and in the few seconds' respite which at most the frail door could give her, Flame knew the attempt would be madness.

In the dark, pressed close against the wall to one side of the bulging door, Flame crouched trembling. The door would burst in at any moment she knew well enough. Neither the wood, the bolt, nor the hinges could long withstand the crushing heaves of the maddened pair outside. Already between the door and its frame the jerking glare of the torch on the other side of the straining planks was sifting broad beams of light into the darkness about her. The wood was yielding. The screws were drawing from their hold. Another instant and....

There was a snapping report of splintering wood. Tearing loose all at once from bolt and hinges simultaneously, the door fell flatly inward with a crashing suddenness that caught the heaving men off their balance and drew them sprawling headlong into the room after it. As they fell, cursing and struggling, Rufe's torch snapped out. And in the sudden darkness Flame leaped, cleared the heaving bodies and the hands which snatched wildly at her, gained the living-room and, not daring time for another attempt at the jammed window, sped back into the kitchen—brushing under the very arms of Slant Galloway as he bounded across the floor to stop her.

Panting and unnerved, confused and spurred on now only by the same blind, unreasoning impulse as a trapped animal, Flame ran frenziedly for the back door of the kitchen. Her eyes were blurred...The room seemed to blacken and go round before her.

Behind her she heard shouts and pounding feet; Jake's feet, Rufe's feet, the feet of Slant Galloway. The door!...the door!...if she could only reach the door! She sprang for it blindly, gropingly...The door! The door!...Oh, God!...

But even as she sprang—even as her frantically outreaching fingers touched the wood—she felt arms close about her suddenly; arms that crushed and pinioned her. As through a mist she saw the scarred face of Martinez the Mexican—heard his chuckling laugh as he dragged her back. And an instant later, as she fought weakly to break loose, she felt Jake's iron clutch fasten upon her; felt herself jerked free from Martinez and shaken till her breath strangled and her head whirled blackly and seemed to snap from her shoulders.

"Damn you! You—!" Jake panted. "Try and brain me, would you!...
you hell cat! I'll fix you!—fix you good an' plenty! The gold, damn
you—the gold—where is it?"

"There's no gold," Flame choked. "I don't know anything about it.
I—"

"Damn you!" With a furious fling of his arm that cut off her words
with a jerk, Jake hurled the girl from him with a violence that sent
her spinning across the floor to fall helplessly through the open door
of her darkened bedroom. "Damn you!" he roared savagely. "You've
spilled that bleat for th' last time. I'm sick o' your lies! Th' truth, damn
you!—out with the truth!"

He flung aside his rifle, and before the dazed girl could rise he was
upon her in a cursing fury, jerking her to her feet with one hand while
with the other he beat and cuffed her about the head and face.

"Out with it!" he raged, shaking her like a rat. "Where's it hid,
damn you?—where's the gold?"

"There...isn't—there isn't any!" Flame gasped helplessly, her
breath coming in sobbing jerks. "I've...told...you...we...never...."

"Damn you for a liar!"—the stinging impact of Jake's palm
across her mouth crushed out the girl's choking words. "Damn you!
he foamed, beating her savagely about the head. "Talk, damn you, or
I'll—"

"Go easy, Jake," Slant Galloway's cold, purring voice cut in abruptly;
"no use to spoil her face. O' course, she's your kid, but if you're aimin'
to bust her up thataways, I reckon the rest of us could have some fun
with her first. She's a right good-looker."

"Go to it then, damn you!" With a sudden wrench Jake jerked the
girl bodily from her feet, hurled her crashing upon the bed behind and
with a furious shove flung Galloway after her. "Get in there, then!" he
roared—"and you!—and you!" With savage fury he jerked the other
two men through the narrow doorway and sent them staggering into
the dark little bedroom. "Get in there and give Slant a hand. Give the
little—hell! An' if the three o' you can't make her talk—well, I'll have
a fire goin' by that time, an', by God, I'll show you a trick that'll make
her."

With a fiendish chuckle, he slammed shut the bedroom door and
lurched towards the stove, fumbling in his pocket for matches.

But Flame heard neither the ghastly threat nor the bang of the
closing door which sealed her helplessness. Breathless and half stunned
from Jake's buffeting blows and from the violence with which he had
hurled her backwards, it seemed to the terrified, half-conscious girl as
she struggled weakly to rise that she was engulfed suddenly in a black
nightmare of horror.

Hands were all at once upon her—powerful, clutching hands against which she beat with frenzied futility. They were holding her—forcing her back—pinioning her down. The crushing semi-darkness of the little room, lit only by the blurred ray of a single torch that had fallen to the floor; seemed suddenly to reel about her—to close in and rush upon her in a hideous, fighting frenzy of foul-breathed panting shapes and leering faces that mocked her frantic struggles in a rancorous din of brutal laughter. Realization of her fate rushed upon the helpless girl in a sudden horror that wrung terror from her lips in scream on frantic scream. Her strength wilted. Blackness spun before her. Limp and helpless she seemed to whirl downwards into a black maelstrom of darkness, crowding bodies, and clutching hands.

But it was for a split second only, as her strength failed; that the black waves of unconsciousness towered over her—they did not close. Of a sudden the numbing darkness that swept upon her brain ripped aside and parted in shattering sound—a crashing fusillade that seemed to jerk back her reason and strength alike in one electric flash. The clawing hands about her were gone suddenly. The torch was out. There was the sound of startled yells—the blundering rush of scrambling men—the splintering smash of glass and woodwork.

As she tottered gasping to her feet there was another rattle of shots; the darkness of the little room glared suddenly with stabbing fingers of fire that leaped vengefully towards the shattered window. Dark pursuing shapes, silhouetted grotesquely against the kitchen lantern-light, came leaping savagely through the narrow doorway—dark, low-stooping, deadly figures that crowded and stumbled together over something upon the bedroom floor and picked themselves up snarling high-pitched curses in a strange tongue. From outside the house, sharply clear in a lull of the wind, came the sound of heavily running feet that receded into the distance amidst a flurry of pistol-shots.

But it was all in one blurred, chaotic whirl that Flame sensed these things. Even as she found her feet and cowered back, still panting, against the bed, the beam of an electric torch stabbed the gloom of the little bedroom and focused upon her with a blinding glare. Two men darted forward from the shadows and clutched her with ungentle hands. Each of them carried a drawn automatic pistol of heavy caliber. And the girl's first glimpse as they sprang forward into the light told her that they were both Chinamen.

∽

CHAPTER 12

Too Late!

Brandon stirred painfully. About him was darkness, the roar of wind and the threshing beat of thorny branches. The headlong plunge down the side of the canyon a few moments before had partially stunned him. He had not lost consciousness, but his senses were blurred. The fall and his whirling roll down the precipitous slope was still clear enough in his mind. He remembered crashing through the small bushes and the tangles of uncovered roots that dotted the face of the slide; they had broken the force of his descent. He remembered bursting through a tougher mat of branches and smashing heavily upon something hard. After that his consciousness was a bit hazy. He had a faint recollection of lights that had stabbed down through the darkness and glared upon the bushes near him. It seemed to him that a second or so ago he had heard rifle-shots, but he was not quite sure. Anyway, the light was gone now and there was no sound above the trampling rush of the wind as it hurtled up the canyon.

Brandon felt hastily about him. His hand struck rocks—water-worn stones, hard earth and the rough, knotted stems of bushes. His body was cramped and jammed in some space barely large enough for it. He was acutely conscious of the bruising hardness of cobble-stones beneath him, and of the scratching jabs of thorny branches that slashed against him with each swirl of the wind. As he moved, squirming violently to extricate himself, his head collided sharply with a smooth, hard stone projecting from the bank beside him. The loose-set bit of rock jarred free from its setting of earth and rolled down behind him with a dull clatter.

Impact with the cold, unyielding surface, painful though it was, seemed to clear his mind. His senses flashed back on him keen-edged.

He realized of a sudden where he was. He lay in a little crevice on the bottom of the canyon—a narrow water-worn ditch that was completely covered over by the interlaced, screening branches of low mesquite bushes. The tough mat of boughs had broken the force of his landing and, save for soreness and bruises, he was apparently uninjured.

Brandon squirmed swiftly to his knees. His suddenly cleared faculties and the realization of just where he lay, brought back knife-sharp the thought of Flame…Flame!—she was up there in the darkness above the canyon lip!—she was up there helpless in the power of those four ruthless fiends!…God! What were they doing to her?…What might have happened to her even in the few seconds that he had lain here half dazed?…

Chilled with a sudden terror, and electrified on the instant to a mad fury of action as the full measure of the helpless girl's plight rushed upon his mind, Brandon leaped to his feet, tearing aside the matted branches above him with a reckless disregard for the slashing thorns that ripped his face and hands. Flame!…She was up there helpless!…He must reach her!…save her! Even at that very moment she might be….

His wrenching hands checked suddenly. Without warning a light had flared near him; the clear, dazzling ray of an electric torch that stabbed through the windy blackness like a sword. Startled, jerked back all at once from the split-second of blind, unreasoning frenzy that had held him, Brandon dropped down beneath the sheltering branches of the mesquites. It came to him like a flash that some of the men above had descended into the canyon and were searching for him. He hunched back deeper into his shelter. The focused beam of light had not touched him. There was a chance that he had not yet been seen.

The moving ray of light came swiftly closer—seeking, playing among the bushes and mounds of earth and stones. Faintly above the wind Brandon caught the sound of hurried, stumbling footsteps and low voices. The searchers were heading directly towards him. The beam of the low-held lights swept presently across the tops of the laced branches that sheltered him; it paused there a fraction of an instant, cutting a sharp pattern of glare and shadow through the twigs. In a moment, however, as he held his breath and hugged lower into the earth crevice, the light moved away. Once more by a scant margin he had escaped detection—the light had not dropped low enough to strike him. But the hurrying footsteps and quick low voices came swiftly closer; they were almost upon him.

Of a sudden Brandon caught his breath, staring startled through the interlaced screen of bush-trunks and branches behind which he crouched. The light had come to rest. A few feet from him—so close that it seemed as though the reflected glow from the downward-turned torch must surely reveal his crouching figure—the searchers had halted. In the glare of the light, which illumined a small circle of ground as clearly as day, and flung into black silhouette the two stooping figures about it, he could see that they were peering downward at a human body which lay sprawled beneath the low-spreading branches of a mesquite bush.

Tense and motionless, scarce daring to breathe for fear of betraying his position, Brandon lay watching. These stealthy men had not come searching for him he realized suddenly. They were none of Jake's gang. He could not see their faces, but as they quickly dragged out the body from beneath the shelter of the bush and bent over it, their low-toned, excited jargon told him that they were Chinese.

Brandon's pounding heart missed a beat at the discovery. Tongsmen!—these were some more of the returning gang of gunmen. The reason for their presence here at the foot of the slid-in bank came to him in a flash—and with it the explanation of his own escape from the fury of Jake and the rest. These Chinamen must have been making their way back along the bed of the canyon just when he had toppled over the edge above. And the light and the recent rifle-shots that were clouded in his memory had been no delusion. That had been Jake and the others shooting down from above to make sure that he was dead. Only it had been into the body of the Tong gunman that Midnight had previously hurled over into the canyon that they had shot, Brandon realized.

Thanks to the speed of his descent and to the friendly screen of branches that had closed over him, he must have been out of sight by the time the brutes above had flashed their light into the depths. And knowing nothing of what had happened before, they had naturally mistaken the body of the Chinaman for that of the man who had just gone over. It had been at this body that they had fired. And these other Chinese had been near enough somewhere to see the lights and hear the reports of the shots. They had come on the run to investigate.

Yes, that was it—it must be! All in a rush, as the mumbling alien voices came to him and the body was dragged out from its shelter, the truth of what had happened leaped to Brandon's mind. An instant later, straining his eyes through the criss-cross screen of twigs, he realized that his guess had been correct. That the body was that of the gunman who had been attacked by the great white hound was plain.

In the pitiless glare of the torch his ripped clothes and horribly torn throat were clearly visible—evidence enough as to how he had met death. But the shattering wound left by a soft-nosed bullet was clear to see also. It had gone in at the back of the head and come out in front. That bullet could only have been fired from the edge of the bank above. The shots which were a hazy memory had been no illusion. Jake and the others had been grimly intent on making sure of him. But they had made a mistake.

The light snapped out suddenly. Scarcely had Brandon taken in all the gruesome details which confirmed his suspicions as to the truth of what had happened than he found himself all at once blinking helplessly into pitch blackness. As his strained eyes struggled to adjust themselves to the gloom he heard the shuffling footsteps receding swiftly into the darkness. They seemed to be hurrying. A loose stone, struck by one of the quick-moving, invisible feet, rolled down into the little ditch and fell close beside him.

The low, excited voices and rapid footfalls were blotted by the wind and the soughing of tossing branches.

For a few seconds Brandon crouched, listening. Caution had come to him. These deadly, prowling figures had been within an ace of discovering him—and he knew well enough that discovery would have meant instant death. The realization sobered him to the odds he faced—odds now apparently increased a hundredfold. The Tong gunmen had returned. Their objective undoubtedly was the house above. If the helpless girl were still alive she would be caught between two fires. Her fate was sealed. There was but one chance in a million now that he could aid her. And that millionth chance—if it were granted him—would not come through acts of frenzied desperation. It could only come through cool caution and by stealth.

Apparently the two men had gone. Brandon's tense-strained senses could gather nothing more from the wind and the darkness; he could catch neither sound nor light gleam. Swiftly, but with an alert caution he wormed his way out of his hiding-place and groped quickly through the shadowy blackness towards where he knew the body of the dead man lay. The gunman had retained his hold on his pistol when Midnight had hurled him into the canyon, Brandon remembered-the spatter of wild shots mingled with the dog's snarling growls that had sounded in the depths had been proof that he had used it in the death grapple. The pistol, therefore, must be lying now somewhere near the body.

But Brandon's hopes of obtaining a gun were swiftly dashed. He could not find the automatic. Neither in the stiffened hand nor anywhere on the ground about the body could he locate the pistol, and a swift search of the dead man's clothing revealed the fact that the Tongsman had apparently carried only one gun. On his heavy leather belt, with its empty holster and three double pouches of extra magazines, there was no other weapon save a long sheath-knife.

Baffled, Brandon removed the dead man's belt, buckled it around himself and turned swiftly away. He had wasted but a few fleeting moments on the search, but every second was precious and he could not delay longer. His failure to find the gun, however, crushed him with a chill disappointment. It must lie somewhere about, he knew, for he was certain that while he had been watching neither of the two men who had just gone had picked it up. The probabilities were that it had been whirled from the dying man's hand in the struggle, and had fallen perhaps yards away among the stones and brush. At any rate it was useless to search further without a light—and he dared not strike any of the few matches which his shirt pocket contained. A match flare in that tearing wind would have been useless. And besides, it would only have betrayed his presence—he had a distinct feeling that the two Chinamen he had seen were not the only ones prowling in the darkness.

Breathlessly, his hands torn and smarting from the slashing scratches of mesquite branches, and stabbed cruelly with the spines of cholla which he had picked up in his vain gropings for the pistol, Brandon stumbled quickly into the darkness, fighting against the furious gusts of the wind as he made his way up the bed of the canyon. To attempt to reclimb the face of the slide down which he had fallen he knew was hopeless; that much he had discovered when he had come down into the canyon with the lantern searching for Amos. The canyon was no easy place to get out of; near the house its sides seemed to be everywhere precipitous. He had had a hard time before, even with the lantern, to pick out a place that could be scaled—and even then it had been no small feat to make the ascent.

Now, without even the feeble lantern-glow to aid him, the difficulty was immeasurably greater. The blanket of cloud that smothered the sky blotted everything—there was not a single star gleam. The night was as black as pitch. He could scarcely see his hand in front of him. What with the darkness and the confusing buffeting of the wind, which here in the canyon bed whirled sand and gravel in his face as he stumbled blindly among the scattered, threshing bushes, it seemed almost hopeless to expect that he could again locate the point where he had climbed out before.

In frantic haste Brandon scrambled on, floundering into ditches and stumbling over bushes and fallen rocks. Flame!—her face seemed to float before him in the darkness; her terrified cries which had rung in his ears as he had toppled backwards over the bank still seemed to echo on the wind. He plunged forward recklessly, his pounding heart strangling with an icy fear. The girl would get no mercy, he knew, from the four human devils who had her in their power—they had already given proof enough of their fiendish cruelty. The plight of a man in their clutches would have been dreadful enough. But the fate of a girl....And there was now the returning Tong gunmen to reckon with...If she fell into their hands and their vengeance....

Cold with horror and tortured with the bitter realization that his only weapon was a futile sheath-knife, Brandon swerved abruptly and scrambled up the steep slope of fallen rock and earth that footed the canyon wall. It was here, it seemed to him, that he had climbed up before. And unless the two Chinamen....

Something leaped suddenly at him from the darkness—something pale and huge that hurled itself without warning, and sent him crashing backwards as from the glancing impact of a battering-ram. For an instant, as he sprawled dazed and breathless, clutching for his knife, he had a glimpse of white fangs and blazing eyes thrust towards him through the gloom. Hot, rank breath beat upon his face; his ears blurred to the sound of a dreadful, blood-choked snarling.

Then, suddenly as it had sprung, the Thing was gone. Like an insane fury the monstrous white shape leaped from him and fled away, crashing headlong through the bushes. The sound of its awful snarling—low, gibbering and continuous—dwindled into the wind as it sped furiously up the canyon.

Midnight! Midnight wounded and gone mad! As Brandon scrambled to his feet the truth rushed upon him. He remembered suddenly that in groping around near the dead gunman in search of the pistol, he had not encountered the big dog's body. In his frenzied haste he had had no thought of the dog. He had somehow taken it for granted that Midnight was dead—the blur of pistol-shots and snarling had seemed to indicate that both dog and man had perished together.

It was plain enough now, however, that Midnight had survived that last spatter of bullets. But he had been wounded, and badly. Brandon had proof enough of that in the dog's queer actions and the fact that its leaping body where it had struck against him had clotted his shirt with the sticky feel of blood. But however badly hurt he had been by the gunman's shots, Midnight had survived. Crazed though he undoubtedly was from the pain of his wounds, he was still alive—a dreadful, suffering thing, ranging the canyon in snarling, mindless fury.

But Brandon at that moment had scant time for thought of Midnight. Even as he picked himself up, thankful that some dim glimmer of belated recognition had prompted the dog to leave him unharmed, there came all at once to his ears the sound of pistol-shots—a muffled burst of reports that came down to him from the darkness above. As he leaped forward, clutching in the inky gloom at rock and bush and swinging himself up the steep side of the canyon, the sound came again, and sharper—the crackling detonations of an automatic that ripped the night above somewhere near the canyon rim.

The Chinese! The Tong gunmen! Recklessly Brandon scrambled upward, conscious of a sick sense of despair. The Tong had struck!—somehow, even in the few moments' start which the Chinamen had had of him, they had gained the canyon lip and attacked the house. No, that seemed incredible—there had probably been others—others who had been already above! The two he had seen could hardly have climbed the canyon so swiftly...Unless...unless there was some easier way out—a way which they knew! They had been running as they went down the canyon bed! Perhaps they knew of a way...perhaps....

Desperately, his mind whirling in a blurred, disjointed frenzy, Brandon clawed from hold to hold, swinging himself up the precipitous bank. He had made a mistake he realized chillingly—this was *not* the place where he had climbed up before. The bank here seemed to overhang; the rocks and shrubs were fewer—loose-set in a crumbling earth that gave and broke beneath his weight. The handholds were more scarce. The wind gusted at him furiously as he fought for toe-grip in the crumbling bank and groped desperately from one breaking handhold to another. This was not the place!...not the place!...This place was too steep to climb, too crumbling. He could never make it!... But he *must*! He was more than halfway to the top now; it was too late to turn back, he had no time. He was too late already—too late!... Flame would be....

The wind roared down in redoubled fury—dashing sand in his face—beating at him as with monstrous wings. A rain of pebbles and stinging gravel cascaded down upon him; the whole bank against which he clung seemed to shake, tremble and sway outward.

Faintly to his ears came the crackle of another burst of shots and the drumming hoof-beats of galloping horses.

But neither the sound of the shots nor the clattering hoofs registered very clearly upon Brandon's brain. For at that instant, as he hung swaying within almost an arm reach of the top, the whole face of the crumbling, overhanging bank against which he clung swayed and toppled forward, sweeping him downward into the canyon in a bounding avalanche of earth and tumbling rocks.

⌀

CHAPTER 13

Pai Lang

The Tong!—the Tong gunmen had returned! Dazed and terror-numbed though she still was and breathless with exhaustion from her struggle against Slant Galloway and the other two, Flame's heart turned to ice with new fear as she realized the identity of these swift, grim men whose sudden attack on the house had saved her. They were Tong gunmen—the rest of the gang who had come back. The thing that, in her hatred of Jake, she had prayed for had actually come to pass. The Tongsmen had returned, surrounded the house and struck with deadly efficiency. She had been snatched from one fate only to face another equally dreadful.

But at that instant, as the triumphant clutch of her new captors fastened upon her arms, there was scarce time for the weak and gasping girl to think—scarce time for her brain to function clearly. From the half-light behind the flare of the torch beam, a voice spoke suddenly in terse command, and Flame felt herself all at once dragged roughly forward. She heard the banging of the outer doors as they were opened and closed; she felt on her face the swirling gust of wind that rushed in from outside; she heard the tramping entrance of more men. The dazzling torch receded into the duller glow of the kitchen lantern-light. Staggering towards it, forced onward by the hands of those who held her, the girl noticed dully that a dead body lay sprawled upon the floor in front of the bedroom doorway. As she was jerked, stumbling, across it, she saw that it was that of the short, one-eyed man who had been called Rufe.

The glaring lens of the torch was almost in her face now. Flame's eyes closed weakly against the intolerable blaze of it. Again, sharp and chilling, came that steely Chinese voice. The girl felt herself jerked round and forced down into a chair. There came the whispering slither of rope. Her arms were twisted back and secured behind her; her ankles were bound swiftly to the chair legs. As the coils of line were passed quickly around her, lashing her securely to the seat, the night outside the house woke in another spatter of savage pistol-shots, followed by the wind-blurred, dwindling sounds of furiously galloping horses. The glaring torch before her eyes winked out suddenly, and an instant later the front door swung open and banged shut. A short, wind-whipped Chinaman, a smoking gun in his hand, spilled into the room from the outer blackness and came leaping across the floor, shouting excitedly.

The lean, steel-voiced man who had snapped out his torch and swung round at the sound of the shooting, listened a moment impassively to the newcomer's excited report. Then, silencing him with an abrupt gesture and a few curt words, he turned swiftly again to Flame.

"Your two friends who dived through the window and escaped us have gone," he said in perfect English; "we prevented them reaching their car, but it seems they found horses somewhere in the mesquite clump. However, it makes little difference. We have you and your father—and we will have plenty of time to finish with both of you before we can be disturbed. We are expert. We shall work quickly—but not too quickly."

Blurred a moment by the sudden switching off of the blinding torch rays that had dazzled them, Flame's eyes cleared. The cold, menacing voice—if anything more steely hard and deadly in its scrupulously correct English than in Chinese—seemed to jerk her faculties back to her as brutally as a sudden dash of ice-water.

"We have you and your father"—the words, charged with a dreadful, sinister meaning, seemed to sear into her brain as though burned there by the white-hot stabs of an electric needle…"We have you and your father"…Wide-eyed, every nerve of a sudden tensed and terror-sharp, the girl's eyes flashed about her. From where she sat, bound and helpless near the back door, she could see all of the dimly-lit room.

The yellow-burning lantern was now its only light, and the flickering rays, writhing and jumping unsteadily as the flame rose and fell in gusty unison with the wind that swirled through the door cracks and the broken window-panes, flung dancing, gruesome shadows from the silent, ghastly shape that swung from the center beam, and from the grim-faced, deadly figures that stood beside it. There were six Chinamen in the room altogether, the girl saw. The lean, wolf-faced man who stood in front of her was obviously the leader. Two of them—one of whom was the outside guard who had just come in—were now engaged in taking down the suspended body.

But it was upon the other three gunmen that Flame's eyes riveted in sudden startled understanding…"We have you and your father"…she understood now, in a flash, the full meaning of those ominous words. Near her, but further back and set against the wall, was another chair. The sight of the three muscular Tongsmen working in swift silence over the limp, bound figure which it contained brought an involuntary shriek of horror from her lips.

"Not yet"—the lean man silenced her with a quieting gesture—"there is now no need of screaming, our vengeance has not yet begun. Those three are engaged only in restoring consciousness to your parent; he is still dazed from the blow which stunned him. But soon he will be awakened. And then"—a malevolent smile flickered across his thin lips—"then you may scream if you wish. You will have cause."

Flame's blood froze. The inflexible deadliness of that polished, merciless voice seemed to chill her heart with a numbing horror—a fear so dreadful that it seemed suddenly to snap her nerves—to blunt all at once her power to feel. It seemed to her that of a sudden she became an automaton; that her body was not really her own, but some insensate thing which she somehow controlled from a distance. An odd feeling of dulled indifference swept through her. This was the end, she told herself. It would be an end more dreadful than she had imagined; but physical agony could not last forever—sooner or later death must come. That would be release.

Death! Of a sudden, Flame found her mind catching at the word eagerly. Death!…it might be good perhaps to die. She had nothing left to live for. She was alone now. There was no one who cared. Amos was dead—he must be. And Brandon was dead too—he had died trying to save her. He had….

Her thought broke suddenly in a stabbing pang of remorse. Brandon!…she had drawn him into this—it was her fault. This had not been his quarrel. But he had come into it for her sake—and for her sake he had gone to his death. He had stood by her; he had fought for her; he had died for her—and at best, after all her suspicion and abuse, she had treated him with but bare civility. She had had no chance to give him one word of thanks…And now he was gone—gone beyond reach of thanks or gratitude for ever; unless—unless perhaps somewhere beyond death there might be….

Of a sudden, Flame was aware that hot tears were trickling down her cheeks, and that there was a deeper and more poignant pang in her heart than anything that was physical. All the pent-up agony which had choked her since the moment when those three deadly rifle-shots had ripped down into the canyon seemed to burst its bounds. Brandon!… Jim Brandon! He had died for her—and Jake had killed him.

"Death is not turned by tears—or fear." The steely voice seemed to cut like a sword across the girl's tortured thoughts. She felt a touch on her arm. Her eyes jerked up to find the lean-faced Chinaman regarding her fixedly.

"I'm not afraid!" With a sharp toss of her head, Flame flung the moisture from her eyes and faced him in dull defiance.

"Then why weep? Is it for your father?"

"For him! For *him*?—when he…Oh, I—I—" Flame's voice choked. With a sudden effort she checked her words and the red flood of hate and loathing that rushed upon her. After all, Jake *was* her father. At this moment, when a dreadful retribution was upon him, it was not for her to be his judge. She held her peace.

But her emotionless questioner had read enough.

"You hate him," he said shrewdly, "yet you will not speak ill. For whom then do you weep? Is it for one of those who fled?"

"No—oh no!" Flame gasped loathingly. "Your coming saved me from them. You were just in time to save—"

"To save you for something much more painful," the merciless voice cut in.

"It will be a cleaner death. I am glad," Flame said simply.

"You do not know—you have never seen." The hard eyes narrowed a little. "Perhaps when you see—and feel—you may change your mind. Death will not come easily."

He stood looking down on her. His face was impassive, emotionless. He seemed to be studying her.

In spite of herself, Flame shivered. There was something cold—merciless—devilish—in this lean, wolf-faced man with the fastidiously correct speech. He was no ordinary Chinaman—no common gunman. She sensed that he held authority far greater than was apparent. He filled her with a nameless dread—yet he roused in her a dreadful curiosity that struggled with her fear.

"I am Pai Lang"—as if in answer to her thought the man before her spoke again—"Pai Lang—White Wolf. I am known—and feared. I am the brother of one of those whom years ago your father murdered treacherously to save himself. In the Tong of the Yellow Dragon I speak with authority. For nine years I have waited for this moment. For nine years my men have trailed and sought. And now the vengeance which I have sworn is mine to take. For it is written into the records of the Tong of the Yellow Dragon that, to avenge those whom your father murdered, every living being with the blood of Templeton in its veins must die—and by torture."

He paused, his cold, metallic eyes searching the girl's features; watching her lips. Flame's bloodless face whitened a shade more. But she was silent.

"I come for vengeance," Pai Lang went on, speaking now more slowly, "and vengeance I will have. Life pays for life! Not till the debt is paid in full, will my task be done. The decrees of the Tong of the Yellow Dragon are always fulfilled. The Tong never sleeps; it never forgets; it never forgives. You must die."

Again he paused, watching her. In the interminable second that those hard eyes scrutinized her, the girl was aware dully of the roaring of the wind as it tore like a living thing at the roof overhead. The yellow lantern flame flickered up and down jerkily. Mingled with the patter of flying gravel against the outside of the house came the low, sing-song jargon of the five other Chinamen who were all gathered now near Jake's chair. Jake was stirring with swiftly returning consciousness.

"Justice has no mercy"—cold and dispassionate Pai Lang's voice came again—"and you must die. Life must pay for life. But there are many things which I do not understand. When your father escaped our first attack and fled on foot into the night, I do not understand how it was possible for him to return so quickly in a motor-car; and bringing three others to assist him.

"I do not quite understand how the two of my men whom I sent back to watch this house, while we were searching in the darkness for your father, came to be killed. I do not understand where you yourself were when we first surrounded this place. I do not understand why, hating your father—as I see plainly that you do—you have yet stayed with him and aided him all these years. Above all, I do not understand why you were in danger from your father's friends...All this I do not understand—and I do not ask. You have not asked me for mercy; I do not ask you to satisfy my curiosity. We have accomplished our purpose. That is enough.

"But there is one thing which I do understand. You are brave. Of accursed blood though you be, you yet have a noble and courageous heart. You are young—and very beautiful. Moreover, you remind me....Once, at the time when I was studying at a great English university, there was one...She was like you a little...It is no matter—it is but a memory. But I am reminded. And for this—and for your courage that you do not cry out weakly against Fate—I respect you.

"In the execution of justice I have no mercy. Life pays for life, and you must die to pay the debt. But in the council of the Tong of the Yellow Dragon, I speak with authority, and I shall grant you a favor. For you I will remit the torture. You shall not die the 'Death of a Thousand Cuts.' You shall die by one swift thrust only. Moreover, you shall go first. You will be spared sight of the fate of your father—and that in itself is a favor for which you may be thankful.

"And now prepare, for I see that your father is already fully conscious—and time presses. Prepare!" He turned away abruptly and strode towards the others.

Flame's head whirled. A sudden dizzy blackness swept upon her. Her breath choked in her lungs. Gratitude, relief—and a frantic terror—merged in her reeling brain. The blood pounded in her temples; her limbs shook. She felt the numbed fortitude that had upheld her slipping away. Death!—death!—it was coming!…Her mind seemed to cloud in a throbbing, formless tangle—stark terror—snatches of broken prayer—blurred and jumbled together meaninglessly. As she fought frenziedly to cling to her courage one coherent thought only held through the dazed blur of her mind…Amos!—Amos had escaped… the Tongsmen were still deceived…Amos had fled and escaped! And now he would be safe—they would never know now. Thank God she had let slip no word from which they might have guessed the truth!

"The time has come!" The cold, level voice seemed to jerk the misty curtain from before Flame's vision. With eyes suddenly cleared and horror-wide she saw that Pai Lang had returned.

But he was not alone. With him was another man—one of the three who had been busied with Jake. A bowed-shouldered, muscular man with sleeves rolled to the elbow, who stood now before her, the lantern-light flickering redly on his flat, cruel face and upon the long, Dragon-hafted knife that he gripped in his right hand.

"Courage! It will not hurt much." Dimly, chilly as the sound of a tolling bell beating across leagues of ice, Flame heard Pai Lang's voice. He seemed, somehow, very far away—miles and miles away. The lantern-light was blurred. She seemed to be drifting slowly downward into a vast space—a space filled with voices and misty faces. Death! Was this death?…It would be good to die. Brandon would be there… Brandon!…She could thank him…She could….

Her brain whirled helplessly. Dimly, as in a dream, she saw the squat, powerful man before her gather himself; saw his right arm draw back; saw the long knife gleam in the lantern-light like a chill ray of silver, pointing straight at her heart…She closed her eyes.

"Now!" said Pai Lang softly.

He made a swift motion to the holder of the knife. The blade flashed forward.

CHAPTER 14

Jake Makes a Bargain

But the gleaming steel did not reach its mark; the awful, life-quench-ing thrust for which Flame waited with tight-closed eyelids did not come. Instead of the numbing plunge of the blade in her heart her whirling senses cleared suddenly to the sound of a bellowing shout from Jake—a shout so frenziedly arresting that it checked even the lunging arm that held the knife. As the girl jerked wide her eyes she had a blurred glimpse of a wavering blade...of a half-extended arm—and of Pai Lang flinging himself forward and wrenching the thrusting knife aside. Jake's shouting voice, almost incoherent in its gabbling frenzy of haste, but savagely compelling nevertheless, came again to her ears.

"Stop!...Stop!" he was bellowing. "Don't kill her!...Wait!...Wait!"

As though enraged that his own startled, involuntary impulse had prompted him to strike the death knife aside, Pai Lang waved back the confused and hesitating executioner with a sharp gesture and wheeled furiously on the shouting man.

"Silence, swine!" he hissed. He made an angry, significant motion with his hands. In instant obedience, one of the two guards who stood beside Jake's chair snatched down a dish-towel that hung on a nearby nail and crumpled it swiftly into a ball.

"No!...No!" Jake's eyes bulged with sudden terror as he read the meaning of the quick movement. "Lemme talk!...Th' gold!...She—"

The doubled towel was forced suddenly between his jaws. His voice choked out abruptly in a strangled gulp.

But Pai Lang had caught the sputtering words. His eyes narrowed. With a quick stride he reached the side of the silenced man and jerked loose the gag.

"What is this about gold?" he demanded sharply. "Speak!"

"You're damn' right, I'll speak!" Fear and a triumphant venom struggled in Jake's gasping voice as he shook his mouth free from the choking cloth. "I'll speak a plenty. It's damned lucky fer you that you didn't bump off that little she-wolf before I come to...I heard some o' your spiel though...Aimin' t' let her off easy, weren't you, eh?...I reckon you kinda fell fer her face an' smooth tongue."

Pai Lang's eyes blazed. "This gold?" he said in a sharp, deadly voice. "Quickly—talk quickly!"

"I'm comin' t' that," Jake snarled hastily. "Gimme time, or it won't do you no good. Joke's on you, anyway—you ain't so smart. You been runnin' on a false scent for nine years. It wasn't me that you been—"

"Hold your tongue, you cowardly beast!" Flame's voice, shrill with a sudden horrified apprehension, suddenly cut short Jake's words. "Hold your tongue, can't you!...Keep quiet for God's sake!"

"Hold my tongue...hell!" There was a flare of venom in Jake's thick tones. "Like hell I'll hold my tongue!" His eyes glittered at Flame viciously..."You pulled a sweet scheme on me, didn't yuh, kid—tellin' me there was only one Chink in these parts when you knowed damn' well there was more. Now you reckon I'm goin' t' hold my tongue so's t' save th' hide o' Amos, eh? Not by a damn' sight! You lied me inta this trap an' I'm aimin' t' see that yuh get a full dose o' your own medicine. If I'm bumped off, you're goin' t' get th' same works...you an' nice brother Amos too!"

"Amos? Who is Amos?" Pai Lang demanded.

"He's th' bird you've been trailin' so smart for nine years," Jake growled triumphantly. "You ain't been huntin' me a-tall. I been hid out in South America—down in Chili. You've been runnin' circles after my twin brother Amos—after him and this brat."

"He lies!...He lies!" Flame shrieked desperately. "He hasn't got a twin brother!...He's just trying to—"

"Silence!" Pai Lang wheeled angrily on the girl. "Silence !" he hissed threateningly. "Hold your peace, or we will make you silent!"

"That's th' stuff! Put th' stopper on her lyin'!" Jake gloated. "She's tryin' like hell t' save Amos's hide—an' his gold cache too."

"So you have a twin brother? I did not know!" Pai Lang's voice was mild, almost purring, as he faced Jake again. "But this girl? I thought she was your daughter."

"You're damn' right, she is—one hell of a daughter, too, I'll say!" Jake snarled savagely. "But I reckon she's been runnin' round with Amos so long she's fergot whose brat she is."

"So!" Pai Lang mused, his eyes smouldering and inscrutable. "So this explains much! So it was your brother Amos who fled from us to-night—there are *three*, then, instead of two who must die. And we have been pursuing the wrong one for nine years—or is it possible that it was the right one after all? Perhaps it was not you who did the slaying?"

Jake snatched at the straw. "It wasn't!" he admitted, as though reluctantly. "I ain't sayin' I wasn't there—but Amos was there too. It was his scheme, them murders, not mine. I warned him what'd happen if we done it. I was fer givin' up an surrenderin' t' th' Government boat an' takin' our medicine. But Amos said no—said he wouldn't go to th' pen fer no boatload o' dirty Chinks. He done th' killin'. An' afterwards—"

"You devil! You lying devil!" Flame screamed, her voice choked with horror and fury. "How can you tell such lies!…Amos was in New Mexico…He never knew a thing about it…He wasn't near—"

"*Silence!*" thundered Pai Lang. He hissed a sharp order in Chinese. One of the gunmen caught up the towel that had been used to quiet Jake, and, springing across to the girl, muffled her outcries with a swift and skillful gag.

"Perhaps you have been a little wronged." Pai Lang's voice was level and disarming as he turned again to the bound man in the chair. "True, you must die to pay the debt—for so it is written in the sentence of the Tong—but it is possible that you speak the truth…This other whom we have hunted may be the more guilty. But what of the gold?"

Jake's bloodshot eyes glittered craftily.

"Loose me up a bit an' I'll tell you," he grumbled. "These damned ropes are nigh cuttin' my wrists and feet off. How th' hell can I talk—sufferin' like this!" He strained and writhed painfully at his bonds.

"*Talk*—and talk quick!" Pai Lang's face hardened.

"See here, pardner"—Jake's tone was of a sudden whining—"you hold th' winnin' hand and I got sense enough t' know it. But you owe me somethin'. If I hadn't told you, you wouldn't never have knowed nothin' about Amos—nor the gold either. You birds have got me hog tied, an' where you want me, right enough. But it seems t' me I ought t' have a break fer what I done. How 'bout a fair trade? Amos is th' one you really want—you can get him easy now that you got trail of him—an' you got th' kid already. The Big Chiefs o' th' Tong up in 'Frisco ain't got no record o' *three*—all they know about is *two*. There ain't goin' to be no one th' wiser if you let me skip out—these boys o' yours will hold their tongues if you pass 'em th' word. How 'bout it? Do I get turned loose if I put you on th' trail o' a snug little gold cache?"

Pai Lang's lips tightened. For an instant his steel-hard eyes lit with a strange glint. He regarded Jake fixedly.

"There would be no need, I think, to make bargains," he said slowly. "I could make you talk fast enough. Still—perhaps…Yes, I think we can make an arrangement. Where is this money? It will help to discharge the blood debt. Talk—I promise you a fitting reward."

"Turn me loose first," Jake begged. "You ain't takin' no chances. I ain't goin' t' try makin' no breaks. You boys all got your guns an' I ain't got so much as a toothpick. These damn' ropes—I'm sufferin' agony." Again he writhed his bound limbs, tugging and heaving stiffly.

"You have my promise of suitable reward," Pai Lang said harshly. "There will be no other concessions until after you have spoken. Where is this gold? Quick now—the truth."

"The girl's got it!" Baffled, and realizing that he could push his temporary advantage no farther, Jake spat out the words venomously. "The girl's got it! It's cached around here somewhere—an' she knows where…God! This rope's cuttin' my wrists in two!" His arms writhed agonizedly.

"Explain!" Pai Lang's tone was suddenly steel sharp.

"It's th' O'Hara gold"—Jake's arms continued to twist and tug— "that bunch o' dust an' nuggets that's been hid somewheres ever since way back in 'fiftynine. You've heared o' that, I reckon."

"Pah! That story is a myth!" Pai Lang exclaimed angrily. "Is it for such idle talk that you—"

"Listen a bit! Listen!" Jake broke in desperately. "It ain't no myth… It's God's truth! I oughta know…I seen th' papers an' old letters…It's true, I'm tellin' you. You don't think I'd a been fool enough t' come back here on no hot-air story, do you?"

"So!" Pai Lang's eyes lit with sudden interest. "So it was for this you came here. You had definite information?"

"You're damn' right, I had. I had th' straight goods. Pedro Martinez…Say, where is Martinez an' Slant? You bumped them off too—same as Rufe?" Jake's eyes flicked round nervously. He stared into the darkened room beyond Rufe's body.

"That is nothing to you," Pai Lang said sharply. "Speak swiftly."

"But Martinez could ha' told you I was givin' you th' straight truth," Jake whined abjectly. "Martinez is th' grandson o' th' Mexican who used t' be hoss wrangler at th' old stage station down here at Vallecitos in 'fifty-nine. Martinez's mother died a short while back. An' just before she died she passed him a bit o' information that she'd got from his grandmother, years ago. She'd been scairt to tell a soul all her life. Th' old woman who told her had scairt her plumb stiff about th' stuff bein' cursed, an' she hadn't dared tell nobody for fear th' ghosts would kill her. But, dyin', she took a chance…an' she told Martinez—an' he told Slant an' me." Jake paused. He moistened his lips, his eyes darting about him furtively.

"Go on!" Pai Lang snapped impatiently.

"Th' night before they got killed tryin' t' hold up the stage, th' Morgan boys give th' gold they got from Captain O'Hara to old Si Slade, th' stage station tender," Jake went on sullenly. "Slade was in cohoots with 'em on th' sly, an' they give him the gold to hide out for 'em. But next day, after th' Morgans had been killed, Captain O'Hara's body was found too, an' there was such a hollerin' raised that Slade was plumb scairt. He had t' find a safe hidin'place for th' gold in a hurry. So him an' th' Mex hoss-tender went out together an' give th' four Morgan boys a nice decent burial. Slade an' the Mex done all th' job theirselves—they was damn' careful not to have anyone t' help 'em.

"Th' old woman what give th' tip t' Martinez's mother had a pretty straight suspicion that they buried the gold in one o' th' graves. But th' night o' th' next day both Slade an' th' hoss wrangler was shot dead in a gamblin' row. Th' old woman was scairt stiff then—she reckoned there was a curse on th' stuff. So she never told no one but her daughter-in-law. That's th' straight o' what happened to th' O'Hara gold. An' that's what brought me here. It ain't no blasted myth."

"But did you find it? Where is it, then?" Pai Lang's contemptuous incredulity had vanished, and his voice was savagely impatient.

"No, we didn't find it," Jake snarled. "It was gone when we dug up the graves. Someone had already took it. Amos and th' brat is th' ones what got it—I knowed that th' minute I found out that they was livin' here. That's what I come after tonight. Amos got it—he's got it hid. An' *she* knows where it is!" He jerked his head viciously towards the gagged and helpless girl.

"How do you know?" Pai Lang sneered.

"Hell! How do I know I'm settin' here? There ain't no one else likely to ha' got it. Amos had th' same old letters an' papers t' go on that I had. What th' hell d'you suppose brung him back here? He come here pokin' an' scratchin' around an' got a hunch, I reckon, an' found th' stuff. Where else d'you suppose he'd get money t' buy a cattle ranch or to live on if he hadn't found it? He was starvin' three years ago, when you had him on th' run."

"If the gold was found it is spent, then," said Pai Lang coldly. "You waste my time only."

"Spent hell!" Jake's fear gave him violent vehemence. "There ain't only th' stuff that they found in th' cache. Th' papers givin' th' location o' th' Lucky Ledge mine was with that cache f' gold—when they found one they musta found th' other. An' th' Lucky Ledge was high grade—old Captain O'Hara done all his own minin' hisself—th' ledge was so rich he usta bust th' gold outa th' quartz with a hammer. Mean t' tell me that Amos would keep a claim like that t' look at? Spent hell! There's a nice fat bunch o' gold cached there somewheres. Th' damn brat as good as admitted it. We'd ha' made her tell, too, if you birds hadn't come buttin' in." He shot Flame a malevolent look.

"And for this—for this information about something of which you yourself do not know the truth—you expect to be spared?" Pai Lang demanded acidly. "Is this the bargain you would make?"

"Play fair with me, mister, fer God's sake!" Jake was cringingly entreating. "I've done all I could. I told you 'bout Amos...I saved you from bumpin' off th' girl—you never could ha' found th' stuff if you'd ha' killed her. I put th' whole key in your hands—all you gotta do now is make th' girl talk, an' I reckon you can do that easy enough. I took your word that you'd play fair with me—you ain't a-goin' back on your word, are you? Cut me loose an' let me go so's I can get away outa hearin' before you start on th' girl. I got some feelin's an' I don't want t' hear her hollerin'. I played fair with you, mister.

Lemme go—you ain't goin' t' break your word, are you? Don't you believe I been tellin' you th' truth?"

"Yes, monster, I believe your story!" Abruptly, and with a new and terrible note to his voice, Pai Lang drew back a pace, as though in utter loathing of the abject, sweat-beaded face which the pleading bully thrust towards him. "Yes, monster," he repeated, "I believe your story—and I shall keep my word!"

"Thanks, mister!...Thanks!" Terrified for an instant by the startling change in his captor's voice, Jake recovered himself in a gulped rush of gratitude. "I knowed you was a square shooter, mister. Turn me loose now an' I'll fan out...'Twon't take you long t' make th' girl—"

"Scum!" Pai Lang thundered, cutting him short. "Slime of Iniquity! Monster of Hell!...I made no promise to set you free! I promised you only a suitable reward. That you shall have—and swiftly! For a monster who would purchase life with the blood of his own child and the blood of his own brother there shall indeed be a suitable reward. The Death of a Thousand Cuts is too easy. But there is one that is harder. By that you shall die—and now!"

He stepped back quickly, rapping out a savage order in Chinese. The clustering Tongsmen darted forward upon the bound man.

But, quick as they sprang, they were too late. Of a sudden, with a madman's strength born of an awful fear, as in a flash he realized what was in store for him, Jake tore his arms free from the ropes which his deliberate writhings had loosened. With a terrific jerk—before any of the crowding men could touch him—he straightened in his seat, snapping ropes and chair legs alike with one superhuman heave of his tremendous, fear-trebled strength. Terror-maddened, trailing broken cords and with fragments of the smashed chair still clinging to him, he plunged like a mad bull through the surprised knot of gunmen, scattering men right and left like straw. In two bounds, untouched amidst a wild spatter of pistol-shots, he crossed the floor and leaped for the front door, freedom almost within his grasp.

Almost—but not quite! For, from out the frenzy of shouts and wild shots as the scattered Tongsmen recovered themselves and leaped forward in a belated, futile pursuit of the escaping man, there stabbed suddenly three sharper reports—detonations so machine-like and rapid that they seemed to blend. Jake jerked—and stopped short. His outstretched clawing hand, almost upon the door fastening, checked suddenly in mid-air. He reeled, spun round drunkenly and, like a felled ox, crashed twitching upon the floor.

With never a second glance at the fallen man, about whom the shouting gunmen were already gathered, Pai Lang returned his smoking Luger to its holster, and, with a swift stride, crossed the floor to Flame's chair. With rapid fingers he slacked the knots and removed the gagging towel from the half-choked girl's jaws.

"Your parent is dead '" he said coolly. "He has cheated justice; he has cheated the end I had in mind for him—and by this I am dishonored in my vow to the spirits of those whom he slew. But he is dead—one-third of the blood debt is paid! And now"—his hard eyes bored searchingly into the girl's white and quivering face—"where is this other one? Where is Amos hidden? And where is the gold?"

"There is no gold." Unnerved and sick with fear and shock, Flame's voice was a scarce audible whisper. "There is no gold," she repeated. "He lied to you. We did not find it."

"Where, then, is your father's brother hidden—this Amos?"

"I do not know."

Pai Lang bent nearer; he laid a hand upon the girl's shoulder. "Tell me the truth!" he said sternly.

"I am telling you the truth."

The hand on her shoulder tightened. Pai Lang's face came closer. "Speak," he said, his voice low and almost entreating, "for your own sake…speak. If you will not speak the truth I must make you—I must—I am bound by my oath of vengeance, and I have no choice. But I wish to spare you from torture. Tell me—tell me the truth. It is not much that you betray—It can make but little difference in the final reckoning. This Amos cannot escape now. We will follow him to the ends of the earth—now that we know he lives."

"There isn't any Amos." Flame's husky voice strengthened; she met Pai Lang's eyes defiantly. "Jake never had a twin brother—he just made up that lie to save himself."

Pai Lang stepped back, his lean face darkening.

"So!" he said wearily. "It is still to be lies! You told that lie before—and but a few moments later you admitted that Amos had been in New Mexico! Lies! Lies! This is a house of lies—a spawn of liars. Between the lying of a woman for loyalty and that of a craven coward who schemes to save his own life there is difference only in motive. I grow weary. I would have given you a death of mercy, but you force me to do otherwise. You are shielding Amos—but you cling to a useless hope. You cannot save him, for from this puddle of falsehood I have nevertheless gathered a few small pearls of truth. I have clues enough. We will find Amos—we will find this hidden mine to which without doubt he has fled for refuge. Speak now—the truth—or we shall wring the truth from you! Come—this is your last chance! Where is this man hidden? Where is this mine—this secret hiding-place of gold to which he has fled for concealment?"

"We have no mine," Flame whispered huskily, "so help me God…I tell you the truth! We have no mine. We have no hidden gold."

Pai Lang shrugged. But in the movement there was something of weariness and regret.

"So be it!" he said coldly. "You are stubborn—you cling to your lies. I would have dealt lightly with you, but you give me no choice. We must see now if the knife can find the truth."

He turned with a sharply cried order that brought the other men running. Dully, as though in some blurred nightmare of horror, Flame felt them crowding around her; heard Pai Lang's sharp, snarling voice issuing commands in rapid Chinese. She saw the kitchen table swept suddenly clear of all but the lantern and dragged up before her chair. She felt the cords that bound her arms behind her cut; felt the sleeves of her shirt slit suddenly from wrist to shoulder; felt her bare arms dragged roughly forward and pinned down upon the table-top; glimpsed the merciless glitter of knives.

"Speak now—the truth!"

The voice was Pai Lang's. Sharp and dreadful as the cruel, bared blades the words seemed to slash aside the coma of fear that numbed the girl's brain. The tone of them—grim and chilling as was the warning touch of cold steel on her arm—tore aside pitilessly the shadows of unconsciousness which had been mercifully closing upon her. The words—the touch of the blade—seemed to jerk her back to life; to jerk her back wide-eyed and unnerved to face a horror that she could not face.

"Speak—and the truth!" Again the flat of the blade touched her.

Flame found her speech with a choking sob.

"I've told you the truth," she gasped. "I've told you that I…."

Her voice broke—and with it the last remnant of her nerve. Her pent-up fear burst its bounds suddenly in one dreadful, piercing shriek of terror:

"Oh, you devils!" she screamed. "You devils! You merciless devils!"

Screaming and struggling, she wrenched backward, fighting in mad, helpless frenzy against the grim, unyielding hands that held her.

In addition to being an artist and a potter, South also made jewelry from silver, often using turquoise

∽

CHAPTER 15

A Desperate Plan

Brandon came to his senses to find himself lying half-buried in a mass of earth and stones. His head ached as though from a blow. Some bounding fragment of the falling bank had struck and stunned him, he realized—though for how long he had been unconscious he did not know. A few moments perhaps—or minutes? He had no means of knowing. The night was still as black as ink. The maddening wind still roared gustily from the darkness.

Brandon shook himself free from the piled earth which pinned him down and scrambled to his feet, thankful in the sudden realization that he had broken no bones. Except for the blow on the head, he had escaped with nothing worse than a shaking. And even his head did not seem to be badly hurt. The skin was broken a little and he could feel a damp ooze of blood. But it was a surface wound only.

But Brandon's thankfulness at the miracle of his escape from injury was blotted utterly by the dreadful knowledge that he had been baffled. The thought of Flame—the thought of what might have been happening to the helpless girl while he had lain there stunned and inert—froze his blood. The horror of it—the mockery of his own helplessness—woke him to sudden frenzy. It was too late now, he realized—too late! Even the slender, insane flicker of hope that had held him before had snuffed out now. Useless now to hope. And yet....

Blindly, scarce knowing what he did, but goaded by a torturing horror that was unbearable, Brandon stumbled across the piles of new-fallen earth and tangle of broken bushes, and, scrambling to the foot of the slope, raced recklessly up the bed of the canyon. All ideas of a further attempt to scale the treacherous walls of the ravine had left him. In his mind now, vaguely at first, but gathering strength and conviction as he ran, was the thought of the two Chinamen who had run in this direction. If they had indeed reached the house above in time to take part in the shooting that he had heard, it was plain that they had taken some way out of the canyon that was infinitely quicker and easier than climbing.

Stumbling and slipping, crashing into bushes and fighting against the wind, Brandon raced up the winding, brush-cluttered ribbon of sand and cobblestones that marked the bottom of the ravine. The harsh, cold whip of the wind on his face and head seemed to clear his mind—to steady him and to bring back strength to his aching limbs. But it brought also a more chilling horror. More mercilessly than ever, as his fevered pulses steadied, hideous pictures crowded upon his imagination—horrid imaginings which he fought vainly to blot out. Flame! What had happened to her?…God!…What *had* happened?

A gusting cross-current of wind eddying among the bushes and the sudden presence of loose-piled stones and tangles of roots and dead branches beneath his feet told Brandon presently that his guess regarding the two Chinamen had been correct—off to the left some-where a side gully opened into the main canyon. It was by way of this, without doubt, that they had so quickly reached the house.

Guided by the old, dry water-channels, and by the cluttering piles of stones and dead sticks, Brandon swung aside and plunged into the darkness, following the course of this narrower branch canyon. Almost immediately he found himself forcing through a thicker press of bushes that crowded so closely upon the dry watercourse that their tops almost met. The wind was suddenly less; the darkness thicker. The bed of the narrow gully sloped sharply upward, but in spite of the clutter of loose stones and the innumerable steps and crevices which periodic rainstorms had cut in the narrow channel, the going was much easier than he had expected. He was climbing rapidly; already, as the growth of brush thinned, the sweep of the wind from the upper rim was beginning to make itself felt. He was certain now that this was the way by which the two Tongsmen had gone—there was no longer anything amazing in the fact that they had been able to reach the top so quickly.

A final stiff scramble up a narrow, rock-cluttered crevice and Brandon found himself in a fringe of scattered bushes on the lip of the canyon. The wind, sweeping across the valley, struck him full force as he emerged from the tangle of brush that masked the head of the gully, and the air was full of stinging grains of sand. As he thrust aside the tossing bush tops and scrambled out into the black emptiness of the wind-lashed night he was aware of a flicker of lightning away behind him to the westward. The reflection of the distant flash broke the stygian gloom about him with a faint, winking tremor of ghostly light.

For an instant Brandon stood, crouched against the whirling gusts of the wind, while his eyes strained into the dark in an effort to get his bearings. The wan gleam of the distant lightning had given him a momentary glimpse of a blotting line of blacker shadow that banked across the night some little distance ahead of him. The bulking, wide-spreading mass of it confused him. He could not locate himself. His eyes searched the wind-swept dark vainly for some ray of light that would indicate the position of the house.

Of a sudden, with a swift sense of gratitude for the distant electric flare that had given him the clue, Brandon realized where he stood. He was away beyond the western edge of the mesquite thicket—the dark rampart that he had sensed for an instant had been the close-packed mass of the trees. It dawned on him that the little gully up which he had climbed had followed a diagonal course; it had carried him farther away from the house than he had expected. He realized now why he had missed this easy way into the ravine when he had climbed down in search of Amos. In his haste then he had taken the most likely-looking spot close to the house. And, frenzied as she had been over the disappearance of her uncle, it was little wonder that Flame had not thought of suggesting this easier, but more distant, way of descent.

Certain now of his position Brandon plunged into the night, heading for where he knew the house must lie. The stony, windswept flat was bare of bushes and he ran recklessly, all thought of caution blotted in a sharper, more dreadful surge of apprehension. The rayless, wind-moaning dark ahead of him seemed pregnant with horror and with death. There was no ray of light; no sound above the hellish gibbering of the wind.

Dust was swirling in chasing streamers across the flat. The fine sand-grains stung Brandon's face and choked his nostrils. Here on the open stretch the wind roared down with unchecked fury. It seemed to blot everything; drowning the sound of his feet striking among the loose stones; buffeting him; confusing him. He strained his eyes into the darkness vainly, his heart cold with a fear that he dared not face. Flame! What had happened to her? What horror was hid in this appalling blackness?

Of a sudden Brandon jerked to an abrupt halt. Before him, almost within arm's length, and bulking up for an instant grotesque and enormous in the wan gleam of another distant lightning flash, had loomed suddenly the darkened and deserted shape of a long and powerful touring car. And beyond the car, dim and merging as a vast smudge of soot against a background of jet, he saw the house.

But the house was not deserted. Even as he glimpsed its shadowy silhouette, Brandon realized with a sharp jerk of his tensed nerves that somewhere behind the close-shut doors there *was* a light in the building; a faint, yellow light which shone dimly through cracks and knotholes in streaks and glow points—gleams so dim that, from his angle of approach, they had been invisible through the hurrying dust-swirls. Light! Lantern-light still in the kitchen! Then perhaps….

Breathless, his heart all at once pounding so furiously that it seemed to choke him, Brandon sprang towards the motor-car in front of him. He was of a sudden shaking like a leaf. Glimpse of those dim threads of light in the house beyond seemed to both unnerve him and fill him with a fury of new strength. It might be that the girl was still alive!…Perhaps in this car he could find a weapon!…

He leaped on the running-board and groped frantically in the interior of the big machine. Whether this was the car in which Jake's gang had come or whether it belonged to the Tongsmen he did not pause to consider. His only thought was that perhaps it might contain a gun of some sort. His hands darted about feverishly, searching.

But the hope died swiftly. His frenziedly groping fingers, feeling in pockets, on seats and along floorboards, encountered no firearms. A coat, flung carelessly down on the front cushions, and in the back of the car a pick and shovel, a tumble of blankets and a round iron can that evidently contained blasting powder. That was all. No rifles—no guns of any description.

In an agony of bitter disappointment Brandon caught up the heavy miner's pick. It was a pitiful and futile thing with which to face well-armed men, but at least it was better than just a sheath-knife. Despairingly, clutching his crude and clumsy weapon, he whirled towards the house.

But, even as he sprang, a sudden burst of yells and shots in the interior of the darkened building snapped him to a halt. There was the smashing rip of splintering wood and the black wall ahead of him winked in a scatter of new light-points. Bullets slashed out through the dry clap-boards and hummed viciously about him. As he jerked back behind the protection of the car he caught the sound of three sharper reports, followed by the dull thud of a falling body. The tumult ceased abruptly.

Horror-chilled, gripped suddenly by an awful suspicion, Brandon leaped recklessly from cover and ran headlong towards the house. No doors had been opened, but though the yelling had stopped and there was no more shooting, he was aware now of movement and voices— even above the wind came the faint sounds which told him that all at once, just inside the tight-shut front entrance of the kitchen, an excited group of men had gathered.

Chilled and sick-hearted with a dreadful conviction of what had happened, but filled of a sudden with a blind red fury for vengeance, Brandon swerved past the black loom of the little porch and in a wide circle—trusting to the wind to drown his footfalls—darted round the house towards the back door.

A glow of light and a suddenly clear babel of speech came to him as he rounded the comer and circled past the shattered panes of the kitchen window, but he did not pause. The window was too high and too far away for him to see anything, and he dared not go closer for fear of discovery. There were bullet-holes in the back door, he remembered. Through them—if the door was closed, as he hoped—he could see into the kitchen without himself being seen.

Panting, clutching his unwieldy weapon with both hands, his mind still a whirling chaos of madness and horror, Brandon sped past the glowing square of the window and plunged into the more furious wind eddies that tore round the back of the house. He was not think-ing—he seemed suddenly too stunned to think. In his mind there was no clear idea of what he intended to do. He had no plan—no sensa-tions save a sick horror and a frenzied blood lust. The sounds of the shots and the falling body seemed to hammer still in his brain...Flame was dead, he told himself dully...But perhaps by stealth—by a surprise attack—he might yet succeed in dashing out the lives of some of the fiends who had slain her.

The back door was closed as he had expected, but through the cracks between the ill-fitting planks, and through the ragged bullet-holes that pierced them, threads and points of light winked out into the darkness. With grim, tigerish caution, his swift, stealthy footsteps muffled by the furious wind-gusts that swept up out of the black depths of the canyon, Brandon made his way to the back step. The door fastening was broken, he remembered—he had smashed it when he had kicked the door open in his ill-fated attempt to save Flame. But there was no danger now that the door would fly open and reveal him. It opened outward and it was a tight fit. The pressure of his hands and body against it would hold it in place more securely, he reflected grimly—hold it until he was ready to jerk it open and fling himself upon the murderers within.

Silently, but with his every nerve quivering in a fever of madness, Brandon drew close to the rough door-planks and pressed an eye to one of the splintered perforations which bullets had ripped in the boards. For a moment, his vision blurred by the change from outer darkness, he could distinguish nothing clearly in the lantern-lit room beyond.

But as he stood peering, his head close against the bullet-shattered wood, a buzzing drone of speech came again to him from within—a low, merged jargon of Chinese, against which his ear caught the sound of a nearer, sharper voice speaking in English.

Brandon tensed suddenly as though from an electric shock. Those English words—distinct and plainly audible in spite of the outer wind—seemed to stab into his fevered consciousness like daggers of ice. His throbbing brain seemed to stand still—to clear. With every sense all at once cool and razor sharp he thrust his head still closer against the pierced door, straining eye and ear into the dim-lit room beyond, every detail of which seemed of a sudden to stand out before him in wire-edged distinctness.

Flame lived—she still lived!...For a split second, as he realized the truth, Brandon's heart leaped in a choking surge of thankfulness. Trembling, gripped suddenly by a relief so vast that it unnerved him, he pressed closer to the peep-hole. Flame was alive!—alive!...He could see her clearly. There, just on the other side of the door—so close to him that, but for the intervening planks, he could have reached out and touched her; the girl sat stiffly in a chair, bound and helpless. The flickering lantern-light fell full upon her drawn white face, revealing its every detail; revealing also in all their keen-cut mercilessness the wolf-like features of the lean Chinaman who stood questioning her sharply.

Brandon caught his breath with a swift, soundless intake, his sudden rush of relief crumbling all at once in a new and more dreadful wave of hopeless horror. Flame was alive, it was true—and apparently she was as yet unharmed. But—and his blood went cold as syllable by syllable his ear caught the words of the English-speaking Chinaman facing her—it would perhaps have been better—much better—had he found her mercifully dead.

Chilled, his fevered madness gone and his whole body of a sudden damp with a dew of horror, Brandon clung against the door, staring through the splintered bullet-hole as though held powerless in the grip of some dreadful hypnotism. Every detail of the scene within seemed to sear into his brain with merciless distinctness. The lantern which burned upon the table gave light enough, despite the dancing shadows with which it fringed the outer edges of the bleak, disordered kitchen.

Away across the room, sprawled motionless upon the floor near the front door, he could see the unmistakable body of Jake, and near it, to one side, a group of five Chinamen, chattering excitedly together and still fingering their weapons. The body of the Tongsman whom Jake's gang had lynched had been cut down and carried to the side of the room; and in the shadows that masked the open door of Flame's bedroom lay the corpse of the one-eyed Rufe. On the floor near the back wall, and not far from the seat in which the girl sat, was a smashed chair amidst a scatter of broken cords; cords which matched those that trailed in ragged lengths from Jake's death-sprawled arms and legs.

It was easy to see what had happened. Vividly, all in a flash, in that nerveless, horror-stricken second that he leaned weakly against the door for support, Brandon understood what had taken place. The Tongsmen had rushed the house before Jake and his gang had had a chance to harm Flame. And the Chinese had captured Jake and the girl alive. By some means Jake had burst his bonds and attempted to escape—it had been he whose body had fallen in the fusillade of shots that had ripped through the front door. But Jake must have talked— must have told some lying story which the Tong gunmen had believed and which had turned a new and redoubled enmity upon Flame.

Already, from the words of her stern questioner, Brandon had gathered enough to know that the girl was being threatened with torture to make her reveal a secret which her captors were firmly convinced she held. The helpless girl was within fleeting moments of a certain and ghastly fate, Brandon realized; nothing now that she could say or do would make these heartless fiends believe that she truly did not possess the information they sought.

Brandon's mind whirled in an agony of despair. He felt of a sudden sick and trembling. In those dreadful, age-long seconds as he crouched against the door his brain seemed numbed. He strove frantically to think—to plan. The fevered blood-madness that had held him before was gone now. In its place was a quivering horror. Somehow—by some means—he must save the girl from the hideous fate which would be hers unless he could snatch her from it. He must save her!...But how?...*How*?...Worse than madness now to burst through that door and fling himself blindly to certain death against the guns of her captors. Counting the man who stood before the girl's chair there were six armed men in the room—*six* of them!...And he had nothing with which to face their guns but a pick and a sheath-knife! Before he could do more than wrench the door open, their bullets would be ripping through him.

No matter what insane fury upheld him, he could not hope to strike more than a blow or two—the chances were that he would go down lifeless without even the opportunity to strike a blow. And his death would not help the girl. His life would be barely sped when these fiends would turn again to their ghastly purpose. No! Any thought of attack was worse than madness; for the girl's sake he must not attempt it!...And yet!...and yet!...God!—was he to crouch here horror-stricken and helpless while...No!...No!...That was unthinkable!...God of mercy!—was there *no* way...no hope?...If only there were some way, some ruse—by which he could decoy those yellow fiends from the house for a few moments…If only….

Of a sudden, clear and lightning-like as though it had been a direct answer to his agonized prayer; a thought flashed through Brandon's mind—a thought that tensed every muscle in his body and sent him leaping back into the wind and darkness with a swift, soundless spring. *The car!...the can of blasting powder!...*

Frenziedly, the glimmer of a mad, desperate plan in his head, he darted from the door and, in a wide circle, raced frantically back from the house.

South's watercolor of Yaquitepec, his home on Ghost Mountain

CHAPTER 16

Fire and Powder

The car!...the blasting powder!—as Brandon ran madly towards the front of the house, the faint glimmer of hope that had leaped to his mind took shape in a definite plan. Like a flash the conviction came to him that the big motor-car which stood outside the building belonged to the Tongsmen. He had seen but one car, and this circumstance, coupled with the fact that there had been no sign of the bodies of Martinez and Slant Galloway in the kitchen, suggested that these two henchmen of Jake's had somehow escaped the attack, rushed to their own car, and fled. If, therefore, the car in front of the house belonged to the Chinese, Brandon reasoned, and he could set it on fire—could cause some explosion that would draw the Tongsmen outside—there was a chance, a bare chance, that in the confusion he could free Flame and escape in the darkness.

Breathless, his every nerve quivering, Brandon reached the car, and, jerking open the door, dragged out the heavy can of powder from beneath the pile of blankets. In frantic haste, chilled now with the dreadful fear that some of the gang inside might come out suddenly and discover him before he could accomplish his purpose, he carried the explosive to the back of the car and with the pick wrenched open the top of the iron container. In his previous search he had found no fuse," he realized. But there was now no time to look for a fuse. There was a quicker way. Snatching out the heap of blankets from the rear compartment he carried them behind the car and with swift blows of the pick, muffling the sound as best he could in the thick woolen folds, smashed jagged holes in the petrol tank.

Half blinded by the wind-sprayed torrent of petrol that gushed out over his hands, Brandon held the tumbled heap of blankets in the spurting flood. Then, swiftly swathing the opened can of powder in the midst of the petrol-soaked mass, he jammed it beneath the rear axle, and, darting to the front of the car, brought back the coat which had lain on the front seat. For a moment he held the coat in the pouring streams of petrol. Then, catching up the pick from the ground, he leaped to windward. Jerking a match from his shirt pocket he snapped it alight in the shelter of his body and thrust its flickering splint against the coat. As the cloth took fire in an explosive flare of wind-whirled flames he hurled the blazing garment into the petrol-drenched tumble of blankets and, with his unwieldy weapon clutched in his hands, ran for his life towards the house.

A red volcano erupted in the darkness behind him—a writhing spout of swirling fire that flattened to the gale in tongues of tattered flame. The night was of a sudden aglow with dancing, ruddy light that flung up in a pitiless, all-revealing glare the house-front, the corral, the stretch of stony earth and the dark loom of the mesquite clump beyond. With a frenzied, half-formed prayer in his heart that the blanket folds would hold the fire from the powder at least until he could reach the back door, Brandon leaped for the sheltering corner of the house.

But even as he sprang—even as the concealing shadow of the building engulfed him—his blood froze to the sound of a woman's piercing shriek. From within the kitchen rang suddenly dreadful screams of mortal terror—screams which, as he raced madly past the glowing square of the window, were blotted out all at once in the thunderous explosion of the powder. Behind him, whirling out beyond the corner that he had just turned, Brandon glimpsed the blinding flash of a monster, fanlike sheet of fire that ripped the darkness and vanished. The house seemed to heave. From its interior broke a babel of yells and a pounding trample of feet as the startled Tongsmen rushed for the front entrance and spilled like angry bees into the night. Panting, his last shred of caution swept from him by the piteous screams that had stabbed through his ears, Brandon tore round the rear of the house, wrenched open the back door of the kitchen and, with clumsy pick poised savagely in his grasp, flung himself recklessly into the room.

For a split second the lantern-light, faint as it was, seemed to blur his eyes. But even the dim haze which for an instant clouded his vision could not hide from Brandon the sudden icy realization that his desperate ruse faced failure. The noise of the explosion had drawn most of the Tongsmen from the room—but not all of them. The wolf-faced, English-speaking man who had been Flame's questioner was gone, and with him four of the others; through the open front door Brandon glimpsed their moving silhouettes as they swarmed about the flaming remains of the car.

But the girl had not been left unguarded. From beyond the kitchen table, which had been cleared of all but the lantern and shoved up closely in front of her chair, a man straightened suddenly—a powerful, bowed-shouldered man with a flat, cruel face who held a knife in his hand. He jerked erect as Brandon burst through the back door, and, releasing the girl's bared and outstretched arms, which he had been holding pinned down upon the table-top, he dropped his knife and leaped backward with a yell, clutching at his belt for a pistol.

It seemed to Brandon that with the wild yell of the startled Chinaman everything happened at once. He saw the bound girl's white face jerk round towards him—heard her gasping, inarticulate cry of hope; saw through the front door the dark shapes of the other Tongsmen turn swiftly at the sound of their companion's warning shout and come leaping back towards the house. Beyond the flickering lantern—beyond reach of a blow and secure for the instant in the protection which the intervening bulk of the table afforded—he saw the flat-faced, evil-visaged Tongsman whip out a heavy automatic—caught the metallic gleam of the weapon as its black muzzle whirled towards him.

There was no time to think—Brandon acted on blind impulse. Quick as a flash as the gun swung up he leaped sideways and, with a strength and accuracy born of despair, hurled his clumsy weapon across the table full at the flat and brutal face of the man in front of him.

There was a stabbing spurt of fire and a report; a report that seemed to blend with the sickening thud of a crushing impact as the iron head of the heavy pick found its mark. Brandon felt the wind of a bullet along his cheek, but at the same instant, through the hot, whirling cloud of powder-vapor that had blurred his eyes, he saw the bowed-shouldered Chinaman reel backwards and go down in a crumpled heap, his face crushed and bloody. And even as he fell, the dry boards of the front porch roared beneath the racing feet of his companions; the black space of the front doorway lit suddenly with the winking blaze of pistols.

With a savage kick, conscious all at once of the humming smash of bullets into the wall-boards behind him, Brandon overturned table and lantern and, as the flickering light crashed to the floor and snuffed out in sudden darkness, he caught up the girl, chair and all, and leaped through the back door. With no time for choice—no instant in which to hesitate or to weigh the dreadful risk; and with the bullets of the yelling Tongsmen cutting the night about him, he clutched the girl tightly against the protection of his body and plunged over the slid-in bank of the canyon.

Locked tightly together and whirling over and over like a barrel bounding down a slide, they-swept with a sickening rush down the precipitous slope into the blackness and threshing bushes at its base.

South's pencil sketch, "mesquite"

༄

CHAPTER 17

In the Dark of the Canyon

Their tumbling descent checked with a crash in the midst of a springy mass of low mesquite bushes in the very bottom of the ravine. And almost before the yielding branches had brought them to a halt Brandon was on his feet lifting the inert body of the girl in his arms. Bruised and breathless though he was, and with elbows and shoulders scratched and raw from the skidding contact with the crumbling earth of the slide, he had nevertheless escaped lightly, thanks to the tangles of pliable roots and the scatter of new-growth shrubs which clung to the face of the declivity and had broken the force of the descent. Flame seemed to have suffered the most. The legs of the chair to which she was bound were smashed and her body, as he lifted it, hung limp and motionless.

The dreadful fear shot through him that she might be dead, but he had no time for pause—no instant to spare. Above in the darkness pistols still cracked wildly, and, in spite of the wind, he could hear plainly the excited shouts of the Tongsmen and the stumbling crash of their bodies as they tripped blindly over obstacles in their mad rush through the unlighted kitchen. There was no second to lose. With the girl's limp body clutched tightly to him Brandon burst through the hampering tangle of branches, and, stumbling and floundering in the pitchy darkness, ran panting down the rocky, brush-grown bed of the canyon.

Of a sudden he stopped—stopped with a jerk and flung himself and his burden full length among the stones and bushes. Behind him, from up on the canyon rim, a beam of light had cut the night—the blinding ray of an electric torch that darted this way and that, probing the blackness of the canyon like a thrusting rapier. From where he lay, pressed close to the ground in the fervent hope that the low fringe of bushes about him would shield both the girl and himself from view, Brandon could see the shifting shaft of light playing over the steep face of the bank down which they had plunged. It was evident that, from the brink, the Tongsmen were examining the slide. In the dim back-glow from the light he could see their shadowy shapes swarming about the edge above; could hear their high-pitched, excited voices. The light switched away abruptly and vanished. Faintly to his ears came the dwindling sound of swiftly running feet.

Brandon leaped up from his concealment, his heart pounding with sudden realization. The Tongsmen had already discovered the ruse!—the ploughing chair legs and the weight of two bodies had left signs enough on the steep face of the slide to reveal what had happened. Maddened though they were they had not dared to follow down the perilous descent. But they were running now for the little ravine which led into the canyon. In a few moments, aided by their lights, they would come racing like a pack of tigers down the canyon bed. Capture, Brandon realized with a sudden chill, was now certain. Trapped as he was between unscalable walls, and hampered by the darkness and by the burden of the girl in his arms, escape was impossible. He could not outrun pursuit—and to hope to gain safety by hiding was futile. With their powerful torches the Chinese would explore every bush and crevice. Discovery would be inevitable, unless....

Gripped all at once by a swift inspiration—a sudden plan that seemed to flash to him from out the very depths of despair—Brandon whipped out his sheath-knife and, quickly severing the ropes that bound Flame's waist and ankles, he jerked loose the broken chair and with a swing of his arm hurled it ahead of him far into the darkness of the canyon. Catching up the girl's limp body he faced about and ran in the opposite direction, retracing the few steps of his halted flight from the foot of the slide. He was heading back.

Instinctively, in the blind fear of pursuit after the crashing descent down the bank, he had fled down the canyon, away from the house and from the direction in which lay the little ravine by which he had previously climbed out. Now he realized he had erred.

The canyon was a death-trap—the only hope was to escape from it. It was this hope, slender and desperate, which drove him forward stumbling and slipping through the black chaos of rocks and bushes as he headed now directly towards the spot from which he knew the maddened Tongsmen would presently come racing down upon him.

With panting lungs and straining muscles, staggering and floundering under the hampering weight of his burden, Brandon crashed on blindly. Crushed tightly in his arms he could feel the limp body of the girl stirring with returning consciousness. The realization that she still lived fired him with new strength—new hope. The plan that had come to him was a desperate one. It was a slim chance, but it might succeed. Fiercely he told himself that it must succeed!...The new, quickening throb of that soft, warm body against him goaded him to a fresh frenzy of determination. Flame lived!...she must live!...Not now, with life and escape almost within her reach, should she fall again into the hands of those yellow fiends.

He was past the foot of the slide now—past, also, he judged, the place where the bank had fallen with him in his ill-fated attempt to scale it. It had been but a few seconds since he had doubled back up the canyon. But though the whole success of his plan depended upon getting as close as possible to the mouth of the little side ravine before the infuriated Chinamen emerged from it, he dared not delay too long in seeking concealment. It would take the Tongsmen a few moments only to reach the head of the ravine, he knew. And, aided by their lights, they would descend it in short order. At any instant now they might come racing down upon him. Unless he were out of sight before their powerful torches began to flash along the main canyon, discovery was certain.

Already, in the windy blackness ahead, his straining eyes could catch the faint, shifting reflections of swiftly moving hidden lights. Breathlessly, with an unspoken prayer in his heart that his desperate ruse might succeed, he swung aside from the bed of the canyon, and, guided only by instinct, scrambled up the broken, brush-grown footstope that lay against its left wall.

The girl in his arms struggled suddenly. As he stumbled up between the thorny, wind-threshed bushes he felt her limp arms tauten all at once and go round him in a frightened clutch; she jerked back to consciousness with a choking, half-articulate cry.

And almost at the same instant, from close ahead, lights flashed. Even as Brandon flung himself and the girl hastily to shelter behind a low clump of tangled chaparral, the darkness of the canyon was aglow with shifting torch-beams. Down the wind came the sound of excited voices and the swiftly approaching clatter of running feet.

"Oh, where—"

"Ssh!" Brandon clapped a quick hand over the girl's mouth and stifled her bewildered gasp. "Ssh!" he whispered fiercely, pressing his lips close to her ear. "Keep quiet—they're coming down the canyon! Keep still, or they'll find us!"

He felt a little tremor run through her; heard her soft, sibilant intake of breath. She seemed to steady suddenly as though there had come to her all at once the full realization of what had happened. In the darkness he felt her hand grope for his and clutch it tightly. The taut, quivering pressure told him more plainly than words that she had understood. She lay tense and motionless. He knew now that she had seen the swiftly approaching lights. Pressed tightly against him as they crouched together behind the screen of the chaparral, he could feel through his thin shirt the throb of her body; the frantic pounding of her heart.

The lights came closer, flashing over the rocks and bushes in the bottom of the canyon and flinging occasional random gleams across the chaparral clumps that fringed the bordering cliffs. Straining his eyes between the interlaced stems of the bushes Brandon could see the quick-moving shapes of the foremost runners, flung into sharp silhouette by the glaring electric torches of those who followed.

The leaders were almost abreast of the low clump where he and Flame lay concealed. He could hear their panting voices; the grinding clatter of the cobblestones that rolled from beneath their hurrying feet. His heart stood still. The Tongsmen were close—terribly close. A chance sweep now of anyone of their lights along the brush-grown foot-slope might spell destruction. The chaparral clump was thick, but it was none too high. Brandon knew well enough that the screen of branches would not suffice to hide the crouching figures of the girl and himself if the searching light-glare should be turned full upon their hiding-place.

But to his infinite relief the Tongsmen—just as he had reasoned they would—were wasting no time in searching this section of the canyon. Perhaps in the hope that the fugitives had been injured in their perilous leap they were making all speed now towards the foot of the slide. Tense, scarce daring to breathe as he peered anxiously through the bushes, Brandon mentally counted the running figures as they darted past. One-two-three-four-five!…Yes, that was all of them—there had been only six men in the house altogether. And one of the six, Brandon reflected grimly—the one in whose face he had hurled the pick—was already doing all his running in another world.

The lights that had passed paused all at once and circled. In a sudden panic of alarm Brandon flattened closer to earth and thrust the girl down lower among the bushes. A chorus of louder cries from the shadowy shapes ahead came back to his ears. Twisting his head he could see the torches playing over the side of the canyon. He realized suddenly that the Chinamen had checked a moment, attracted by the new-piled earth and stones where the crumbling bank had caved under his previous climbing. They were examining the foot-slope carefully. Brandon's heart chilled. Had he sought shelter just a few yards further back—anywhere in the vicinity of the fallen earth—discovery would have been swift. As it was, the Tongsmen might search round—they might retrace their steps.

But with the delay of only a few seconds the lights and dimly silhouetted figures turned away from the slope and dwindled swiftly along the canyon. The sounds of voices and footsteps died in the wind.

Brandon leaped to his feet and, catching up the weak and trembling girl in his arms, despite her courageous, low-gasped protest that she was uninjured and already recovered enough to walk, he scrambled down the slope and continued his interrupted flight up the bed of the canyon. For the moment his ruse had succeeded. But he knew well enough that each instant now, until he could turn aside and gain the shelter of the little side ravine, was charged with deadly peril.

Behind him the glowing lights were clustered already about the foot of the slide down which he and Flame had plunged. He could glimpse them moving to and fro, probing the bushes. They were even yet no great distance away from him—a torch-beam turned back along the canyon, either by accident or design, would be sufficient to reveal his burdened, staggering figure. Moreover, he was now on the windward side of the searching men. An accidental crashing fall; the clatter of a tolling rock—the sound of any mischance—would be almost certain to carry to their ears.

Swirling gusts of fiercer wind sweeping upon him all at once, and at the same time the crunching yield of dry, flood-piled sticks and leaves beneath his feet, told Brandon presently that he was opposite the narrow ravine. He swung aside thankfully, glancing back over his shoulder as he struggled swiftly towards its shelter. The glowing lights were a little dimmer. They were moving still farther away and flashing from side to side of the canyon. He drew an easier breath. It was probable that the searching Tongsmen had discovered the broken chair, and—as he had hoped they would—had jumped to the conclusion that the fugitives had fled beyond it, heading down the canyon.

But Brandon's swift sense of relief was short lived. Even as he plunged towards the little gully the windy distance behind him was suddenly an uproar of shouts and shots. From down the canyon, despite the blurring roar of the wind, the excited cries of the Tongsmen came to him plainly. And mingled with their yells and the cracking of their pistols was another sound—a strange and dreadful sound that seemed to grow out of the night and come racing up the canyon; a terrible, long-drawn, bubbling, snarling outcry that swept swiftly closer. The torches in the distance jerked around as though by common impulse, their beams of a sudden bathing rocks and bushes in a blinding, far-reaching flood of light—a flood of light through which, pursued by pistol-shots, a great white shape came racing insanely up the bed of the canyon. As Brandon leaped with the girl into the sheltering screen of thick bushes that choked the mouth of the narrow gully he heard, away behind him a sudden louder, more furious outburst of yells.

South's linoleum block, untitled

✑

CHAPTER 18

Flight

"They've spotted us!" Brandon panted as he crashed his way deeper between the sheltering bushes; "we've got a start on them, though! Gully's narrow here—think you can climb alone?"

"Yes—oh, yes!" Flame gasped. "I—I'm not hurt—hardly any! I was just stunned…I'm all right now!"

With a swift twist, as he paused a moment, she slipped from his arms and found her feet. He felt her hand at his back as her fingers clutched into the loose cloth of his torn shirt. "Go on!" she whispered breathlessly, "I can follow. Oh!—what's that awful noise?"

"That's Midnight," Brandon said grimly. "He's wounded…gone mad. It was him racing up through that gang down the canyon that drew their lights this way or they'd never have spotted us. He's scented us maybe, and he wants to follow. God! If I only had a gun! His crazed yammering will draw those devils on us wherever we go. Come on! Quick!…"

With the panting girl at his heels he plunged off through the bushes, leading the way up the steep and rapidly narrowing dry watercourse.

The triumphant shouts of their pursuers raced swiftly closer. In the hushed shelter of the narrow gully the wind-blurred sounds coming up from the main canyon rang with a sudden terrifying nearness. Already, as he scrambled on desperately, helping the breathless girl up through the piled boulders and narrow crannies of the steeply rising channel, Brandon could see the reflected gleam of the quickly approaching torches touching the tossing bush-tops that screened the gully's mouth. Startlingly close now, drowning almost the yells of the men behind, came the ghastly, snarling outcry of the demented hound.

Even as Brandon lifted Flame clear of the last narrow crevice and felt the sudden lash of the upper wind upon his face, the depths of the gully below rang with hideous bubbling snarls. There was the sound of a heavy, leaping body crashing through the bushes…scrambling and charging over the stones. Barely had they gained the lip of the canyon and emerged into the wind-swirled fringe of bushes that masked the gully head when, with a rush, the panting, snarling hound was upon them—a dreadful, dimly seen white horror of glaring eyes and hideous outcry that came rocketing up out of the blackness. As Brandon swept Flame behind the protection of his body and snatched frantically for his knife the huge shape reared and hurled itself headlong towards him.

"*Midnight!*—Midnight! Behave!" Flame's voice was sharp with terror, but the sound of her cry, shrill even above the slash of the wind, seemed to halt the leaping beast like the impact of a bullet. Checked almost in mid-air the great hound shrank back, flattened down upon his belly and crawled forward, his blood-choked snarling changed suddenly to a piteous, sobbing whine.

But there was no instant then for delay. Even as Flame's hand reached out in swift sympathy towards the dog's huge white head the darkness of the little gully below lit with the glare of torches and echoed suddenly with shouts and the noise of running feet. Midnight leaped up and faced about with a dreadful, coughing roar. As Brandon whirled Flame around and raced her away across the windswept stony flat towards the mesquite clump, the darkness again rang with the big hound's hideous snarlings.

"Oh, damn that dog!" Brandon breathed savagely. "He'll draw them on us all the time."

"He's not following!" Flame gasped. "Maybe he'll hold them in the gully."

"He won't!" Brandon answered bitterly. "He can't hold back men with guns! Besides, he won't try, he doesn't know now what he's doing! His mind's gone, he's as likely to turn on us as on them. God! If we can only reach the horses!"

"What horses?" Flame panted.

"The ones we left tethered in the mesquite clump."

"Th—they're gone," Flame gasped breathlessly, clutching tightly at his sleeve as she stumbled blindly over a low bush, "there's no horses there now. Slant Galloway and Martinez escaped. They took the horses."

Brandon jerked to a startled halt. The girl's low-panted words seemed to stun him. Gone! The horses gone?…For an instant, gripped by a numb despair, his heart seemed to stand still. The last desperate hope—a hope that had come to him as he had scrambled with Flame up through the black depths of the gully—crumbled and vanished. He remembered now the clatter of hoofs which he had heard the instant before the bank had caved in and swept him down into the canyon. In the frenzied chaos of happenings that had followed he had forgotten that tell-tale sound utterly.

So the horses were gone! Martinez and Galloway had taken them...Then Martinez and Galloway had not escaped in Jake's car, as he had thought...Probably, then, it was Jake's car and not that of the Tongsmen which he had destroyed...His brain seemed suddenly confused. For a moment, oblivious both to the ghastly tumult of the wounded hound and to the swiftly nearing shouts, he stood irresolute, too crushed to think, his whirling mind dully conscious that away to the left of him in the darkness redly glowing fragments marked the position of the burned car; and that ahead, indicated by a belt of more impenetrable blackness and by the wiry whistle of the wind through the thorny branches, was the mesquite clump.

But it was only for a fleeting instant that despair held him. A glow of light reflecting up out of the gully behind and a sudden more frantic outburst of Midnight's gibbering snarls jerked him back to decision and swift action. The horses were gone, but the mesquite clump still offered a temporary concealment from the searching electric beams of the pursuing Tongsmen. Catching Flame's arm in a fierce, steadying grip he raced her towards the sheltering trees, heading around the clump on the side farthest from the house.

He found himself among bushes suddenly, the fringe of low bushes that bordered the edge of the trees. Running at top speed, their eyes helpless in the confusing darkness, he and the girl blundered through them blindly. Flame stumbled, and in a violent effort to save her Brandon lost his footing also. They went down together with a crash in a tangle of low, thorny branches. And almost in the same instant, before they could gain their feet, lights flashed up over the canyon rim. As Brandon and the girl flattened hastily to the ground behind the poor shelter of the straggling bush, there was the sound of shouts and of a sudden Midnight's mouthings changed to a swift-moving, hideous yammering that told plainly that the maddened hound was again racing frantically away from pursuit. An outburst of triumphant yells rang behind him. But there was no shooting.

"Here he comes!" Brandon groaned, his fingers locking in sudden desperation about the haft of his knife. "He's coming straight this way—and they're right after him. They've guessed he'll lead them to us—that's why they're not trying to shoot him any more. He's bringing...."

"He's not!—he's not!—" Flame broke in excitedly. "Listen!...he's not coming this way...he's headed away from here!...He's racing away up along the edge of the canyon—and they're following! Look!...Look at the lights!"

But even as Flame uttered her hoarse, gasping whisper, Brandon had himself sensed what was happening. His heart bounded with a sudden new hope. He leaped up and lifted the girl to her feet. "Come on!" he breathed. "Quick!..."

He caught her hand and led swiftly, feeling his way through the tangle of low growth that skirted the gloom-blotted thicket of trees. Midnight's long-drawn, dreadful yelling was dwindling quickly into the wind. The dog, as Flame had said, was heading up along the edge of the canyon. How long the wounded brute's unhinged intelligence would hold him to his present course Brandon could not guess; but he prayed fervently that it would be for long enough to draw the Tongsmen well away.

Glancing back as he forced a passage through the bushes Brandon watched the dancing lights anxiously. They were still close—so perilously close that he could hear plainly the cries of the running men. But they were moving each moment farther away, following swiftly in the wake of the racing dog who was already far ahead of them. If only Midnight's course would hold! If only he would continue to draw pursuit for a few minutes!...

A thicker blackness overhead and the sudden slash of whipping branches across his face told Brandon that they had gained the outermost trees. He dropped thankfully to his knees, drawing Flame down after him. Together they crept swiftly into the cavernlike shelter of the matted thicket.

Brandon drew a swift breath of relief. For the moment, hidden by the closely interlaced branches, they were safe from view even should any of the torches of their pursuers happen to sweep in their direction. But the advantage was temporary only. They had not an instant to lose. At any moment the witless hound might come racing back...or the Tongsmen might discover that they were upon a false scent. In speed now—in gaining a long lead over the infuriated Chinamen—lay the only hope.

With an encouraging whisper to the girl who followed closely at his heels, he wormed his way quickly forward, threading between the rough, twisted trunks. Overhead the wind roared in a muffled fury through the tossing tree-tops and the black, draughty darkness that he traversed was clamorous with the creaking groan of rubbing branches. Once, as he paused to wrench aside a low, tough bough that blocked their progress, a pale gleam of light, striking down of a sudden through a rift in the close-wove thorny limbs overhead, brought his heart into his mouth and caused Flame to catch her breath with a little gasp of terror.

But the wan, fleeting glimmer winked out as abruptly as it had come. It was a lightning flash, Brandon realized—another of those distant flashes such as the one which had previously revealed the ranchhouse and the standing car to him. He set his teeth. He had forgotten about the lightning—in the dark depths of the canyon it had been unnoticeable. On the open ground, however, the minute he and Flame should emerge from the shelter of the mesquites, these intermittent, revealing gleams would imperil still more their chances of escaping unseen.

The note of the wind became dearer. Eddying sand grains and dead leaves swirled about Brandon's face. The trees were thinning out. He found himself abruptly on the outer edge of the mesquite clump. There were but few bushes here to break the whirling gusts that swept round the thicket and the flying dust almost blinded him. He remembered that the trail to the corral and the house passed around this edge of the thicket. The hurrying streamers of dust and sand that drove up upon him were proof that he had not lost his direction crawling through the trees. He was now on the edge of the beaten road.

Brandon reached a hand to Flame and together they rose swiftly to their feet, peering into the darkness through the stinging dust swirls. Away to the right the bright gleams of the torches were still darting and flickering along the edge of the canyon. They were considerably farther away now. But the dog's gruesome outcries seemed to have ceased. The wind bore only the sound of faint shouts. Pressed close against him as she stared into the windy blackness, Brandon could feel Flame quivering. Her hand was gripped tightly upon his. "Midnight's silent," she whispered hoarsely. "I can't hear him any more. Maybe they've shot him."

"They wouldn't do that," Brandon said, "they're banking on him scenting us out. More likely he's quit yowling of his own accord and sneaked off somewhere. He was away ahead of them, anyway. He can outrun them easily—they'll never catch him. Chances are, though, that he'll come racing back here presently, yelling for all he's worth. We've got to make time. What's the country like straight ahead—out across the valley here? Any shelter?"

"It's just desert," Flame answered. "It's scattered with greasewood and chollas and yuccas. They're pretty thick in places. But there's lots of open spots."

"We'll risk it," Brandon said with sudden decision, "we've got no choice. Come on!"

He led the way into the darkness, leaving the sheltering fringe of the trees and heading directly into the windy obscurity in front. He felt the worn ruts of the trail beneath his feet as he crossed it, and a moment later found himself among scattered bushes. The ground underfoot was hard and strewn with small, loose stones. He glanced back. The lights of the Tongsmen were still farther away, and, even as he looked, they vanished utterly, blotting out one by one as though swallowed into the earth.

Halted by Brandon's abrupt pause and sudden exclamation Flame looked back just in time to see the last light disappear. The girl gave a low cry of relief. "They're going back into the canyon!" she said breathlessly; "there's other gullies away up there where they are that they can climb down through. Midnight must have led them down one."

"That's likely what's happened," Brandon agreed. "Still, it may be only that they've decided to switch off their torches. Anyway, it gives us a better chance. We've got to make the best of our time now."

He led off again through the night. But of a sudden, reassured somewhat by the disappearance of the lights, halted again abruptly, checking the girl with a sudden steadying hand:

"Flame," he whispered anxiously, voicing the fear which still gnawed at him despite the girl's previous denials, "you aren't hurt, are you? Those devils didn't harm you, did they?"

"They—they didn't have time," the girl answered with a shudder. "The Chinese attacked the house just in time to save me from those brutes of Jake's. And then, just as the Chinamen were going to torture me, you came…Oh, Jim!…I—I thought you were dead.…" Her voice broke in a little sob.

"But the fall—the fall down the canyon?" he persisted hastily. "You—you haven't got any broken bones or anything, have you? I reckon you're too plucky to tell the truth, but that fall must have given you an awful shaking. If you're hurt anywhere bad or if you've broke any bones or anything you've got to tell me, because—"

"Because then you'd want to carry me, I guess," she cut in with a little flare of temper that was strangely softened by an odd choke in her voice. "No, I'm not hurt—honest I'm not!…not any more than you, anyway. I guess I'm better able to walk than you are."

"Then come on!" he said abruptly. "The farther we can get away from here before those devils come searching this section the better chance we've got. Keep close to me—and steer clear of the chollas if you can. They're hell to fall into."

"But you?"—she gripped his arm and her voice was sharp with anxiety—"how about you? Are *you* hurt? Tell me the truth!"

"Nothing but a bump or two and a few bits of bark knocked off," he assured her lightly. "I reckon I was born lucky. Come on!"

He headed once more through the bushes, forcing swiftly through the denser patches and running wherever the ground was open enough for speed. For the first time since this blurred nightmare of horror had engulfed him he was conscious of a vast relief. There had been sincerity in Flame's assurance; he was convinced now that the girl, although she was undoubtedly as stiff and bruised as he was himself, was not seriously harmed. This realization fired him somehow with new life—new courage. Despite the peril of discovery which still shadowed them—a peril which would continue to menace them until they had passed far beyond the range of the searching torches and of the risk of the crazed hound's unwitting betrayal—he felt suddenly easier and more confident.

Flame was alive and unharmed. Somehow, for the moment, nothing else seemed to matter much.

South's pencil sketch untitled

∽

CHAPTER 19

Across Terrible Valley

There was no reappearance of the lights in the blackness behind—
no further sound of Midnight's cries. Pushing close to Brandon as
they ran swiftly across a little open space Flame spoke suddenly:

"I guess they're searching up along the canyon," she said. "We
could circle away around after a bit and strike the road to Gus's place."

"That's too risky," Brandon answered. "That's just what they'll
think we've done if they don't find us; and after a while they'll go
searching along that road in their car. They must have their car hid out
somewhere. I thought I'd destroyed it, but I reckon I made a mistake. It
must have been Jake's machine that I put the powder under."

"Then that noise—that explosion—" Flame gasped: "You did that?
That was your work?"

"Yes," he assented. "I found a can of powder in the car. I'd looked
into the kitchen through the holes in the back door and I'd seen you. I
had to work some scheme to draw those devils out of the house."

He heard her catch her breath with a sharp intake. "You saved my
life, Jim," she breathed—and again his ears caught the queer little break
in her voice. "You—you don't know what you saved me from."

"No," he said grimly, "I reckon I don't—not quite. I saw enough,
though, to guess more than plenty. But it wasn't much of a rescue. I
came near to breaking your neck, rolling you down into the canyon
like I did."

"I—I guess I wouldn't have minded dying like that," she said in a
low voice. "Oh, Jim!...when you burst in through the back door I was
sure you were a ghost...I thought I'd gone crazy! I was sure Jake had
killed you when he shot down at you after they'd knocked you into the
canyon."

"He made a mistake, that's all," Brandon said dryly. "It wasn't me he plugged those bullets into. It was the Chink that Midnight killed."

Again he heard her thankful intake of breath. All at once, as they stumbled hastily onward through a sudden thickening of the bushes that crowded them for a moment closer to each other, he felt her arms go about him impulsively, checking him to a halt. Close to his ear her voice came in a low-pitched, choking whisper:

"Jim," she breathed, "I—I'm sorry!…I'm sorry I was so rotten to you…back there on the trail when I first met you. I—I treated you awful! I suspected you of being a crook…I thought that you'd come there spying, you know…digging in those graves…And I—I…Oh, Jim!…I'm sorry…And—and—"

Her voice broke. Of a sudden her face was buried against his shoulder. She clung to him, shaken with choking, uncontrollable little sobs.

For an instant, as his arms went swiftly around her, Brandon's senses blurred. Her choking, half audible words—the clinging clutch of her hands—the warm, electric throb of her lithe young body against his—seemed of a sudden to snap something deep within his soul—something which released in one headlong flood all the passionate, pent-up emotion and vague, dimly sensed yearnings which had been gathering there from the moment when he and Flame had first met.

For a moment, standing there in the black darkness, ringed by the whipping tops of the creosote bushes, it seemed to him that the world stood still. The weariness of his body; the torture of his swollen, blistered feet; the screaming rush of the wind; the horror through which he had passed, and the menacing peril which still lurked in the ghostly blackness of the night behind—all alike were for the moment forgotten. He was conscious only that Flame was in his arms and that he was crushing her fiercely to his heart—conscious only that the faint, sweet fragrance of her hair was in his nostrils; that he was comforting her—whispering in her ear—whispering broken, disjointed, blundering words which were as inane and unneeded as had been her own stammering, overwrought apology for something which had passed and been forgiven hours ago.

His words were choked, husky, half uttered—but there was no need for speech. Here, of a sudden, before they were yet secure from the merciless death that searched the darkness behind them, something within each of them had snapped. Beneath the whelming pressure of overtaxed nerves barriers had given way. Words were useless and foolish. Something stronger than either of them seemed to have caught them up and locked them together; something that, stronger all at once than the fear of death, had wrapped them about suddenly as with a strange, warm breath of invisible fire, sending the blood racing deliriously through their veins and blotting their minds to all save the throbbing, tempestuous speech of their suddenly yearning hearts.

"Jim!...Oh, Jim!..."

"Flame! Flame, girlie!..." Hungrily, tenderly, he raised her head. He felt her arms tighten about his neck—felt her face lift eagerly towards his in the darkness. "Flame!" he breathed passionately, "Flame, darling, I—"

A dazzling sheet of fire split the sky suddenly. Startlingly and without warning, before even their hungry lips could meet, the heavens above them lit in a blinding, blue-green flare that was closer, and ten thousand times more brilliant, than any of the pale, distant flashes that had preceded it. The desert all about them leaped out from its cloak of darkness in sudden, naked vividness. For one instant, dazzlingly distinct and sharp-edged in a pattern of silver and ebony, Brandon saw the wind-bent tops of the creosote bushes, the scattered, grotesque, sentinel-like shapes of the yuccas—and away behind, chillingly distinct across the pale sweep of tossing bushes, he saw the mesquite clump and the ranch-house. The flash snapped out in a down rush of dazing darkness and a deafening crash of thunder.

But it was more than the startled realization that this merciless light-blaze might have revealed their whereabouts to the searching Tongsmen which caused Brandon to recoil—jerking back sharply before Flame's yearning, upraised lips could meet his own. In the all-revealing light of the flash, clearer and more vivid even than had been his glimpse of the ghostly desert about him, he had seen Flame's pale, upturned face; had caught the glint of her glorious hair; read the surging passion of trust and self-surrender in her wide eyes and quivering lips. The girl's fresh, clean beauty had struck him like a blow—chilling him—jerking him back brutally to his senses.

He was a cad, he realized suddenly—he would be a low-down cowardly skunk to accept thus the love of this girl who lay in his arms. He had no right! Though his heart was of a sudden bursting with a worshipping love for her he had no right to accept her affection. Circumstances, and not he, had been responsible for the service he had done her. The girl's nerves were unstrung and overwrought, he realized. He had no right to take advantage of the situation—no right to accept this priceless gift which she offered him in her impulsive gratitude. He was but a drifter—without possessions—without prospects.

Besides, there was this other, this Ted Davidson of whom old Gus had spoken—to him Flame's heart was already given. After a while—when her strained nerves had quieted—she would regret bitterly this madness of gratitude which had swept her into the arms of a drifter whom she had known only for a few hours.

Chilled, stunned at the bitter truths which crowded upon him in a flash sudden and merciless as that of the lightning itself, Brandon drew back, breaking free almost fiercely from the clinging embrace which Flame's involuntary start of terror at the flash and thunderclap had loosened. He caught the girl's arm:

"Quick!" he gasped hoarsely, "run!—we've got to hurry! That flash was as bright as daylight—they'd see us easy if they were anywhere near. The storm's getting closer! Come on!"

He plunged away recklessly through the bushes, bursting a path through which he swept her almost roughly after him. He felt himself shivering as though from a violent chill. His heart was suddenly cold and his head throbbed. He was somehow dully thankful all at once for the peril which gave him excuse for violent, wordless haste. Beside him Flame struggled onward in silence. Save for a startled exclamation when the lightning had flared, and a little gasp as he had put her from his arms and whirled her after him through the bushes, she had not spoken. But his fierce, tight grip upon her arm told him that she was quivering. He had a dull, aching feeling that she understood—that to her also had come realization.

Another lightning flash, scarce less vivid than the last, tore the blackness above them; the thunder rolled in a deafening roar across the valley.

The peril of the all-revealing light served, in spite of himself, to wrench Brandon's mind away for a moment from the torturing thoughts that filled it. In the ghostly, swift-vanishing blaze he saw, close ahead of him, rising up abruptly beyond the stretch of scattered creosotes and chollas, a rocky, canyon-riven mass of low hills.

"That's the spur of foothills that shuts off this little valley from the main valley to the east," Flame panted, answering his hasty question. "They're not very high or wide, but they're all rocks and canyons. We could hide there."

"And beyond—on the other side of them?" Brandon demanded.

"That's where the main valley is," Flame answered, "the valley that the old stage road runs through. It's not so far, through here in a straight line, to the road. We're about opposite where the old stage station is—the way we're headed now."

"But that's miles away—by the trail we rode up tonight," he objected.

"I know it is—by the road from Gus's," she answered breathlessly. "But the road twists like a snake—it's the only way you can get into this inside valley on horseback. Our ranch house isn't near so far from the old station in a straight line, but these little hills ahead are mostly rocks on edge. Horses can't make it. There's no way through these but an old foot trail that the Indians used to use—and that's fierce climbing."

"A foot trail—?" Brandon caught sharply at her words. "Do you know it?"

"I've never been over it myself," the girl answered, "and it is seldom used nowadays. But it cuts through hereabouts. There's two rocky peaks ahead here somewhere, on the summit of the ridge. The trail leads up between them—through what folks call Dead Man's Gap. It ought to be right in front of us…but I can't tell—dark like this. If we only had daylight…."

"Thank God it's not daylight," Brandon said fervently. "We've got quite a while yet before dawn, I reckon—I hope so, anyway. We wouldn't last long if it was light. Maybe, though, with the next flick of lightning we can get our bearings, and—"

The darting, electric blaze swept the heavens like a sword even as he spoke. Flame cried out, gripping his arm and pointing, her words for the moment drowned in the windy crash of the thunder. Dead ahead of them, on the crest of the sere and naked ridge, Brandon glimpsed two huge and jagged rocks that, for an instant, stood out whitely like monstrous fangs against the black background of the sky behind. The night rushed down again in stygian darkness.

"That is it!" Flame gasped. "That is the Gap!"

"We'll try for it," Brandon said with decision. "Our best chance now is to try to get through here to the stage road, then strike down that to the nearest place where we can get help. I reckon we'd better keep away from Gus's place. Those yellow devils will be searching all along that road for signs of us. It's too risky to go anywhere near there. Alone, Gus couldn't help us much, anyhow, and we'd only bring trouble on him. Where's the nearest place outside of Gus's?"

"Smoky Springs," Flame answered, "the Davidsons'…the place I was coming home from when I ran into you this evening. It's an awful way, though—on foot. We'll never make it."

"We've got to try," Brandon said shortly. "I reckon we'll get there somehow. You got to get somewhere to help and friends pronto. Those Chinks are like bloodhounds. They aren't going to give up searching."

He pushed on swiftly, holding a course as near as he could judge direct for the landmark that he had glimpsed ahead. His heart was of a sudden heavy again—mention of the Davidsons had again brought back upon him in full force the crushing torture of his thoughts. From beside him, as they hurried onward through the inky gloom, Flame spoke all at once.

"Jim! They didn't get Amos! He escaped!"

"Escaped! How do you know?"

"That English-speaking Chinaman told me. Amos got away some-where in the darkness when they first attacked the house."

"Thank God for that!" Brandon said. He pushed on without paus-ing. Somehow he was a bit staggered at the sudden realization that, till this moment, he had forgotten about Amos. Under stress of the hideous danger which had shadowed Flame he had forgotten her uncle utterly. Somehow, now, the fate of Amos seemed relatively unimport-ant compared to the dread peril from which Flame was still far from secure. He was glad though, for the girl's sake, that the old ranchman had escaped.

They hurried onward in silence, struggling forward in a toilsome progress which was an interminable succession of blind gropings and stumbling collisions with the scattered bushes. It was impossible to avoid the chollas; in the black darkness they blundered repeatedly against their bunched masses of needle-like thorns. Brandon's clothing was hung thickly with detached sections of the brittle, vindictive cactus and his hands smarted acutely from the stabbing spines. He knew well enough that Flame was no better off. But the girl struggled on gamely and without complaint.

Once in a while, by the jerky, fleeting flares of the lightning, he caught glimpses of her. Her lips were tight-set and determined. Somehow, from those vanishing gleams of her pale face, he sensed that there was more than the thought of their immediate peril in her mind. He seemed to feel about her the tenseness of a reaction. He guessed that already regret was upon her for the madness of that impulsive moment when she had clung so passionately to him.

And in Brandon's heart there was neither the words nor the mood to rouse her from her spell of dogged silence. His own brain was a maelstrom of torturing thoughts—a misery which even the increasing conviction that they had, for the time being at least, successfully eluded pursuit, failed to lighten. To him it seemed that his heart was of a sud-den dead. Fate had cheated him; made him the victim of a heartless, ironic jest. There had been bitter irony in the train of circumstances which had lured him down here to this devil-haunted region in order to pit him weaponless and bare-handed against a mixed collection of armed and ruthless fiends.

There seemed something devilish and uncanny in the fact that in this whole cycle of horror he had been robbed time and again of the chance to secure a gun—that he had been denied everything in the shape of an effective weapon, when a weapon would have meant so much. And, to cap all, Fate had toyed with him in gloating, fiendish jest by awakening in his heart this blinding, passionate love for Flame, fanning it to fever heat, and then, in the very instant when all his wildest, most impossible dreams were in the moment of realization; forcing him of his own will to deliberately thrust the girl's love from him. This had been the supreme cruelty. It was more than he could bear. Stumbling onward with eyes that were blinded by more than the darkness, Brandon was conscious of a torturing agony of spirit that blotted utterly all sensations of physical suffering.

And yet—and yet he had been right; he told himself fiercely. There was nothing else to do—no other square and decent way! A penniless drifter—no folks—no prospects—not even now a saddle and cowpony to call his own! A fine sort of prospect that to offer a girl like Flame! A fine sort of hombre he'd be to take advantage in this way of a terrified girl's impulsive gratitude.

It didn't make any difference now, the fact that he'd always had crazy dreams in his head; it made no difference now the extra bits of education he'd struggled to get—the books he'd ploughed his way through page by page in spare moments in an effort to add to the plain and simple schooling that had been his. It made no difference now that he had had ambitions to some day…No. It made not a sliver of difference what he *hoped* some day to be. He was a penniless cow-poke *now*, and that was all that counted. He would be a low-down skunk to let this blue-eyed girl's gratitude sway her towards him. He wouldn't do it; he loved her too much.

"Jim! You—you're not married, are you?"

Flame's question came from the darkness so abruptly that it startled him, checking him almost to a halt. He recovered himself as from an unexpected blow. "No!" he told her brusquely. "No, I'm not married!…Don't ever expect to be!"

He forced on savagely through the bushes. He was conscious of a bitter flame of resentment—resentment mixed with a sharper, more unbearable misery. Why had she asked him that question? He had enough to bear without this torturing stab which was like thrusting a knife into an open wound. Married…Married…God! Why had she asked him that now?

But somehow the very pain which the girl's unexpected question— a question which she made no effort to follow up—served to wrench him back to a steadied grip of himself. He was a cheap piker, he told himself in savage accusation—nothing but a spineless dummy packed chock full of self-pity! Flame was alive—that was all that mattered. And he had saved her! Helped though he had been by some Power infinitely greater than himself he had been the instrument which had snatched her from a hideous fate. It was reward enough that he had been able to render her that service.

He was suddenly ashamed of himself—ashamed and thankful. He loved her too much, he realized, to take from her an affection to which he was not entitled, but at least he could serve her still. The menace of a dreadful death overhung both of them too closely to count yet on safety. But if flesh and blood could do it, he told himself determinedly, he would get the girl out of this tangling net of hell somehow, and safe among her friends.

South's oil painting of a desert wash

༖

CHAPTER 20

Through Dead Man's Gap

With a steadier mind, fighting down with every ounce of his will the torturing thoughts that pressed upon him, Brandon faced the problem which was now his sole concern. That the only safety lay in getting Flame well clear of the little valley and into the care and protection of friends he had already determined. The Davidsons' ranch at Smoky Springs was the logical place. He remembered what Flame had said about the expected return of old man Davidson and his son—by this time they were probably back. There was the chance also that the messenger who had been sent off to notify the deputy sheriff of the theft of the horse would bring back that officer with him. All this was to the good. If he could get Flame somehow to the Davidsons, Brandon had little doubt that, for the time at least, she would have ample protection.

But the problem of getting there was staggering enough. The rocky hills ahead had to be crossed. Beyond them there lay another stretch of desert slope, then the interminable length of the old stage road back to the bandit graves where he and Flame had first met. And Davidsons' was away beyond the section where the graves were—how much far-ther beyond he did not know. But it was a long way, because it must be on the far side of the place where, earlier in the day, he had struggled out of a foothill canyon and struck on to the road.

The prospect of traversing all this country on foot was appalling even to Brandon's grim determination. Had he and the girl been fresh and unwearied it would have been bad enough. Handicapped now, as they both were, with a dreadful exhaustion of body which only the press of danger served to hold in check, the thing loomed almost as a physical impossibility; somehow, however, it *had* to be done. To make matters worse, there was also against them the question of time. Unless they got well away from the little valley while the darkness held, the chances of discovery and capture by the searching Tongsmen would be fearfully increased. Darkness was their salvation. But just how long would the darkness last?

Anxiously Brandon swept his eyes about the inky, wind-filled gloom that pressed upon them. He tried to figure back, but somehow he could find nothing for his mind to lay hold of that would serve as a base for calculation. He hadn't the faintest idea of the time.

The blurred tempest of horror through which he and the girl had passed seemed, somehow to have taken an age—yet he knew well enough that it could have covered altogether but a short period. It had been a frenzied period crowded with a lifetime of terror, but in actual clock-time it had been short. Happenings had followed upon each other in dazing succession, but actually it had not been so long ago that he and Flame had ridden up to that black and silent house of horror and tethered their horses in the mesquites. All that had happened after that—the search of the house for Amos—Flame's breathless explanation—the fight with the first two Chinamen—the coming of Jake— the maddening struggle to climb the caving bank of the canyon—the blowing up of the car—the rescue of Flame and their narrow escape together up the ravine—all this had happened swiftly, horror crowding upon the heels of horror.

But it had in actuality not taken much time, Brandon realized. Just exactly how much he could not tell. But he guessed that the night had still far to run before dawn. Moreover, dawn, he reflected thankfully, would be later than usual in coming, unless in the meantime the impenetrable blanket of clouds that blotted the sky should break up. He was all at once grateful for the wind and storm. The blackness was their only hope. The lightning, now that they were so far away beyond the range of searching eyes, was no longer a peril—it had become a help. But in the cloaking gloom of the night lay their security. With daylight the desert would lie clear and bare. Under the searching sweep of binoculars, or even of sharp, unaided eyes, their moving figures would not long escape detection.

The ground underfoot was rising now, lifting towards the hills in a swiftly mounting stone-strewn slope. The bushes were thinning, their places taken more and more with fallen boulders and jutting outcrops of rock. The wind gusted more furiously as it tore up from the brush-scattered floor of the valley and whirled hurtling up among the rising ledges ahead. The lightning was by now more frequent, playing almost continuously in flickering tongues amidst the hurrying cloud masses that seemed to crush down menacingly from the inky sky. Scattered drops of rain, swollen and driving down through the wind with the pattering impact of bullets, fell occasionally. The thunder had settled to an intermittent, sullen roll that filled the valley like the uneasy growlings of some monstrous beast.

"There won't be enough rain to hurt us any, I guess," Flame said, answering a sudden anxious remark of Brandon's. "It's just one of those dry thunderstorms. There won't be more than a sprinkle."

"I hope not," he said. "We've troubles enough without rain—here among these rocks."

"I wish I knew something about this old trail," the girl said regretfully. "Amos went over it once, just to find out what it was like, but I never asked him much about it. All I remember is that he said it was awful rough and that it led up a narrow; rocky canyon and through between the two peaks on the summit."

"Must be this gash right in front of us, I reckon." Brandon's eyes were strained ahead at the tumbled piles of rock which leaped to view and vanished with each lightning flash. "That's the most likely place for a trail. Looks like it'll be tough climbing, but thank God there can't be so much of it. These ridges aren't so high, by the looks."

"They're high enough," she said. "You ought to see those rocks by daylight. They're fierce."

"They're mean enough looking to suit me as it is," he said grimly. "But we're going to get through 'em, just the same. I reckon you're dog-tired though, aren't you?" His voice was suddenly anxious.

"I'm lots fresher than you are," she evaded stubbornly. "I can keep going as long as you can. I've been riding all day. You've walked."

"Then we'll keep right on moving," he said. "We've got no time to lose. We'll strike straight up this gorge. We'll get through somehow. Thank God for the lightning. It'll give us a sight of things every once in a while."

He pushed onward, leading the way up the slope, which had suddenly become acutely steep. About them all at once, grim and grotesque in the jerky, inconstant flares of the lightning, rose piles and masses of jagged rocks that thrust sharply upward in pinnacles and inclined planes of weathered stone. The whole ridge, Brandon suddenly realized, was a mass of ancient stratified rock, tilted on edge by some vast convulsion of Nature and upthrust above the desert floor. It was not astonishing that no horse trails crossed these ridges; it seemed impossible that they could be passed even on foot. As he clambered up a mammoth boulder and drew Flame up after him into the narrow, sheer-walled gorge that the lightning had revealed. Brandon's heart faltered. The climb, he realized, was to be a more appalling task even than he had thought.

And quickly enough it was forced upon him that his worst misgivings had been amply justified. The black, cliff-sided gorge up which they now picked their way was narrow—little more, it seemed, than a crack that had split in fantastic windings into the very heart of the ridge. The floor of it was choked with masses of stone which had fallen from the heights above, and its length was scattered with treacherous steps and water-worn hollows which the scouring freshets of centuries had carved in the stubborn rock.

There was no semblance of a trail underfoot—but that Brandon had not expected to find. In the stygian darkness, which here between the narrow walls the lightning penetrated only in wan gleams, no evidence of an old foot trail would have been discoverable. But there was no choice of routes. The narrow cleft seemed to have no side outlets; it wound on in ever ascending course between close-crowding cliffs. There was nothing to do but to struggle onward and upward—or to go back.

Panting and exhausted, feeling their way foot by foot in the impenetrable darkness, Brandon and the girl toiled forward, crawling and slipping on the water-polished, precipitous slides and clambering painfully across the jagged piles of fallen boulders. It was hushed here in the depths of the narrow chasm—strangely hushed in spite of the wind which screamed far overhead and the hollow echoes of the thunder that rolled from cliff to cliff along the summit of the ridge. It seemed to Brandon that the climb would never end. For an age it seemed they had toiled on in silence, too wearied for speech, helping each other past difficult places in an utter exhaustion that was too breathless for words.

The possibility that perhaps the winding chasm was leading them along the ridge instead of to its summit had already begun to worry him seriously when, all at once, as they paused an instant with laboring lungs on the flattened summit of a huge rock which had taxed their strength to the limit to scale, he felt Flame's hand upon his arm in sudden warning grip. "Listen!" the girl whispered tensely. "Listen!... We're followed!"

Startled, his every nerve taut, Brandon froze motionless, peering back into the black chasm behind them. He could hear nothing but the dulled note of the wind and the muffled echoes of the thunder. The hush of the close-crowding rocks seemed to weigh down upon everything.

"There!" Flame whispered breathlessly. "There it is again!"

But this time Brandon had heard also. To his straining ears, out of the depths of the inky crevice, had come the faint sound of a rolling stone. He heard the fragment go bounding downward from rock to rock till its clicking impacts died in the darkness. But, as the noise of it dwindled, there came to him plainly another sound—the slithering scrape and pant of a heavy body climbing swiftly among the rocks.

Seized with a sudden consternation Brandon caught, the girl's hand, and, with a low-breathed word of caution, drew her after him in a reckless scramble up the rocks ahead. There had been no illusion in the sounds he had heard—the noise had been too distinct. Though the unseen climber was still well below them he was coming on with savage speed. Their sole hope, Brandon realized desperately, was to win out from the confines of the narrow crevice before pursuit overtook them.

Gasping and out of breath they clambered on frantically, not daring an instant's pause. And presently, to their infinite relief, progress became easier. The floor of the crevice sloped upward still more sharply, but gradually the stones which littered it were becoming smaller and more scattered. Of a sudden their feet were gritting upon gravel and pebbly fragments; the rocky walls which hemmed them narrowed, turned sharply to the right, then to the left.

Abruptly Brandon felt the tearing rush of the wind upon his face. The barriers on either hand were gone. He found himself all at once out upon a level, windswept ledge, his hands clutching instinctively at the girl at his side to steady her against the furious gusts that whirled up from the valley below. Before him, gaunt and forbidding in the ghastly, blue-green flare of a lightning flash, there leaped out from the darkness two towering pinnacles of stone.

"The Gap!"—Flame gasped thankfully—"the Gap!"

Together they raced towards it, spurred to frenzied haste by fear of the unseen peril mounting so swiftly through the cleft behind them. Only beyond the narrow Gap, Brandon realized, could they hope to find some place of concealment, for the same flash that had revealed the huge, twin fangs of rock had shown him also, that the bare ledge across which he and Flame now ran offered no hiding places. One side of it was bordered by an unscalable mass of overhanging cliff—which was an extended footing of the southernmost of the two peaks—while the other edge was a sheer drop into black space.

The dazzling blaze of the lightning came again as they reached the narrow portal. But, even as they plunged into the gusty blackness between the giant pillars of stone; a wild cry lifted in the night behind them—a ghastly yell that, reverberating it seemed from the very depths of the rocks, froze Brandon's blood and wrung a choked sob of fear from Flame's breathless lips: "Jim!" she gasped. "Oh, Jim! What in God's name can it be? That awful cry wasn't human! It sounded like…"

Thin air was suddenly beneath their feet. The girl's words strangled off in a sharp shriek of terror. Abruptly, on the farther side of the two huge monoliths, the level stretch of ledge that led through the narrow neck had ended. Brandon felt himself falling. Clutching the girl desperately in a vain effort to save her he was conscious of the jarring impact of hard, smooth rock beneath him—a violent glancing contact with a sharply inclined plane, down which, like a toboggan on a slide, he and Flame shot feet foremost into the darkness, fetching up an instant later, almost without shock, in a yielding stretch of soft, drifted sand. As he picked himself up and snatched the girl to her feet the dreadful blood-curdling scream, terribly close this time, lifted once more in the darkness. Then the lightning flared. Above him, framed for an instant between the towering pillars of Dead Man's Gap and distorted to monstrous size by the flickering, unearthly light of the flash, Brandon saw a huge white shape—a shape that, as the light winked out, gave tongue once more in a hideous, nerve-shattering cry.

South's oil painting of Blair Valley facing Ghost Mountain

∽

CHAPTER 21

In the Clutch of Fear

But there was no mistaking the nature of the terrifying apparition which the lightning had revealed. Realization came to Brandon and the girl in the same moment.

"It's Midnight! It's only Midnight!" Flame gasped, a choke of hysterical relief in her voice. "Midnight!" she called impulsively. "Come here!"

"Let him alone!…Let him alone!…" Brandon cried sharply. Alive instantly to the peril which the dog's presence suggested, he snatched at the girl's arm and drew her after him in swift, floundering flight down the yielding slope of sand. "Let him alone! For God's sake don't call him!…" he panted. "The whole gang's probably at his heels!… God!…Here he comes!"

A clawing, scrambling rush, as the hound swept down the smooth rock incline, sounded in the darkness behind them as he spoke. Even above the gusting of the wind the muffled thud as the huge beast's body landed in the sand drift was clearly audible. They ran on frantically, expecting each instant a repetition of the hideous, screaming cry or to hear the galloping rush of the great dog's feet over the sand towards them. But, strangely, Midnight neither gave tongue nor appeared. The blackness of the windswept night seemed suddenly to have muffled everything. No further sounds of movement reached their ears.

"I don't believe there's anyone following him," Flame whispered, as they plunged heavily across the soft, foot-hampering sand of the dune. "He was way ahead of them, you know, when he led them back into the canyon. He probably gave them the slip there, then circled round and trailed us. They couldn't possibly follow him in the dark unless they had his yowling to guide them. And he hasn't been making a sound while he's been trailing us across the valley—if he had we'd have heard him. Those yells he gave just now when he found he was close to us are probably the first in a long while. I don't believe there's anyone with him."

"Maybe not," Brandon admitted. "It might be that he's alone. I hope to God you're right!"

He checked his pace somewhat, listening intently. The total absence of all hint of pursuit was reassuring. He drew an easier breath. It seemed likely, after all, that the girl's surmise had been correct.

"I can't hear Midnight either," Flame whispered uneasily. "There hasn't been a sound of him since he slid down the rock." "He's maybe hurt himself, poor brute," Brandon said. "He was wounded pretty bad, I reckon, to begin with. And like enough this last jump...."

"Oh, Jim!"—with an impulsive clutch Flame caught his arm, checking his words and progress alike—"let's go back and find out. Poor old Midnight. Maybe he's dying back there, all alone."

"We couldn't do any good," he protested. "Besides, we can't risk it! For all we know those yellow devils may be...."

"They're not!" she broke in with conviction. "I feel certain they're not anywhere near. I can't stand the idea of leaving Midnight if he's lying there helpless. I'm going back to find out!"

"You'll not!" he said sharply, catching her arm with a restraining grip as she faced abruptly about. "I won't have you going back there! The dog's mad, I tell you! He's likely to tear you to pieces if you go near him."

"He won't!" In a sudden flash of temper she struggled to wrench her arm from his grasp. "Let go of me!" she panted. "He's my dog! He saved our lives once tonight...I'm not going to leave him to die like this without trying to...."

A deafening clap of thunder drowned her words as the heavens cracked suddenly open in a darting, many-branched fracture of fire. For one flickering instant the weird blue light lit the desert in vivid, unearthly glow, revealing the rocky ridge, the towering pinnacles of Dead Man's Gap and the long, shelving surface of the sand dune underfoot—revealing also to the startled eyes of Brandon and the girl a dreadful, silent Thing that, with bared fangs and stiffly bristling hair, stood motionless and menacing on the wind-furrowed sand scarce a dozen paces from them.

The glimpse was fleeting, blotted out swift as it had come in a down rush of thunder-sullen blackness. But it had been enough. Flame shrank back against Brandon with a little sob of terror: "Jim!" she gasped. "That can't be—that can't be Midnight?"

"I—I reckon it is," he said, his voice of a sudden tight and breathless. "An' he's not dying, either. Not by a long shot!"

He stood staring into the sooty darkness, one arm protectingly about the girl, the other instinctively upon his knife. The thing that he had seen had startled him and for the moment shaken his nerve. There had been something ghastly and uncanny about the monstrous white beast that had stood there stiff-legged and motionless watching them, its glowing eyes fastened upon them with an awful intentness and its great teeth bared in a dreadful snarl.

In the fleeting glimpse which he had had of the horror it had seemed to Brandon's startled eyes that Midnight was twice his former size; every hair of the great hound's body had seemed stiffly erect; by the glare of the lightning he had appeared to glow with a ghastly luminosity. In spite of himself Brandon was conscious of a chilling, uncanny fear. If this dreadful, insane Thing should hurl itself upon them a knife would be about as effective a weapon as a straw.

"Jim! Oh, Jim! What's changed him like that?"

Flame's scared whisper jerked Brandon back to himself, snapping the momentary spell of horror that had gripped him. He drew a quick breath.

"I don't know," he said in a low voice. "The Chink that he knocked over into the canyon—one of those first two who attacked us in the house—shot him. There's a bullet lodged somewhere in his skull, maybe, and pressing on his brain...or maybe it's a bit of bone that was driven in by a glancing shot. I don't know. But I do know that he's stark, staring mad—and he's dangerous."

"Oh, Jim!" she whispered. "He looked awful! I'm afraid of him."

"So am I," he said frankly. "But there's no help for it—we can't stand here all night. We've got to go on—and I reckon he'll follow us, if he doesn't do worse. Thank God, though, it's only him we've got to worry over—seems like there's no Chinks trailing him after all. But we'd better be moving. Got any idea which way we ought to head from here?"

"Follow on down the slope, I guess," Flame answered. "The way we were going when we stopped. The old stage road is right east of this ridge; it runs along the bottom of the valley. We're over all the ridges now—there's no more rocks. The land on this side slopes up from the valley almost to the top of that ridge we just came through—it's different altogether from the other side. If we keep going down the slope all the time we can't go wrong."

"Then let's go!" he said. "Just forget about the dog. He'll probably let us alone if we take no notice of him."

He turned away resolutely and led off into the pitchy blackness, heading by instinct and by the sloping feel of the sand underfoot. But this time it was his left hand that he gave to Flame. He wanted the other for his knife. A low, menacing snarl out of the dark behind him as they had moved off had not escaped him. There came to his ears, faintly but unmistakably, the *pad, pad* of the huge hound's stealthy, following feet.

The soft, wind-piled drift ended presently, giving place to a steep slope on which patches of stunted bush alternated with cactus-dotted stretches of gravelly sand. The going, Brandon soon discovered, was now much easier; the bushes were lower and less dense than in the little valley they had just left, but the wind, hurdling the ridge behind, seemed to slash down with redoubled force as they drew away from the sheltering lee of the rocks. There was no let-up to the windstorm. As they stumbled downward, following the dip of the slope as it merged swiftly into the broad, sandy wash of the valley, the gale increased.

But Brandon gave little thought to the flurries of dust or to the stinging sand-grains that drove against his face as he and the girl struggled wearily onward. An uncanny sense of depression and fear was upon him—a strange, invisible pressure more exhausting than anything physical, which seemed to weigh him down more relentlessly with every step, filling his mind with a nervous, intangible foreboding which he strove in vain to shake off.

Again—but stronger this time—there pressed upon him the queer, formless apprehension which had unnerved him that evening just before he had encountered Flame. Again, unbidden and against all the resolute strength of his will, there crowded upon him all the wild, fantastic stories with which old Seth Ross had filled his ears in Jacumba—tales of the Ghost Horse—of the Lost Woman of Carrizo—of the grinding wheels and beating hoofs which passed by night over these old valley trails without leaving trace or track behind…All this, and more, pressed upon him despite his savage efforts to shut his mind to such superstitious absurdity. The darkness—the wind—the unearthly flickering of the lightning and the sullen mutterings of the thunder—all seemed to conspire to torture his worn nerves with uneasy misgivings.

He remembered that the road towards which he and Flame were struggling was the old trail along which, more than sixty years ago, the lurching Butterfield stage coaches had run in regular schedule. This desolate valley had been a wild place then. Lives had been cheap. Flame had spoken of the many graves that were scattered along the old road. She had given voice also to her belief that the valley was haunted… Well, it wasn't hard to believe that it might be. In this gusty darkness, filled with the ghostly gibberings of the wind, and rendered infinitely more terrible by the constant menace of the dreadful slinking brute that trailed their footsteps relentlessly, Brandon told himself it would be easy to believe anything.

And, to add to his growing uneasiness, the actions of Midnight were causing him more and more apprehension. Keeping always behind them—slackening pace when the bushes checked them, and quickening it again when they hurried forward across the open spaces—the hound was following them with grim purpose. Though he skulked always far enough behind so as to remain utterly hidden, except when the intermittent glow of the lightning revealed his huge slinking shape, the crushing twigs, deep, coughing breaths and occasional low, menacing snarls, gave hint enough of his constant presence.

Nor was this all. More and more, as Brandon and the girl made their way towards the bottom of the valley, the dog had developed the habit of making occasional ferocious side-rushes—leaping away savagely into the night to right or left, where, in the Windy blackness, he would claw and fight viciously with the bushes, panting and snarling horribly as though in mortal combat with unseen foes. But always, when the crazed fit of fury had ended, he returned to his grim trailing. It seemed to Brandon that always, as they stumbled onward, he could feel the great beast's eyes burning hungrily upon them from the darkness.

"Jim!"—Flame's voice was full of fear as she broke abruptly the silence which for a long time had held her—"what makes him do that—that fighting?"

"He's crazy, that's all," Brandon answered, forcing an indifference he was far from feeling; "he's having fits."

"I—I don't think so," she said uneasily. "They don't sound like fits to me. It sounds like he's fighting something."

"It's just fits," lie assured her hastily. "He sees the bushes moving in the wind and springs for them. He's likely to spring on anything. He'd throw himself at an express train just as soon. He's stark mad."

"I think he sees things," she said stubbornly. "They say dogs can."

"There's nobody here," he said shortly, in a determined effort to mistake her meaning. "If there was anyone following us we'd know it quick enough."

"I didn't mean living people," she said in a low voice. "I—I meant other things…You know what I mean."

He knew what she meant well enough. But he thrust aside her suggestion with a forced carelessness.

"It's nothing but the wind," he assured her again, "just this everlasting wind and darkness and that crazy dog that's got on your nerves. There's nothing hereabouts to be scared of. We're clear away from the Chinks now. We'll strike the road pretty quick. Then it'll be clear traveling."

He slackened pace a little and reached out a reassuring, steadying hand, drawing her closer to him as they plodded on across the open, windswept stretch. The girl's words, added to his own uneasiness, had shaken him more than he cared to admit. The gruesome notion that the insane hound was making his savage runs at some ghostly, invisible thing which hovered constantly about them was not Flame's idea alone. Slowly, in spite of himself, that very conviction had been growing upon Brandon also. There was something grim and purposeful about those sudden rushes which Midnight made—something horrible in the fury with which he leaped each time at the unseen object of his attack.

For the second time within a few hours Brandon was beginning to feel his healthy disbelief in the supernatural breaking down. It was somewhere about here, he recalled, according to the old stories, that Captain O'Hara had been murdered. The thought was distinctly unpleasant. It flashed upon Brandon that if motion-picture film and gramophone records could reproduce movements and speech it was perhaps possible that the scene of a crime could, under certain conditions, produce a ghostly replica of the tragedy and its actors. Unless everyone, including Flame and old Gus, had been deceived, the phantom of Captain O'Hara and his white horse still haunted this section of the valley. And if one ghost was possible, so also were many. It seemed likely, after all, that Midnight, with the dissolving forces of death creeping slowly through his numbed brain, was sensing among the tossing bushes grim, lurking shapes that belonged borderland of another world.

In spite of all his efforts to control his overtaxed nerves Brandon realized that he was on the verge of panic. A dread sense of impending calamity gripped him. It seemed to him that the last dregs of the desperate hope and strength which had carried him thus far through a nightmare of horrors were ebbing away. It was all a mockery, he told himself wearily—the hideous, mocking jest of some vast and evil supernatural intelligence which had, from the first, engineered this web of deviltry with the express purpose of watching, like a gloating spider, the misery and impotent struggles of its victims.

Escape!...Safety!—it was all a devilish torture of hope. What chance was there of winning through to safety from a nightmare region like this where the very darkness seemed alive with the malignant spirits of the dead. The whole valley was haunted!—more than haunted, it was accursed! The O'Hara gold, if indeed it existed, was accursed also. It was the fatal bait which lured innocent and guilty alike into a merciless net of death from which there was no escape once the meshes closed.

And, for the exhausted girl at his side, for Amos Templeton, and for himself, Brandon realized, the meshes *had* closed. Temporary respite there might be, but no escape. Chillingly it dawned upon him that this was but the beginning. Even if he succeeded in getting Flame clear of this devil-shadowed valley and got her to the Davidsons she would not be safe—she would never be safe anywhere so long as she lived. The vengeance of a Chinese Tong was deathless and tireless. They were closing in now on the victims which they had hunted for years, and the blood that had been spilled this night would add tenfold to their fury.

Escape?—the hope was a dreadful illusion. There was now, for Flame, not even the faintest chance of escape; the whole world now held no hiding-place strong enough to protect her. Delayed a little perhaps, but nevertheless relentless, the intangible hand of Death was already reaching towards her. With a cold horror the thought leaped to Brandon's mind that the stealthy approach of this shadowy doom was the thing perhaps which Midnight sensed. Dogs, he had read somewhere, could see death.

Spent and weary, chilled with the dreadful realization of futility and fighting savagely against the formless terror which had undermined his worn-out nerves, Brandon trudged doggedly onward, steadying the stumbling girl and straining his eyes ahead into the shadows in anxious expectation of the road.

The storm was passing. The wind roared with unabated fury, but though the flickering sheets of lightning still lit up the desert from time to time with momentary glares of all-revealing light, the intervals between the flashes were each time more prolonged. The booming of the thunder was fainter and more distant, rolling away across the sky like the sullen guns of a retreating army. The hurtling squadrons of cloud overhead were thinning. It was growing lighter, Brandon realized. Dawn was coming slowly. The dense gloom was lessening bit by bit. Already the dim outlines of the closest bushes and the pale glint of the sandy earth underfoot could be discerned through the ghostly, wind-whipped sea of shadows. Behind, slinking sullenly from cover to cover, the huge form of the grimly trailing hound was faintly visible.

The dim bulk of a mesquite tree loomed suddenly out of the thinning darkness ahead. Beneath Brandon's feet was the feel of yielding earth that was crusted with alkali. The mournful whispering of tules was about him all at once. Flame gave a cry of relief:

"The road!—thank God we're almost to it!" she whispered. "It's just the other side of these tules. We're right close to the old stage station now."

Mud squelched suddenly beneath their feet as they forced onward through the whipping reeds; there was the scattering splash of an ooze of shallow water. But beyond the marshy stretch the ground hardened and sloped gradually upward. The tules thinned and a scatter of ghostly, wind-heaved mesquites bulked out ahead. Abruptly, stretching across the shadowy earth at his feet, Brandon glimpsed all at once the pale, wheel-rutted course of the road.

"The old stage station's close here somewhere," Flame said, peering into the thinning gloom as they turned thankfully down the trail. "We can't be far from it."

Brandon strained his eyes ahead. The darkness was breaking up, but, though it was already light enough to follow the winding of the sandy trail easily, dim obscurity still wrapped everything that lay at a little distance. Somehow the dread, depressing fear which weighed upon him had not lessened with the lessening dark. He would feel better once they were well past the grim and haunted old ruin, Brandon told himself uneasily. He wished fervently that he could see better. Despite the added peril of discovery which daylight would bring he felt that, somehow, he could stand but little more of these eerie, horror-breeding shadows.

"Here's the turn-off—the road that leads to Gus's place and our ranch," Flame said all at once, pointing to the right. "I knew we were close to the stage station. It's right ahead."

Midnight snarled suddenly—snarled and in two tremendous bounds flashed past them and sprang into a bank of shadow that lay to the left of the road and almost opposite the turn-off trail. As Brandon jerked to a startled halt he glimpsed, in the half-light, the outline of a tremendous, dark bulk that lay sprawled there upon the ground. There came the sound of smashing twigs and the mad hound's infuriated, worrying growls.

"It's—It's only a pile of dead mesquite branches and tules!" Flame gasped, recovering from the sudden start of fear with which she had shrunk back against Brandon. "Gus was here about a month ago, cutting mesquites and tules for a shed he was building. He left a big heap of stuff lying here. I—I guess you were right about Midnight—he'd spring at anything. It's only a heap of brush this time."

A vast relief was in her voice—relief that struggled still with terror. As they stumbled on, leaving the crazed dog to his senseless fury among the dry, snapping branches, Brandon could feel her pressing closer to his side. He put his arm around her protectingly. He knew well enough that the same indescribable fear that was upon him held her also, and that the reassuring words which he forced himself to utter sounded as hollow to her ears as they did to his own.

"Jim! Jim! Listen!" Abruptly, with a sudden frightened clutch, the girl caught at him, checking him once more in his tracks. "Listen—there's a horse coming!" she whispered. "Hear it?"

Brandon's heart seemed to stand still; a cold thrill like the passage of an icy hand ran along his spine. Faintly, coming down the wind from the shadows to the right of him, he heard the thud of hoofs.

"There's someone riding through the tules," he said in a low voice.

"People don't ride through the tules," Flame whispered, her breathless words suddenly dry and tense—"they—they'd use the trail. Any—and in the dark like this there wouldn't be anybody riding thr—*Oh, Jim!...Look!...*"

Her voice leaped to a cry of terror—a cry that was crushed out by the deafening detonation of a clap of thunder. Blindingly, dazzlingly, as though the dying storm had gathered itself in one last flare of fury greater than all the rest, lightning had arched the sky from west to east. Ghostly blue in a shimmering mantle of fire the desert for one instant had flashed up clear as day. Straight ahead of him, hunched amidst its scattered fringing of trees, Brandon saw the grey-brown bulk of the ruined stage station, and away to the right of it, tossing like a weedy sea and backed by another belt of trees, was the dark stretch of the tules.

But it was neither the old ruin nor the desolate sweep of writhing reeds that held Brandon's horrified eyes. It was something else—something which seemed to choke the breath in his throat and to raise the hair prickling along his scalp. There on the far edge of the tules, flitting swiftly between the clustering mesquites and heading straight towards where he and the girl stood, was the thing that had brought the choking cry of fear from Flame's lips—a dim and shadowy rider astride a huge white horse.

CHAPTER 22

The Ghost Horse

The glimpse of the ghostly rider which the lightning had given had been but momentary, but it was more than enough to shatter the last remnant of Brandon's overtaxed nerves. Panic seized him—a blind, unreasoning panic which, as the lightning glare snapped out and left his dazzled eyes helpless an instant in pitchy blackness, was intensified a thousand-fold by the sound of a faint, unearthly cry that swept down to him from across the wide stretch of wind-tossed tules. With a sudden strength born of mad fear, he gripped Flame's arm and ran, sweeping the terrified girl along with him in headlong flight up the trail, conscious, as he did so, that the dread cry had been answered by a deep and terrible snarl—that, from somewhere behind, Midnight had hurled himself across the road and, in great leaps, was smashing his way furiously into the shadowy stretch of reeds.

But even in that surge of blind panic, as Flame and he fled up the trail with terror-winged feet, Brandon's mind was working. In the flash-glimpse which he had had of the ghostly shape on the far side of the tules he had realized that it was slightly to the rear of them. To run back, therefore, along the trail which they had already traversed would be to hasten their meeting with it; to turn aside and seek safety in a flight through the foot-hampering bushes and cactus of the open desert was equal madness. There was no choice but to follow the road straight ahead past the old stage station, and he had taken that course instinctively. Still in his fear-numbed brain, as they ran madly onward, was the queer thought that he had held before. If they could only get past the stage station—the reputed haunt of this ghostly terror—they would be safe.

Swaying mesquites, starting from the shadows, were about them all at once; out of the greyness lifted the dark-bulk of adobe walls as abreast of them, on the left hand side of the trail, the ruined stage station loomed up suddenly, fringed in its circling gloom of trees. The wind, sweeping down across the valley, seemed to eddy about the old building, beating in their ears with a fury that drowned utterly all sound of the drumming hoofs behind. The creaking mesquites closed in and hid the back trail.

"It's coming!" Flame gasped. "Oh, Jim, it's coming!…I can hear—"

"You can't!" he panted savagely, his arm tightening about her and half carrying her onward as she staggered exhausted. "That's only the wind!…We'll be past this shack in a minute, and…."

He did not finish the words. Even as he spoke a dark figure ran out of the shadows of the mesquites a little distance ahead and blocked the trail; the lens of an electric torch glared all at once from the greyness. As Brandon and the girl checked terror-stricken, swerving aside instinctively from the dazzling beam of light, there came a sudden thick oath of astonishment and triumph—an oath that was followed almost instantly by a spurt of fire and a deafening report. Brandon felt his shirt rip and the searing scorch of a heavy bullet as it grazed the skin of his right side. The pistol crashed again viciously, and the blinding beam of the torch leaped closer as the man ahead sprang forward with a hoarse shout.

Keyed to panic though he already was by the ghostly terror behind and staggered with the instant realization that in their flight from it they had blundered straight into an ambush, Brandon acted, nevertheless, with the swift impulse of instinct. Even as the gun ahead flamed he jerked the girl round and darted with her towards the ruined, lintel-fallen doorway of the old adobe that bulked but a few yards to the left of them. The black, silent mass of the old stage station had given no hint of human presence; its thick walls offered at least a momentary shelter from bullets.

But close as the old building was it was not close enough. In the same instant as he raced the breathless girl towards the huge, roof-high, ragged-edged gap that had once been the doorway, Brandon realized that hope of shelter or of escape was futile. There was no time! The blazing glare of the light was upon them; there was the sound of running feet and panting breath, and, as Brandon reached the gaping doorway and thrust Flame to shelter, the gun roared again, almost at point-blank range.

Half-blinded by the glaring electric light and by the spurt of dust and earth that flew from the adobes as the bullet buried itself in the raw edge of the wall beside him, he snatched out his knife and spun round to face the leaping figure that rushed upon him. But even as he did so there came a yell and the charging trample of feet from within the darkness of the room itself. Flame cried out in terror, and, as Brandon swerved sharply to the girl's assistance, the pistol behind the dazzling light exploded almost in his face.

Dazed, he struck out blindly, but at the same moment someone seized him from behind. He went down with a crash, rolling back into the black gloom of the earth-floored room with the weight of a clutching, heaving body on top of him.

"It's th' damned son of a— that Jake heaved in th' canyon come t' life again!" a voice panted. "It's him an' th' kid!...they musta got away!...Kill him, Pedro!—kill th' damned—! I've got th' girl!—she's all we want!"

Brandon lashed out furiously, struggling to free himself. Half-stunned though he was by the concussion of the shot which had come within an ace of blowing out his brains, the thick panted words came to him clearly—and with them came instant realization. These men were not Tongsmen! As he heaved upward in a desperate effort to fling off the pinning weight of the man who had fallen atop of him, and whose pistol, by blind chance, he had somehow managed to grip and wrench aside, he had a glimpse of them. The electric torch had been dropped upon a pile of smashed adobe that lay on the floor inside the doorway and by its light, which now flooded the interior of the big, ruined room, Brandon saw that his panting antagonist was the scar-faced Martinez, while the taller figure that struggled with Flame in the farther corner was Slant Galloway.

"Slant! Queeck! Queeck!" the Mexican shouted. "The ch— holds my *pistola!*...He has a knife!—and if I let go his hand...."

"Hold him! Goddammit, hold him!" Galloway roared. "I'm a-comin'!...There, you little—, take that!...That'll gentle you some!..."

There was the sound of a blow and a choking gasp. Wrenching back in a desperate effort to break his knife-hand free from the iron grip which Martinez had fastened upon his wrist, and at the same time to hold off the wavering muzzle of the Mexican's pistol, Brandon saw Flame stagger back from the impact of a brutal fist and fall helplessly across a heap of broken adobes. With leveled gun Galloway came leaping across the floor.

"Hold th' son of a—, Pedro!" he snarled gloatingly. "I'll fix him this time so's he don't play 'possum no more. I'll blow his damned...."

But his words were never completed. Even as he stooped, lunging his arm viciously forward, his voice was drowned in a hammering thunder of hoofs and an awful, blood-freezing cry. To Brandon, hurling himself sideways in a violent attempt to avoid the black muzzle of the six-shooter that Galloway was thrusting savagely at his head, it seemed as though suddenly and without warning the dirt floor beneath him heaved and trembled and that from the gusty gloom outside all the grim terrors of the valley swept down upon the old adobe in one furious, roaring blast of trampling din and raging wind.

All in one fleeting, fractional second, as the light seemed to blur, everything appeared to happen at once. He saw Slant Galloway spin round with a startled oath; saw Flame—struggling at that instant to her feet—cower back with a piercing shriek of terror; felt the weight above him and the iron clutch on his wrist removed suddenly as Martinez released his hold and leaped away with a choking yell of fear: "*The Horse!...The Horse!...*" The Mexican screamed wildly, "*Madre de Dios!*—it is the Horse!..."

Something white came hurtling through the ruined doorway— something white and monstrous that crashed into the room and checked itself in a whirlwind scatter of flying earth as it reared upward with snorting nostrils and flailing fore-feet beneath the gap of the half-fallen roof. The light swirled and crunched out under the smashing hoofs. But even as it vanished the shadows ripped in two blinding flashes of fire and the room reeled with the deafening crash of a double detonation. There came a dreadful, suddenly silenced scream and a hideous trampling.

"Flame! Miss Flame!...Where are ye? Are ye hurt?"

Out of a swirling darkness, acrid with the bite of powder-smoke and gruesome with animal snortings and the faint, swiftly stilling rustle of spasmodically twitching bodies, came an anxious, oddly familiar voice coupled with the creak of leather and the sound of a dismounting rider. A match flared, revealing the outlines of a big white horse, and beside it, peering into the darkness, a lean, slightly stooped figure with a bushy-browed, weather-beaten face. As Brandon scrambled unsteadily to his feet, his confused senses whirling in desperate effort to grasp the unbelievable thing that had happened, he heard from the farther corner of the room Flame's hysterical gasp of recognition:

"*Gus!...*Oh, my God!...Gus! Is—is it you?..."

"Me an' old Baldy, that's all—there ain't nothin' t' be afeared of!...I reckon I got both th' skunks all right. Are ye hurt?"

"No! No!" Flame panted, staggering forward. "But Jim?—where's Jim?..."

"I'm all right." As the match-glow shriveled out Brandon leaped across the floor and caught the tottering girl in his arms. "I'm all right, honey! But you?..."

"No, no!" she snatched at him, clutching him tight in a passion of breathless relief, "I—I'm just dizzy...and scared....Oh, God, that was awful!...Gus, how did you....Oh, what happened?"

"Well, I jest nach-rally shot th' two skunks as I come through th' door." The old man struck another match and peered again with satisfaction at the two sprawled forms that lay dark and still upon the dirt floor; "that there thingamadoodle they had lyin' on that heap o' dirt give plenty o' light an' I jest had time to let fly at 'em as Baldy stomped it out. I reckon I made two clean bull's-eyes. I ain't been wastin' cartridges a-rollin' tin cans fer nothin'."

"Oh, God!" Flame shivered. "I—I thought...."

"So did they, I reckon," Gus said grimly; "they was too scairt t' think o' shootin'. 'Pears like me an' old Baldy can give a pretty tol-able immytation o' Cap'n O'Hara an' his hoss. I reckon I come nigh scarin' th' two o' you stiff too when I hollered at ye as I was comin' across th' tules. That flash o' lightnin' give me a clear sight o' ye both as ye was comin' down th' road, an' I rec'nized ye and hollered. But I reckon you thot I was somethin' else. You both lit out hell-bent, an' there weren't nothin' t' do but t' take after yer. Then I heared th' shootin' an' I guessed what was happenin', an' I come a-tearin', jest in time t' plug these two varmints. But come outside, we gotta get away from here. What in God's name's been a happenin' Miss Flame? How'd you get here?"

"We've walked...we came across the ridge...through Dead Man's Gap," Flame answered, her words coming in nervous, unsteady jerks as she and Brandon followed the old man and the stumbling horse across the fallen adobes and through the yawning door-gap. "Oh Gus, we've been through hell!...The ranch was...."

"I done seen it," Gus cut in, checking his big-boned mount in the windy shadows just outside the building. "Things is shore a muss up there. There's dead men lyin'..."

"You—you've been there?" Flame gasped, "*to the ranch?* But the Chinese? Weren't they...."

"Weren't nothin' but dead Chinks there, two of em' lyin' in th' kitchen—them an' two other dead fellers, one of 'em lookin' like enough t' your uncle that I was certain, fer a minnit, it was him till I seen by his clothes an' a close look at his face that it weren't. I hadn't nothin' t' see by except strikin' matches, but the looks o' things plumb upsot me an' I couldn't find hair nor track o' you nor your uncle nor this here young feller neither. So I come lickin' down this way hell-bent, headed fer th' Davidsons' place so's t' give th' alarm. I was afeared t' tackle that old cut-off trail through th' hills in th' dark—old Baldy ain't so surefooted as he used t' be over rocks—so I come this way. But

I was sure makin' time an' cuttin' all th' corners I could. That's why I was short-cuttin' through th' tules when you seen me."

"My God!" Flame breathed. "The Chinese must all have been away up the canyon searching for us when you were there. You must have just missed them. It's a miracle you got away alive. Whatever made you go up there?"

"Well, I got t' worryin' 'bout things after you'd left my shack—you'd acted kinda queer. An' after you'd been gone quite a while another big car went past, headed up your way. An' quite a piece after that agen I heared two riders come a-tearin' down th' trail. They went past my place hell-bent in th' dark, headin' towards th' stage station. It got me plumb nervous. I worried about it fer a long time an', finally, I rode up your way t' investigate. I found a-plenty. How come all this happened, Miss Flame?"

"It was the Tong," Flame answered; "the Tong and Jake! You might as well know the truth....It—It doesn't matter now...."

In a snatch of breathless words she told the old man briefly what had happened, revealing also her own true identity and the reasons why she and her uncle were linked both with the Tong vengeance and with the O'Hara gold.

"Well, that kinda explains things," Gus said as she finished; "that kinda explains too why Slant an' Martinez come down here an' hung around—they weren't quite sure what'd happened up there, an' bein' too scairt t' go back they jest hung round waitin', thinkin' t' mebbe find out. An' mebbe they had some idea they could kinda ambush th' Chinks as they come past—mighta had some sich notion. Yes, sir, that 'splains things. An' I reckon I know now who stole my little pinto hoss, Flapjacks, from th' pasture."

"Flapjacks stolen?" In spite of her exhaustion there was a startled surprise in Flame's voice.

"Yes'm—that's what made me a whole lot later gettin' up t' your ranch. When I went up t' th' top pasture t' get him I found that th' outside gate had been opened an' shut agen powerful careless. Th' spare bridle that I keeps a-hangin' on th' mesquite tree jest inside th' gate was gone—an' Flapjacks was gone too. I couldn't find him nowhere, an' it took me a powerful long time t' ketch Baldy in th' dark."

"Oh, it must have been uncle took him!" Flame exclaimed in sudden excitement. "When uncle got away from the ranch he must have run up the canyon and then struck across to your pasture and caught Flapjacks. Then he probably rode straight for the Davidsons by that old cut-off trail. He thought you were away in Julian, anyway, so he never went near your house. I guess he thought I'd decided to stay all night at the Davidsons', so he took the shortest way there."

"Must ha' been," Gus agreed. "Yore uncle was th' only other man, essept me, that Flapjacks would come to when he was called. Yes, it must ha' been yore uncle. Well, him an' all th' Davidson bunch'll come a-tearin' back this way soon's he finds you ain't there. We gotta get movin' an' head down their way—'tain't nowise healthy stayin' round here nohow…Gawd! What's that a yellin' out there?"

"It's the dog," Brandon said, recovering from the momentary jerk of alarm which the sudden outburst of wild, blood-curdling yowling away off in the tules had given him. "He was wounded up at the ranch. He's been off his head ever since."

"Gawd! It sure sounds like it," Gus muttered uneasily. "I thot they was somethin' th' matter with him, th' way he come a-tearin' through th' tules an' lep at me as I was ridin' t' catch ye. I thot for a second he was goin' t' maul me. But jest as he jumped he kinda swung off and went tearin' away inta th' reeds—musta rec'nized me, I reckon. My Gawd, that's shore a awful sound he's a makin' now!…Come on, let's get away from here!…Them two skunks musta left th' hosses they rid tied around here some place—somewheres in th' mesquites, I reckon!…We got t' find 'em!"

He moved away, leading his horse and peering to right and left among the shadowy trees.

Flame and Brandon followed, their eyes searching the gloom. The wind still blew with undiminished fury, but though the light of the slowly coming day had increased a little, revealing still more plainly the winding white stretch of the road and the nearer bushes, the dark bulks of the swaying mesquite trees were still cloaked in dense shadows that betrayed no trace of tethered horses. Across the tule swamp in spasmodic, furious outbursts, came the ghastly yelling of the demented hound. There was something terrifying in the sound of the dog's outcry—something ominously warning.

Shaken and unsteady as he still was from the effects of the last few minutes of horror, Brandon was conscious all at once of a fresh thrill of dread. That Gus had, by some miracle, escaped being seen by the Chinese while he was at the ranch was doubtless true—but what if some of the Tongsmen, scouting in the vicinity, had *heard* him? Undoubtedly the motor-car which they had first come was parked in some hidden place within their easy reach. And if by any chance they had heard the hoof beats of Gus's horse speeding down the trail towards the stage station they would naturally suppose the animal was being ridden by one or other of their intended victims. And in that case they would.…

But the dread thought that leaped to Brandon's mind had no time for completion. Even as he jerked around, gripped by a sudden terrifying conviction, a long, dark automobile, unlighted and with the sound of its speeding tires muffled utterly by the wind, came racing into view through the gloom of the mesquites that hid the back trail. A spotlight flared. There came a savage, triumphant yell.

There was no time for thought—no time for anything but the lightning-quick action of instinct. With a frantic shout to Gus, Brandon clutched at Flame, and, half-blinded in the sudden, all-revealing glare of the light, leaped with her towards the sheltering walls of the old stage station. But, even as he leaped, he realized with a chill flood of despair that that wild, malignant yell that had seemed to freeze his blood had been Chinese.

South's oil painting of the Vallecito Stage Station ruins

~

CHAPTER 23

Cornered

"**B**ack t' th' 'dobe!" Old Gus's stentorian bellow as he jerked round in his tracks, startled by the sudden glare of the spotlight behind him, seemed almost to blend with Brandon's warning shout. "Back t' th' 'dobe!" the old man yelled in instant realization, "Th' varmints are...."

A crashing fusillade of pistol-shots drowned the words as the shadows behind the spot-lamp ripped in stabbing fingers of fire. To Brandon, as he darted with the girl across the deadly, light-flooded stretch that separated them from the old building, it seemed that the air was of a sudden alive with the savage hum of bullets. Spurts of flying gravel whipped up from the earth about his feet; the light-bathed adobe walls ahead patterned in little jets of dust. As he plunged headlong with Flame through the gaping doorway he heard the thunderous detonation of Gus's heavy Colt and a split second later the old man, gun in hand and hatless, leaped to shelter beside them.

"Back!" Gus shouted breathlessly. "Git back under cover! Th' varmints are goin' t' rush us!" Yells and a pounding scramble of feet gave instant confirmation of his warning. The car had stopped. The glare of the spotlight—augmented now by the blaze of suddenly switched on headlights—beat cornerwise through the ragged door-gap and the narrow window opening, illuminating the interior of the big room with a dim, reflected glow. Brandon had scarce time to spring across the floor and snatch up the six-gun that lay beside Martinez's dead body when, with hoarse, triumphant cries and a furious spatter of pistol-shots, the Tongsmen poured recklessly to the attack.

"Th' side door!" Gus shouted. "Take care o' th' side door an' th' winder! I'll 'tend t' this one an' th' other side!...An' you, Miss Flame—you keep down under cover!...You can't do...."

His words were blotted in a deafening thunder of sound as his own gun and Brandon's leaped into action. The big, half-ruined room seemed to fill suddenly with swirling smoke and darting tongues of orange flame as the roar of the powerful six-shooters hurled back the crashing reports of the heavy-caliber automatics. Dark, scrambling shadows were all at once at the side door, at the window, at the front door-gap and in the dimness that lay beyond the rear door—dark, clawing shapes that jerked to view, spat fire and vanished.

Crouching low in the angle of the sheltering wall, his gun smashing blazing answer to the vicious red flares that stabbed through the dim openings of the ruined doorway and the window, Brandon was suddenly aware that Flame was at his side—that with a heavy six-gun which she had wrenched from the dead hand of Slant Galloway she was shooting back savagely at the pistol-flashes that darted from the gloom beyond the rear door. Everything was a blur—a frenzied, frantic blur of yells and shots and the thudding smash of bullets ripping into adobe. The world seemed to heave up and topple over in a thunderous avalanche of deafening noise, blinding smoke fumes and stabbing tongues of fire.

And then, as suddenly as it had begun, the volcano of sound dwindled and died in a ragged scatter of shots. There came quick, stumbling sounds of swiftly retreating feet. The glaring car lights were abruptly switched off.

Through the sudden, blotting gloom, thick and choking with the acrid fumes of powder, Brandon groped frantically for Flame. But the girl's quick, panted whisper lifted the icy fear that had clutched his heart. Miracle though it seemed, neither she nor Brandon had been hit. And the tinkle of empty cartridge-cases, coupled with Gus's cautious voice, brought assurance an instant later that the old man was likewise unscathed.

"Hell—but that was warm!" Gus whispered hoarsely. "Varmints sure slipped up an' took us by s'prise. If it weren't fer this here 'dobe we'd all ha' been dedder'n pizened pups by now. As 'twas, they couldn't do nothin' but blaze away wild—they didn't dast show theirselves too plain. How many of 'em is there, anyways?—they was dancin' round here like a bunch o' crazy terantlers."

"Five," Brandon answered breathlessly; "there were only five of them left when we got away from the ranch." Feeling with swift fingers in the gloom he was stripping the cartridge-belts from the bodies of Galloway and Martinez. He passed one to Flame.

"Well, there ain't but four o' th' varmints now," Gus growled grimly. "I stopped th' dancin' antics o' one o' 'em for good. But th' rest'll be back on some new devilment afore we can turn round. How many, cartridges ye got?"

Brandon snapped back his refilled cylinder and ran his fingers along the belt in rapid count. "Nineteen and a full gun—twenty-five all told," he announced. "How about yours, Flame?" "I've got a load and fifteen left in the belt," the girl whispered. "Hell! Them fellers weren't packin' none too much ammunition!" There was a sudden worried note in Gus's voice. "That cuts us pretty short. An' myself, I ain't got but two shells left after reloadin'. I was figgerin' on gettin' more cartridges when I went inta Julian. Like a fool, I let myself run low—never expectin' nothin'. I got a scad o' rifle-cartridges, but that don't do us no good. Them yaller varmints jumped us so all-fired suddent I never had a chance t' grab th' rifle outa th' saddle scabbard. Baldy rairt up an' I had t' let him go and bolt fer all I was worth. There ain't no tellin' where he's lit out fer."

"What size is your gun?"—Brandon was making a swift mental calculation.

"Forty-five."

"So's these. And we've got fifty-four cartridges all told between the three of us. So we'll just split up in even shares. That'll eave us each with a full load and twelve extras apiece."

The division was swiftly made. In the ghostly shadows of the old room the three crouched tense and alert, straining their ears for any sound above the skirting gusts of the wind that swept round the old building and worried at the sticks and ragged edges of the broken earthen roof overhead. That the respite was only temporary they did not doubt. It seemed too much to hope that, beaten off in their first rush, the remaining four Tongsmen would give up the attack.

"Now ain't it a hell of a note," old Gus reflected in an apologetic whisper, "all this here's my doin's. If I hadn't ha' gone up t' th' ranch this wouldn't ha' happened. It was hearin' me lickin' down th' trail thisways that musta brung these varmints. If I'd ha' jest had sense enough t' stay quiet at home—"

"We'd have been murdered by Slant and the Mexican," Flame cut in. "Shut up, Gus—don't talk foolish! Your coming was the only thing that saved us."

"Might ha' done that, in a way," the old man admitted grudgingly. "But that don't make th' fact no better that I brung all these varmints...."

"Sh—h!" Brandon warned sharply. Through the drumming blur of the wind had come a slight noise. As they tensed, listening, it was followed by the unmistakable whirring note of a starter and an instant later by the churning throb of a motor.

"They're going!" Flame whispered excitedly. "They've had enough!"

"Goin' nothin'!" Gus growled. "Like hell they'd be goin'! They're fixin' some new devilment, that's what. Keep back, Miss Flame; lemme take a obsevashun." He wormed his way cautiously to the edge of the door-gap.

"They've turned round and they're going back the way they came," Brandon announced, peering warily through a chink between the adobes in the bottom corner of the window opening. "There's all four of them in the car."

"Danged if they ain't," Gus admitted, his head craned round the edge of the door wall. "Dang their ornery hides! I'll put a shot in their hindquarters t' keep' em goin.'"

But as though this possibility was precisely what they had feared the Tongsmen were taking no chances. In a burst of speed, before either Gus or Brandon had a chance to thrust out a gun, the big car whirled down the trail and vanished, from view beyond the fringe of mesquites.

"They've gone! They've gone!" Crouching beside Brandon, her eyes strained across the lower edge of the window opening, Flame half-rose in her excitement, "Oh Jim, they've gone! It's getting broad daylight and they don't dare to wait! They've given up!"

"Keep down!" Brandon cried sharply, snatching at her. "You don't know what they're up to! We can't see where they've gone and the bushes and mesquites are too close up here to be safe. There's light enough outside for 'em to shoot by right now."

"You're danged right!" Gus growled. "There ain't no tellin' what th' varmints is up to. Like as not it's jest a scheme t' fool us, an' they'll come sneakin' back under shelter o' th' bushes. You keep down under cover, Miss Flame, fer Gawd's sake, an' don't take no chances. We'll lay low right here till we knows jest fer sartin what's goin' on…Hell! Ain't that th' dawg hollerin' agen?"

"Yes—yes, that's him!" Flame caught her breath shudderingly at the gruesome outcry that had lifted in the distance. "He must be hiding in the tules!"

"Yeh, an' he's spotted them varmints agen," Gus said, listening. "They're up t' no good!"

The savage yowling of the hound dwindled presently, blotted in the threshing of the wind. With nerves keyed taut the three crouched listening and waiting. The dawn was broadening fast. Even in the big, half-ruined room it was now light enough to see everything clearly. The piles of fallen adobes stood out sharply; sprawled a little distance apart the bodies of Slant Galloway and Martinez lay grim and rigid and, darkly distinct, some thirty feet beyond the gap of the front doorway, the form of the Chinaman whom Gus had shot lay huddled motionless upon the sandy earth.

Sheltered well back behind the friendly adobes Brandon crouched tense and expectant beside the window opening. The realization that all his hopes of getting Flame to safety had been shattered by this staggering reappearance of the Tongsmen crushed him with a numb sense of despair. Though the strengthening daylight dispelled somewhat the press of ghostly horror which had charged the darkness, it brought no relief from chill forebodings of some swiftly impending tragedy. He could not free his mind from the conviction that, despite the seeming advantage of their position, they were trapped. He shared with Gus the firm opinion that this seeming retreat of the Tongsmen was but a ruse. He did not believe that the Chinese would give up so easily. Now, when they had their quarry cornered, it was not within reason to think that they would so soon admit defeat.

Carefully Brandon studied the details around him. The old stage station was tumbling into ruin, but the thick walls, built of a natural root-bound adobe that had been cut out in the form of bricks from the nearby swamp, offered a perfect, barrier against bullets. There had been originally three rooms in the building—the main one, running clear across the front, and two others, a central and a rear, which were much smaller but which likewise extended from side to side of the structure.

With the two smaller rear rooms, however—the outermost of which was nothing but a roofless ruin of fallen walls—Brandon was not concerned. It was the big front one—the one in which he and the others sheltered—that claimed his attention. Seen in the wan light of dawn this main room was a forlorn wreck enough. Almost half of the old roof—fashioned of close-laid sticks and saplings lashed together with rawhide and covered with a thick layer of earth—had fallen in, leaving a wide gaping space through which the wind raged gustily. But the thick walls were still in fair shape. Despite a small window opening and the high, ragged gap in one corner, where the collapse of the lintel and part of the front wall had transformed the old doorway into a wide breach, there was still enough of the wall standing to afford ample protection from in front.

The sides and the rear, however, were a different matter. Each of the side walls was pierced with door openings and these, together with the low doorway which connected with the central room—and through it, owing to the fallen walls beyond, with the outside—constituted a real peril. Only by crowding back into the extreme corner of the front room and sheltering in the angle of wall between the narrow front window and the side door was it possible to obtain partial shelter from bullets coming through these doors. And, even so, if the attackers could get close enough among the mesquites, the corner would be exposed to shots fired in through the door on the east side.

With his first glance Brandon was quick to see this danger. He realized that the old stage station was at best a treacherous shelter—one that was likely to prove a death-trap. While the ammunition lasted it would, perhaps, be possible to prevent the Tongsmen gaining a position from which their shots could rake the building. But when the ammunition was exhausted?...

"Dang it, I wish I had th' rifle!" As though in proof to Brandon that he was not the only one whom the question of ammunition was worrying, old Gus's hoarse whisper of a sudden broke the tenseness. "Dang it!" the old man muttered, "I got plenty rifle cartridges here in th' belt an' they ain't no manner o' good t' us. I wonder where old Baldy lit out to."

"He maybe went home," Flame suggested.

"No'm, I don't think so—he never run in that d'rection. An' I ain't heared him go past here since—he'd have t' go this ways if he was headed home. An', anyways, now if them yaller varmints is parked up there blockin' th' trail he wouldn't have no chance to go home. He'd have t' pass 'em t' do it an' he wouldn't try no sich thing. He's got sense—even if he ain't nothin' but a hoss."

"The Chinese may have gone," Flame said. "They've lost heavily. There's only four of them left now—and there's three of us, and we're under cover. They haven't got much advantage. Besides, they probably won't dare to stay around here in daylight. They'd be I afraid someone would come past." She spoke with forced hopefulness.

"I reckon they've spied around this here district enough so's they won't be worryin' any over people passin'," Gus said dryly. "They'd know well enough that there ain't nobody travels on this road in a coon's age 'ceptin' it's us what lives in these parts. An' us they've got corralled up here nice an' proper. Besides, I don't reckon they'd stick overly much at slittin' a few more throats. I'd be kinda sorry fer any pore feller in a flivver what'd happen t' come along right now."

"But if uncle got to the Davidsons' he'd be coming back this way," Flame persisted, "and he'd be bringing all the Davidson bunch with him."

"That's right 'nuff," Gus agreed; "but it ain't humanly possible fer 'em t' get here fer a while yet, no matter how fast yore uncle traveled— Smoky Springs is a long ways from here."

"Everything seems quiet now," Flame argued, "except for the wind. Maybe the Chinamen really did go, Gus."

"Mebbe so," the old man admitted grudgingly, "but we ain't goin' t' do no strollin' 'round an' lookin'—not fer a whiles, anyways. How do we know that they ain't crept back here through th' mesquites? It don't signify nothin' that we can't hear 'em. Rattlesnakes kin be powerful quiet too—when it suits 'em. You lie low, Miss Flame, an' don't you get rastless. We ain't missin' no bisness 'p'intments by waitin' here."

Followed another period of listening and waiting. The minutes dragged slowly and the light of dawn broadened. The murky pall of clouds overhead was breaking up in wind-blown tatters. Through the gap of the ruined roof streaks and patches of cold grey sky were visible. The wind swooped through the doorways of the old adobe, skirling little eddies of dust on the trampled earthen floor. There was no other sound besides the wiry whistle of the gusts through the trees and the slap and creak of branches.

In spite of himself Brandon began to wonder if, after all, he had over judged the Tongsmen's qualities of persistence. There was no hint of their presence anywhere. The strips of wind-waved trees and the thick crowded bushes which he could glimpse through the doors and window gave no sign; apparently nothing but the wind moved through their thick-laced branches. On the edge of the thicket opposite the east door a wind-blown Butcher-bird, battling the buffeting gusts in early search of breakfast, dropped down and perched a moment on a swaying branch of mesquite before whirling away across the grey tangle of bushes.

The vicinity of the stage station seemed utterly deserted. Perhaps, after all, Brandon reflected, the Chinese had had enough. Discouraged perhaps by their losses, and by the fact that their intended victims were now armed and securely entrenched, they had fled-anxious to escape before broadening day rendered their retreat more hazardous.

"I reckon mebbe they pulled out after all," Gus speculated presently, impatience and uncertainty evident enough in his tone." They're keepin' powerful quiet if they ain't. It might be that the varmints has...."

He checked his whisper abruptly, his hand suddenly raised in a sharp, warning gesture. Even as he had spoken there had come from the mesquites at the rear of the old building a noise of movement and snapping twigs. Flame and Brandon tensed, their hands tightening on their guns. The sound came again, nearer and clearer—a shuffling *clump!...clump!*...mingled with a faint, metallic jingle.

Gus's face suddenly cleared. "'Tain't nothin' but old Baldy!" he exclaimed in vast relief, "th' old fool's comin' back here lookin' fer me,

I reckon. I might ha' knowed he wouldn't go far. Mebbe now I kin get th' rifle." He straightened to his feet, peering cautiously.

"Gus, take care!" Flame whispered warningly. "Make sure it's him!"

"It's him all right—I kin spot th' old cuss from here a'ready." Gus had moved over and was peering sideways through the east doorway. "He's right close t' th' little lean-to shed that's agen th' back end o' this wall. An' I can't see no hide nor feather o' nothin' else. 'Pears like th' Chinks skipped out after all. Anyways, I reckon I'll risk t' sneak out an' ketch him. We needs that rifle bad, anyhow."

He craned his head around the edge of the door, his eyes searching the silent bushes. "I reckon everything's clear," he said with sudden confidence. "But you two keep back—'twon't take me but a minnit."

He stepped boldly out of the doorway and strode swiftly towards the big white horse which, head down and with trailing reins, was cropping leisurely at the dry grass among the nearer bushes.

Stiff from their cramped crouching Brandon and Flame scrambled to their feet. Already convinced in his own mind that it was nothing more than unfounded fear that held them prisoners, Brandon was ready enough to accept Gus's opinion that the coast was clear. The torture of his swollen and blistered feet and his aching muscles had made the period of tense crouching and listening seem an interminable agony. Followed by Flame and giving scant thought to Gus's caution to keep under cover, he moved towards the door through which the old man had just stepped. He saw the white horse lift its head and stand waiting as Gus strode quickly towards it.

"*Jim! Gus! Come back!…Come back!* They're there—*there in the bushes!…*"

The words were a scream—a frantic scream of warning that broke suddenly from Flame. On the threshold of the door, in the very act of stepping out into the windy, open stretch beyond, Brandon felt the girl's hands snatch at him frantically, jerking him violently backwards and whirling him aside into the shelter of the wall: "*Get back!…*" the girl screamed, "*They're in the mesquite!… I just saw.…*"

Her words were drowned in a deafening blur of detonations as, of a sudden, the bushes opposite the east door shook violently and parted in a vicious slash of pistol-shots. Bullets smashed chips from the adobes and hummed through the doorway. All in a flash, as he reeled backwards, jerked to shelter by Flame's frenzied clutch, Brandon saw the figure of Gus crumple and fall—saw the startled horse whirl about and plunge snorting into the mesquites—saw two Chinamen with automatics in their hands break from the screen of bushes and come racing towards him.

And in the same instant, even as he swung up his gun and fired point blank at the leaping figures, there came to his ears from both front and rear of the old building the sound of shouts and shots. Bullets ripped in viciously from the front door and from the back, as from both front and rear simultaneously the other two Tongsmen burst out of the mesquites and came charging to the attack.

Photo of the Vallecito Stage Station ruins (used with permission California State Parks)

℘

CHAPTER 24

A Grim Barricade

Thced here was no time to choose shelter—scarce time even to realize
what had happened. With a rush, from all sides at once, came the
vicious crash of automatics and the sound of infuriated shouts.
As he and the girl flattened back in the poor protection of the wall
between the front and east doors, it seemed to Brandon that in the
twinkling of an eye everything had become a crazed blur of yells and
deafening reports and flying chips of adobe—a maddened, smoke-
strangled chaos through which his gun and Flame's, moving with the
darting speed of cornered rattlesnakes, spat fire to front and rear and
side in lightning succession.

But the margin of warning, scant as it was, which Flame's quick eye
and frantic scream had given had been enough. Discovered and forced
to action before they had succeeded in drawing all their victims into
the open, the Tongsmen were at a disadvantage which they seemed
to realize the instant they broke cover. In the clear light of dawn they
offered a plain target, and the swift burst of shots, that met their charge
was staggering. Dimly, his eyes blurred an instant by a bullet-flung
spurt of dust from the wall beside him, Brandon saw one of the men
who had come leaping out of the thicket opposite the east door stop
short and pitch forward on his face. His companion swerved frantically aside and plunged back into the mesquite. And almost at the same
instant the other two, racing towards the front and rear doors, checked
precipitately and, turning, bolted into the bushes.

Taking instant advantage of this check in the attack Brandon and
the girl darted back into the one comer of the room that offered a
degree of safety. Though the partial protection of the wall near the east
door had saved them from the hasty shooting of the excited attackers,

Brandon knew well enough that their respite now would be only a matter of seconds. Infuriated by the failure of their ruse, the Chinamen would waste no more time. At any instant might come another concerted rush.

Flame was panting as she hastily crammed fresh cartridges into her gun. "Oh, Jim!" she gasped. "Gus?"

"They got him!" he told her breathlessly as he snapped the refilled cylinder of his six-shooter into place. "They got him with their first shots. They…."

There was a sudden sharp report. From the bushes opposite the east door a bullet whammed across the room and thudded into the wall a hand-span above their heads, showering them with dust. Almost instantly came another that struck short and tore a fountain of flying dirt from the earth floor.

"Down—lie down!" Brandon shouted; "get way back in the corner among the broken 'dobes!" With lightning swiftness he crashed three answering bullets at the hidden marksman, and in a sudden flash of inspiration born of the desperate need, sprang across the room and snatched at the sprawled body of Martinez.

But before he could thrust it into place as a shelter for the exposed corner there came another shot. Flame flattened to the floor with a sharp gasp, but recovered on the instant. Her gun hurled lead into the bushes in rapid detonations. Through the screening film of smoke Brandon dragged up the body of Galloway, shoved it against that of Martinez and dropped hastily to shelter beside the girl just as another bullet, ricochetting along the floor, buried itself in the grisly barricade with a sickening thud. Flame's gun roared answer in a stabbing flare of shots that ended abruptly in a dull clicking.

"Get hit?" In an agony of apprehension Brandon gripped the girl's hand as she fumbled at her belt for more cartridges.

"No!" she panted; "but one was sure close—through my hair. That devil's got our range." "Well, we've got shelter now—of a sort. Keep down low, for God's sake!"

"I don't think these will stop their bullets," she whispered. With her smoking gun, as she refilled it, she motioned shudderingly towards the grim bulwark that protected them.

"No, but they'll help a lot. And with some of these broken 'dobes…."

Another vicious shot ripped from the thicket. There was the sound of a slashing impact. Something whizzed past Brandon's cheek and struck the bricks in the corner. He fired back, quick as a flash, and was rewarded by seeing a sudden commotion in the bushes that was not due to the wind. Before the movement had subsided he planted two more swift shots. His gun went suddenly silent.

"That one came clean through!" Flame breathed.

"I know it!—but I think I winged one of the devils," Brandon answered breathlessly. He hastily refilled his gun. The sudden realization that this was his last load and that his belt was empty gave him a startled chill. As his hands worked swiftly, dragging together fragments of the broken adobe bricks and piling them against the inner side of the protecting bodies, he whispered an anxious question.

"I've only got one left in the belt," Flame answered soberly. "I used five in that first rush—and another load just now. But I've got a full gun."

"So've I," he said, "but that's all I have got. My belt's empty. We mustn't waste a single shot now—we've got to save these against another rush. God! I hope I got that devil out there!...that'd leave only two of 'em."

The shooting from the bushes had stopped. Stretched prone among the litter of smashed adobes that strewed the corner and both working with feverish haste to pile up a ridge of fragments that would render more bullet-proof the gruesome barrier behind which they lay, Brandon and the girl strained their ears desperately for sounds of movement. Once more the dreadful grip of suspense had fastened over everything. The wind worried at the broken roof and whistled mournfully through the mesquites. But there was no other noise. The bushes opposite the east door seemed suddenly to have been deserted.

And then, just as Brandon had begun to feel certain that his last shots had accounted for at least one of the hidden snipers, the firing from the thicket suddenly recommenced, more viciously than ever. Bullets zipped across the floor, ripping spurts of dust from the wall behind or thudding savagely into the yielding barrier in front. More than once the low ridge of broken adobes which Brandon and the girl had piled behind the bodies jumped and crumbled ominously as bullets, penetrating all else, checked against it with a dull shock.

And suddenly Brandon was aware that the shots were coming from a different angle—they were coming from higher up. The low barricade—all too low and inadequate to begin with—had all at once lost more than half its sheltering value. Bullets were whamming across the top of it and striking terrifyingly close. It was evident that somewhere, screened by the branches, one of the Tongsmen had climbed into a mesquite tree and from this vantage-point was pumping a steady stream of bullets into the corner. That he had not already scored a hit was apparently only because the shadow of the side walls and of the overhanging roof hid the corner and made shooting from the outside a matter of guesswork. But Brandon realized grimly that unless this sniper could be promptly ousted from his new position it would be a matter of a few seconds only before the fight would come to a grim and sudden end.

"I see him!" Flame whispered; "there—in that big mesquite to the left! He's up in the fork—behind that big bunch of mistletoe."

"Keep down!" Brandon cautioned sharply. "I've spotted him! You keep under cover!"

He sighted carefully and squeezed the trigger. With the roar of the gun the mesquite branch shook. Something dark dropped hastily from behind the tangle of interlaced stems and vanished into the cover of the lower bushes.

"You got him!" Flame cried triumphantly.

Brandon shook his head. "I don't think so," he said, crestfallen. "It was a clean miss. That was the branch I plugged—not him. I aimed too far to the right—couldn't see which was which, he was so well hid. But I scared him out of there, anyhow. These Chinks aren't keen on being shot at themselves."

He tried to speak cheerfully, but to himself he swore in bitter chagrin. He had had a chance and he had bungled it—and wasted a precious cartridge. There were but twelve cartridges now between them and annihilation. Cartridges!—if only they had a few more—enough at least to keep up a scattering reply to the attackers' fire. This sudden necessity for hoarding them was increasing the peril tenfold. The Chinese would speedily interpret the real meaning of these sparing and careful shots. And while it was apparent that the surviving Tongsmen had become exceedingly cautious about exposing themselves, they would be quick to sense the dwindling ammunition of their victims and to take instant advantage of it.

The sniping from the thicket opposite the east door had ceased abruptly when the sniper had dropped from his perch. But presently it began again, this time from the lower bushes. It dawned on Brandon suddenly that all the shooting from this quarter was being done by one man—stopping when he was dislodged from each position and beginning again when he had established himself in a new one. And with this realization Brandon's hope that he had accounted for one of the snipers faded. It was evident that his previous shots, despite the agitation of the bushes that had followed them, had done no more execution than the last. Apparently it had been the same man at whom he had fired. But if so where were the other two Tongsmen?

Yet even as the question flashed to Brandon's mind it was startlingly answered. A stealthy footfall beyond the wall behind him and the faint scrape of a boot against adobe caused his heart to check with a sudden jerk and his eyes to flash to the window just in time to see the black muzzle of an automatic stab through the opening, swing towards him and explode in a deafening, blindly aimed burst of shots. And almost at the same instant, mingling with the roar of his own gun as he fired back, there came a ripping blur of point-blank detonations from the west doorway—a savage smash of sound that was drowned by the answering crash of Flame's gun. Chips of adobe flew from the walls in all directions. The air was a sudden blinding whirl of dust and powder-fumes.

And then, from door and window alike, as suddenly as they had appeared, the belching guns were gone. Another bullet whammed in through the east door and glanced from the floor with a vicious note. But from outside the walls came the scuffling noise of retreating feet and the dwindling sounds of high-pitched Chinese voices calling to one another. As the gusting wind whipped back and scattered the swirls of dust and powder-fumes, Brandon saw, with a stabbing catch at his heart, that Flame had dropped her gun. Desperately, hampered by her prone position, she was trying with her right hand to staunch a trickling flow of blood that had already crimsoned her fingers and forearm.

"It's—it's only my left arm," she gasped as he caught at her in a cold fear. "It's nothing—it isn't even broken—it's only a scratch. That brute at the door got me with his first shot. But I slammed back at him so quick he didn't get another chance to aim—damn him!" With the ragged sleeve of her shirt she struggled bravely to check the spreading red flow.

"You can't do it that way," he whispered, his voice suddenly tight and choking. "I'll fix it."

"No," she panted; "there isn't time! They'll be back!"

"Not for a minute or so—we made it too hot for 'em. They've sneaked off. Turn this way—quick!"

With swift fingers, as she twisted obediently towards him, he tore the ripped sleeve from her shirt and quickly fashioned a rough, but effective bandage that would stop the bleeding. The numb terror that had clutched at his heart lifted a little when he found that she had spoken truly. It was a slight flesh wound only—in the upper arm midway between elbow and shoulder. He bound it up quickly, his hands suddenly trembling.

The shooting from the bushes opposite the east door had stopped, but he was only vaguely aware of the fact. For the moment the throbbing feel of the girl's soft white flesh under his hands swept all else from his mind. The realization that it was her blood that was staining his swiftly working fingers seemed to unnerve him—the thought of the relentless doom which was reaching so swiftly towards this clear-eyed girl for whom he would gladly have given his own life a hundred times over wrenched him with a sudden agony of grief.

"There," with hands that shook so that he could hardly use them he managed somehow to get the last knot tied; "there! That'll hold it till we can make a better job."

"I guess I won't need another one," she said softly. And then, with a sharp catch of her breath, "Jim—you big fool! What in hell's the matter with you?...you're bawling."

"It's the powder-smoke," he said hastily. "These doggoned guns...."

She reached out suddenly and caught his hand, squeezing it fiercely. "You're an awful good liar, Jim," she breathed huskily; "a damned good liar. But it don't do you no good. I—I can...Oh, Jim, you're such a d—darned honorable fool!...But I like you a whole lot better for that too. You're so d—darned honest that...that you...you...."

She choked suddenly on her own words, and releasing his hand abruptly dashed her unwounded arm across her eyes. "It's no use, Jim," she said with a dry, nervous little laugh, "our goose is cooked—and we both know it, I guess. I've only got two cartridges left in my gun—just three altogether." She reached towards her belt for the odd one.

He stopped her with a quick motion: "Leave that one be awhile, honey," he said chokingly. "You—you might need it—that last one. Don't put it in your gun yet."

"I—I guess you're right." She caught her breath as she read the grim meaning in his eyes. "It's sort of cowardly, I guess, but I—I don't think I could stand what almost happened before. You better save one too—just in case...How many have you got?"

"Only two—I had to make it hot for that devil at the window. If he'd dared get his head above the bricks so's he could see what he was shooting at he'd have got both of us sure."

"Well, it's a cinch we can't stop any more rushes," she said hopelessly. "The quicker it's all over the better now. What did they quit for? Another shot or two and they'd have had us."

"They don't know just how short of cartridges we are," he answered. "We're pretty well sheltered here, and they know what they're up against. They know that as long as our ammunition lasts we'd have a good chance of wiping out the whole bunch if they tried a rush. They've got to be cautious. They didn't do more than shove their guns around the corner and blaze away blind till they'd emptied a clip apiece, hoping that they'd hit us."

· "There's still three of them," she whispered. "There was one shooting from among the trees all the time the other two were here."

"Yes; worse luck. I thought once I'd got one of 'em, out there in the bushes. But it seems I didn't."

"She was listening intently. "I wonder where they are," she said in a hushed voice. "I can't hear a thing but the wind."

He was straining his ears also, his every sense tensed. "They're up to something," he said grimly. "Maybe that last flurry was just to test out how much ammunition we'd got. Thank God we gave 'em a generous dose—they'll think we've got plenty left. Maybe we can keep 'em bluffed. Somebody may come to help us."

She shook her head hopelessly.

"Nobody'll come, except Amos brings help—that's if he really did get through to the Davidsons. But that'd take time. This is a lonesome road—and those brutes out there know it."

Close together they lay listening. There was no more shooting from the thicket and no sound of footfalls or movement. Yet there was a grim sense of something impending; of unseen eyes that watched; of stealthy hidden shapes that crept closer. To Brandon, his nerves a-quiver with the almost impossible task of watching every point at once, and dreading each instant a new attack from some unexpected quarter, the strain was almost unendurable. His head was throbbing, his heart pounding with a feverish, labored action that made every beat seem a dull twinge of agony.

Seconds seemed all at once to lengthen themselves to hours. It was not long, he knew, since the sounds of the shuffling horse had lured Gus out to his doom. Somehow that first unexpected volley that had blotted out the old man's life seemed to have been an age ago, yet he knew it had only been a few minutes.

It was a little lighter now—but not much lighter. Beyond the building things were clear enough, but beneath the old, sagging roof the shadows lightened slowly. He wondered how long it would be to sun-up—and in the same instant caught himself on the grim thought that this sun-up was one which he and the girl beside him would probably never see. They were trapped—and with the ending of their cartridges would end their last desperate hope. With the next rush of their relentless foes must come the final tragedy of this dread cycle of horror. And Flame...Flame would be....

He checked the thought savagely. His racing brain, stunned suddenly with the stark realization of the inevitable, recoiled in a surge of frantic rebellion against the merciless fate that reached out so devilishly towards the girl at his side. She was too young to die—too young and sweet and beautiful to be blotted out thus in a feud in which she was utterly innocent. If only there were some way—some way to hold out against these implacable fiends until help came...If only they had a few more cartridges....If only....

Desperately, gripped of a sudden with all the frantic, unreasoning impulses of a trapped animal, his eyes swept round the old room as though by some miracle he expected to find within its crumbling desolation some clue to help. But his feverish scrutiny served only to crush him with a bitterer sense of despair. The old, time-worn, bullet-marked walls seemed to mock him. The smoke-blackened, hide-lashed sticks and poles of the roof seemed suddenly to have gathered blacker and grimmer shadows along the curve of the great, sagging ridge beam.

With an involuntary shudder he noticed for the first time that, bedded flush with the adobes of the wall, between the window and the front door gap, was a rectangular framework of timbers that had evidently once been the back-frame for shelving or for a cupboard of some sort. It was tall and narrow and, somehow, grimly suggestive of the outline of a coffin standing on end. And on the top cross-piece, burned deep in the wood and still startlingly visible despite the years that had passed since it had been done, was a charred outline that had been made by a queer, grim cattle brand—the brand of a Death's head.

"It isn't any good, Jim," the girl whispered softly, as though reading his thoughts. "There's no dodging Fate—and I guess it's got us. I've always sort of felt that this darned haunted old ruin would be where I'd end up. But it's not fair that you've got to go too. It's my fault. I dragged you into this—I—I'm sorry."

"You didn't," he said huskily, "I—"

"Yes, I did!" She brushed his denial aside. "I oughtn't to have let you come with me. But it's no use crying now over what's done. I guess we've all got to go some day. Only I—I wish that you…that I.…"

She broke off abruptly and lay silent, her head held tense as though listening, but her eyes were brimming with tears which she could not hide. His left arm went round her shoulders tenderly and his pulse thrilled to the quick, answering pressure with which the fingers of her gun-free left hand reached up and gripped his. Eddies of dust swirled in through the front door-gap and swept bleakly across the littered floor. Under the roof, against the farther wall, a long, half-broken fragment hanging from the rotting, close-laid sticks of the ceiling, scraped back and forth across the adobes with a low, dry creaking.

"There's a curse on it," Flame whispered, speaking in a hushed, almost inaudible voice as though to herself; "there's a curse on this place. God knows how many these old walls have seen die. No wonder it's haunted; no wonder the whole valley's haunted.

It's sure queer, though—queer how things work round—how they wind up sometimes just where they began. Close to seventy years ago Captain O'Hara was murdered for his gold and Si Slade and Martinez, the horse tender, hid it somewhere. And now, after all these years, a

Martinez—the last survivor, I guess—is dragged back here by Fate to die along with the last living being that has O'Hara blood in its veins. It's uncanny…It seems like…."

"Hush, honey, hush!" he whispered chokingly. "Maybe it won't come to that—lots of things can happen yet. If your uncle got through he'll be coming back, bringing help and…."

His whisper checked, unfinished. Out of the distance had burst suddenly a gruesome yowling that was unmistakable. There came the sharp sound of a pistol-shot—then another. The outcry lifted in a frenzied note and grew swiftly clearer. From the mesquites, both at front and side of the building, broke a wild spatter of shots. A second later, before either Brandon or the girl had clearly realized what was happening, a huge white shape, streaked with mud and slime and traveling like a cannon-ball, flashed in through the front doorway as though in blind search of shelter, crossed the floor at a bound and vanished into the dim recesses of the inner room. The old adobe echoed suddenly to the sounds of a heavy body hurling itself about, snapping and howling in a maddened frenzy of pain.

"It's Midnight!" Flame gasped. "He must have attacked them and they've wounded him again. They've…."

A rattle of pistol-shots, ripping from the thicket opposite the east door, clipped short her words. In swifter succession than ever before came the vicious thud-thud of bullets striking into the wall behind. And there came another sound. Mingled with the din of the suffering dog and the sharp detonations of the rapidly fired automatic was the sudden throbbing of a motor. As Brandon flattened to the floor and pressed Flame down into closer shelter behind their frail barricade he was aware that somewhere just outside the front wall a big car had stopped. There came a curious scraping, cracking noise like the dragging and snapping of a heavy mass of dry sticks—a sound that was followed a moment later by a clearer, splintering impact as though a great bundle of dry brushwood had been flung down before the front door gap. And almost in the same instant, from somewhere in the mesquites in front of the building, another gun opened fire. A bullet hummed through the window opening, another—striking a little lower—tore a spurt of fragments from the mud bricks of the frameless sill. Faintly, through the racket of mingled sounds, came the scraping crackle of dry brush being dragged and piled.

CHAPTER 25

Blazing Brushwood

Faint though it was, the brittle crushing sound as the dry, dead branches were heaped together was unmistakable. Brandon's heart stood still. Explanation of this new activity on the part of the Tongsmen flashed upon him in the instant. Dry brush! Fire! They were to be smoked out! Ignorant of the defenders' lack of ammunition, and not daring with their diminished numbers to risk defeat by attempting to end matters by a rush attack, the Chinese had hit upon a more certain and less risky method. Taking shrewd advantage of the wind, which was just in the right direction to drive smoke and flames back into the building, it was the Tongsmen's scheme to force their victims into the open where, from the shelter of the surrounding bushes, they could be shot down with ease. The reason for the sudden furious fusillade through door and window was now apparent. While two of the tonsgmen poured in a stream of bullets that would keep the defenders close under cover, the third Chinaman—sheltered by the wall from any shots from within—was piling the brush.

"What are they doing?" Flame whispered, forcing her lips close to Brandon's ear to make herself heard.

"Piling dead branches in the front doorway. They're going to try to smoke us out."

She shook her head. "It'll take them too long to collect enough dry stuff. Oh!"—she caught her breath in startled recollection—"Jim!—that pile of brush and tules that Gus left—the pile Midnight jumped at in the dark! They must be dragging that up here with the car! There's an awful pile of it—and it's dry. If they're bringing *that....*"

He nodded soberly, answering the sudden consternation in her eyes with a tighter pressure of his arm about her shoulders. He had not thought of the brush heap. The time it would take the Chinese to collect dead branches and inflammable bushes, even from the close encircling thicket of mesquites, had occurred to him also. Subconsciously, even in the moment when their purpose had dawned on him, he had counted on that as a factor that might defeat their scheme. The sudden realization that just a short distance down the trail was a huge pile of tinder-dry fuel, ready cut and needing only the hauling, staggered him. By piling their car full and also by passing a rope around huge bundles of the light, dead branches and dragging them, the Tongsmen could haul up great quantities at a time.

Here was instant explanation of why they had brought up their car—explanation also of the sudden reappearance of Midnight. The brush-laden machine, dragging its mass of dry, snapping wood and coming slowly up the trail, had drawn the attack of the crazed hound, who had probably been lying among the tules cooling his fevered body in the muddy seepage. And, beaten off and wounded afresh, the anguished dog had fled blindly for shelter.

Brandon's teeth set grimly. That infernal pile of brush! Its presence there beside the road had been deadly. It was probably the sight of the heap of dry branches and tules close to where they had left their car when they had retreated the first time that had suggested the scheme to the Tongsmen; it was the abundant amount of fuel that the pile contained which would make the plan horribly certain of success.

The dreadful outcry of the maddened dog and the thudding sounds of his frenzied struggles ceased suddenly, to be succeeded by a low, strangled moaning. More clearly, between the steady cracking of the guns and the vicious impact of the bullets on the adobes, came the snapping noise of breaking twigs as the hidden worker piled up the brush. That there was already a considerable heap of the dry stuff in the doorway was apparent. Risking a swift glance above shelter Brandon could see the lower edges of the pile projecting into the room. From where he lay, looking along the wall, he could not see through the door-gap, but the section of the pile that had overflowed into the room was an indication that the load of brush and dry tules that the Tongsmen had dragged up had been a large one.

Brandon thought fast. More chillingly than ever now he realized the utter certainty of the girl's fate and his own. If their position had been hopeless before it was now doubly so. The wind that sucked in at the doors of the old building would drive the smoke and flame of the fire directly into the corner where they lay—the dust swirls that from time to time had eddied across the floor and drawn up under the roof had been enough to tell him that. Once the fire was started their position would speedily become untenable. Unless they chose to remain where they were and meet a dreadful death by heat and suffocation they would have no choice but to dash blindly out into the open—to be shot down by the gunmen crouching ready behind the screen of bushes. In either case the end was sure; there was no way to avoid it. To attempt to change position now would be suicide.

The daylight had increased by this time and the shadows beneath the old roof were less, so that the marksman shooting from beyond the east door had a much better view of his target. To attempt now to move from behind shelter would only be to invite death more speedily. Narrow and low as their gruesome barricade was it was nevertheless a fairly effective protection so long as they remained behind it. To abandon it would be madness—there was no other section of the old building which offered anything like as much security. The middle room, where the wounded hound had found refuge, was not to be thought of, owing to the ruined walls beyond. Even if by some miracle they succeeded in running the gauntlet and reaching it alive they would be in an infinitely worse trap.

Nor was there a chance—as for the moment in mad desperation the thought flashed to Brandon's mind—of making a quick spring to the window and shooting down the Tongsman who was piling the brush. To do so meant exposure not only to the bullets coming through the side doorway but also to the fire of the man who, from the bushes in front of the building, was sending a steady succession of shots through the window and into the adobes about its edges. There was nothing to do, Brandon realized bitterly, but to lie waiting, like trapped rats, for the doom which they could not avoid.

The throbbing motor of the hidden car stirred suddenly to swifter life. There was a whining mesh of gears and the faint receding sound of twigs and gravel crushing under moving tires.

"It's going!" Flame whispered.

"Going back for another load of brush," Brandon said grimly. "One of 'em's doing the hauling while the other two keep us cornered." With the departure of the car the shooting from both front and side ceased abruptly. The faint noise of the retreating machine faded into nothingness down the trail. The gusting of the wind and the low, moaning pant of the suffering dog were of a sudden the only sounds that broke the tense hush of expectancy which seemed to settle over the old adobe.

"Maybe they've all gone with the car," Flame suggested.

"Not likely. They've stopped shooting because there's no need now—all that before was to prevent us trying to pick off that bird who was piling the brush. And maybe now they think we'll be fools enough to believe they've gone again."

He raised his head cautiously for a view of the bushes. But, on the instant, a gun cracked from the mesquites. As he flattened down with a jerk a bullet ripped across the edge of the barricade and buried itself in the bricks behind.

"*Jim!*" With a gasp of terror Flame clutched at him.

"No, he didn't get me; but he came dam close. Looks like they ain't by any means gone. Hombre out there can see better now, I reckon. He's got our range about perfect."

Satisfied apparently that his shot had gone close enough effectually to discourage any further movements on the part of the concealed pair, the marksman in the bushes did not fire again. Grimly tense, Brandon and the girl lay listening. From the inner room the dreadful, blood-choked sobbing of the dying dog came with increasing clearness. The wind skittered among the broken sticks of the roof. Little swirls of dust danced across the floor and drove eddying into the corner. Of a sudden Flame sniffed sharply. "I smell smoke!" she said.

Brandon stiffened. Even as she had spoken he had smelled it also. The air seemed full of the hot, acrid whiffs. Long, swirling tentacles of whitish-yellow vapor were reaching in through the door-gap and billowing through the window-opening. From beyond the wall, growing swiftly in volume, came the fierce crackling sound of fire eating into the dry sticks.

"Chink with the car must have lit it before he left," Brandon said shortly. "The heap's smothered down with green tules and branches, I reckon, an' the fire's just now taking hold. Maybe it'll burn itself out before he can get another load here. We'll just lie low."

He spoke with forced courage, but his voice was hoarse and his arm about the girl's shoulders tightened. Now that the brush piled against the wall and in the doorway was already alight he realized that the end was upon them. He knew well enough that there was no chance that the fire would die down before it could be replenished. With the huge heap of ready-cut brush to draw upon, it would be but a matter of moments before the car would be back, dragging up a fresh supply. And it was quite possible that a fresh supply would not be needed.

With the wind as it was and with the gaping doorways sucking smoke and heat greedily back into the old building, it would be but a matter of a few scant minutes before it would be untenable. The old ruin could not burn, it was true, but with its shattered walls acting as a flue to the raging fire that was swiftly growing in the yawning door-way no living thing could remain within it. Already the smoke had increased startlingly. In choking clouds—proof enough that masses of wet, green tules had been mixed with the dry fuel—it poured now through the door-gap in a billowy flood that swirled back with the wind and eddied up in ever-thickening masses beneath the overhanging section of the roof.

The air became stifling and almost unbreathable. The whole pile of tinder-dry brush seemed of a sudden to have burst into flames. Tongues of fire, dully red through the smoke, were flaring in wind-torn streamers through door and window; glowing fragments and flying flakes of hot ashes poured back into the corner in a blinding, swiftly increasing shower. The heat was already intense and the whole big room was a murk of rolling smoke.

"Jim...we...we can't stay...We've got to make a break for it!" Flame gasped.

"It's better to be...shot than...this...." Her panting words strangled in a fit of coughing.

"The smoke's thickening," he told her hoarsely, his mind stirred of a sudden with a new glimmer of desperate hope. "If we can stick it out a bit longer it'll be thick enough maybe so's we can make a break through the back door under cover of it. Maybe, if we make a sudden rush, we could reach the bushes at the back without getting hit. And then—"

A snarling cry, smoke-strangled and dreadful, lifted of a sudden above the crackling roar of the fire. From the rear room came the sound of a terrified, blundering rush, the impact of a heavy body colliding blindly with the adobe wall and another blood-choked animal scream of frenzied fury. Through the dense swirls of smoke that hid the rear doorway Midnight, his jaws dripping with blood and froth, his eyes wide and glaring in fire-maddened terror, catapulted suddenly into the front room, checked an instant on rigid, stiffly braced legs, and then, as though in one last mighty burst of dying strength, cleared the floor in a bound and with a scrambling plunge and a hoarse, demoniac yell of agony leaped through the window and vanished.

Sharply above the crackle of the fire came the sounds of a sudden spatter of shots and a furious snarling, that dwindled swiftly as the maddened dog sped away down the trail. The retreating outcry blended with another low sound which grew louder—the splintering crackle of a dragging mass of dry branches mingled with the faint throb of a slowly approaching car.

"Come on." Scrambling to his feet, half-blinded by the dense choking clouds of smoke that had of a sudden closed about them, Brandon reached helping hands to Flame. "Come on!" he panted. "The car's coming with more brush—we'll have to make a break before it gets here...We'll try to reach the mesquites at the back. And...and maybe...."

His voice broke. With a swift, instinctive movement he crushed her to his heart. "Honey," he whispered huskily. "I—I reckon this is good-bye. An'..."

His words went unfinished, blotted suddenly in the sound of a dreadful cry—a cry that on the instant was lost in a deafening roar as of a powerful motor jerked violently open to the limit. There came the splintering crash of dry branches; the rip of breaking bushes; a whirled blur of frantic cries. Hurtling forward from somewhere close at hand, as Brandon leaped back in alarm, snatching the girl once more into the protecting shelter of the corner, a terrifying tornado of crazed sound and roaring speed seemed to hurl headlong towards the old building.

"*The car!*" Flame gasped in terror. "*Midnight! He must have sprung....*"

There was a rush—a roar—the jarring impact of a thunderous shock that shook the old adobe to its foundations. Almost within reach of Brandon's arm as he was hurled violently backward, snatching the girl clear, a hurtling mass—dark and enormous and traveling at terrific speed—crashed through the wall like the ramming-bow of a racing torpedo-boat and, in a smoke-blurred inferno of scattered firebrands, whirled sideways and rolled over, stilling suddenly in a dreadful screeching crash of wood and metal. As he whirled the girl back into the corner, sheltering her with his body, it seemed to Brandon that heaven and earth rushed together and went down into chaos in a smoking avalanche of dust and fire and tumbling walls.

∽

CHAPTER 26

Out of Fiery Chaos

Through a blinding blur of smoke and a rain of dust and falling earth Brandon and the girl fought their way clear of the debris. Above the corner which had protected them still stretched a shattered, sagging remnant of hide-lashed sticks and trickling earth. But the balance of the old roof, together with the whole section of wall between the window and the front door-gap, had fallen, burying the floor beneath tumbled heaps of ruin among which, half hidden in the huge mass of dry brush which it had been hauling, the big touring-car lay bottom up.

Already in a dozen places flames kindled by the burning brands which it had hurled with it in its plunge, were licking hungrily at the pile of dry fuel which surrounded it. From somewhere, blurred by the choking clouds of dust and the snapping crackle of the scattered fire that blazed fiercely along the outer edge of the fallen wall, came an agonized, high-pitched screaming.

But at that instant, as they staggered half-blinded through the smoke and dust, Brandon and the girl had scant time to realize the ruin which lay around them. Even as they stumbled out of the debris-choked corner the dust-clouded chaos ripped apart in a vicious slash of shots as from front and side, charging in recklessly through the whirling pall of smoke that wrapped the wrecked car, the other two Tongsmen flung themselves towards them, shooting as they came.

There was no instant to think of shelter. To Brandon as he jerked up his gun it seemed as though in the very moment of his first glimpse the two infuriated Chinamen were upon him. The smoke was a sudden spinning blur of action—of everything happening at once. He felt the wind-spurt of a bullet along his head—the hot graze of another across his thigh; heard the crash of his own gun and the swift double detonation of Flame's as the girl pulled the trigger twice in lightning succession. Through the smoke, as he fired again, he saw the nearer of the two Tongsmen crumple forward in a sprawled, lifeless heap; saw Flame, in the same instant, stumble in a treacherous tangle of debris from the fallen roof and go down with a crash; saw the remaining Chinaman swerve savagely towards her, leveling his automatic; heard, in the same split-second as he whirled to the girl's aid, the dull, hopeless click that told him that his own gun was empty.

Quicker than thought, and with the strength of desperation, Brandon hurled his empty weapon and leaped. The heavy gun struck the Chinaman full in the chest with a force that staggered him, spoiling his aim and sending the bullet intended for the helpless girl crashing into the opposite wall. Before he could recover himself or pull trigger again Brandon was upon him with a smashing blow that whirled the Chinaman from his feet and sent him toppling backwards. Clutching desperately at the Tongsman's pistol and unable to check his own headlong leap, Brandon fell with his antagonist. Through a blur of smoke as they went down together among the tumbled bricks of the fallen wall he glimpsed Flame scrambling to her feet and snatching at her cartridge-belt.

But even as they crashed, struggling, to the floor, Brandon realized that his momentary advantage was gone—his worn strength was no match for the startling surge of trained muscles that heaved suddenly against his own. Almost in the instant of the fall the stocky-built Chinaman squirmed sideways with the agility of a cat. Brandon found himself caught suddenly in a cunning lock-hold. His right arm was pinned helpless and his neck constricted in a vice-like grip. He felt the muscles of his left arm giving slowly; felt his left hand, which had gripped desperately about the pistol, slipping before the surge of a strength greater than his own. As they writhed savagely in the choking heat that drove in from the fire he felt the wavering pistol of a sudden wrenched from his hold and jabbed viciously towards him.

But in the same split second, and before the Tongsman could pull trigger, Brandon's ears deafened to the crash of a shot that ripped from another quarter—a shot fired so close that the flash of it seemed to sear his cheek. The strangling hold upon him released with a jerk. He broke free from the suddenly limp body of his antagonist and staggered to his feet to find Flame beside him, a smoking gun in her hand.

"Oh, Jim!" With a choking sob of thankfulness the girl reeled towards him. "It was the last cartridge. Th-thank God I hadn't put it in the gun before. But I—I was almost too...."

He caught her in his arms, stilling her broken words in a swift, crushing pressure of gratitude. There was scant time for words. Even the realization that the impossible had happened, and that, with this sudden blotting out of their enemies, they had been snatched from certain death, was for the moment blurred in Brandon's mind by the necessity of swift escape from the fiery menace about them. The heat was intense. Already the tumbled mass of brush piled about the wrecked car was blazing fiercely. Half carrying the girl he stumbled across the debris-littered floor towards the side doorway. But even as he did so there came to his ears the moaning, agonized scream that he had heard before—this time weaker—more strangled. Through the smoke that swirled from the swift-spreading flame he had a glimpse of a head and shoulders projecting from beneath the overturned car—a glimpse of a lean, pain-twisted face; of a hand and arm that beat in frantic, futile effort.

"*Jim! Quick!*" With a horrified cry as her eyes fell upon the trapped man, Flame whirled free of Brandon's steadying arm and sprang back impulsively towards the fire-licked car. "Quick!" she screamed, as, utterly careless of her wounded arm, she tugged and thrust impotently at the ponderous bulk. "Quick! Help me! We've got to get him out! Oh, my God! He'll be burned alive!"

With a bound Brandon was at her side. "Get back!" he shouted frantically, "you'll be killed! The petrol tank! If it explodes...."

But even as he cried out he was tugging and heaving, aiding the girl's strength with every ounce of his own in a desperate attempt to tilt the massive wreck. The dreadful plight of the trapped man filled him with a horror as great as that which had gripped Flame, and for the moment he forgot all else; he could not abandon even one of these relentless fiends to perish in this hideous fashion.

But the heavy car, wedged and jammed among fallen piles of adobes, resisted every effort of their straining muscles. The smoke was all at once blinding and filled with licking tongues of fire. A sudden gust of wind drove a whirling sheet of fire in their faces and sent them staggering back with arms flung up to save their eyes. The trapped man, half-hidden now in a pouring flood of smoke that rolled from beneath the wreck, caught feebly at Brandon's feet and cried out piteously in faint, incoherent English.

"It's Pai Lang!" Flame gasped. "He was the best of the lot. He's burning. We've *got* to get him out...." She flung herself once more against the scorching car.

Brandon dragged her back fiercely. "You can't do anything that way," he panted. "We can't lift it. We've got to have...."

He broke off with a choking exclamation as his glance, darting desperately about in search of a lever, fell suddenly upon the long section of a snapped roof beam. He leaped across the tumbled bricks and with a herculean effort dragged out the heavy, hand-hewn timber, and, tilting it down across a handy ridge of fallen adobes, he thrust one end beneath the lower edge of the wreck and heaved. The car stirred and lifted. But of a sudden the crest of the ridge of adobes which supported the beam crumbled. The big machine settled abruptly. The pinioned man shrieked in agony.

"Raise the lever!" Flame screamed frantically. "Raise it! I'll fix...."

Shielding her face against the swirling fire with her arm she darted forward, dragging at a long, narrow frame of timbers that lay half embedded in the fallen bricks. She wrenched it clear and, scattering aside the broken adobes which the beam had crushed, thrust one side of the frame back in place of them as a bearing to distribute the weight. "Now!" she gasped, "you lift. I'll drag him out!"

Once more, with all his strength, Brandon heaved down upon the lever. The wreck tilted up slowly. Beneath grinding weight, despite the timber which Flame had placed, Brandon could feel the ridge of adobes crumbling. Then the subsidence stopped as though the heavy lever had come to rest upon a solid rock. He forced down upon the bending beam desperately. Half-hidden by the blinding smoke Flame was stooping beside the car, pulling and tugging. Dragged by her straining arms a limp, silent shape suddenly drew clear from beneath the edge of the swaying mass.

"Hold it!" the girl screamed: "hold it a second! He's clear, though he's fainted. But there's something else...." She was on her knees again, peering and groping. As he struggled with the groaning lever Brandon could see her feeling and dragging at something that still lay beneath the car. She staggered back suddenly with a hopeless gesture.

"It's no good!" she gasped. "Let go! It's Midnight. He's there too. But he's stone dead—crushed...I can't get him out. Let go!" She stooped once more to the sprawled shape at her feet.

Brandon released his hold on the lever and sprang to her aid. Between them, stumbling blindly in the smoke, they carried the limp body across the piled debris and into the clear air beyond the side door. The Chinaman's shirt was gashed and torn about the shoulders and there was a trickling red slash along his throat that had obviously been caused by the dog's slashing fangs. He gave no sign of life as they laid him hastily down on the sandy, windswept ground beside the outer wall.

"I reckon he's passed out after all," Brandon said grimly. "He was crushed pretty bad, I reckon—but, anyway, he wasn't cooked alive.

Well, thank God, that's the last of the devils, and...*Flame! Stop!* My God!—where are you going?..."

"Jim! The box! We've got to get it!" Heedless of his shout and wrenching clear of his snatching hand the girl was darting back towards the smoke-belching doorway through which they had just emerged. "The box!" she cried over her shoulder. "Quick! Help me! We've got to get it out!" She vanished recklessly into the smoke.

He plunged frantically after her, chilled with the sudden conviction that she had gone crazy. It was almost suicide to venture back into that raging inferno, which each instant was gathering new fury. He shouted hoarsely, clutching wildly at her as she ran stumbling towards the blazing car. Even as he reached her side, half-blinded in the licking fury of fire and smoke, he saw her hurl the heavy lever aside and drop on her knees, tearing frantically at the tumbled ridge of adobes on which it had been balanced. "It's an iron box!" she panted. "I saw it hidden when I fixed the lever! It must have been hidden in the wall... and when that fell...."

He was on his knees beside her now, hauling and heaving in an excitement as great as her own. Choked and dizzy, in a searing, blinding heat, he dragged at the heavy, oblong shape that lay buried among the broken adobes. His fingers locked suddenly about an iron ring and, with a tremendous heave, aided by the panting girl, he dragged the heavy metal box free of its earthy bed. It was not large, but the weight of it staggered him; even with Flame's aid he could hardly lift it.

Scorched and gasping, their combined strength taxed to the limit by their burden, they stumbled towards the doorway, groping blindly through a whirling tempest of smoke and driving sparks—a searing whirlwind which, even as they reeled out into the open air, split suddenly apart behind them with a glare and a deafening roar. Raging tongues of fire hurtled skywards. The interior of the old abode was in a twinkling a seething furnace of blazing petrol.

But at that moment, as they staggered well clear of the smoke-vomiting doorway and dropped their weighty burden to the earth, neither Brandon nor the girl had a thought for the flaming death that they had so narrowly escaped. Gripped in a sudden fierce excitement that for the moment swept away even their utter exhaustion, they fell on their knees, tugging together at the lid of the earth-grimed iron box—a box which Brandon saw now was of the type that had been used in the late 'fifties for gold shipments. The fastenings were stubborn with rust, but it was not locked.

"It must have been hid in the thickness of the wall," Flame panted, as with excited fingers she wrenched at the stiff clamps; "somewhere behind the frame of that old cupboard, in a hole that had been bricked up again with halved 'dobes. And when the car hit and the wall fell...."

The creaking catch slid back suddenly. With a quick tug Brandon swung the lid open. Flame uttered a sharp cry, snatching eagerly at the flap packet of time-yellowed documents that lay on the very top of the collection of bulging, tightly tied little canvas sacks and the scatter of loose, gleaming nuggets with which the box was crammed.

"The will!" she gasped joyfully. "Oh, Jim, the will! See! See!..." With shaking fingers she straightened out the discolored sheets, searching eagerly through the close lines of faded but still legible writing. "Look!—here's the signature—Terrence O'Hara. And here's the map of the mine! Here on this separate sheet!...Oh, Jim, we've found it! We've found it!—the O'Hara gold—the 'Lucky Ledge'!...We'll...."

"*Hands up!—both of you!*"

Sharp as the crack of a whip and hard as steel the command came suddenly from behind. Whirling about, startled, as he and the girl jerked to their feet as from an electric shock, Brandon found himself looking straight into the black and ugly muzzle of a leveled Luger— and behind it, hunched against the wall for support, his lean, wolf-face stamped with a diabolical expression of triumph and his icy eyes glittering venomously, crouched the Chinaman whom they had dragged from the blazing car.

South at the restored Vallecito Stage Station, 1947

⚈

CHAPTER 27

The Final Reckoning

For the fraction of a second, stunned with dismay, Brandon wavered. In the excitement over the discovery of the old iron box he had forgotten utterly this lean, wolf-faced Chinaman whom he had believed dead. Now, as the appalling realization of what their impulsive act of mercy and subsequent carelessness was likely to cause them, his heart seemed to stop. Coupled with the sickening knowledge that he and the girl were out of cartridges and utterly defenseless, was a bitter chagrin that, in the mad haste to escape the fire, he had not had the presence of mind to snatch up one of the slain Tongsmens' weapons to replace the empty gun which he had flung at Flame's antagonist. For a split second he wavered.

"Hands up!—both—quick! And stand still—both of you! The first one that makes a move I will shoot the *other!*"

The words snapped out with a sharp, hissing venom. Brandon's muscles, already tensed for a mad, reckless spring, wilted. There was no mistaking the grim meaning behind that shrewd and deadly threat. Following the example of the startled girl his hands went slowly aloft.

"That is better—stand like that! And remember—if either of you makes a move towards me I will instantly shoot the other one!"

"Pai Lang"—Flame found her voice with a sharp, choking intake— "you are a contemptible cur! You are...."

"*Silence!*" With a deadly note in the harshly rasped word the Chinaman cut her short. "Silence! Do not waste breath in insult. Lower your left hand slowly. Unbuckle your cartridge-belt, let it drop to the ground, then kick it towards me. But do not let your fingers make even the slightest move towards your gun while you do so. I can shoot swiftly."

"Come and get it yourself!" Flame snapped defiantly.

"I am in pain," Pai Lang said in a low, deadly voice, "or perhaps I would do so. But though I am injured I am not so injured that I cannot end that which I set out to do. And I am accustomed to being obeyed. Quick—*do as I say*—or—" His gun-muzzle shifted a fraction towards Brandon.

"There!" In a flash of panic the girl hastily undid the buckle and kicked gun and belt across the sand. "Take it—it's empty, anyway!"

"So I had suspected," said Pai Lang coolly. "And your friend, I see, has neither gun nor cartridges. Fate has planned wisely, it seems, to turn all things to my advantage and to deliver you into my hands in the end in spite of all your attempts to escape. Remains now only to settle the score. But first, I am curious. Why did you risk your lives, both of you, to get me out of the wreck in there?"

"You've got no call to feel flattered," Brandon said contemptuously; "we'd have done it lots sooner for a dog."

His muscles were tensed. He was watching the Chinaman narrowly. Only the fear that this wolf-faced fiend would make good his threat, and shoot down the girl the moment he made a spring, held him. But it came to him that if he could somehow infuriate the Tongsman and draw his first fire, then perhaps....

But the deadly eyes behind the gun did not flicker. Pai Lang betrayed no sign that the insult had gone home. Instead, he nodded grimly.

"You have good cause to think highly of dogs. It was the attack of the white hound just now which caused me to lose control of the car. His weight, when he sprang, hurled me from the seat and wedged me down so that my foot was jammed, forcing the accelerator wide open. Had it not been for that—for the crazed attack of a wounded dog...."

He paused, his thin, cruel lips tightening over his unfinished words. From his position, half-sitting, half-lying against the adobe wall on the windward side of the smoke-belching doorway where they had hastily laid him down, he regarded Flame and Brandon with hard, steely eyes that seemed to glitter like those of some deadly snake. For a full half-minute, his lean wolf-like face an inscrutable mask, he studied them in silence, his flickering gaze taking in also the open iron box, and the yellowed, wind-fluttered papers that Flame had dropped beside it. Abruptly he lowered his pistol.

"Go your way in peace," he said brusquely. "Life pays for life. Go your way together and fear no more. And may your path be prosperous."

Dumbfounded, scarce able to credit his ears, Brandon lowered his hands. Flame caught her breath in an astonished gasp:

"You mean?"—the girl's voice was husky and incredulous—"you mean that the Tong...."

"I mean that the debt of blood is paid in full," Pai Lang said quietly. "Justice has been done. He whose hands slew my brother and the others has received death in payment. You who risked your lives to save mine are paid with life—you and all others of the blood of Templeton who may yet remain. By your act of mercy to a deadly foe you have gained something which you could in no other way have attained.

"The Tong of the Yellow Dragon is deathless—its vengeance is not swerved by obstacles; it is patient as Time and relentless as Death. Had you left me to perish you would have gained safety for a month, perhaps. But the Tong does not lose track of those who do its bidding. When I and those who were with me did not return there would swiftly have come others, aflame with added fury, to avenge us. And after them—if necessary—still others yet. The decree of vengeance would have been fulfilled to the uttermost. You could not have escaped.

"But now...Well, I am not ungrateful—and you are worthy—both of you! In the councils of the Tong of the Yellow Dragon I speak with authority. I shall make my report. The blood of my companions whom you have killed in self-defense shall not be held against you. The record is clear at last. You have earned your lives and your safety—and in my heart I am glad that it is so. May your feet walk always in prosperity, and may this treasure"—he gestured towards the open iron box—"of which it seems your parent, did indeed speak truly—bring you happiness. Perhaps it also is the reward of mercy, since it seems that I was instrumental in uncovering its hiding-place. May you enjoy it and may peace and long life be yours."

With a swift motion he holstered his pistol in its hiding-place within his shirt, and, with a violent effort, despite a wrenching twist of agony, tottered to his feet. "Good-bye!" he said, his hard, steely tones of a sudden hoarse with pain, "I am going! I have far to go and—"

"But not so fur by a dang sight as ye come nigh goin', hombre!" said a grim voice. "Ye come almighty near hittin' th' cinders o' hell more'n a minnit ago!"

"Gus!" Startled at the abrupt, gruff words which, with their first syllables, had jerked Pai Lang around with a snarl, his Luger once more in his hand, Flame stared unbelievingly at the lean, grizzled-haired figure which had suddenly come round the front corner of the building. "Gus!" she cried, almost in terror. "My God! I thought—"

"I reckon I thot so too fer quite a piece, Miss Flame. But what with these here varmints bein' sich poor shots an' me havin' a extry tough head I waren't no more'n creased, I reckon. Only one bullet hit me an' that one didn't do no more'n cut a neat trail through th' hair an' hide atop o' my head. I reckon it made me sorta sleepy. Leastways, I woke up jest now an' sneakin' round this ways...."

"Up with your hands!" snarled Pai Lang. "Quick!"

"Hands nothin'!" Gus growled impatiently. "There ain't no time t' waste in sich foolishness. D'ye think if I'd ha' wanted t' shoot ye I'd ha' walked out here like a galoot with my gun in my belt like this? It's you that's had th' narrer escape, hombre. I was jest squeezin' th' trigger on ye from between the jints o' th' corner 'dobes when ye lowered yer gun an' begun t' talk amiable-like. I've had th' drop on ye ever since—all th' time I was squattin' there listenin'.

"If it weren't fer me havin' good ears an' bein' able t' savvy your grade o' Chinese you'd ha' been waltzin' with th' devil quite a piece back. Never mind about holdin' up hands, hombre—th' thing fer yer to do is t' travel, pronto. They's a hell-bent cloud o' dust comin' up th' trail from Smoky Spring's way what's goin' t' look plumb unhealthy t' you when it gets here, 'cordin' t' my way o' figgerin'. Yuh better put that gun away an' fan out!...If them riders pulls in here afore you've melted inta th' sticks you ain't gonna have half th' chanst o' a snowball in hell. They're liable t' act powerful suddent."

Pai Lang's eyes narrowed. Contemptuously, without speaking, he holstered his gun and turned away. But almost at the second step he staggered. Without Flame's quick clutch and Brandon's steadying grip he would have fallen.

"Gus! He's hurt—hurt bad!" Flame cried frantically. "The car crushed him—he can't walk!"

"A few broken ribs—a little pain," Pai Lang said hoarsely. "It is nothing...I can crawl to the reeds and hide."

"Hell!" There was consternation and remorse in Gus's explosive exclamation. "I didn't have no idee th' pore cuss was hurt that ways—an' me invitin' him t' hit the trail. He can't travel hisself—that's sartin...an' in a few minnits!...Hell! We gotta do somethin'...'tain't likely that bunch what's comin' will let him go—an' if th' deputy's along with 'em—he'd *have* t' arrest him, regardless...Here, Miss Flame—you an' th' young feller kinda keep a eye on him! I'll be back in a minnit!"

Weaving a little unsteadily on his feet, but nevertheless astonishingly active notwithstanding his recent close call, the old man vanished around the corner of the building. He was back almost immediately, leading the big white horse.

"I seen Baldy nosin' this ways when I was hid back o' the corner jest now," he explained briefly. "I reckon, like me, he ain't got sense enough t' keep outa trouble. Listen, hombre!"—he turned briskly to Pai Lang—"reckon you kin stick on a horse fer a whiles—busted up like you are?"

Pai Lang nodded coldly. "Better perhaps than I could walk. But why trouble? You are breaking the law."

"Hell, yes!" Gus's tone was savage as he tightened the cinches and swiftly unknotted a couple of long leather thongs from behind the saddle. "I reckon I'm compoundin' a conspiracy or aidin' a writ o' have yers corpus or some sich. But I ain't no lawyer an' I dunno whether the law would class ye as a murderer or jest a Chinaman. But I do know that it'd be plumb murder t' let ye go limpin' away here in th' desert with yer timberin' all caved in like it is. Besides, I reckon from that speech o' yourn what I overheard that you're worth a whole lot more alive than dead. It ain't fer you that I'm a doin' this—it's fer th' sake o' the little girl here that I want t' get you back t' yer Yaller Laundryman's Associashn so's you can give 'em th' high sign t' keep their murderin' hands away from her fer th' future. That's why I'm taking a chance on ye. Hold still now, an' between us we'll hoist ye inta th' saddle!"

With a desperate effort, aided by three pairs of arms and fighting back his agony with a will-power that was almost uncanny, Pai Lang mounted. With a few swift loops and knots Gus tied him into the saddle.

"There! I reckon that'll hold ye—even if ye should happen t' faint a bit. An' I've fixed it so's you kin untie yerself easy when ye get there. See that little bald hill over there a piece? There! See?—jest t' th' left o' th' trail t' my place?"

Pai Lang nodded.

"Keep yer eye on it—that's where ye got t' head fer. Right at th' foot o' that hill, jest where th' trail swings round, there's a big lone rock standin' in th' mouth o' a little rocky gully—you kin see it from here if ye look hard."

"I can see it." Pai Lang's eyes had lost some of their cold hardness.

"Well...when ye get there untie yerself an' git off an' give Baldy a clip on th' rump so's he'll light out fer home. Then you crawl up th' gully. Jest behind that big rock a ways you'll find a old prospect tunnel that I druv inta th' side o' the hill once—crawl inta it an' hide. They won't nobody find ye there—an' if ye get thirsty there's a spring o' purty good water a short ways up th' gully. Soon as I get a chance I'll come up there an' do what I kin fer ye, an' I'll find some ways o' gettin' ye down t' old Sam Wing's ranch near Westmorland. He's a countryman o' yours an' a square shooter. I reckon he'll see that you get a doctor an' he'll keep you hid out till you kin travel.

"That's th' best I kin do fer ye. Now beat it! That bunch'll be here in a few minnits, an' bein' excited an' law abidin' they'll probably fill ye full o' holes fust an' arrest ye afterwards. But if ye can manage t' hang onta Baldy an' if ye put a move on ye can make it an' get hid afore they shows up. From where they are they can't see th' trail you'll be a fol-lerin'—this fust spur o' hills hides it. An' by th' time they gets here you ought a be under cover. Now git!"

Pai Lang leaned swiftly and touched Flame's shoulder. For a mo-ment the mask of wolfish cruelty seemed to slip from his face. "Good-bye," he said huskily; "we will never meet again. But I shall not forget. May your life be happy."

The next instant he was gone. Reeling in his seat and clinging desperately to the saddle-horn as the white horse raced away down the trail he vanished among the wind-tossed mesquites. A few seconds later, as the three stood watching, they saw the big horse—sharply white and distinct in the first glow of the sunrise—flash up on the far side of the tules and go galloping up the distant trail. The injured man was still holding gamely to the saddle.

"Oh, Jim!" Flame caught Brandon's hand nervously as her eyes followed the dwindling path of white. "Oh, Jim—do you think he'll make it?"

"You bet your danged boots he'll make it," Gus growled, taking it upon himself to answer. "Th' devil hisself'll see that he makes it—ac-count o' not wantin' a hard-faced cuss like him in hell. I reckon I had oughta plugged him full o' lead. But I kinda figured...."

Thank God you didn't!" Flame said fervently. "He's grateful—and through him maybe this awful blood feud will be stopped forever. Oh, Gus—do you really think that dust down there is uncle and the Davidson bunch? That would mean for sure that uncle got through all right."

With eyes shaded against the rising sun, which was already stab-bing the grey sky with hot shafts of light, the girl studied the swift-approaching dust-cloud anxiously.

"I reckon it's yore uncle an' th' bunch all right, Miss Flame. That's hosses raisin' that dust—an' there wouldn't be no other riders likely t' be comin' this way so hell-bent. I reckon that, as per usual, Davidson's ole flivver ain't percolatin' jest when they needs it most—prob'ly they busted hell outa it comin' back from Brawley—that's why they had t' light out fer here on hosses. They're makin' time too—I reckon they kin see this here- smoke...'Twouldn't be humanly possible fer 'em not to—they's enough of it. Sure seems like th' two o' ye wrecked this old 'dobe purty bad wrastlin' with them Chinese varmints, Miss Flame. A powerful lot o' things must ha' happened in them few minnits whilst I was out there slumberin' with th' angels. An' ye found th' old Cap'n's gold too, seems like."

"It was in the wall," Flame explained breathlessly, as she ran back towards the iron chest and caught up the fluttering papers that lay beside it. "It was hid in the wall—somewhere behind that old cup-board frame, I guess. And when the car hit…" In scattered, snatchy words, she told all that had happened.

"Well, I'll be danged!" As though scarce able to believe the evidence of his senses Gus fumbled at the box and its contents incredulously, picking up a nugget here and there and squinting at them profes-sionally. "Well, I'll be danged! It was Si Slade an' that ole hoss tender, Martinez, what hid this away right 'nuff—same as some folks suspi-cioned. That there Death's Head what was burnt on that frame that was in th' wall was a brand what Si Slade used—there usta be a heavy cupboard built agen that framework, I've heared, where Slade kept his own private stuff.

"But bit by bit, what with some folks pullin' th' boards offen it lookin' fer clues an' others usin' it fer firewood, if plumb vanished years ago—all but th' back-frame. There don't seem t' have been nobody with sense enough t' think o' diggin' inta th' 'dobes behind it. I dunno why, but I never even thot o' such a possibility myself…Seems kinda like th' old Cap'n's ghost sorta pertected that *cache*—pertected it so's it would come t' th' rightful owner.

"In a case like this findin's keepin' I reckon, an' it's yourn, Miss Flame, anyhow. But t' back up your rights there's this here will." He peered judicially at the bunch of time-faded documents that Flame had thrust into his hands. "An' you bein'—as I allows from what you told me a while back—th' rightful heir, it's yourn all th' more. An' th' 'Lucky Ledge'—that's yourn too!…Hell!…we gotta record that pronto—that's if we can locate it from this here map. Gotta be careful too—there mustn't be another soul outside o' yore uncle get wind o' where it is until you've got it all tied up legal. Le's see, now. I wonder jest whereabout it's at."

He thumbed the yellowed old diagram, peering at it intently. "I can't hardly make it out," he complained; "what with th' faded ink an' my ole head achin' fit ter split. No, sir—can't hardly make it out a-tall. This here'd be th' main mountain range, I reckon. An' this"—he traced a grimy finger along another line—"this'd be th' canyon that runs behint yore ranch-house.…Hell!—'cordin't' th' place where he's got marked as 'Lucky Ledge' th' outcrop an' th' old workin' had oughta be right in th' bed o' th' canyon, 'bout a mile an' a half due west o' yore house…But.…Hell!—that must be wrong!…I *know* there ain't nothin' there!—I been over every foot o' that ground an' I ain't never seen nothin' but th' reg'lar scatter o' non-payable color what that crick carries…Must be some mistake. There ain't…An', hell!—there ain't no 'abandoned Indian encampment; many old meal-grinding holes visible in rocks'…He's got that marked right agen where th' mine's supposed to be…But it just ain't there! I been there!…Sumpin's outa kilter with all this….

"Hold on-what's this!…'Side of canyon rises above ledge very high and steep. Big saddleshaped rock on opposite bank'…Say—I've seen that rock!…But th' bank on the other side from it ain't neither high nor steep—it's a long tumbled slope o' boulders…An' below it.…Hell! I got it now—I got it!…

"Looka here, Miss Flame!…See here!" With sudden fierce excitement he thrust the time-stained paper closer towards the eager eyes of Flame and Brandon. "Looka here! You rec'lect what th' banks o' that canyon are like, don't you, Miss Flame—right east o' this little crick that's marked here?…They're plumb rotten—allus slidin' in. Well, th' 'Lucky Ledge' is sitooated right in that section that's li'ble t' bank slides, an'…."

"You think the mine and everything is there?" Flame cut in excitedly. "You think that it's been—"

"Hell! I don't *think* nothin'!" Gus exploded triumphantly. "I know!…An' I know now why th' 'Lucky Ledge' ain't never been found since it was lost…Th' whole bank above it has slid in—a extry big slide o' rocks an' boulders what's buried th' outcrop an' th' old Injin camp an' the' whole danged I shootin' match. It must ha' happened years an' years ago—close up after th' time when th' Cap'n was murdered, an' long afore anyone even thot o' establishin' a ranch in them parts. I rec'lect now—th' canyon bed is plumb choked with rocks at that pint. They's been a awful big rain some time that's brung down the whole side o' th' canyon like a avalanche—or mebbe th' ghost o' th' old Cap'n pushed it in hisself, jest for spite…Anyways, all we gotta do now is t' sink a shaft…Terrible Valley'll be a boomin'…Y' can instal machinery, Miss Flame, an'…."

"*I* won't"—with a sudden weariness Flame cut short his bubbling enthusiasm. "*I* won't instal any machinery! That'll be your job, Gus—you and uncle will have to tackle that. Because, if the mine is there, you're in on it too, you know—equal shares. But I'm through. I—I don't want ever to see Terrible Valley again. I'm—I'm going away… back to New Mexico. Uncle had a ranch there once…the place where I was raised before all this hell started…I was happy there, and I've always dreamed that maybe, some day, I could buy the old place back and…and…maybe—"

"I reckon you can, honey." Old Gus's voice was suddenly full of sympathetic understanding. "They's enough gold in that there box t' give ye quite a good start towards it…an' I reckon th' 'Lucky Ledge' will take care o' th' rest. An' if that there dang Chinee keeps his word—"

"He will," Flame said quietly; "I know he will. Look, Gus!—Look!...'Way up there along the trail—just by that hill where you told him to stop! Isn't that white patch Baldy standing still?...There!—there he goes again!...He's galloping away without anyone on him!"

"Yeh, that's him! Chink done exac'ly like I told him." Gus was shading his eyes with his hand. "I kin see th' varmint crawlin' up among th' rocks. I reckon he won't die—but I reckon, judgin' by th' speed that cloud o' dust back there was a makin', that he's got under cover none too soon. All we gotta do now is t' fergit jest exac'ly how many Chinks they was altogether in th' fust place. I kin take care o' that all right—bein' a born liar—but you an' this young feller want t' remember an' not be drawed into no matheymettical statements while you're restin' up an' settin' round th' Davidson place. Ole Ma Davidson is a powerful talker...an' if it should leak out what we done—helpin' that Chink t' escape...."

"I guess I know how to hold my tongue," Flame said confidently. "There's no danger of me saying anything. And it isn't likely that Jim...."

"I don't aim to stay around, anyway," Brandon cut in. "I'm goin' on to Yuma. And...."

"You're...going...to...do...*what?*" Flame demanded, startled.

"I'm goin' on to Yuma," Brandon said steadily. "I was headed that way to begin with and the quicker I—"

"*Yuma—hell!*" With a sudden flare of hysterical temper that was the reaction of utter exhaustion and shattered nerves Flame flung herself at him; with fingers clutched suddenly into the torn cloth of his shirt she tugged and shook at him furiously. "*Yuma!*" she exploded. "*Yuma!* You got the nerve to say you're going on to Yuma, after last night? After all we've been through? And you'd go to *Yuma?* You'd—"

"But—but, honey," he stammered' stubbornly, "I—I've got to go...I—"

"*Damnation!*" With a darling leap, snatching at the belt which lay on the ground near her, Flame caught up her gun and, forgetful utterly of the fact that the weapon was empty, jabbed it savagely into his ribs. "Try it!" she stormed; "just you try to go and I'll blow the living daylights outa you so quick...Yuma!...Yuma hell!...You're not goin' to Yuma—you're goin' to marry me...an' you're goin' to New Mexico...an'...an'...Oh, Jim!" Her anger collapsed in a choking cry as I she dropped the gun and flung her arms about his neck. "Oh, Jim, you big fool, you! What's got into you?...You're brave as a lion—and yet you haven't got sense enough to know—to know that I—that I—"

"B-but, honey"—he faltered helplessly—"you know it ain't—it ain't right. I'm only a drifter. I—I ain't got a thing!...An' you...An'

now.…An' this here Davidson feller that you're going to marry.…
An'.…"

With a smothered sob that was half laughter, half tears she dragged his face down to hers: "Oh Jim—you big, wonderful fool! I—I knew that was it! I guessed it last night the minute you acted up like you did and wouldn't kiss me. Listen, you big boob!…It's *you*—not what you've got—that counts…See!…And there isn't anything to that Ted Davidson stuff—that's only just family kidding and Gus's teasing… Ted doesn't give a hoot for me, outside of being good friends, and I don't for him…And.…"

There was a sudden thunder of hoofs upon the trail; a blurred roar of noise and voices; and from Gus—who, after stowing the precious map and documents safely away in his pocket, had discreetly retired out of sight around the corner—there came a stentorian bellow:

"Here's yore uncle, Miss Flame…an' th' deputy…an' Ted Davidson…an' th' whole dang outfit!"

But Flame scarcely heard his shout. Almost fiercely, with neither eyes nor thought for the crowding bunch of dust-grimed riders that drew rein suddenly before the smoking ruin, she pulled Brandon's face down closer to hers.

"Jim—you big fool!" she whispered softly. "Kiss me—kiss me quick! I've waited long enough! You're not going away to Yuma and you're not going to leave me—not *ever*—I *know* it!"

…And as his arms tightened about her and his lips met hers hungrily he suddenly knew it also.

THE END

ROBBERY RANGE

by

MARSHAL SOUTH

Originally published in 1943:
    The World's Work (1913) Ltd.
    Kingswood, Surrey
    Great Britain

Printed in Great Britain:
    Windwill Press
    Kingwood, Surrey

ROBBERY
RANG[E]

by

MARSH[ALL]
SO[UTH]

Aut[hor]
"Child[...]"
"Flame of T[...]"
Valley[...]"

A [...]
TH[...]

Spine:
ROBBERY RANGE · MARSHALL SOUTH

Facing page (partial newspaper text, left margin):

[...]s
[...]e

[...]rey
[...]pilot
[...] the
[...]way

[...] Sale
a fifty-
[...]eautiful.
[...]d across

CHAPTER 1

Relics of an Outlaw

It was a mean and dirty little shop on a frowsy, deserted side street. In the night shadows, with its shabby front dim in the murky glow of the infrequent street lights, it looked almost sinister. Rodney Kent, still too recently arrived from the clean, wide spaces of the cattle country to be used to city grime and dinginess, eyed the place a bit suspiciously. But there was no mistake apparently. The shop bore the number he sought and the lettering on the dirty window, illumined by the glow of a dusty light-bulb, was plain enough:

HOLTZHAUSER'S BOOK AND CURIO STORE
ANTIQUES AND LIBRARIES BOUGHT
OPEN EVENINGS

Yes, this was the place, right enough. In the dim light that filtered out from the window Kent glanced once more at the brief little three line ad that he had clipped that afternoon from the columns of the San Diego *Evening Tribune.* Then, without further hesitation—suddenly glad that in his present clothes there was nothing save his suntan to stamp him as a cowboy—he stepped briskly into a dimly-lit interior piled with junk of every description and musty with the smell of ancient, decaying books.

"I've come to look at the stuff you advertised," he said, addressing the tall, cadaverous individual with sour, spectacled eyes and black cloth sleeve protectors who was obviously the proprietor. "—Those Hesfor relics."

"Vell, there they vas—on der counter here!" with almost a resentful snarl the man jerked a hand at the junk-littered central table beside which he stood. "But there vas not many left—nearly all iss sold already yet."

He turned his back sourly. And then, for the first time, Kent saw that he was not alone. Beyond him, half-hidden in the dimness of the ill-lighted shop, was a girl—a girl of about, eighteen, dressed in a dark suit. Another customer evidently—the only other one in the store.

Kent's eyes ran swiftly over the table the sour-faced man had indicated. He was disappointed. From what source the relics here displayed had come the advertisement had not stated. But from a first glance Kent was inclined to think that they were fake. Wolf Hesfor, the outlaw, had been hanged way back in 1860. If the miscellaneous assortment of battered odds and ends that lay here had actually been part of his personal possessions, Kent wondered where they had been during all the intervening years. He had never heard of any such collection before.

"…But—but weren't there any books—any papers?" It was the girl who was speaking. Purposely lowered, but still distinctly audible to Kent's sharp ears, her voice came from the shadows at the other end of the table. "—I tell you I'm not interested in these old pistols and leather things. Weren't there any letters or papers—any books? Those are the things that I collect. Surely there must have been *something* like that?"

"But I tell you, Miss, there vas not. This man Johnson, whose people sell me this collection, vas nod that kind of man. He vas an oldt soldier. He get these things vot vas handed down from relatiffs of his. There vas a Johnson who vas guard in der prison when this tief Hesfor vas hanged. He get these things. Undt he pass them along in der family. Now all are dead who care for them. I tell you there vas no books—no bapers—noddings but an oldt Bible that Hesfor iss given for reading before he iss hanged. It iss nodding vorth—all spoiled mit scribblings and figures. It iss so bad I throw it mit der rubbish oudt."

"*Oh!*" the word was almost a gasp. "Oh—it was something just like that I wanted! I would have bought it! You—you *threw it out?*"

"Veil, berhaps I can look. Maybe der trash man iss not yet come." Stirred very obviously by the sudden notion of possible profit, the vinegar-featured shopkeeper began to betray some interest. "Vait. I vill see."

He hurried away and vanished in the dim, junk-crowded rear of the store.

The girl stood waiting. She was nervous. Kent could see that plainly—and deliberately he affected an intent examination of a rusted old cap-and-ball six-shooter that lay on the table. But he had of a sudden lost interest in the rather mediocre assortment of junk before him. The words that he had not been able to avoid hearing had eclipsed everything else. Who was this girl, he wondered. And what did she so desperately want with books or documents that had belonged to the dead stage coach robber? She was not a book collector, certainly. And she didn't look like the sort who would be interested in morbid relics either. Unquestionably she was an outdoor type. Her skin was tinged with a golden bronze that was a product not of rouge and crafty powder, but of genuine sunlight and wind. And she was distinctly pretty. Her hair and eyes were dark and there was a firmness and decision to her chin and mouth that spoke of character. What would a girl like that want with books or papers of the blood-thirsty Wolf Hesfor, who had been hanged over seventy years ago?

The sour-faced, spectacled man came hurrying back.

"It vas still there," he said, holding out a battered, age-worn little black volume, moldy and with wisps of packing excelsior clinging to it. "I take it from der trash barrel oudt. How much you vill giff?"

"Oh !—" with almost a snatch the girl caught the ragged little book from his hand. "—Oh, let me see it!" Nervously she jerked off the perished rubber band that encircled it and opened the cover. Kent saw her start. For an instant a flash of something like incredulous joy lit her face. But it was only for a fleeting instant that her emotion betrayed itself. With a sharp side glance at Kent she shut the book hastily.

"How much?" she demanded.

"How much you vill giff?" the cadaverous man's sour eyes gleamed greedily behind his glasses.

"Five dollars," the girl said. She unsnapped her purse.

"It vas vorth more," the other hesitated calculatingly. "I vill take ten dollars. That vas der least I could take. It vas—"

"See here!" the girl cut in sharply, "you were going to throw it out! You wouldn't have got a cent! Five dollars is a good price." She held out a note.

The lean-visaged proprietor's eyes narrowed—then lifted suddenly to a sound. Two men had entered the store. He waved the note aside and reached a claw-like hand for the book. "Ten dollars or nodding," he said with sudden determination. "Here comes some odder customers. They giff more maybe."

"Well then, take your ten dollars," the girl said hastily. She shrank back, clutching the book tightly to her, and with a nervous glance at the approaching newcomers snatched another note from her purse. "Here's your money. I can't stand here arguing all night."

But already, as though sensing something, the foremost of the newly-arrived pair had come up with a quick stride. His glance flickered swiftly from the little black book that the girl held to the money that she was extending. His harsh, brusk voice checked the shop owner's greedily reaching hand like an electric shock.

"I'm lookin' fer any books or papers what's in this here Hesfor collection yuh advertised—an' I'm willin' t' pay handsome." His hard, black eyes, roofed under bristling black brows, seemed to snap at the girl as though in challenge. With obvious intent he planted his heavy-set bulk squarely in the aisle. His companion, a bullet-headed man with the face of a thug, pushed closer and flanked him. The girl's way out was blocked. Kent, fumbling and pawing with studied unconcern among the scatter of relics on the table, saw her face whiten suddenly. He edged closer.

"Let me pass, please!" With quick determination the girl flung down the two five-dollar notes on the table, and clutching her book turned swiftly. "Let me pass."

The heavy-set man with the wolf face and beetling eyebrows hunched forward a trifle. He did not budge.

"Vait!...vait!" The storekeeper's voice came in a shrill, hasty cackle. "—Der book!—maybe these chentlemen giff more! Der iss no more books or bapers—just this Vun!"

"Hell!—sure I'll give more'n ten!" the black-browed man's eyes snapped contemptuously from the two notes on the table.

"Make it twenty. I'll take it." He hauled a wad of currency from his pocket.

"I was here first—and I've bought it already." Jerking back from the eager clutch of the lean storeowner's hand as he reached for the book she held, the girl faced him, white-faced but defiant. "It's mine. There's your money. I've paid for it already."

"No! No!—I haf not accepted! Take it back!" He thrust the two notes toward her. "—Dese chentlemen—"

"Then *I'll* give you twenty myself," the girl gasped. Her words were choked and desperate. "Here!" She fumbled swiftly at her purse.

"Thirty!" the wolf-faced newcomer snapped harshly.

"Th-thirty-five." The girl was almost crying. "Here! Here!" She thrust forward a handful of paper money. "Here!—this—this is all I've got! And I want this book. Please!—I was here first!" Her voice was frantic, pleading.

"I reckon I want it too," the black-eyed, wolf-featured man was plainly gloating at her helplessness. "It's worth forty bucks t' me. Here y'are. I reckon it's mine, sister." He began to peel notes from his roll.

Kent decided to take a hand. "I think the book belongs to the young lady," he said quietly. "I'm a witness to the fact that she bargained for it and produced the asked price before you gentlemen attempted to buy it. It's hers by right and law."

"Huh!—an' who th' hell are you?" savagely the black-browed man wheeled on Kent.

"Start something and you'll find out!" Kent snapped. It flashed on him that if he could pull a bluff on these two bullies it would simplify matters considerably.

"Huh!—a dick, eh?" the big man's black brows drew together in a calculating scowl. "Well, this ain't none o' your business. This here book b'longs t'—"

"No! No! He vas nod an officer!" With a shrill, cackling chatter the sour-eyed proprietor recovered from his moment of astonishment. "He vas nod an officer! He vas chust a customer. He come to buy—"

He got no further. On the mad impulse of the moment, nerved by the frantic appeal in the girl's eyes—and warned of danger by a sudden, swift and menacing movement on the part of the thug-faced man who was nearer to him—Kent leaped.

With a smashing, knock-out blow that landed squarely he sent the bullet-headed thug sprawling backwards to the floor, while at the same time, with a terrific kick, he hurled the rickety center table toppling across the shop. As the table whirled crashing, spilling its piled junk in a clattering avalanche into the book bins along the opposite wall, he drove in another sledge-hammer blow that flung the wolf-faced man staggering against the terror-gripped store owner. With a snatch, pulling the girl free in the suddenly-widened floor space, he raced with her towards the door. "Run!" he 'panted. "Beat it! We've got to run for it!"

But she needed no urging. Frightened and gasping, but still clutching tight to the little black book, she darted on winged feet for the entrance door and, with Kent but one jump behind her, gained the sidewalk and dashed for the shelter of a dark alley that led from the next corner. Quick as they were, however, they were not quick enough. Almost as his running feet hit the pavement Kent heard the trampling charge of pursuit. With a bull-like yell of fury the black-browned man came leaping from the shop door and with a slashing swing of a hand that gripped something heavy and hard hurled Kent aside and plunged like a whirlwind after the speeding girl. Of his partner, the bullet-headed thug, there was no sign. Evidently he had been knocked completely out.

∽

CHAPTER 2

"Run! Don't Argue! Run!"

Dazed only for a split-second by the impact of the heavy six-shooter, which had struck him a glancing blow across the head, Kent tore after his hulking assailant. The wolf-faced man, almost in two jumps, had overtaken the girl and with a brutal snatch and a menacing flourish of his pistol had wrenched the little book from her grasp. Kent heard her wild, frightened scream. But the sound of it was blurred in his ears for, almost at the same instant, as the bully swung round to make off, he hurled himself upon him, fastening a clutching grip on the gun and driving with his other hand a smashing blow at the jaw. The big man staggered and reeled back with a gasped oath. The age-molded little volume jerked from his grip and went whirling across the pavement, shedding its decaying cover and landing in the gutter in a scatter of fluttering leaves.

"Run! Run!" breathlessly, as the girl sprang to recover the torn book, Kent shouted at her. "Run!" With no time for the niceness of ring etiquette he followed up his temporary advantage with a lusty kick and another trip-hammer upper-cut which, as he wrenched the heavy gun free from the ham-like hand, drove the black-browed bully against the wall. "Run!" he yelled again. "Run! Beat it quick! I'll 'tend to this bird!" He jabbed the captured six-gun savagely at its former owner. "Reach high, feller!" he snapped. "Reach high—and stand right there!"

"But you ?—But you?" Pantingly, as she sprang back from the curb edge, the ragged remnants of the little black book clutched in a disordered bunch in her hands, the girl's words came in a gasp. "What'll you do? I've got a car down here. But you—"

"*Beat it! Beat it!*" he shouted at her almost savagely. "I know this place. I'll get away all right! Don't argue! *Run!*"

And indeed there was scant time for argument. People were coming. Running feet sounded on the sidewalk. Somewhere a police whistle blew. From the door of the little curio shop a lean, spectacled figure suddenly spilled out into the dimly-lit street and plunged yelling towards them. The girl hesitated no longer. "Oh—but thank you!... thank you!" she gasped. "I—I—"

She turned and ran—ran like a deer, darting down the darkness of the side lane. Kent whirled, lunging with sudden menace at the cursing ruffian before him. "Now, beat it back there, you coyote!" he snapped, jerking his head towards the shop and its onrushing, yelping owner. "Pronto now! Hoof it!"

He clenched the order with a shot that ripped dust and chips from the brick wall behind. The bully needed no second urging. With a gasped curse he swung about and fled, crashing into the lean shop owner who, at the report of the gun, had turned tail with a yell and bolted for the shelter of his store. From up and down the pavement came a chorus of startled cries and the noise of feet swinging hastily about and stampeding in frantic flight. In a twinkling, it seemed the dim street was deserted.

Kent wheeled and darted for safety. Across from him was the dark mouth of another narrow lane, black in the dense shadow of a drooping pepper tree. He jumped towards it. But as he sprang across the dusty roadway a flutter of paper almost at his feet caught his eye. Part of the little book probably, he guessed—something that the girl had missed. On the impulse he snatched it up and, abandoning his intended line of flight, darted about and raced down the dark side alley where she had gone.

But he was too late. Even as he turned into it he heard, from further down the alley, the protesting roar of a suddenly wide-open Ford engine. Through the pale glow of a street light on the further intersection a battered little model T. roadster fled suddenly and swung around the corner. The girl had made a clean get-away.

ᗧ

CHAPTER 3

A Sheet of Yellowed Paper

With a queer sense of chagrin that he had missed her, but with his own safety now to think of, Kent stuffed the bit of tattered paper into his pocket and ran—doubling down a branch alley that led past a high fence and a huddle of Chinese quarters. For a moment his eyes darted about for a good place to throw the six-gun he still held. But, on a second impulse, he decided to keep it as a souvenir, and thrust it to safe hiding inside his shirt.

He ran on. There was quite a racket back in the street he had left— the noise now augmented by the swiftly approaching scream of a police siren. But the alley he traversed was silent as the grave and the hubbub was fast dwindling behind him. There were no indications of pursuit. He slackened his pace presently, straightened his coat and tie, adjusted his cap and sauntered nonchalantly out into a quiet but well-lit street. A policeman stood under the lamp at the next intersection, evidently listening. "What's the row?" Kent queried, innocently pausing.

The patrolman shrugged. "I dunno. A fire or a drunk or something. Was that a shot just now?"

"Search me," Kent said. "It sounded like one, but it might have been some car or truck backfiring. I guess it wasn't much. Seems to have all hushed up again."

He strolled on, fished in his pocket for a cigarette and made his way up-town toward Broadway. But for all his careless exterior his mind was moving fast and his heart was thumping. He had set out that evening in the hope merely of perhaps picking up an interesting souvenir of a bandit who, in the late Fifties, had terrorized the old coaching routes. And instead he had blundered head first into something that had held all the elements of a perplexing mystery—an adventure, too, that might well have ended by placing him behind the bars. He wondered what it was all about. Who had the mysterious girl been? And who was the wolf-faced man who had seemed viciously determined that she should not gain possession of the ancient little Bible that had once served the supposed purpose of easing the villainous Hesfor's hours before execution? Neither the girl nor the man were book collectors—of this much he felt positive. What then was it all about? Curiously, with a swift glance up and down the street to see that he was not observed, he drew out a small tattered sheet of yellowed folded paper that he had picked up at the scene of the scuffle, and opened it beneath the glow of a street lamp.

And then, of a sudden, he started—started violently, while his staring eyes, steadying all at once to the lines of faint, faded scrawl upon the time-stained sheet, widened in incredulous astonishment. All at once he *knew*. He knew now why the girl had wanted the book—knew also why the black-browed, wolf-faced man and his thug-visaged partner had wanted it. That little book had held the key—the key to the buried and never discovered loot of Hesfor's last—and biggest—robbery. Both the girl and the black-browed ruffian had in some way known that the decaying little Bible had held the clue—a clue which, by the mocking irony of fate, neither of them had succeeded in getting. For the clue had been written on this yellowed sheet of paper—this folded sheet, which had slipped from between the scattered leaves, and which the girl had failed to pick up.

Startled, Kent stared at it. His heart was suddenly thumping again violently—the scrawled, dim lines of handwriting seemed to writhe and jumble together in the lamplight. He swallowed hard. With sudden briskness, his pulse wildly pounding, he stowed the yellowed scrap carefully away in an inner pocket and headed swiftly for his lodgings.

∽

CHAPTER 4

Kent Makes a Decision

When he called for his key at the desk of the cheap but clean little hotel where he roomed, Kent found that he had a letter waiting for him. One glance at the envelope told him that it was from El Paso—from a big cattle company to whom he had written regarding a job. He had been eagerly awaiting an answer for days. Now, however, his mind was full of something else. He went up to his room and, tossing the unopened letter indifferently on the table, sat down to study the queer scrap of faded yellow paper that had come so strangely into his possession.

And a second and more careful scrutiny did nothing to lessen his excitement. Whether the rest of the Hesfor relics had been fakes or not, he felt absolutely convinced that this scrap of worn and ragged paper was genuine. He had seen once, in a Los Angeles museum, a letter that had been written by Wolf Hesfor, and the style of the peculiar angular script had impressed itself on his mind. There was no doubt whatever that the writing now before him was actually Hesfor's. Even had it not been for the odd fact that the message on the sheet was in the form of verse—a peculiar habit that had distinguished not only Wolf Hesfor but also "Black Bart," another early-day California coach robber—Kent would have been willing to wager his life that the scrawl was genuine.

Again and again he scanned the queer rhymed lines—reading them over and over while his pulse pounded with excitement:

> *"Flowers on the cactus. Bones on the sand.*
> *Gold in the reach of the dead man's hand.*

Black in the shadows. White in the sun.
Death stands guard with a dead man's gun.

Over the catclaw. Under the cave.
When you find it, fool, you'll have found your grave.
"S4."

Kent continued to study the thing as though fascinated. Even as poetry it wasn't bad—and that was another proof of its genuineness. Wolf Hesfor had been a well-educated ruffian. He had been no illiterate cut-throat. His career of crime had been distinguished not alone for cold-blooded and merciless cruelty, but also for brains and careful planning. His odd way of writing his signature as "S4" was also characteristic. It was an unmistakable brand. More than once it had been found slashed with a knife-point on the foreheads of slain men—marking that particular victim as a man against whom Hesfor had nursed an especial grudge.

A long time Kent sat staring at the paper. Meaningless though the lines would have been to most people, to him they carried a distinct clue. He had made a hobby of reading up on the careers of Western outlaws. Down in a San Diego storage warehouse, together with some boxes of books, his saddles and riding gear and a collection of mineral specimens, he had a trunk that was crammed with odds and ends that were relics from half a hundred old-time road agents. He happened to know many events in the history of Hesfor's depredations. He knew, too, as the result of several prospecting trips, a good deal about the desert section of San Diego County that had been Hesfor's particular territory and hide-out. And from this knowledge of the ground he jumped instantly to the conclusion that the words "the dead man's hand" referred not to the actual hand of a dead man but to a weird and sinister hand-shaped rock that stood on the rim of a desolate and almost inaccessible canyon, situated on the borders of the old-time Robbery Range cattle outfit, in the lone and barren Vallecitos Mountains. Rumor had been rife that Hesfor had cached much loot out in the desert. But the popularly believed stories had always placed its location as somewhere in the lower badlands or along the foot-slopes of Coyote Peak. The scrawled lines on this yellowed paper were the first hint that Kent had ever come across that pointed to a hiding-place that was in exactly the opposite direction. It was no wonder, he realized, that scores of search-parties had hunted for the Hesfor loot in vain.

But Kent saw clearly enough that though the paper gave him a definite clue, he was still far from knowing the whole secret. He sensed well enough that there was a wealth of meaning in those cryptic lines of verse—meaning that held mockery as well as sinister threat. Again and again, as he strove to recall to his memory every detail of the desolate little canyon into which he had penetrated more than two years ago, he re-read the line:

"Over the catclaw. Under the cave."

His brows drew together in thought. Yes, when he had been there he had noticed a sort of cave near that gruesome-looking hand-shaped rock. And there certainly had been lots of catclaw growing close by— he recalled sharply enough the vicious thorns that had torn at him as he pushed through it. But the lines about the "dead man's gun" and the "grave" were puzzling and sinister. In spite of himself he could not repress an odd, chill feeling. He remembered that, sure enough, there *had* been a scatter of old sun-bleached human bones and part of a skull lying on the sand at one point of the little canyon bed. Altogether the canyon had been an eerie sort of place—made somehow more lone and ghostly by the crumbling ruin of an ancient adobe hut and traces of old-time mining operations. The towering walls of the gorge and the sullen look of the grey rocks had depressed him, Kent remembered, and he had got out in a hurry. Later he had not been surprised to learn from old Jeff Crossman, the eccentric hermit-like cattleman and miner, who was the present lessee of the old Robbery Range property, that the little canyon was supposed to be haunted; that according to legend the old-time miner who, in the early Fifties, had built the hut and driven the tunnel into the canyon side had been murdered.

But, save for the conviction it gave him that he knew now the general locality where the Hesfor loot was buried, Kent wasted little time on back memories of the lonely little mountain canyon. The burning point in his mind now was the connection which the mysterious girl and the two men had had with this scrawled clue that had been hidden in the little Bible. The men had displayed all the ear-marks of bullying ruffians. But the girl had been different. If he had stopped to analyze his feelings Kent might have admitted that it was the girl who had gripped his interest far more than the treasure. She wasn't just an ordinary girl, he told himself. Certainly, in character, she and the wolf-faced man had seemed as far apart as the poles.

Puzzling, hoping to get some hint that would help him, Kent picked up the heavy six-shooter that he had captured in the fight. He had tossed it on the bed when he had entered the room. Now he examined it closely. It was a thoroughly modern double-action Colt .45. But, barring a small W.H. crudely cut with a file on the under side of the trigger-guard, there was nothing about it that told him anything of the owner. With a shrug and but a brief second glance at the roughly cut letters, he laid the weapon aside again. A man who would scratch his initials on his gun, he reflected, had either nothing to fear from the law or else belonged to that particular class of cock-sure ruffians whose egotism eclipsed their caution.

Baffled in the hope of getting a clue from the gun, Kent turned back to the yellowed paper. That paper rightfully belonged to the girl, he realized. She had paid for it—had, in fact, been shamefully robbed in her purchase of it. Clearly it was his duty to return it. But how? He did not even know her name. To advertise would almost certainly result in the advertisement being seen by one or other of the ruffians from whom she had escaped, and to return to the little book store in quest of information was not to be thought of. Besides, it was almost certain that the sour-eyed, cadaverous store proprietor knew no more of the girl than he did himself.

"I'll bet," Kent reflected, half aloud, "she's hot footing it back to the desert, right now. She looked like a girl that's used to living out in the open. And the little old car she was driving seemed as though it was all sun-blistered and battered up. Bet that's where she lives."

He ran a hand through his thick brown hair, his grey eyes perplexed and thoughtful. It came to him that the girl probably had no notion that an important part of the clue had been lost to her. It was quite possible that she hadn't known of the existence of the folded sheet of paper that had been between the pages of the little book. All she had looked at, when she had opened the old volume, had been the inside cover and the fly-leaf. And in the swift glance that he had taken, Kent had seen figures there—figures and lines of writing. And he recalled now, with something like a start, that he had seen a sort of sketch which then he had made little of. Now, with the clue of the verses to give him the hint, he realized that it had been a crude drawing of a hand.

"And I'll bet she knows the desert and all about where that hand-shaped rock is," Kent reflected. "She knows what she's about all right. She's most likely been working on this for a long while—and she's probably got a hunch, anyhow. And now she thinks she's got the whole secret. And the chances are a hundred to one that she's heading back, straight for that very canyon, right now. She wouldn't be likely to waste any time—not after the way those bozos acted tonight."

He picked up the paper again and read the verse through once more. Again, in fancy, the face of the girl in the dim-lit shop rose before him and somehow, with the memory of her standing in clear-cut distinctness upon his mind, the last line of Hesfor's verses struck him with a queer, cold chill. There was something sinister about that Dead Man's Hand Canyon, anyway. And in her ignorance, failing perhaps the very hint that this paper gave, there was no telling what the girl might run into.

"There's only one way," Kent said to himself uneasily. "I've got to take a chance and follow her."

He rumpled his hair once more, frowning and worrying. Then, with a quick, nervous motion, reaching for the unopened letter that still lay on the table, he ripped the envelope open and straightened out the crisp folded sheet it contained. It proved to be just what he expected and his eye flicked over it swiftly, catching words and phrases.

"…Your age, twenty-seven, is about right, and in view of the fact that you have had considerable experience as top-hand and foreman… We have an opening on one of our cattle properties in the State of Chihuahua, Mexico…The position carries a salary of $150 gold per month and the Company furnishes board and living quarters… Contract for two years…Wire immediately if you accept, and come to El Paso by first possible train."

Kent frowned again, and let the letter fall from his fingers. Here was a chance for which he had waited a long time—a connection with a big cattle outfit in Mexico, a company with which perhaps he might establish a permanent position. One hundred fifty dollars per month clear. The promise of a two-years' job. Chances like that did not come every day. He had been out of a position a considerable time. His cash had dwindled down now to exactly sixty-five dollars and eighteen cents. This job came as a saving hand. There was no time to quibble. He must accept or reject at once. And if he turned this down it was pretty certain that he would never get another offer from the same company.

He just had to accept it, he told himself, nervously pacing up and down the little room. All this stuff about the Hesfor treasure that he had stumbled on to was probably fake and a hoax…a false alarm as all the many "clues" that others had worked on in the past had been. And, anyhow, this girl was nothing to him…Besides, that was all rot about her running into any particular danger. That sinister last line of the verse on the old paper was bluff, anyhow—a lot of bunk. The devil with the treasure!…And let the girl look after herself. He'd try to send her the paper some other way. He didn't have to throw up a good job— a splendid opportunity—just for a wild goose chase…And, anyhow—

He scowled, hesitating. And then, with sudden decision, his mind was made up. With a quick stride he crossed the room and jerked the telephone receiver from its hook.

"Give me Western Union," he said crisply to the drowsy voice at the hotel switchboard. "I want to send a telegram." And a few moments later he was dictating it:

J. C. Rogers,
Texas & International Cattle Co., Inc.,
El Paso, Texas.
　　　Regret cannot accept offer. Stop. Leaving for
　　　desert in morning on urgent personal business.
　　　Stop. Will write on return.
　　　　　Rodney Kent.

A Model A Ford in Box Canyon (used with permission California State Parks

CHAPTER 5

Into the Desert

L ate afternoon of the day following found Kent far out in the weird grey solitudes of the silent desert. He had lost no time. Once his mind had been made up he had acted with a brisk swiftness that was characteristic of him. Early that morning, with the friendly co-operation of an acquaintance who worked in a second-hand auto yard, he had invested fifty dollars of his capital in a battered-looking but reputedly sturdy old model T Ford. It was a machine that had been stripped down to the barest essentials and as such promised, despite its junk-pile appearance, to give good service over the rough, sand-drifted country that Kent knew he would have to traverse. The purchase of it gave him no pleasure. By nature an ardent lover of horse-flesh, Kent had a hearty aversion to all gasoline-burning mechanical contraptions. But this time he realized he had no choice. No horse, however good, could get him to his destination fast enough. For now—now that his mind was made up, he was of a sudden desperately anxious to find out if the mysterious girl whom he had met in the bookshop had re-ally headed, as his hunch told him, for the ominous little canyon of Dead Man's Hand. With the few dollars of his capital left over from the purchase of the machine he had therefore filled up on gas and with a gallon can of oil, a five-gallon container of water and two five-gallon cans of extra gasoline lashed firmly down in the car as a precaution against emergencies, had driven his time-battered auto out of the city and headed eastward across the mountains. Stowed away inside his shirt was the heavy Colt pistol that he had taken from the hulking, black-browed bully of the night before, while on the seat beside him were a hundred rounds of extra ammunition which he had hastily pur-chased at a sporting goods store. It might all be a piece of foolishness, he told himself. But there was no telling. He didn't quite know what he was heading into. But if the actions of the pair with whom he had tussled the previous evening were anything to go by, there was no sense in taking chances.

And now, with the mountains passed, with the day already far spent, and with the grey reaches of the desert greasewood all about him, Kent, despite the weight of weariness from his long drive, felt his sense of apprehensive excitement steadily mounting. Perhaps it was the desert, he told himself uneasily, as, clinging desperately to the steering-wheel, he guided the jouncing, panting car over the dim, sand-drifted apology for a trail. Perhaps it was the long, sinister shadows which the sinking sun was flinging eastward from the towering mountain rampart on his left. Perhaps it was the hazy, voiceless vastness of the great grey stretch of desolation that swept away from him on every side. Perhaps it was all this—perhaps it was just his own imagination. But somehow over everything there seemed to hang a brooding, sinister ominousness. He was conscious of a feeling of uneasy foreboding which he could not shake off. Thunder-clouds were gathering along the mountain tops to the westward. Probably, he told himself, in excuse, it was just the electric atmosphere of the prospective storm that had unsettled his nerves.

The glow of the afternoon sun was already dulling towards evening when, rounding a dense clump of yuccas, he came suddenly upon the sun-blistered shack of "Chink" Halloran—a dreary, unkempt shanty which, suddenly, he remembered from his previous prospecting trip. On the impulse he stopped the car and got out. "Chink" Halloran was a desert rat of more than doubtful reputation, whose "mining" operations were declared to consist chiefly of smuggling Chinese across the International Line. But his shack was right beside the trail. If the girl had passed that way Chink Halloran would certainly have seen her. He might, Kent reflected, be able to give some information.

But the red-bearded, slovenly figure, of which Kent all at once recalled a memory, did not appear in response to his knock. Instead the carelessly latched shanty door swung open, revealing a one-room sordidly furnished interior that held no human occupant. That the shanty still had Chink Halloran for its tenant was plain enough from a new grub-box crudely but recently lettered with his name, and from the scatter of tin cups and plates and the remnants of a recent meal which littered the dirty table-top. In the open fireplace fag ends of mesquite roots smoked faintly. But the place was deserted. It was evident enough that Chink Halloran was not at home.

At the moment, however, it was not the realization that the sordid little shack was untenanted which struck Kent so much as the very evident fact that its unsavory, red-bearded owner had recently been entertaining company. The dirty, rough-boarded table bore witness of that. From the array of tin cups, plates and knives and forks it was plain that four persons had sat there to eat. Moved by a sudden impulse which he could not quite have explained, Kent stepped into the earth-floored shanty to examine the table more closely.

But a more careful inspection told him nothing save that the four persons who had eaten there had all been men and that they had apparently left the cabin only a few minutes ago. The first of these facts he learned from a glance at the foot-marks on the earth floor and the second from the hot coffee which still remained in the battered coffee-pot. Without wasting further time he turned away, and closing the shack door returned to his car. As he climbed into the seat, however, he noticed something else—the recent tracks of a big automobile. Judging from the deeply-rutted traces in the sand the machine had stood parked for a time before the shack door and had then headed off up the trail in the same direction as he himself was bound.

With sudden energy, and conscious all at once of a queer apprehensive chill, Kent stepped on the starter and swung his battered, protesting little car hastily along the tracks of the heavy machine that had preceded him. For some reason he felt oddly startled and worried. Coupled with the evidence supplied by the uncleared table in the shack, those big car tracks seemed all at once strangely suggestive and sinister. All foolish, of course, he told himself uneasily. It was probably just a hunting or prospecting party—men who were acquaintances of Chink Halloran and had stopped off for a few minutes, eaten a meal at his shack and then taken him along with them. There was no cause to attach any significance to the fact that they were headed up along the Robbery Range trail. Might be friends even of old Jeff Crossman, cattlemen or prospectors who were driving up to pay the old man a visit. There wasn't any need to get all worked up over things. Lots of cars, and big ones too, came out here into the desert. He was just keyed up over nothing, that was all.

But even as he argued thus against his steadily mounting uneasiness, Kent knew well enough that his excuses were a bit flimsy. In the first place Chink Halloran's acquaintances were likely to be cut out of the same ruffianly cloth as Chink himself—and in the second there was no love lost between Chink Halloran and old Jeff Crossman. Crossman hated the ruffianly, desert rat Border smuggler. He had told Kent as much. In fact, at the time of Kent's previous visit, the eccentric but sterling old hermit had stated bluntly that if Chink Halloran ever had the nerve to show up on his range he would shoot him like a dog. Scarcely likely, then, that Chink or any of his acquaintances would be heading up to pay Jeff a friendly visit. Yet that apparently was where they *were* going—because this latter section of the trail was exclusively Crossman's. It went nowhere else and came to a dead end at his shack. And plainly enough, from the evidence of its wheel-marks—deep sunk above all lighter tracks—the big car had passed up along it. Oh well, friends of Jeff Crossman's perhaps. But then Crossman had almost no friends. And would friends of his be friends of Halloran also?

South's ink sketch "Desert Shack"

∽

CHAPTER 6

Murder

Feverishly, in the steadily waning light, Kent drove on, his eyes searching the sandy trail now for some hint that would bear out his hunch
that the girl whom he had met in the bookstore had also driven
her machine over this route ahead of him. But the rutty little desert
roadway refused to answer his question. There were other car-tracks
on the trail, it was true—light car-tracks of uncertain age which the
traces of the bigger machine had all but obliterated. But these tracks
told nothing. Jeff Crossman, too, had a battered little Ford in which he
made his infrequent trips to EI Centro or San Diego for supplies. The
smaller tracks in the sand might be his.

The afternoon was almost dead. And presently, just as Kent
rounded the curve where the ancient but now impassable road to
the original Robbery Range ranch-house branched off to the left, the
sun went down in a blaze of glory among the storm-clouds that were
massing along the summits of the western sierras. Blue shadows filled
the vast bowl-like valley in which the crumbling, dimly discernible
ruin of the old ranch-house lay. It had long since been deserted, Jeff
Crossman, when he had leased the property, having preferred to make
his headquarters farther to the north, in a little cabin which he had
built away up in the spurs of the barren desert mountains into which
Kent was now heading. The change of location was one which only
an eccentric old man who loved solitude would have made. Skirting
now the shoulders of the hills and with the broad wide valley with
its crumbling old adobe ruin below him, Kent found it a bit hard to
understand why Crossman had not built his shack at least somewhere
near the old location.

But, still a prey to the odd fever of uneasiness that had taken hold of him, Kent found time for little more than a passing thought on Crossman's eccentricities. The trail, winding now into the heart of the Vallecito Mountains, was rocky and steep and at times taxed both his driving skill and the power of his little car to the uttermost. The greasewood of the lower desert had been replaced by cactus and a sprinkling of junipers. Long-wanded ocotillos, green with new leaf and tipped with the flame of scarlet flowers, swayed beside the wheel-ruts, and here and there the curved thorns of a close-bunched catclaw whipped viciously at the car as it brushed past. Evening had closed down. Dim mists of grey and purple were filling the rock-walled canyons and sink-like little valleys with a haze of ghostly shadows through which, here and there, rough-coated grazing cattle, singly or in isolated little bunches, looked like dim, slow-moving phantoms. But there were not many cattle. Extensive as the Robbery Range territory was, Jeff Crossman, who now leased the run-down property for a song, ran it in only a small way, employing no help and keeping no more stock than he could attend to himself. Mostly the wild trail that Kent now followed was as utterly devoid of animal as it was of human presence. A lone, grim trail, Kent reflected—a fit setting for deeds of murder and violence. Was it possible after all that the girl he had aided the previous night had headed out this way as his hunch had told him? And the other car, the one that had pulled out from Chink Halloran's shack? What was that doing here? He had had no glimpse or sound of it, but he knew for certain that it was still ahead of him. Plain enough, in every patch of soft earth or sand, the marks of its heavy tires stood out distinctly in the evening shadows.

And then, of a sudden, as he jounced breathlessly down across a stony creek bottom and sent his sputtering little machine at the steep grade beyond, Kent had even his forebodings and uneasiness swept for the moment from his mind. For all at once his laboring engine leaped to life with a furious racing roar while abruptly, at the same moment, the car slowed. Losing way almost instantly on the steep slope the machine, still with racing engine, stopped dead and then began to slide swiftly backwards down the grade.

Like a flash, realizing from instant, instinctive pressure that the foot-brake no longer worked and that the car was out of control, Kent cut the motor and swung the steering-wheel hard over. With a lurching crash, its momentum scarcely checked by the emergency brake which he had jammed on at the same instant, the car swerved rear end first into the steep bank at the left and came to a dead, lifeless halt.

Hastily, thankful enough that his quick action had resulted in the car crashing into the hill-side instead of toppling over the fifty-foot drop on the other side of the narrow trail, Kent climbed out. A few experiments, however, convinced him that the first thought that had leaped to his mind had been the correct one. The car had stripped its drive-shaft pinion. Its engine still roared merrily at his will. But the car itself remained immovable despite all coaxing. As far as a means of transportation went, it was utterly and hopelessly dead..

Bleakly, knowing well enough that without help he could do nothing with the machine, Kent unwrapped his package of pistol cartridges, stowed the two fifty-round boxes away in his pants pockets and headed up the trail on foot. It couldn't be more than two or two-and-a-half miles to Crossman's shack, he reflected. Lucky the machine had hung out thus far. Had the mishap occurred away back in the open desert it would have been much worse.

Walking briskly he presently topped the rise and saw that his estimate of the distance had been approximately correct. Dead ahead of him, across a narrow valley, the dark dump of rocks and trees that marked the site of the little spring where Jeff Crossman's shack was located stood out in dim but unmistakable outline against the steep grey lift of the towering, shadow-wrapped cliffs and ridges that rose directly behind. A moment held by the weird wildness of the scene, Kent stood gazing across the valley, his eyes instinctively seeking out the darker, thread-like gash which, behind Crossman's place and a little to the left of it, cut into the grim ramparts of Piñon Peak. That black shadow-filled gash was the mouth of the wild gorge that led back into the glim little canyon of Dead Man's Hand—the canyon where, as he now believed, Wolf Hesfor had cached his treasure. A wild and desolate enough setting, anyway. The great black shadows of the massing storm clouds to the west were fast blotting the remaining light of evening. A thin rustle of wind moaned suddenly up the valley and struck Kent with a quick chill. Hastily tightening his belt and settling his hat more firmly on his head, he struck off with increased pace towards his goal.

The walk, however, proved longer and harder than the seeming nearness of the cabin had led him to expect. The tramping, especially when he had crossed the dry wash and begun to ascend the opposite slope, was hard and rough. Twilight had faded almost to darkness by the time he reached the outskirts of the straggle of cottonwoods that fringed Crossman's shack and spring.

There was no light in the cabin—at least none that Kent, peering ahead through the intervening tree shadows, could discern. But it was still comparatively early, he reflected. Old Jeff was probably puttering about the barn or corral tending his three saddle-horses and few chickens. Or he was more probably sitting outside on the bench smoking and talking to the occupants of the big car, which must long since have arrived.

Quickly, but with suddenly cautious steps as he remembered the heavy machine that had preceded him, Kent began to pick his way through the shadowy scatter of cottonwoods that rimmed the little spring. The spring was lower down than the house. He could save time by taking a short cut instead of following the trail.

And then, suddenly, as he came around the comer of the big rock that stood close by the dark little pool, Kent saw that neither of his guesses as to Crossman's whereabouts had been correct. Old Jeff had come down to the spring for his evening pail of water. And apparently the sound of approaching footsteps had already caught his sharp ears, for, with his battered old galvanized bucket already set at the water's edge, he had straightened and stood peering across the pool in Kent's direction.

"Evening" Jeff!"—suddenly grateful for this chance opportunity to have a private word with the old cattleman, Kent swerved his steps towards the peering figure. "It's me—Rod—Rodney Kent. My car broke down away back on the road. So I had to come in afoot. How's everything? An'—"

He stopped—stopped short, halted in his tracks by a queer sense of sudden fear that strangled even his purposely lowered voice in his throat. A moment, held by a chill clutch of uncanny terror, he stood irresolute, staring at the silent, suddenly ominous figure that had neither spoken nor moved. Then, mastering himself with an effort, he stepped forward and touched it—touched it, only to recoil on the instant, a startled gasp of horror breaking from his lips.

Old Jeff Crossman was dead. Dead and cold and stiff, with his battered old water-pail gleaming palely on the edge of the dark pool at his feet, he was standing against the slender trunk of a young cottonwood and peering with glazed, unseeing eyes into the weaving shadows. And around his throat, its strangling silken strand deep sunk into the sun-tanned flesh, was twisted tightly a woman's stocking.

༄

CHAPTER 7

Silent Shadows

For perhaps the space of a dozen seconds, his mind stunned by his gruesome discovery, Kent stood there in the ghostly whispering shadows, staring in incredulous horror at the rigid, erect corpse of the old cattleman. The startling suddenness with which he had come upon this ghastly evidence of cold-blooded murder had for the moment unnerved him. Dead! Sterling old Jeff Crossman dead! Standing there dead and cold and sightless in a ghastly travesty of life. Jeff Crossman dead! Murdered!—and by a *woman*....

It was this last thought—the thought of that deadly strand of feminine silk—which of a sudden roused Kent as by an electric shock. A woman!—a woman's stocking!...God!...did that mean that the girl whom he had befriended in the bookstore had had something to do with it? Had it been *her* hands which had wrenched tight that strangling cord? Jeff was old and comparatively feeble, and she was an active, athletic girl. Was it possible that after all...

Feverishly, gripped all at once by a sudden frenzy of suspicion that for the moment blotted caution and the thought of possible personal danger, Kent dragged out the tiny flashlight that he always carried in his pocket and began a swift examination. Yes, it was a silk stocking all right—a stocking of a sort that might easily have belonged to the girl he had met. Dark brown in color, the deadly silken twist of it encircled both the old man's neck and the slender trunk of the young cottonwood against which he stood. It had been wrenched tight and knotted securely at the back of the tree. It was this vise-like strangling tie that held the body erect against the tree trunk. Kent was unable to determine whether the old man had been surprised while he had leaned against the tree or whether he had been stunned or strangled first and then trussed up in this gruesome position and left to die. On this score there was no definite evidence. But in the soft ground near the water edge and at one side of the base of the cottonwood were the distinct prints of a girl's shoes.

Shaken and horrified, scarce able to believe his eyes, Kent stared at the tell-tale tracks that the tiny flash-beam revealed. The thing they shouted to the world was obvious. But, sick with the gruesome real-ization of their damning evidence and the ghastly way in which they wrecked all his illusions, he continued to search around for further traces that might in some desperate way reverse the awful conclusion to which the stocking and footprints forced him. But search as he would, he could find no further signs. With the exception of the small patch of soft earth near the water edge and to one side of the tree base, most of the surrounding territory was rocky—a dry creek bed, floored with flat, water-worn, granite rocks, in the gaping cracks between which the cottonwoods had thrust their roots. A score of persons might have wrestled and fought here without leaving traces. If the girl had had accomplices, which he was now inclined to doubt, he could find no tracks of them.

Sick at heart, but fired now with a slowly mounting fury that was of a sudden tempered by stealthy caution, Kent snapped out the little flashlight and, treading stealthily, began to pick his way up the tree-dotted creek bed in the direction of the cabin.

Everything, save for the faint rustle of the wind among the trees and rocks, was silent. No sound of voice or movement broke the shadowy gloom as, treading cautiously between the boulders and cottonwoods, Kent came presently within view of the house. Dark and apparently deserted, the rough little boarded cabin, over-topped by the greater bulk of the barn that stood behind it, loomed silent and ghostly in the dimness. Even from his first glimpse some inner sense told Kent that the shadowy buildings harbored no human presence, but he did not permit that conviction to relax his caution. Stealthily, pistol in hand and peering keenly ahead into the grey obscurity, he skirted the house and came around into the little open stretch of yard which lay between the cabin and the barn. And here, behind the sheltering trunk of a cot-tonwood, he stopped short, his heart of a sudden pounding violently. For just ahead of him, bulking huge and black in the dimness, was parked a big automobile—a long, powerful car that seemed as utterly deserted as the buildings.

Cautiously feeling his way step by step and in taut-keyed readiness to meet any surprise, Kent moved forward in stealthy exploration. A few minutes of careful maneuvering, however, served to assure him that his surmise had been correct. The big closed car concealed no occupants. He did not dare yet to light his flash, but by peering and feeling he discovered that the machine bore Arizona license plates.

Satisfied that from the car at any rate he had nothing to fear, Kent turned his attention to the cabin. The door, under the shadow of the rough little porch, stood open and the interior was as silent as the grave. After a cautious interval of strained listening and the unresultant experiment of pitching a couple of pebbles into the cavern-like blackness, he moved close to the dark doorway and with his flash held low, shot a beam of light for an instant into the one-room building.

But the simple little shack that had served Jeff Crossman for a home sheltered now nothing in human shape. Like the car, it was deserted, but unlike the car, it had been systematically ransacked. Even the first gleam of his light, which satisfied Kent that no danger lurked within, was sufficient also to reveal in startling fashion its wrecked interior. Blankets strewed the floor; boxes had been emptied; shelves had been broken down and the articles they had held scattered. The little cupboards that had held old Jeff Crossman's books and his treasured mineral collections had been wrenched from the wall and their contents dumped in tumbled confusion over the floor and table. Even at first glance it was plain enough that ruthless searchers, in quest of something, had gone through the place from end to end.

In his present keyed state, however, his nerves taut against more deadly surprises, the ransacked condition of the cabin did not greatly astonish Kent. Subconsciously he had expected something of the sort. With no more than a hasty glance around to be certain that the little building at least concealed no lurking foes, he quenched his flashlight and turned his attention to the barn.

The crudely built, shed-like structure, partly open along one side, was not quite as silent as the cabin had been. But the faint sounds that his cautiously approaching footsteps woke from its dark, shadow-shrouded depths were not of human origin. The querulous mutterings of disturbed chickens and the stamp and snuffle of horses held no menace of danger. Instead the sleepy movements of the stock, quiet until then, served to assure Kent that he himself had been the first individual in some time to attract their attention. Feeling reasonably certain, therefore, that he ran no great risk, he switched on his little flash, and skirting the wire-fronted chicken-house and the stalls where Crossman's three saddle horses were rummaging at their hay, made his way to the farther end of the building where the old cattleman had kept his car.

And here, as the beam of the flash cut into the darkness, Kent stopped short. There were two cars there, standing side by side in the gloom of the closed-in space. One was Jeff Crossman's old tattered-topped Ford touring and the other was the sun-blistered little roadster which had been driven by the girl who had figured in the adventure of the night before.

But it was not his recognition of the girl's car that startled Kent so much as another fact, which in the same instant the glow of the flash revealed. Rough hands had been at work upon it. The hatch of the rear compartment—which as he saw in the same glance had been secured by a stout, home-fitted hasp and padlock—had been battered open and a scatter of articles, which the compartment had evidently sheltered, had been dragged out and flung in confusion upon the earth of the barn floor. Most conspicuous among these miscellaneous articles was a worn little black leather suitcase which had been wrenched open with the same savage violence that had been used on the car. Battered and torn and empty, it lay now partly propped against the rear wheel. And there at his feet, among the scattered, dust-trampled little pile of feminine articles and under-things that had been emptied from it, Kent saw a stocking. A long, dark brown silk stocking. A stocking that was the mate of the one that had choked out old Jeff Crossman's life.

South's watercolor painting of his pottery

CHAPTER 8

Gathering Storm

But Kent's startled surprise at sight of the looted car and the tell-tale stocking was blotted almost at once in a surge of tremendous relief. In one flash, as he read the meaning of the open suitcase and its ruthlessly scattered contents, the whole nightmare fabric of unwilling suspicions which he had entertained vanished. The girl was utterly innocent. Whatever the meaning of those feminine footprints which he had seen near Jeff Crossman's body the girl at least had had nothing to do with the old man's death, for it was only too evident that her car and Jeff Crossman's cabin had been searched by the same hands. The same cold-blooded villainy that had snuffed out the old cattleman's life menaced her also.

Suddenly cold with a new chill of apprehension that was not for himself, Kent snapped off his light. It was all plain now—plain as large print. Standing there in the inky black gloom of the barn he reconstructed the whole happening. The girl had come here. His hunch had been exactly right. She *had* headed back here immediately after her get-away from the bookstore fracas. And the black-browed bully and his bullet-headed crony had known well enough where she was going and had followed her. Theirs had been the big car that had stopped at Chink Halloran's. They had probably arrived at Crossman's during the old man's temporary absence and had seized the opportunity to ransack the girl's car—looking, of course, for the battered little clue-containing Bible. They had not found it, but for some queer reason they had annexed one of her silk stockings, which had been used later with murderous effect in a surprise attack on old Jeff at the spring. Then they had ransacked the cabin in a hasty search that had doubtless been equally fruitless. And now....

But Kent did not follow to its conclusion a train of reasoning that was all too dreadfully obvious. Instead, abruptly, he snapped the swift rush of his thoughts and spurred himself into action. The chill, deserted silence of the vicinity was now only too grimly explained. The gang was away on the trail of the girl. She must have got well ahead of them. She must already be somewhere in the Canyon of Dead Man's Hand.

Without pausing to consider, but in the grip all at once of a fevered apprehension, Kent swung about and strode swiftly towards the exit of the barn.

Of a sudden, however, struck by the quick thought that the little roadster might still hold something that might aid him, he retraced his steps and with the flashlight made a swift but thorough examination of the machine. But there was little more to be learned. Beyond the fact that the registration certificate bore the name of Marie Banniston, he learned nothing fresh in regard to the girl who had driven it. The address given on the certificate was a post office box in El Centro. A little disappointed at having wasted precious moments fruitlessly, but with a queer thrill of satisfaction that at least now he knew her name, Kent switched off his light and hurried out into the night.

It was quite dark by now—dark with a gloom far deeper than the usual starlit dimness of the desert night. The storm clouds to the westward had massed and spread, drifting eastward from the sierra crest in a rolling, rapidly widening canopy that was already blotting the stars overhead. Wind was coming down from the mountaintops in moaning, fitful gusts and, as he stood a moment hesitating at the corner of the corral which adjoined the rear of the barn, Kent was dazzled suddenly by a sheeting green glare that flamed and vanished in the turgid cloud-wrack to the west. The low, ominous roll of thunder boomed across the sky. Close beside him, with a slapping patter, fell a scattering of heavy raindrops.

But Kent just then had neither eyes nor ears for the gathering storm. Eclipsing all else in his mind at that moment was the thought that somewhere out there in that darkness-hidden tumble of cliffs and canyons was the girl whose car stood now in the barn behind him. She was out there somewhere—and she was in deadly peril. It was up to him, somehow, to reach her and aid her.

✍

CHAPTER 9

An Ancient Trail

It was from the black depths of the storm cloud's to the westward, however, that Kent suddenly drew his cue for action. For, as he stood that moment undecided at the corral corner, the blue-green flare of the lightning again tore the sky from west to east. Clear for an instant in the ghastly glare his eyes caught the glint of a speck of white far up the rocky slope which rose steeply almost from his feet. That glint of white decided him—for on the instant he knew what it was. It was a little cairn of white stones—a trail-marker which, at some time in the forgotten past, had been placed there by the Indians to indicate the course of one of their mountain pathways.

Breathless with a sudden excitement Kent began a rapid scramble up the stony hill-side. The sudden sight of that ancient trail-marker had recalled the fact, which he had temporarily forgotten, that Jeff Crossman had once said that an old Indian trail led into the ill-omened Dead Man's Hand Canyon. It was a much shorter trail than the one up the gorge which Kent himself had followed on his prospecting trip. But it was so precipitous as to be practically impassable accept to agile climbers. Kent recalled now that the old man had pointed out this lone white rock cairn, far up the hillside, as being the point where the actual trail began. Toiling now with hasty scrambling foot-holds up the hill shoulder in the direction of the ancient landmark, Kent breathed a fervent prayer that the old trail might still be passable; that in the darkness and storm some Power might aid him in the appalling task of following its dim windings.

But, mad as the attempt seemed, Kent knew well enough that it was his only hope. The other trail into Dead Man's Hand Canyon— the trail which undoubtedly the girl and her pursuers had taken, was much longer—following as it did the sinuous windings of the deep gorge which cut into the flanks of Piñon Peak. Its great length more than counter-balanced its easier going. For, though heart-breakingly rough, it was still possible with trouble to get pack-donkeys through on it. This short cut, however—according to what Crossman had told him—was passable only on foot.

Panting and out of breath, Kent scrambled on. The ascent of the slope was harder even than he had expected. Huge boulders impeded his passage and the ground underfoot was slippery and treacherous with a mass of broken stony fragments amidst which, to hamper his advance, bulked spine-embattled clumps of low-growing cholla cactus and mescals. He was suddenly thankful now for the black ranks of the storm clouds rolling overhead, for it was only by the green flame of the lightning which from time to time ripped the stygian gloom that he was able to keep his direction. Maddeningly, the pale gleam of the little white cairn seemed to recede as he struggled towards it. The whirl of the wind gusts, charging down from the bleak peaks above, seemed to force him back with a buffeting hand. Desultory raindrops whirled in the blasts and stung his face like flying pebbles.

But the ancient trail monument, when he reached it, offered re-ward enough for all his effort. Merely a bleak little column of white stones, piled there by brown hands that had long since crumbled into the dust of a forgotten past, it marked the beginning of a distinct gash that scored diagonally across the steep face of the mountain. Even in the gloom that reigned between the lightning flashes this ditch-like gash was comparatively easy to follow. The narrow channel which provided a run-off for the waters of the infrequent desert storms had been scoured deeper and deeper with the passing years. There was no possibility here of straying from the trail; with each forward step the side banks seemed to become steeper as the little ravine cut deeper and deeper into the mountain.

Spurred by new hope at this fortunate beginning, Kent hurried on, clambering up over the steeply pitched ledges of the dry watercourse with a feverish energy and excitement. His mind was a whirling chaos of apprehension and speculation into which almost vainly he strove to bring order. Banniston...Marie Banniston...So the girl's name was Banniston. That seemed to recall something—something dim which refused to take definite form. He'd heard that name somewhere before. But where? And what did the fact of her leaving her car at Crossman's signify? Obviously enough, Crossman's was the end of all possible progress for a car. But was this her first visit to the old man's place or was she in the habit of stopping there? Was it possible that she had struck out from Crossman's on foot for Dead Man's Hand Canyon or had she pack donkeys with her? These and a hundred other tormenting and equally unanswerable questions surged through Kent's mind as he climbed on. In any case, he reflected, whether the girl had gone on foot or with donkeys, she must have got many hours' start on the gang whom he believed were trailing her. If the evidence at Chink Halloran's shack meant anything, it meant that the men who had murdered Crossman could not have reached the old cattleman's cabin very long ago. And if the girl had left San Diego the previous night, as he felt confident she had, she would have reached Crossman's some time in the morning hours. She must at least have a good start on them. Then, too, what did the El Centro post office address signify? Not much probably. El Centro was possibly only the point where she got her mail.

But before long Kent had other and more immediate matters than fruitless speculation to tax his mind. The fury of the stormy wind gusts, tearing down from the rugged desert peaks above him, was increasing with his advance and, of a sudden, the trail had become more precipitous and difficult. The steep hemming walls of the little ravine were still a reasonable assurance that he was following the right path, but underfoot the bed of the channel had changed. In the dark Kent found himself repeatedly confronted by steep, slippery faces of rock, worn by centuries of intermittent storm waters. Tremendous boulders that had fallen from the heights above blocked the way at increasingly frequent intervals; and most dangerous of all were the deep, treacherous water-worn holes, to avoid which, in the pitchy blackness, demanded unceasing vigilance. The rain flurries were now becoming more frequent and with his exertion and in the cold chill of the heights, Kent became increasingly aware of the fact that he had eaten but little that day. He had had a light lunch at midday on food that he had brought along from San Diego. And though he had had the foresight to take along a small supply of canned provisions in the car, they had been left in the machine when he had abandoned it. He had subconsciously counted on getting something to eat at Crossman's. But events there had swept all thoughts of food from his mind.

Thought of physical exhaustion, however, did not long hold Kent's attention. The little ravine he had been following came of a sudden to an abrupt end. Rounding a huge boulder and clambering up the steeply-pitched ledge beyond he found himself without warning on a bleak, plateau-like summit across which, amidst a pathless desolation of tumbled grey rocks, the wind roared with the buffeting fury of a legion of unleashed fiends. The trail had utterly disappeared.

❧

CHAPTER 10

The Thing in the Dark

Cold and shivering, clinging to the side of a friendly boulder for support and crushed suddenly with an overwhelming sense of utter helplessness, Kent peered out into the grey, windswept bleakness that seemed, in every direction, to roll away into a boundless inky void. Fruitlessly, waiting with anxious impatience for the winking flare of the lightning, he scanned the vicinity for another rudely-piled monument that would show the direction of the trail. But the ghastly, blue-green flashes that for a fleeting instant illumined a terrifying wilderness of distant peaks and precipices, failed to reveal one glint of anything that even remotely resembled another stone cairn. The trail had vanished.

Heavy hearted, realizing only too well the probable utter futility of the attempt, Kent began to circle out into the wind-threshed dark, picking his way from rock to rock, scanning his surroundings feverishly, and aiding the glare of each succeeding lightning flash by the feeble, impotent gleam of his tiny pocket torch. But his stumbling search was fruitless. The wind mocked him and the rain, dashing with increased gusty flurries, blurred his feeble hand light and soaked him to the skin with a bitter chill. And presently he discovered that in his circlings he had gone a long distance from the point where he had emerged from the head of the ravine. He could no longer find it. The discovery was a staggering shock. Sickeningly he realized that after all his attempt at a short cut had been madness. Amidst that grey sea of rocks and the howl of the wind and lash of the chilling rain he was hopelessly lost.

Just how long he wandered in that maddening wilderness of desolate, rain-dashed boulders Kent did not know. He had no watch and he was aware only of the torturing fact that considerable time was elapsing—and that every passing minute was destroying, with chilling finality, the sole advantage of time which had induced him to attempt this treacherous short cut. He had been a crazy fool, he told himself bitterly. Better by far to have traveled the old trail that he knew. Perhaps by hurrying he might at least have caught up with the gang which he believed to be trailing the girl. Now, by yielding to a fool impulse, he had wrecked all hope. In this ghostly, eerie chaos of rocks and darkness he could not hope to find a trail until morning—then it would be too late. Maddened by the thought, filled with a fury of hopeless desperation, he stumbled on and on; breasting the wind and driving rain squalls, peering frantically into the shadows for some signs of a guiding mark.

At just what moment the notion came to Kent that he was being watched and followed he had no clearer idea than he had of how long he had been hopelessly on the rocky crest. But, bit by bit—faintly at first but growing in strength as he blundered on from rock to rock— the creepy conviction came to him that he was not alone. Someone or something—hidden and invisible in the windy dark—was near him, dogging his footsteps. More than once, in the darkness behind him, he heard distinctly the sound of dislodged stones. But when he wheeled, staring out over his back tracks in the ghastly, cold flare of lightning flashes, he could see nothing but the grim grey wilderness of wet rocks. The thing, whatever it was, remained invisible.

In spite of himself, Kent began to feel the chill clutch of a queer terror fastening upon him. He was no coward. There was nothing physical of which he was afraid, and as far as anything supernatural went he had always worked on the theory that infinitely less was to be dreaded from the dead than from the living. Like most cowboys he had heard one or two tolerably convincing ghost stories and he was not ready to deny absolutely the possibility of such things. But never until this time had he ever felt the queer thrill of eerie terror which, fight against it as he would, seemed to reach out to him from something that followed him through the ghostly, storm-swept darkness of that desolate ridge crest.

But, fight against the feeling all he could, Kent soon became convinced that the thing was no trick of the imagination. He was being followed. Out of the darkness somewhere he was being watched. Step by step through that gusty blackness something was clinging to his trail. The sensation was becoming unbearable. In spite of the chill of the rain a new cold sweat began to dew his body and little gusty electric currents to play up and down his spine. It was nothing, he told himself desperately. A mountain lion, likely…A coyote perhaps—or more improbably a wolf that had strayed into this region…Nothing to be scared of….

In the same breath, however, he knew that he lied to himself. It was nothing on four feet that was out there in the dark. It was something else. All the stories of old prospectors dealing with ghosts of murdered men came crowding back upon him. These desolate Vallecito Mountains held, even by daylight, a grim, weird atmosphere. This had been a wild section in the early outlaw days of the west. Queer tales were told about the things that had happened here. And then Crossman—old Jeff Crossman—had spoken very definitely of the legend of Dead Man's Hand Canyon being haunted.

And then—then all of a sudden—just as the thought of old Jeff Crossman, whose cold, dead body stood even then down by the dark waters of the little spring, rushed back upon him with a cold shock— Kent saw the thing that followed him. All in one fleeting, ghastly instant, when the whole world seemed to glow blue-green in the chill glare of a terrific flash of lightning; he saw it. And the sight of it brought a choking cry from his lips and sent him cowering back in terror, clutching at the face of a giant boulder for support.

For the thing that followed him was *white*— ghastly white as the white of desert bleached bones. There in the shelter of a rock, not ten paces behind him, it stood watching—a grim, dreadful travesty of a human figure, that with staring eyes and forward thrust head stood peering at him through the gloom. And the grim, drawn face-aglow with an unearthly phosphorescence in the electric glare—was the cold, dead face of *old Jeff Crossman.*

South's pencil sketch of "Señor Quien Sabe."

∽

CHAPTER 11

A Ghastly Guide

For a moment stark terror at the fearsome thing that the lightning flash had revealed held Kent rigid. And in that moment, as he stood there flattened back against the rock and utterly incapable of movement, he was aware that in the gloom, the thing had glided past him. In the glare of the next electric flash that tore the sky he saw that it was standing now some fifteen paces ahead and that its right arm was raised in a rigid, beckoning gesture. Even as the light-flare blotted out he saw that, regarding him with fixed stare over his shoulder and with stiff, beckoning arm still upraised, it had begun to move away.

And, drawn by some weird, uncanny power which he was powerless to combat, Kent followed. Stumbling, breathless, with chilled blood and every hair on his body tingling with cold, electric draughts of uncanny fear, he moved out into the gusty, rain-whipped dark, following like a numbed automaton at the heels of his dreadful guide.

But slowly, as he blundered on through the darkness, following by the glare of every succeeding lightning-flash the unearthly thing that seemed to draw him as a magnet, his first sense of petrified horror passed. Fear took its place—but a fear that was more closely allied to wondering amazement than to actual terror. His mind—stunned by the first shock—was beginning to function again. He did not doubt that the thing he was following was Jeff Crossman. And he knew, moreover, with equal certainty, that Jeff Crossman was dead. This, then, if it was really something more than just a dreadful hallucination, must be Jeff Crossman's ghost. If so, why had it appeared to him? It must have some purpose—and it could not logically be a sinister one. In life old Jeff—even for the little he had known him—had always been a good friend. It did not seem reasonable that after death he would be imbued with any malevolent motives.

And of a sudden, even as reason fought with his dread, Kent's heart bounded. All in an instant, in one sweeping surge of grateful realization, that for the moment blotted all fear, he understood the motive which had actuated the shadowy thing in front of him. For suddenly, as the skies lit with a greater sheet of flame than usual, he saw a guide cairn—and almost on the same instant as he glimpsed the little monument of piled stones his eyes caught the dim, time-scoured channel that had once been a foot trail. His aimless wanderings were over. The ghost of old Jeff Crossman had guided him to the right path.

Almost incredulous, overwhelmingly thankful and with his every nerve a-tingle with a breathless, uncanny sensation that had nevertheless been robbed of almost all terror, Kent plunged down the new-found pathway. There could be no mistake now.

Even if it had not been for the pale glint of the grim thing that, still visible in each light-flash, floated before him, he would have had no doubts. Guide stones there were now in plenty. Single stones, double stones, little piles at the turns. The ancient trail had here been well marked. With rapidly-beating heart and his former dread practically obliterated in a fevered urge for haste, Kent hurried on through the storm.

It was a weird and ghostly journey—an experience which, under normal circumstances, Kent would have scouted as being utterly impossible, as some crazed freak of an overwrought imagination. But here, in this weird, grim setting of storm and lone desolation, the thing, oddly enough, seemed less impossible than it was nerve-shaking and amazing. Firm held in the strange, uncanny sensation which had been slowly gathering force within him all that day, Kent had come easily to an unquestioning acceptance of his unearthly guide which, under normal circumstances, would have been utterly impossible. Strangely the grim thing that guided him held his thoughts less than did a fevered eagerness to hurry—an unceasing speculation as to what really lay ahead of him in the grim little canyon which his sense of direction and location told him he was rapidly nearing.

Troubles enough, however, beset his progress. Old Jeff Crossman had indeed spoken truly, Kent realized, when he had said that this short-cut was impassable except to an active climber. For, presently, plunging downward from its winding course along the ridge-top, the trail crossed a chasm-like ravine and swung up along the almost sheer face of a cliff beyond. The going here was perilous in the extreme. The hand-holds and foot-holds and the narrow ledges were all but impossible to discover in the rainy blackness, and often as he groped for them

Kent's heart-stopped short to the yielding feel of some crumbling rock or loose stone which gave away under his hand and went thumping down the sheer wet face of the cliff below him. The lightning flashes were here all too far apart and, in the bewildering gloom, it was the grim flicker of ghostly white which moved always just ahead of him which, more than anything else, seemed to keep up his courage and constant effort.

And then of a sudden, scrambling up over an overhanging rock, Kent felt the wind strike him with a new, unleashed fury. Before and below him rolled a sea of empty blackness—a sea of shadowy dark which, an instant later in a blinding electric glare, took form as a deep, rock-filled chasm stretching back into the depths of the mountains. The flash winked out and the dark rushed back. But even as he passed the summit and scrambled downward, fighting against the roar of the mountain wind as he followed down the steep declivity at the heels of his unearthly pathfinder, Kent's heart was bounding with triumph. He had won through. He had succeeded. The ancient trail had well served. For below him, filled with the trumpeting raging of the wind that howled and skirled in unchecked fury through its narrow, gash-like depths, lay the Canyon of Dead Man's Hand. Triumphantly, heartened by a sudden new vigor and courage which even thought of the weird, grim thing ahead of him could not damp, he slid downward, swinging, in the glinting glare of the intermittent lightning flashes, from ledge to ledge along the wet, treacherous face of the cliff.

And then, all without warning, disaster rushed upon Jim. For, of a sudden, sharp and piercing and borne upward on the wind from the black depths below him, there came to his ears the sound of a girl's scream. And even as his limbs went rigid and his blood froze to the dread significance of it, the tiny ledge of water-soaked rock to which he clung gave way.

With a choking gasp and with hands clutching wildly at thin air he toppled and fell downwards—downwards in a hurtling plunge to a sudden stunning shock and the black silence of complete oblivion.

〰

CHAPTER 12

The Girl in the Canyon

"**O**h please!…please speak to me!…Are you badly hurt?"

Kent opened his eyes. Like a cool waft of wind, fanning aside the dark mists that had clouded his brain, the soft, oddly-familiar voice seemed of a sudden to bring back his senses in an abrupt, tumultuous rush. With a quick, twisting jerk, raising his aching body on his arms, he sat up, blinking dizzily into the bright glow of a flashlight that someone beside him in the rainy dark was holding close to his face. He felt a supporting arm all at once about his shoulders; caught a glimpse of a slim hand and of a girl's anxious face.

"Oh, please—are you much hurt?" Again, in breathless concern, she repeated her question. In the glow of the flashlight, as she bent closer scanning his features, Kent's eyes confirmed what the sound of the voice had already told him. It was the girl whom he had met in the bookshop. It was Marie Banniston—the girl whose looted little car stood now away back at the foot of the mountain, in the silent shadows of old Jeff Crossman's barn.

"No—no, I'm not hurt, miss! Nothing to speak of. Nothing but a shaking." Kent found his voice and at the same moment scrambled a bit stiffly to his feet. "I guess I didn't fall far—I sort of slid. And I must have hit a soft place."

"Soft place?" the girl echoed the words with a gasp. "Why, you struck solid rock. Look!" She turned her flash an instant upon the glistening wet granite underfoot. "And you fell far enough—right from that ledge there." She swept the light beam across the face of the steep-sloping cliff.

"Then I guess it's a good thing I struck on the end I did," Kent rubbed his head wryly. "If I'd have lit on my feet or anything delicate I'd have probably hurt myself. As it is everything's O.K."

"Are you sure?" She eyed him anxiously.

"Positive." To satisfy her he gave himself an investigative shake. "A headache and a few bruises, but that's all. There's not a thing broken."

"Oh, thank God! Thank God!" There was heartfelt relief in her voice. "I saw you in the lightning flashes, as you were coming down the cliff. I thought you were father. I was so startled, I screamed. And then you fell…Then—then, when I'd climbed up here, I recognized you the moment I flashed the light on you. But I was afraid you were dead. You were unconscious for several minutes. How did you get here?"

"I had a hunch. I guessed that this was where you'd headed for, so I came out here on chance. You lost part of the clue last night—an important piece—" All in a rush, as his mind steadied and swung back to complete realization, the words tumbled from Kent's lips. "But quick, snap out the light. They may see it!"

"Who?" Her voice was sharp with alarm as she obeyed. "Who'll see it?"

"The bunch that's trailing you. They're out here somewhere. They left their car back at Crossman's. It's probably that hard-faced ruffian and his gang—the hombre that tried to get the book away from you last night."

"Oh—" Even through the swirl of the wind he caught the fear-sharp gasp in her voice. "You—you mean Wolf Hesfor?"

"No—no! I mean—. That is—" Startled, his pulse checking to a sudden staggering suspicion, Kent's words blundered confusedly. "I mean the wolf-faced hombre that—that…Why, good God!…Wolf Hesfor was hanged in 1860. He's been dead over seventy years."

"This man is his grandson." Through the dark the girl's voice came low and tense. "He bears the same name; he has the same character. From everything I know of him he's the exact duplicate of his grandfather, except that he lacks the finish and education—and that's only because he's been an outlaw in Mexico all his life…Oh!…Oh, are you sure that he's really followed me here?"

"Well, I haven't set eyes on any of them, but I'd lay a strong bet that he's one of the four, miss." Himself considerably staggered by the startling information she had just given him, Kent spoke quickly. "They're a bad bunch." Swiftly, judging this to be no time for concealing ugly facts, he told her in a few words what he knew and all that had happened at Crossman's.

"And so—so they've murdered poor old Jeff!" She spoke haltingly, almost stammeringly, breaking with evident effort the stunned, horrified silence in which she had listened. "Poor old Jeff...Oh, the brutes!—the brutes!...Oh...Oh, if only—if only—"

Her voice strangled out in a dry little sob, and for almost a minute, standing there in the ghostly, wind-swept gloom, she was silent. But when she spoke again it was with a new, breathless determination and purpose. Almost fiercely she snatched at Kent's arm. "Come!" she breathed, "come! We must get down out of here quickly! We've got to find father and get him to safety. If those devils find him, they'll murder him too. Oh, please, please, let's hurry!"

She was of a sudden frantic. Even as she panted the words she was tugging at his arm, drawing him after her, guiding him down what was evidently to her a well-known path that zigzagged down the precipitous slope. In a sheeting blaze of lightning Kent saw, as he scrambled swiftly after her, that they were still quite a distance from the bottom of the canyon. But the going was much easier. He had already passed all the really perilous points of the trail.

"Where—where is your father?" Snatching an opportunity between the furious wind gusts that seemed all at once to have redoubled their force and frequency, Kent put a hasty question. "Where is he?"

"I—I don't know." Almost in a sob her wind-blown voice came back to him. "He's—he's sick! But he's in this canyon somewhere. Oh, we must hurry!...We've just *got* to find him!"

The wind roared down and put an end to speech. Puzzled, still a bit stiff from his fall, but with the throbbing ache in his head almost miraculously gone, Kent hurried after her. Not yet, in spite of his feverish conjectures, could he bring order to the weird chaos of happenings into which fate seemed to have plunged him. This last complication of a sick man, of whose actual whereabouts the girl seemed to have no clear idea, was utterly beyond him. The whole affair was steadily becoming more and more weird and incomprehensible. But of this somehow he did not feel great concern. At that moment, blotting everything else in his heart, was a strange tingle of gladness. He had won through. He had achieved his purpose. This girl at his side, to whom his hunch had so strangely guided him, was still safe. Somehow, together, they would see this thing through.

They would see it through together. The thought gave him a queer, fierce thrill of joy. And only then, even as his heart surged to the thrill of it, was he aware of something which, in the excitement of the last few minutes, he had quite failed to notice.

The weird, grim thing that had guided him across the treacherous section of the trail was gone. Since the moment of his fall it had utterly disappeared.

CHAPTER 13

Marie Explains

They reached the bottom of the canyon presently and the girl halted. The wind broken by the clutter of mighty boulders that filled the narrow channel, was here less violent. Sheltered by the bulk of a great rock beside which they had stopped, the girl peered out into the darkness in desperate uncertainty. "Oh." she breathed, "—Oh, if it were only daylight! But in this awful dark…Oh, how can I hope to find him?"

"How did he happen to get lost in the first place, miss?" Kent questioned puzzled. "Did he come here with you? Haven't you any idea where he went to?"

"No, he didn't come here with me. You don't understand." As though sensing for the first time his bewilderment the girl spoke in quick explanation. "We live here—way up there near the far end of the canyon," she gestured into the darkness. "There used to be an old ruined house there and we rebuilt it. We've been living there almost a year. Father's in poor health—he has periodic sick spells. I found him in one when I got back home, late this afternoon. He was in bed in a deep stupor from a native drug that he takes. I had to go up the canyon to the spring for some water. And when I came back his bed was empty. I couldn't find him anywhere and most of this canyon's so rocky, I couldn't even find any track marks. He'd just vanished. I've been hunting him ever since. When I saw you away up the cliffs here, I thought you were he."

"But it was still daylight when you first missed him, wasn't it?" Given something definite to go on by the girl's words, Kent put the question quickly. "There's no possibility that—that someone might have taken him away while you were away getting the water?"

"Yes, it was still daylight. It was pretty late afternoon—almost evening, in fact. But there was still lots of light. You see, I was late getting home here from San Diego. I had trouble with the car last night and that delayed me so much that I didn't reach Jeff's place till way late today. Then by the time I'd put the car away, changed into these hiking clothes and tramped up here by the long trail, it was late afternoon. Then it was quite a while after I got home that I left father to go up to the spring, so you see it was late when he disappeared. But at that I'm positive that no one else came to the cabin in my absence. I wasn't away more than a few minutes. And anyway, from what you've told me, Wolf Hesfor and his bunch couldn't possibly have got here. Why, by that time they wouldn't even have been at—at poor Jeff's." She caught her breath in a little shudder.

"Then I guess he must have just wandered off somewhere, miss—folks often do that in a delirium. We'll find him. He's bound to be close around here somewhere." Kent spoke with assumed confidence to hearten her. "What was that native drug that you said he'd been taking for his sickness?"

"*Toloache*"—for just a fraction of a second, as though the admission came a bit unwillingly, she hesitated. "You know, that sort of wild melon-vine with the big, purple-white flowers. *Toloache* is its Indian name, but some people call it Jimsonweed."

"Oh," Kent said, startled, but trying on the instant to hide it. "Yes, I know the stuff. What was your father's sickness, miss—asthma?"

"Oh no, nothing like that. It was his heart. He's had a bad heart for years."

"I—I never heard of *toloache* being used for heart trouble," Kent said slowly, hesitating and trying to choose his words while his mind raced on puzzled with grim possibilities. "That—that stuff is—is…." He checked himself, realizing that his words were floundering awkwardly and that he was perhaps making a mistake.

"Yes, I know—it's a deadly poison," low voiced, but realizing what he was trying to say, she bravely completed the sentence for him. "Yes, I know that. But—but I don't think that that's what has happened. Father knew his business. He's a professor of chemistry. He was an instructor in the university at Berkeley for years—until we came down here. You may have heard of him—Banniston—Professor Walter Banniston. I'm Marie Banniston."

"No, miss, I don't think I ever heard of your father. It wouldn't be likely. I've followed the cattle business—and university news don't always filter down to the range. But at that the name's somehow familiar. Maybe I read it somewhere. And your name, yes, I knew that already. I got it from your car at Jeff's."

"Oh," she said, and in spite of the splashing raindrops and the gusting of the wind he caught a sudden eagerness in her voice: "Oh—so you're a cowboy. I thought so—I guessed as much. There—there was something about you—about the way you acted there in that book shop last night. I was certain that you belonged out in country like this and not in a town. And, oh please forgive me, I haven't thanked you yet for the way you got me out of that trouble. Oh, you were wonderful. And, and I'm so grateful! I do appreciate it. But I've been so worried and—"

"Oh, that—that wasn't anything, miss," hastily, feeling sudden embarrassment, Kent cut her short. "It was just—just a sort of coincidence, my being there in the store. It wasn't anything, and anyhow—"

"And I suppose it's 'just a sort of coincidence' you being here to-night," she cut in. "Do you really think that there's such a thing in this world as 'just coincidence' Mr…Mr…Oh !—" she broke off in confusion, "Why, I don't even know your name yet."

He told her.

"Rodney—Rodney Kent." Gravely, thoughtfully, as though appraising it, she repeated it after him. "Oh, I like that. It's got a clean, big ring to it. No wonder you follow an outdoor life—with a name like that you just couldn't do anything small and petty. Oh, Mr. Kent, but I do want to thank you for your help last night." Through the darkness her hand reached out and touched his in a quick, impulsive movement.

"Call me Rod." Tingling all at once to a sudden odd thrill, Kent caught her fingers a moment in swift pressure. "Call me Rod—the Mr. is too much of a handle."

"No," she said, "I'll call you Rodney—I like that better. But you've got to stop calling me 'miss'—my name's Marie."

"All right," he agreed heartily. "But say!"—with sudden realization he snapped back to a facing of the grim immediate present—"we've got to be moving. Do you suppose that maybe your dad would have headed down the trail towards Crossman's?"

"N—no," she said, and despite the falter in her voice there was a conviction in her tone that did much to dispel the pang which shot through Kent at realization of his tactless blunder. "No, I don't think he'd go that way. I don't think he'd leave the canyon. He—he's probably wandering around among the rocks somewhere. Oh I—what was that?" She caught his arm and, suddenly rigid, stood listening.

"Nothing—nothing but the wind and a rain-loosened stone rolling down the slope." Kent strained his ears and eyes out into the dark. "The chances are, though, that your dad has headed home by this time. Even if he's been temporarily out of his head on account of an over-dose of that dope he's been taking this rain and wind and the cold of the night would bring him 'round. Then he'd naturally go back home. I think our best bet is to look for him there."

"Then let's hurry." With sudden feverish anxiety she led the way out into the swirling gusts of the storm. "Follow me—I know this trail up the canyon best, I guess. Oh, let's make haste. We've got to find father before those other devils get here. And in this dark God knows how close they may be to us."

Kent made no answer. Close at her heels, following her slim, swift-moving figure which, in shirt and whipcord breeches and high-laced boots, looked very slender and boyish in the occasional lightning flashes, he was thinking hard. That very question that she had voiced had occurred to him also. Just where, he wondered, was the black-browed ruffian, whom Marie had called Wolf Hesfor, and his gang. There was no earthly means of knowing. It was impossible to tell just what start the gang had got from Crossman's, or how fast they had traveled. He himself had been a long time negotiating that treacherous short cut. In the dark and storm everything was uncertain. Was it possible, he asked himself uneasily, that while the girl and he had been away up the slopes of the canyon side, the gang had passed up the canyon bed and got ahead of them? Was it possible that they had already reached the house? Were the girl and he, in this seemingly hopeless search for her delirious parent, walking directly into a trap?

There was no means of knowing. To this and a hundred other questions Time only held the answer and Caution the only safeguard. But as he followed the shadowy lead of the swift-moving girl up along the rocky canyon bed it was with a sense of considerable comfort that Kent felt the weighty rubbing pressure of "Wolf Hesfor's heavy Colt that was tucked away inside his shirt. Whether the girl carried a weapon or not he did not know. But at least with this heavy six-gun and the hundred rounds of ammunition that he had with him they would not be entirely defenseless.

∽

CHAPTER 14

Ken Learns Some Details

But the realization that somewhere the stormy darkness hid a deadly peril could not altogether keep Kent's mind from running on other things as he followed the girl's lead up the canyon. She had told him several details that were puzzling. There was that fact of her father habitually taking *toloache*. There was something decidedly queer about that—especially for a man bothered by heart trouble. And then, according to Marie, she and her father had lived in this weird mountain chasm almost a year. Obviously, it wasn't altogether for health reasons. The only logical conclusion was that they had in some way got a suspicion as to the whereabouts of the treasure and had settled here in a determined effort to find it. That they had evidently been unsuccessful up to the present would explain all the more the girl's eagerness the previous night to locate some more definite clues. And thinking of this he recollected suddenly that in the excitement of other things he had forgotten the verse-inscribed sheet of yellow paper which was the direct reason for his presence here. It was still tucked away in a leather notecase in his pocket. Seizing his opportunity as the trail widened presently, he quickened his steps with the notion of giving it to her.

But almost in the same moment, as though her mind had been running in a similar vein, she slackened pace and dropped back beside him. "You spoke of a clue," she said, forestalling his words before he could utter them. "Some important part of the clue that I missed last night. What was it?"

He told her briefly, reaching at the same time for the notecase in his pocket. But she stopped him with a checking hand. "No, you keep it—at least till we get some place safe. You can take care of it better. Say!—that's a queer thing...queer and ominous—" Reflectively, almost to herself, she repeated scraps of the verses that he had quoted to her. "Yes, I think you're right. It must be a vital part of the clue. Oh, it was wonderfully good of you to go to all that trouble to try and get it to me. I don't know, however we'll be able to repay you enough. But say!"— there was a sudden wondering curiosity in her voice—"however did you know anything about the Hesfor treasure—the details I mean?"

"I've—I've read it up a bit," steading a moment against a breath-taking gust of wind that swept past and roared away down the canyon. Kent made the admission a bit sheepishly. "I'm a sort of crank on the history of road-agents."

"Oh," she said, and in the almost hushed lull that succeeded the wind swirl, her voice as she walked at his side sounded strangely thoughtful; "oh—then that accounts for your being so interested in that book store collection. But surely—surely, if you've read up the accounts of Hesfor's robbery, you must remember something of the name of the man whose property it was he stole—the man for whose murder Hesfor was hanged?"

"Banniston!…Banniston!" Startled, stopped dead in his tracks by a sudden rush of amazed recollection Kent caught his breath on the name. "Banniston—Judge John J. Banniston…Why, of course!— what a fool I was not to think…I've been so interested in Hesfor and the story of his buried treasure that I'd almost forgotten where that treasure came from in the first place. Why sure! John J. Banniston of the Robles Ranch—the old pioneer California Judge who incurred Hesfor's special enmity. I'd all but forgotten that. But no wonder—the name seemed familiar. Banniston!— Then—then you must be-must be….?"

"A direct descendant," she said quietly. "John J. Banniston at the Robles Ranch was my great-grandfather. Only they don't call it Robles Ranch any more. Since the hold-up and murder the name's somehow been corrupted to Robbery Range. But it's the same place."

"Then you still own all this desert range?" Amazed, his mind struggling to grasp the full significance of the thing as they pushed on through the windy dark, Kent put the question almost incredulously. "Then it was from you—from your father—that old Jeff Crossman had it leased? I remember now he said it was from some folks near San Francisco."

"Yes," she said, "he leased it from father, for a mere trifle. It wasn't worth much—it's run down. And—and father liked Jeff. Yes, we still own all this country. It's never been out of the hands of the family. But it's brought no luck with it since the robbery. It's been a white elephant—especially to father. He's had such poor health. And we're awfully poor now. That's—that's why we're here now—looking for the treasure." She caught her breath in a hard little gasp that was almost a sob.

For a while, side by side in the wider section of the trail, they tramped on through the gusty dark in silence. Of a sudden, however, abruptly, the girl spoke again. "Poor old Jeff," she half-whispered, almost as though thinking aloud, "strangled—down by the spring. Oh, it's awful! 'It's too terrible almost to believe. Why, I ran down there to get a drink myself, just as soon as I got the car in the barn—before I'd changed my clothes even. And to think—to think that just a little while later…Oh!…She broke off shudderingly.

"Yes, I knew you'd been down there. I saw the tracks," Kent said. "I couldn't help seeing them. They were plain in that patch of soft earth."

"And—and I suppose you thought *I'd* done it?" Instantly, sensing what his reaction must have been, she put the question bluntly. "You couldn't help think that—after seeing the stocking."

"I know it couldn't possibly have been you when I got to the barn and saw the way your car had been searched," Kent said hastily. "I knew then well enough what had happened."

"It must have been Halloran that did it," she said. "I've heard ugly rumors about him being a strangler. He's been in the Orient and he's had lots to do with Chinese and Hindus. That's probably where he learned it. Somehow…somehow I've always been afraid of Chink Halloran. Perhaps more so even than of Wolf Hesfor. Halloran's Hesfor's crony. They're partners in the Chinese smuggling racket. Halloran lives on this side of the Line and Hesfor takes care of the Mexican end of the business. The old-time Wolf Hesfor had a hide-out in Mexico—in Baja California—and that's where his son grew up. This present man, the first Hesfor's grandson, has been raised most of his life in Mexico. He's a thorough scoundrel. But it was Halloran who first tipped him off about our coming here, and Halloran has been keeping him posted as to our movements. They're certain—since we began to live here—that we have a definite line on the treasure. I've always suspected that they were just waiting, like wolves-waiting for us to do the hard work of finding it. You've no idea just how much you've done in getting ahead of them like this to warn us. However did you manage to get across that old Indian cut-off trail? It's terrible enough in the daytime. But in the dark—why, I'd have said it was absolutely impossible. How did you find your way along it?"

"It—it was hard—it wasn't an easy job." Hesitant, suddenly reluctant to confess the utterly improbable, mysterious experience, through which he had passed, Kent floundered for words. "But there are lots of trail markers. And then there was the lightning. Anyway, I got here—head first, it seems, at the end." He forced a short laugh. No, he thought desperately, he could never tell her *that*. The thing was a crazed madness—something which already he was beginning to disbelieve himself. To tell her that Jeff Crossman's ghost had led him?… Never! In this eerie solitude of storm and terror the girl had enough to frighten her without *that*.

"Yes, you got here," the girl agreed gravely, but something in her almost-whispered tone gave Kent the startled feeling that she had been following his thoughts. "But—but there must have been something… some Power that led you. This is a queer country. I don't know. Since I've been living here somehow I've come to believe a whole lot of things that once I didn't think about. I remember you spoke once tonight of coincidence. Rodney, there's no such thing as coincidence. No such thing as chance. I'm beginning to think, Rodney, that there are a whole lot of things about life and death in this world we live in that we don't begin to understand. You somehow get close to things like that out here in these desert solitudes."

Again she became silent and for quite a long while, tramping along at his side, a dim shadow in the tempestuous dark, she made no further effort to talk. The lightning flashes, though as blinding as ever, were now less frequent. The storm was changing position. The rain squalls were fewer and the steady rush of the wind leaped less often into the violent skirting gusts that formerly had been almost overwhelming. They must be getting near the end of the trail, Kent reflected. Remembering the lay of the canyon and the position of the old ruin, which the girl had told him she and her father had rebuilt, he reasoned that they must now be very near the end of their journey. In the gloom he could sense the closing in of the canyon side walls. About here, he remembered, the canyon contracted, then opened into a wider space, then contracted again.

Already, peering into the darkness, he was waiting for a lightning flash to reveal the outlines of the grim, hand-shaped rock that stood on the south rim of the gorge, when suddenly the girl spoke:

"Here's the house," she said in a low, tense whisper, "—and there's no sign of a light in it!"

✍

CHAPTER 15

Trapped

Checked by the girl's sudden words and her quick clutch as she drew him to a halt, Kent stood peering into the darkness, aware all at once of the black, blotting mass of a building which seemed abruptly to have taken form in the gloom ahead. So suddenly had it appeared that even though he had been momentarily expecting to come upon it, its nearness startled him. It was so close that almost he could have reached out and touched the shadowy walls. The wind whistled down the canyon and skirled around the dim bulk of the building with a lonely whine, and flying gravel from the cliffs above rattled on the roof with a dreary patter. The place seemed as dark and lifeless as a tomb.

"See—there's not a ray of light any place." As though hushed with the chill atmosphere of lone desolation which seemed to envelop the black, lightless mass, the girl spoke in a whisper. "That doesn't seem as though father had come home—unless he just came back and went to bed without lighting the lamp. We'll have to go in and look. Take care. There's a deep gully right here." Reaching back a quick, guiding hand, she led the way cautiously around the corner of the cabin.

"Be careful with the flashlight," Kent cautioned. "A light would show a long way."

"I know. I can find my way well enough in the dark. But you watch out for that gully on your right. It's deep and it's full of catclaw."

Stealthily, their cautious steps soundless enough in the blurring rush of the wind, they made their round of the house. The shadows were black, but even through their cloaking gloom Kent could see that the girl's warning about the ravine had been justified. One side of the house paralleled the edge of it with only a space of some six or eight feet between the wall and the dark edge of the drop. The wiry whistle of wind through thorny branches came up out of its depths and, peering, Kent fancied that he could see the dim, swaying tops of the catclaws that choked the bottom of the channel. A few steps farther and they turned another corner, meeting the full force of the wind that came sweeping across a wide leveled stretch of hard ground that had seemingly been cleared of stones. The girl halted. "Here's the door," she whispered.

"Then you stand back a bit and let me try it." Kent reached past her. "We don't know just what's inside—and there's no sense in taking chances." Fumbling cautiously he found the latch, stood a moment listening and then, tensed and with ready-drawn pistol, swung the creaking barrier inward.

But no sound, save the gusty inrush of the wind, came from the black, cavern-like interior of the little shack. Swiftly, following the same tactics that he had employed at Crossman's cabin, Kent reached for his tiny pocket light to dart an exploratory beam into the room. It was, however, no longer in his pocket, and he realized all at once that he must have lost it in the fall down the cliff. Reaching back, with a swift whispered word, he took the girl's more powerful torch and, hiding the back-glow as much as possible with his hand, illumined for an instant the dark silence within the doorway.

The cabin, however, like Crossman's, was apparently empty of all human occupants. Unlike Crossman's, however, it had not been ransacked. Rough built and crude though it was, Kent saw plainly, even in the transitory wink of his light, that there was a certain homely neatness to the interior which no rough hands had disturbed. Not all of the inside had been revealed by the light-flash, for one end of the little building was closed off by a canvas partition and a curtained doorway—the girl's room evidently. But from the orderly condition of the place Kent was instantly certain that the gang who had searched Crossman's had not yet reached here. He was also equally certain that the girl's father had not returned. A rough bunk that was obviously the sick man's stood to one side of the little stove. But the blankets were disarranged and the bunk was empty.

"He's not here. He hasn't come back." Hastily, as he snapped off the light, Kent whispered to the girl. "But we'd best look in that other room to make sure." "That's my room—he won't be there." There was a sudden utter dejection in her voice as she swiftly followed him inside. "Oh, God! Whatever can have happened to him? However will we be able to find him in this storm?"

Kent made no answer, but groping in the dark made his way to the doorway in the partition and drew aside the curtain.

"See—see, he's not there. I knew he wouldn't be." There was hope-less despair in the girl's voice as the flash for an instant illumined the tiny little room with its narrow but neatly made bed. "He's not around here any place. He's—he's just gone…Vanished." Her breath caught in a stifled sob.

"Then we'd best get out of here—and quick!" Kent said grimly. "There's four in that gang. They're headed here for certain and we 'don't want to be caught in a trap. Is there anything you want particu-larly to save? If there is you'd best take it along. They'll ransack this place from top to bottom."

"Oh, the book—the book I got last night." In a sudden panic of recollection she caught at his arm. "Yes!…yes! Quick! Give me the light! I'll get it! They mustn't find *that!*" Hastily, snatching the torch from his fingers, she darted to a corner of the front room and flung up the lid of a stout but time-worn trunk. "It's here," she said breathlessly, "hidden down among father's books…I put it here when I came home. Here! please hold the light a second! I've got to dump all this stuff out first before I can get at it."

"Hurry," Kent urged. "Hurry—every second we stay here is dan-gerous. We don't know just where…."

The word's died away in his throat. For even as he bent to help her, stooping with back turned to the open outer door as he held the light over the book-filled trunk, there shot startlingly from the dark-ness behind him the streaming, blinding glare of a powerful electric torch—a light glare that was blended with the crisp snap of a sudden harsh command:

"Up with yer hands, hombre!" barked a thick, familiar voice. "One false wiggle, an' we'll blow yer whole back off!"

CHAPTER 16

Wolf Hesfor's Gang

For a fleeting instant, staggered by the blinding light and harsh snarled words as though from a viciously dashed pail of ice water, Kent froze rigid. The surprise had been utter and complete and the realization that they were trapped stunned him. For one light-swift moment that passed slowly as an age, he felt as though he had turned to stone and the whole world with him. It did not seem real. It was like some fantastic tableau in which he was not an actor but a spectator. In the blinding glare that streamed from the open doorway behind him he saw himself, flashlight in one hand and gun in the other, standing low-bent but rigid over the open trunk. Just across from him, her arms laden with books and her face half turned towards the door in an expression of startled terror, was the girl. Everything was motionless, frozen. Time and movement seemed to have stopped.

But it was only for the space of one hasty heart-beat that the spell lasted. Of a sudden the girl screamed, dropping her armload of books in a tumbling heap as she staggered back against the wall with a sharp, piercing cry. And as though her first movement had closed the switch which sent swift thought flashing through his brain in an electric flood, Kent too awoke. Acting on a lightning impulse that seemed to come from somewhere outside himself, he checked his natural urge to wheel and shoot, and instead lunged slightly forward, dropping his gun into the trunk where on the instant it was buried in the girl's spilled armful of books. Released from the pressure of his arm as he swiftly raised his hands aloft, the trunk lid shut with a crash.

"Yeah I—that's right, hombre. Stick up yer paws—an' keep 'em up!" Gruffly from the doorway, as Kent straightened, the thick voice came again. "An' you too, sister—you just stand agen the wall there as y'are. Don't try t' get smart, neither o' you. This ain't no Sunday school party."

Feet scrunched heavily upon the earthen floor. Slowly, arms upraised, his left hand still holding the flashlight, Kent turned to face the blinding light beam which was still trained upon him. Despite the dazzling glare he could make out well enough the figures of the hulking bully of the bookstore fracas and his bullet-headed companion. With lowered but ready rifles in their hands they stood just inside the shack door, close beside another man, who held a powerful electric lantern. A fourth man, who from his slouching, slovenly figure Kent guessed to be Chink Halloran, was just entering the door. All of the gang, he saw in the first glance, carried rifles.

"So here y' are agen, Mister Buttinsky." With heavy, lurching gait the black-browed man strode forward. "Pleased t' meet yer. Fond o' buttin' in t' other folks' business, ain't yer? Feel like startin' somethin' agen t'night? Haw haw!" With a thick, malevolent guffaw he jabbed Kent's ribs savagely with his rifle-barrel.

"Stan' aside, Wolf, an' lemme paste 'im one"—as the other three crowded up the bullet-headed man spat a vicious oath. "I owes that bird somethin' from las' night."

"Wait a bit—wait a bit," impatiently, with a none too gentle shove of his rifle-butt, the wolf-faced man pushed the glowering thug back. "Y'can have a crack at him before we get through—an' mebbe at th' gal, too. Haw haw! But hold yer hosses a bit. Business before pleasure. Keep yer mitts t' yerself a while. But take that there flashlight he's a holdin'. He might do some damage with it."

" 'Ell! 'E's probably got a gat on 'im besides," a bit sulkily the bullet-headed thug jerked the electric torch from Kent's upraised hand. "An' th' skirt, too. Likely she's packin' one on 'er as well."

"Well, frisk 'em both—an' look lively," Wolf Hesfor snapped. "An' one o' you fellers go see where th' old man is."

"You keep your hands off that girl," in a sudden surge of apprehensive fury that scattered caution to the winds Kent surged forward. "She hasn't got a gun. Leave her alone."

"Back—damn yuh!...An' keep 'em up!" With a savage, lunging prod of his rifle muzzle Hesfor checked the movement. "An' shut yer trap. We ain't hurtin' her—yet. But we'll find what we're lookin' fer if we have t' pick every rag off o' both o' yer."

"Girl ain't packin' no rod nor nothin'." From the wall where he had stepped briskly to run a swift, practiced hand over the girl's rain-soaked clothing, Chink Halloran spoke up quickly. "She's all right, I reckon. I never knowed her t' pack any shootin'-iron, anyways."

"Well, this bird's been packin' somethin'," the bullet-headed thug who was going over Kent grunted triumphantly. "'Ell! 'Ere's two boxes o' pills fer a forty-five gat." He dragged the two heavy little pasteboard boxes from Kent's pockets and set them down upon the top of the closed trunk.

"Yeah-that'd be fer my shootin'-iron. He snaked it from me last night," Wolf Hesfor growled. "Hand it over here."

"'E ain't got it on 'im," puzzled, the searcher prodded and felt Kent over once more. "'E ain't got nothin' more on 'im but a few odds an' ends, an' this 'ere billfold."

"Huh!" Wolf Hesfor's heavy hand closed over the rain-damp leather case that the other extended. "Where's th' gun, Buttinsky?" he demanded shortly, jabbing again at Kent with his rifle.

"I lost it." His heart pounding now with the certain knowledge that his action in concealing the weapon had gone unnoticed, Kent met the questioning stare unflinchingly. "I dropped it. I slipped over a cliff getting here in the dark."

"Oh yeah?" Wolf Hesfor drawled dangerously.

"That's the truth," Kent said shortly. "You can take it or leave it. If you don't believe me, maybe you'd like to feel the place I lit on." With a shrug and an indicating gesture he lowered his head.

"Huh—yuh did raise quite a hen's egg—didn't yer." With one finger of the hand that still held the note-case Hesfor made a rough, sceptical exploration. "I wish t' hell you'd broke yer blasted neck. Well, yuh may be tellin' th' truth, or yuh may be lyin'. But it don't make much difference. Yuh ain't got no shootin'-iron in reach o' yer mitts now, an,' that's th' main thing." He moved back a pace and, fumblingly, with a suddenly greedy light in his eyes, began to open the billfold.

"Old geezer ain't around no place," slouching back from a tour of inspection which he had conducted by the aid of the flashlight taken from Kent, Chink Halloran made the announcement laconically. "Mebbe he's crawled off and died somewheres from over-excitement." He gave a hard, cackling laugh.

"Where's yer old man?" Pawing through the contents of the note-case with hands that were hampered by the rifle he held, Hesfor glanced up to shoot the girl a brusk, harsh question. "Where's he got to?"

"I—I don't know," haltingly, her face still white from the sudden expression of agonized fear that had shot across it at Chink Halloran's brutal suggestion, the girl broke the numb, stony silence that had held her since her first scream. "He's disappeared—he disappeared some-where this afternoon—while I was away from the house. I—I don't know where he is."

"Huh!…Fell down a cliff in th' dark an' got lost—same as th' gun, I s'pose, huh?" Wolf Hesfor's voice was a snarl. "Think agen, sister. Two o' them stories don't go."

"I reckon, mebbe she's tellin' th' truth, Wolf—but she ain't tellin' all th' truth," Chink Halloran emitted another of his cackling chuckles. "Probability is that the old geezer has got one o' his bug-house spells on. Th' old fool heared somewheres from th' Indians that eatin' that damn Jimsonweed—*toloache* some calls it—gives yer second sight. He eats a dose o' it every so often an' goes into a bug-house trance, lookin' fer th' treasure. Th' girl won't never acknowledge that to no one, though. Claims th' old man's heart is bad." He chuckled again.

"His heart *is* bad and—and you know it, you beast," the girl cried vehemently. "It was on account of his heart that he had to give up his profession. Any shock, anything sudden, is liable to kill…him…And what if he does take *toloache*? He's studied that and—"

"Aw shut up—who cares?" savagely, but with his face all at once alight with a fierce new triumph, as he looked up suddenly from something he had been laboriously reading, Wolf Hesfor silenced him. "But looka here, boys, here's somethin'—somethin' Mister Buttinsky was a packin' 'round with him. Looka here!" Triumphantly he displayed the old yellowed sheet of paper. "Here's th' clue we're a lookin' fer, boys, an' all wrote out in my ole granddad's own handwritin.'"

CHAPTER 17

Terror

"**A**w 'ell—that there's poetry—that ain't no clue." Peering, with craned neck, across Hesfor's shoulder as all the others came, crowding up, the bullet-headed man snorted disgustedly. "Clue—'ell! That's just some slop wrote to th' skirt by this 'ere." He jerked a derisive thumb in the direction of Kent.

"Oh yeah!…Smart, ain't yer," Hesfor snarled. "Jest shows what sort o' mud yer brain's made of. Listen here, boys." Thickly, stumbling and halting over many of the words, he read the verses aloud. "That there's clear as yer want it," he said when he had finished. "All the landmarks is told plain. Come daylight we'd oughter be able t' locate the cache first crack."

The gang fell into excited discussion. Watching them Kent felt a stir of hope. Would it be possible, he wondered, while their attention was engrossed over prospects of the treasure, to drop his' aching arms, wrench open the trunk and gain possession of the gun? It seemed a madman's scheme, for, in addition to their rifles, all the gang with the exception of Hesfor carried six-shooters as well—slim chance for but one man against such an arsenal of weapons. Still it might be the only desperate hope. Sight of the silent, white-faced girl, shrunk back against the wall within arm reach of him, was good enough for any attempt that held even the faintest chance of success. With tensing muscles and suddenly pounding pulse he watched for his opening. The bearer of the lantern, a lean Italian with a sinister, pock-marked face, had pressed forward among the rest. His attention now was less on the management of the light than in an attempt, with slowly tracing finger, to spell out for himself the words on the paper in Hesfor's hand.

But all at once Kent's dimly forming hopes went glimmering. As though warned by some sixth sense of what was passing in the prisoner's mind, Chink Halloran suddenly straightened up. "Well, I reckon it's mebbe O.K., fellers," he said, squaring his slouching shoulders with an abrupt shrug. "So what are we goin' t' do with these two? We won't want 'em no more. Mebbe we can find some more gal's stockin's hereabouts." He emitted one of his ugly chuckles and swept the two captives with an evil glance.

"Aw, no yer don't," wheeling, the bullet-headed thug shrilled sharp protest. "I'm goin' t' 'andle that bird a bit. An' besides, th' skirt...she's a good looker an'—"

"Shut yer trap." With thick-voiced savagery Hesfor cut him short. "We would be a bunch o' nit-wits t' bump off these two before we gets a holt o' the stuff. No tellin' what more they knows about it. An' besides, this paper ain't all. There was that little book—the one that all th' scrappin' was about last night. Where's that got to? How about it, sister?" He shot a questioning glare at the girl.

"If you'd use yer 'ead, you'd know damn well it was in that there box," sourly, without waiting for the girl to make answer, the bullet-headed man pointed to the trunk. "They wuz both 'andlin' th' books in there when we come in, wasn't they? That's where yer blarsted book is."

"Then hop t' it an' dig it out!" Hesfor snapped. "G'wan now. Le's see if th' mud in yer head's workin' this time or not."

But the bullet-headed man's lunging movement to comply was never completed. Before even his reaching hands could move the two boxes of cartridges which stood upon the trunk top, and while Kent's sharp-caught breath was still checked by the chilling realization that now the concealed gun must surely be discovered, there rang suddenly from the wind-whistled darkness outside a dreadful, blood-freezing sound—a sound that swung every face in the room with a startled jerk towards the black rectangle of the open door.

"Gawd A'mighty!" Hesfor gasped. "What th'...."

Again, clearer, sharper, blotting his stammering words as it swept through the shanty on the beating pinions of a wind gust that roared down the canyon, the ghastly sound came again—the high-pitched sound of a wild, unearthly laugh, a laugh that was more the gibbering scream of a triumphant demon than the sound of any earthly creature. The wild, malevolent shriek of it seemed to ring in every corner of the cabin at once, to swirl freezingly on the wind across the roof; to pulse echoing through every cave and hollow of the canyon depths. Kent felt his heart stand still. The girl shrank back against the wall with an involuntary, terrified cry.

And then, all at once, out of emptiness it seemed, there was a *Something* in the doorway. A Something tall and ghastly and white as sun-bleached bones. A Something that, framed against the ebony black of the outer night, seemed both to stand firm and to billow and drift upon the howling wind that was of a sudden sweeping down the canyon. It was standing there glaring into the cabin—glaring with deep-sunk, ghastly eyes that seemed to glow coal red in the flooding rays of the electric lamp. Malevolently, dreadfully, lit with a terrible hate, those flaming eyes gleamed in the shrunk, set face—a face that was a drawn and ghastly death-mask of the face of old Jeff Crossman.

And then, then suddenly out of a momentary blackness of stunned terror, Kent was aware that the Thing—its left arm with rigid pointing finger leveled accusingly at Hesfor—was speaking. Words shrieked upon the driving eddies of the wind; words dry and whistling as though hissed through fleshless jaws, but words vibrant with some awful compelling power that seemed to check the blood, to still the heart, to turn tensed muscles to powerless stone.

"Wolf Hesfor—I know you!" dreadfully through the little room rang the terrible voice. "Murderer! Scoundrel! Now in the appointed time shall vengeance be fulfilled! Here in these grim solitudes in which you thought to hide your crime and your stolen wealth shall justice overtake you. In that place where you chained me to die of hunger and of thirst shall you die also. On this canyon bed where my bones have bleached yours also shall lie. Fool! Here shall you learn that life is an endless book and that its pages are always balanced. Learn now that for each stolen thing there is a reckoning; for each taken life there is full payment. Go!…Go now into the wind and darkness. Go now and prepare!"

The voice had leaped to a shriek—a shriek that ended suddenly in a deafening, shattering crash. Dazed, jerked sharply forward as though the numbing, paralyzing spell that had gripped everyone in the little room had snapped and released his muscles in an involuntary surge, Kent was aware that the white, ghastly figure had all at once flung forward its right arm—the arm that till then had been invisible amidst the white, billowy mist. Fire was flashing from it—fire and the deafening crash of heavy detonations. The light went out in a splintering smash. Blackness and wild pandemonium seemed to whirl suddenly over everything. The room was filled with shots and shrieks, the red flashing of guns and a yelling tumult of terrified oaths. Leaping like a madman, scarce knowing what he did, Kent wrenched back the lid of the trunk, plunged his hand among the tumbled books and clutched the heavy six-shooter.

"Gawd A'mighty!...Outa here!...Outa here!...Gordam! Get outa...!"

Lightning tore the night outside—a sheeting, sky-shattering flash that flamed across the mountains on the heels of a bellowing down rush of wind. In the cold, glinting glare Kent had a fleeting glimpse of surging forms leaping for the doorway, of rifle-muzzles that licked orange jets of flame across the dimness, of something ghastly white that pitched forward and fell sideways into the room. And even as he swung up his own gun and fired, slashing a spatter of bullets into the plunging shapes of the ruffians silhouetted against the flare-lit outer night, he heard the girl scream something. The next instant, as the lightning flash winked out and the dark struggling forms vanished through the doorway in a wild, cursing plunge, she whirled past him. He heard the door slam, the crash of a shot bolt, the bumping thud of a heavy wooden door-bar being dragged hastily into place.

South in Julian

CHAPTER 18

Dead Man/s Vengeance

"**Q**uick! Quick!"—in the sudden momentary hush that followed the slamming of the door the girl's voice came hoarse and panting. "Help me with this bar. It's jammed somewhere, and the bolt alone won't hold!"

Groping feverishly in the dark Kent found her tugging hands and threw his strength also to the task. The bar, evidently unused for a long time, was warped a little and one end was stubborn about fitting into its socket. A desperate heave with their combined power at length forced it into place. But even as it did so something heavy, hurtling from the night, struck the outside of the door with a crash that seemed to strain every plank. The bar groaned, but held. In the same instant, to a rattle of rapid reports, bullets flew through the side walls, hurling a cloud of dust and splinters through the darkness of the room.

"Down! Down!"the girl gasped. "The lower part's 'dobe—bullet-proof. Top's just mud and sticks."

Flattened beside her as he followed her example and dropped prone upon the earthen floor, Kent's groping hands found that this was so. Beside him, rising to a height of a little more than thirty inches above the floor level, was a low, solidly built base wall of heavy adobe bricks. Above that, as his cautiously exploring fingers told him, the cabin walls continued upward as a flimsy barrier of ocotillo stalks plastered with mud. Through this, as through a screen of paper, bullets from the cracking rifles of the gang outside were now slashing like angry hornets. It was evident enough that Wolf Hesfor and his partners had in a measure recovered from their wild panic. They were now blazing away rapidly, pouring in bullets with a random fury that caused Kent's mind to leap instantly to the thought of peril from the direction of the windows. With a quick sense of relief, however, he remembered that the only two windows which the cabin possessed were tight closed with board shutters.

But even to the savage fusillade which was riddling the cabin from end to end Kent had scant time to attend. Almost as swiftly as she had dropped to cover, the girl had crawled away somewhere in the darkness. He heard her hands fumbling along the floor. Something rolled and scraped. An instant later, light lit the dusty floor earth in a blinding glow—light that was accompanied by a choked, breathless sob.

"Shut it off!... Shut it off!" Startled, the peril of the revealing light for the moment sweeping everything else from his mind, Kent reached towards her with a snatch. "That gives 'em a target—they can see that light through the bullet-holes. Shut it off."

But even as he cried out and, as in obedience, darkness snapped down again over the little room, Kent realized that it had not been the finding of the flashlight Halloran had dropped on the floor that had occasioned the girl's low cry. For in the momentary flood of radiance he, too, had glimpsed the thing which evidently she had been seeking—a long shape of ghastly white that, with outflung arms, lay sprawled on the floor to one side of the doorway. Across from it, on the farther side of the room, and visible for just an instant in the transitory light-flash, another prone form, dark, but equally motionless, was stretched upon the floor dust. But for this second shape the girl had evidently no eyes.

"Father! Father!...Oh God, dear God, please...please don't let him be dead!"

The words were a low, sobbing wail of anguish. Kent's mind, still whirling with the hideous unreality of the last few frenzied moments, seemed to suddenly clear. With a swift movement, the cold, dreadful sense of uncanny horror scattered all at once by one light-swift rush of realization, he was at the girl's side, his hands groping with hers along the outlines of the silent, still form that, beneath the voluminous folds of some thin, cloak-like covering, lay motionless on the earthen floor.

"Oh, Rodney! Rodney—he's dead! They've killed him! Oh, God!... Oh, what shall we do? Oh, what shall we do?"

"The light!—the light!" Hoarsely unnerved and cut to the heart by the terrible intensity of her grief, Kent felt about in the darkness. "Give me that flashlight. Quick!"

"Here, here!" She thrust it into his hand. "Oh, Rodney, please—please...Save him! Oh, do something! Don't—don't say he's dead."

Her pitiful grief was heart-wrenching. With fingers that were all at once trembling like aspen leaves, Kent pushed forward the flashlight and, mindful enough that the peril of attracting deadly bullets would allow him to risk no more than a hasty glimpse, switched on the light for an instant and then, as abruptly, shut it off.

But that one momentary glimpse was enough. A man lay there on the floor beside him—a man who was flesh and blood and no ghost. Drawn-faced and ghastly, his long lean body wrapped in the winding folds of what was evidently a bed sheet and with the hand of his bare, extended right arm still locked about the butt of a heavy revolver, he lay very still and rigid staring up into the darkness with wide, unseeing eyes. The face was white, gleaming in the flash-glow with almost the same ghastly pallor as the white winding sheet. But in the centre of the pale forehead was a dreadful red wound that marked the course of a heavy bullet. Kent needed no second glance to tell him that the motionless, sheet-clothed figure was beyond all human aid.

"He's dead, Marie." Gently, dazed now of a sudden with the abrupt realization of what it had really been that had guided him across that perilous mountain trail, Kent whispered the words. "But—but that isn't your father. That's old Jeff Crossman."

"No, no…Oh, you don't know…Oh, you can't understand." Stranglingly, without need of his words to tell her what her own eyes had already seen in the momentary flash-glow, the girl's voice came in a broken sob. "It's father. I—I didn't know him till the very last moment. Those sheets—he must have taken them from his bed. It's father—not Crossman. Jeff Crossman and he were doubles—they looked like twin brothers. But this—this is father. Oh, God!…Oh, God, that he should die like this!"

She broke down utterly. Grief-wracked and sobbing, utterly unmindful of the hum and slash of the vicious bullets that still searched through the cabin, she crouched huddled beside the still form, weeping her heart out in a terrible, uncontrollable flood of grief.

At her side in the black darkness Kent knelt in stunned, helpless sympathy. The girl's torrent of suffering crushed him. Her agony of sorrow wrenched his heart. But he could do nothing. Only too well he sensed that there was nothing he could say at that moment that would ease her grief. Speech just then would only have added to her torment. In the dark, with his hand closed comfortingly over hers, he sat silent.

But even above the poignant ache of his sympathy his mind was racing. Many things were now clear that had mystified him. But even now, with this logical and human explanation of events that had seemed terrifyingly supernatural he could not rid his mind of a certain sense of the uncanny. That it was quite possible for the girl's father, while under the influence of *toloache*, to have wandered in a trance-like state and have guided him over the trail, he did not doubt. He had heard things of a similar order. He had heard that certain old-time

Indian witch-doctors were able to go into trances by the aid of tiny doses of this deadly, poisonous herb and thus locate missing persons or animals or discover water. That part was possible enough. But there were other queer things. Not the least of these was the startling resemblance which the dead, sheeted form beside him bore to Jeff Crossman. Side by side the two men could hardly have been told apart. It did not seem possible that two unrelated individuals could so closely resemble each other. And then there was an odd and uncanny fact. The dead man's frenzied words and his accusingly pointing finger had been directed at no one but Wolf Hesfor—yet the bullets from his suddenly drawn gun had been fired not into Hesfor, but into Chink Halloran. And the aim had been deadly, for even in the transitory gleam when the girl had first found the flashlight, the prone shape that lay further across the room had been unmistakable. That was a queer thing. Why had Halloran—of all the four—been especially singled out as a target by the terrible, white-sheeted figure? Was it vengeance? Halloran was undoubtedly the murderer of Jeff Crossman. But how did Banniston, the grim, white figure that had been wandering in the storm, know that? Was that again all the doings of *toloache*?

Uneasily, disturbed more than he liked to admit by these flooding speculations which seemed to drive for the moment even the girl's grief and their present desperate peril from his mind, Kent crawled softly away in the dark and groped for the other body. He felt positive that his first fleeting glimpse had not deceived him, but he wanted to make doubly certain. Besides, he wanted to assure himself that no possible peril was to be expected from that quarter.

A brief wink of his flashlight, however, answered both questions with finality. It was Chink Halloran, and he was stone dead. It seemed plain enough, even in that momentary glimpse, that the entire contents of Banniston's six-shooter had been poured against him. At least two bullets had found their mark in his evil face and others, judging by the welling stain of blood, had torn through his heart.

Awed and startled by this evidence that Halloran had been deliberately singled out, Kent swiftly removed the dead man's cartridge-belt and six-shooter, buckled them about his own waist, and picked up the rifle which lay on the floor beside the body. With a distinct sense of something uncanny—something that even the trance-inducing properties of the deadly *toloache* did not quite explain—he crawled silently back towards the girl. Just before reaching her side he paused a moment and, with a little difficulty, removed also the heavy six-gun from the white-sheeted' figure's stiffening fingers. The gun was empty, as his sense of touch quickly informed him. But from the same groping examination he judged that it was a weapon of forty-five caliber. At least now, he realized, they had armament that was more on a level with that of the ruffians outside.

"Toloache" or Jimsonweed—Datura wrightii *(Photo: Diana Lindsay)*

∽

CHAPTER 19

The Stealthy Digger

"**R**odney, we're trapped! We'll never get out of here alive!"

It was the girl's voice, tear-choked but steadier. Somehow, by what supreme effort of will Kent never knew, she had fought down her racking tempest of grief and, even in the few moments that he had been away examining the body of Halloran, a great change had come over her. It was as though somewhere in her mind, by sheer force of will, she had closed a door and, closing her grief and tears behind her for the time, had turned bravely to a facing of the immediate present. Her voice was shaking and husky, and it somehow sounded infinitely older. But she had regained her nerve. Kent's heart lightened. Realization of her grit sent a sharp thrill of admiration through him.

"We're trapped, Rodney. We'll never get out of here." Again, more steadily, she repeated the words, reaching at the same time towards him in the darkness.

"It's all right, Marie—sure we'll get out." In the gloom Kent's hand closed over her searching fingers with a sudden, warm, tender pressure. "You just keep up your heart. We've got that bunch beat already. And with all these extra guns—why, they're simply out of luck."

"Rodney, I'm not a kid." As though in rebuke for his forced optimism, her answering whisper was grave. "You don't have to try to fool me. We're in a bad place. This is a box canyon, as you know, I guess, and right here the cliffs are unclimbable. Also this place is away off in the wilderness. No one ever comes here. They've got us bottled in. They can shoot us out or starve us out—no one will ever disturb them. Even if we manage to keep them off while it's dark, daylight will make things worse for us. And it must be getting towards daylight already."

"Yes, I know—but things aren't nearly so bad as they might be," he tried to reassure her. "They've got us cornered right enough. But there are only three of them now. Halloran's dead—over there on the floor. Your dad got him."

"Oh!" She caught her breath. "Is it Halloran? Well, that was justice. Father must have known he killed Jeff. Father was awfully fond of Jeff. He—he was just like…" Her voice faltered and choked, but with an effort she regained her calmness. "They've stopped shooting, Rodney," she whispered. "They're up to something."

But already, warned by the cessation of the fusillade, Kent's every sense was keyed in taut expectancy. For some moments the shots from the windy darkness had been slackening. That they had stopped altogether was ominous.

"Maybe, on account of our not shooting back at 'em, they've got the notion that they've wiped us out," Kent whispered. "Can you use a six-shooter?"

"Yes—oh yes. Father and I used to go hunting rabbits together. I—I'm a pretty good shot." She struggled bravely to hold her voice steady.

"Then take this gun." He thrust one of the revolvers into her hand. "And come along with me. We've got to get some cartridges for it."

"This—this is father's gun, isn't it? It feels like it." As she crawled stealthily after him in the inky blackness, her whisper came low and strained.

"Yes"—with a stabbing sense of having made another blunder Kent spoke hastily. "But I can give you this other one. I'll…."

"Oh no, no!" with a tense fierceness she cut him short. "I—I'd much sooner have this one. It's the one I've always used. Poor father, he must have taken it with him when he slipped away from here. We always kept it in the book trunk so I never missed it. But we've no more cartridges for it. We were just out. Those in the gun were all we had left."

"It's a forty-five, isn't it?" Kent was groping on the earth floor for the two boxes of shells that had been dumped there when he had flung back the trunk lid during the melee.

"Yes."

"Then these will fit it." He ripped open one of the boxes that his feeling hands had suddenly encountered and passed it to her. "Load up, and put the rest in your pockets. I've got another box here. And maybe you'd better take one of these other six-shooters as well. One's Hesfor's—that I took last night. The other's Halloran's."

"No—no," she gasped, and even in the dark he could sense her shudder of revulsion. "It would be a crime against father's memory—his gun in one hand and the gun of one of those murderers in the other. This gun will be enough for me. And I only hope…." She did not finish her words. But in the black gloom there came to Kent's ears a sharp, vicious click, as with deadly purpose she snapped the loaded cylinder of her gun back into place.

Kent was busily replacing the shells he had discharged from Hesfor's gun, and in assuring himself that both Halloran's six-shooter and rifle were fully loaded. The rifle was a 30-30 Winchester and the feel of it gave him greater confidence than the two six-shooters combined. He paused a moment, listening. But he could hear nothing but the gusting roar of the wind and the occasional patter of squall-driven gravel rattling upon the roof.

"Better come over here." He reached out and touched the girl's arm. "—Over this way, in the corner. We can shove out this book trunk a bit and get behind it. That'll give us quite a bit more protection if we keep low down behind it."

"Yes—that and the stove," she agreed. "The stove's on this other side, you know. It's an old cast-iron one. We brought it in here in sections."

"Uh-uh—I was counting on that as well. It'll be a pretty good bullet stop." Already Kent was tugging at the trunk. "Here—you get in here—this way. Close against the wall."

Silently and swiftly, working and tugging together, they dragged the heavy, book-filled trunk out on to the floor and arranged themselves in the corner behind it. Here, defended on two sides by the low adobe base wall and on the other two by the stove and trunk, Kent felt that they would be reasonably safe from flying bullets, provided they kept low-crouched and near the floor level. Several minutes had now slipped past without any sound of the men outside. Save for the buffeting tumult of the wind the black outer darkness, illumined by an occasional glare of lightning that glinted green into the cabin through cracks and bullet-holes, seemed empty.

And then, all at once, as Kent crouched tense and listening, there came a sound—a faint, scraping, pecking sound, that seemed to come from the wall just behind their heads. Kent put out a quick hand and touched the girl's arm with warning pressure.

"Ssh!" he breathed softly. "There's someone outside—digging with a knife at the wall. Get ready—but don't shoot till you can't miss."

The pecking, prying noise continued, ceased, and then, after a short, cautious interval, began again. It was evident that the besiegers had made a prowling examination of the outside of the cabin in the dark, and finding everything tight barred and shuttered had determined on the plan of cutting a hole through the flimsy upper wall, possibly with the notion of turning the beam of a flashlight through the opening and inspecting the interior. The foolhardiness of the scheme puzzled Kent a little, for, though the silence within the cabin might very reasonably have convinced the attackers that their random bullets had accounted for its occupants, yet they could have no definite guarantee of that fact. With this in mind, Kent wondered which of the three was doing the digging. Not Wolf Hesfor, he felt certain. Wolf was far too shrewd. His might have been the plan, but undoubtedly it was one of his under-studies who was carrying it out. Grimly Kent wondered whether it was the bullet-headed thug or the lean, sinister Italian whom Hesfor had bullied into thus inviting destruction.

The cautious pecking and digging continued, but now more swiftly, as though the man outside in the darkness was drawing confi-dence from the fact that his operations had drawn no response from within. Clearly to Kent's ears, despite the gusting rush of the wind that tore around the house, came the noise of falling hunks of dry mud as the swift-working knife blade pried them loose. He heard presently the slashing hacking of the steel cutting at the dry *ocotillo* stalks that formed the thin wall's core. Close by his head a big hunk of the mud plaster broke loose from the inside of the wall and fell to the floor with a resounding thud. He heard the girl beside him draw a low, quick breath as she moved slightly to a better facing of the attack. Tensely, with ready guns, they crouched side by side in the blackness, listening and waiting.

And then, all at once, there came the sound of a savage tugging slash and the sharp snapping of *ocotillo* stalks. Another big section of mud plaster tumbled into the room, accompanied by a gusting inrush of wind. Almost between them and a little above the level of their heads, a ragged patch of dimmer gloom appeared upon the inky blackness of the wall—a ragged patch of murk that was of a sudden outlined a cold, blinding green in the flare of a lightning flash that blazed an instant above the canyon and blotted as swiftly into the raging dark.

But that brief, winking flash, as though timed by some directing Power to the exact fraction of a second, had served its purpose. Clearly for a moment, as they crouched with eyes glued in dreadful fascination to the new-made wan opening, there came to both Kent and the girl the fleeting glimpses of a lean, pock-marked face, a pair of glittering eyes and a long, dark hand and arm that came swiftly reaching into the room.

CHAPTER 20

A Foiled Attempt

The glimpse of that sinister, inreaching hand had been but a transitory flash, but it had been long enough to show Kent that the lean, dark fingers grasped a small electric torch—and also that the man outside was close pressed against the wall, his eyes peering into the opening. Like a flash, certain now of his target, Kent swung up his gun and pulled the trigger. A deafening roar beside him that seemed to unite with the report of his own pistol told him that the girl also had fired. Blended with the sudden ripping detonations as the orange flashes of the close-held guns stabbed against the wall, there came from outside a wild startled shriek—a shriek that blurred out in the sounds of a thudding, struggling fall, over which the roar of the wind closed like a muffling blanket.

"Flatten down—flatten down again close to the floor." Breathlessly, half stifled by the acrid powder fumes and wall dust that the inrush of wind through the opening had flung back in their faces, Kent pulled the girl down under shelter. "Keep well down! Don't take chances! They'll begin shooting again now."

And scarcely had the words passed his lips when, from somewhere outside, the darkness woke in wind-muffled reports. Again, hungrily, seeking bullets whined viciously through the shack. Beside them an iron pot leaped suddenly from the stove top with a resounding clang. Dry mud plaster fell from the wan in a pattering shower.

"We got him—we got him," the girl breathed. "But—but it wasn't Hesfor."

"No, it was the Italian," Kent answered. "Hesfor's far too foxy to have taken a foolhardy risk like that. But he likely bluffed or bullied this man into the job."

"That would be typical of Hesfor," she said in a low voice. "He's probably figuring already on how to avoid sharing the treasure. He's still got that paper with the clue on it, you know. Unless he lost it in the stampede when they thought father was a ghost."

"I don't think he'd let go of that—no matter how badly scared he was," Kent said reflectively. "Anyway, we've only two of them to deal with now."

"If there was only one we'd still be at an awful disadvantage here," the girl said practically. "Even one man could hide in the rocks and keep us bottled in this canyon till he either shot us down or forced us to surrender—which would be the same thing. Thirst would soon get us. The spring is up the canyon. When we've used up the little water there is in the house we'd be forced to expose ourselves in order to get more. That would be the end."

Kent made no immediate answer. In his own mind he knew well enough that the girl spoke truly. If it came to a siege, to venture out of the protection of the cabin by daylight would amount to suicide. They would be an easy mark for a rifleman concealed among the giant boulders which cluttered the base of the canyon walls. And there was no telling whether the affair would even develop into much of a protracted siege. The vicious whang and spatter of the bullets that ripped through the cabin from end to end was an ominous indication of the determination of the two men outside to end the business as swiftly as possible. For a brief space he considered the possibility of abandoning the cabin and making a bold attempt to slip away down the canyon in the darkness. But he dismissed the notion. With the intermittent lightning flashes which were still, from time to time, ripping the sky with their all-revealing glow, the attempt would be entirely too risky.

"I'm sorry it wasn't Hesfor that I shot at just now," the girl said abruptly, breaking in upon his silent speculations. "I'd die happy if I could shoot him first."

She spoke calmly, in a low, deliberate voice that was vibrant with grim purpose. In spite of himself, Kent was conscious of a sudden startled sense of admiration and respect. He realized all at once that his first judgment of this girl had been correct.

At heart she was all loyalty and gritty determination. What it was costing her to preserve her calmness with her soul torn by the agonizing knowledge that but a few feet away her father lay on the floor a cold corpse he could not tell. But in the intensity of her low spoken words he could read something of her inner misery and her thirst for vengeance. There had been an uncommon bond of sympathy and understanding between Marie Banniston and her father, he realized. And, crouching there in the black darkness at her side his heart bled for her. He reached across and touched her hand. "It's—it's all right, Marie," he whispered awkwardly. "You just keep your heart up. It'll all come right."

The words were foolish, and he knew it. But he knew also that she understood, for her fingers closed round his with an understanding pressure.

"You—you're awfully good, Rodney," she said huskily. "And it's too bad that you've been dragged into this dreadful business. For father—for me—well, it couldn't be helped, I guess. We're part of it. It's our affair. But for you...."

"Now see here," Kent broke in quickly. "That's not fair, Marie. You've got to quit feeling like that. I wasn't dragged into this—I just naturally butted myself in. And it was the best thing, I guess, that I ever did because—because—" his words became all at once stumbling and awkward. "Because—I'd sooner be right here with you, no matter what happens, than any place else. Oughtn't to say it, I guess, but I mean that, Marie. An' I want you to believe that, because it's true."

"Thanks, Rodney," she said softly, but the quick warn pressure with which her hand tightened upon his for an instant told him infinitely more than the whispered word's. "Thanks...And I—I guess it's not so strange after all...From the first moment I glimpsed you in that book-store last night I—I had a feeling...that—that somehow...."

Her unfinished words trailed off in a soft, wistful sigh. But again, quickly, her fingers closed over his. Side by side, crouched low behind their sheltering defenses, they remained for a long time without speaking, straining their ears into the gusty rush of the wind that whirled round the cabin and drove fierce eddies through the ragged hole just above their heads. The whanging bullets had ceased slashing through the walls. The firing had stopped.

"Rodney, you're cold—we're both cold." Breaking at length what seemed to Kent an interminable period of tense, fruitless listening, the girl spoke abruptly. "There's no telling what those two brutes outside are up to or where they are, and there's no sense in getting ourselves exhausted. I'm going to get you something to eat and drink."

"You stop right here," Kent said hastily. "I don't need a thing. And besides, if you make a movement they might...."

"No," she cut in, "I don't think they're close—not this minute. So I'm going to take the chance. I've a good hunch that you're need-ing food—and I know that in these rain-sopped clothes we're both wretchedly cold. We can't light a fire or anything, but there's a bottle of brandy in the cupboard. Father always kept it in case of emergency. I'm going to get that—if the bullets haven't smashed it. And I'll get something to eat."

"Hold on there!…Take care!" With a sudden clutch as the girl rose briskly to her feet, Kent caught at her. "Get down under cover. I'll go get…."

"Why look—look! They've got a fire!" With a sharp exclamation which cut him short the girl seized his arm. "Look!—Way down there along the canyon."

In the darkness she was stooping close to the ragged hole in the wall and peering out. Already on his feet beside her, Kent bent forward and looked also. He saw at once that she was right. Among the rocks, at a considerable distance down the canyon, the leaping glow of a fire was plainly visible. The distance was too great and the flames were too well sheltered among the massive boulders to allow any possibility of discerning any silhouettes of human figures. But the fire was visible enough.

"They've made camp," the girl said, "down in that narrow neck of the canyon where they know we couldn't possibly get past them without being seen. They've got us bottled in, and they know it. Well now, I'm going to get you something to eat. We'll be safe enough here for a while."

"Take care all the same, and don't make any noise," Kent whispered. "That fire may be a dodge—just to make us reckless. They may be up to something else."

"I know," she agreed. "But we've got to take a chance. Come on. You can help me."

Silently, but briskly, she drew him after her into the gloom, and groping swiftly along the wall had soon swung open the door of a small cupboard.

"It's here," she gave a low exclamation of thankfulness, "and it's not smashed. Here, Rodney"—feeling, she passed a bottle into his hand—"you hold it and' I'll get a couple of cups and a can of beef."

❧

CHAPTER 21

Shadows from the Past

The sketchy, impromptu meal which they ate presently, when once more installed in the comparative security of their barricaded corner, did much to put heart into them both. Not until he actually began to eat did Kent realize just how long he had been without food or how much he had needed it. In addition to the can of corned beef the girl had found a large package of pilot biscuit, and these they munched gratefully, washing down the dry food with sparing sips of brandy and water. The brandy was of good quality, and the warming glow which it presently sent through their veins did much to counteract the wretchedness and chill of their rain-soaked clothing. Crouched side by side in the darkness, using fingers for knives and forks, and each suddenly too hungry to talk, they ate for the most part in silence, their ears strained only to the rushing swoop of the wind and the loud skittering rattle of gravel that bounced and rattled on the peaked roof of the unceiled cabin.

"It's just the wind—it always makes a noise like that when it's stormy," reassuringly as a particularly loud scraping clatter overhead caused Kent to tense, the girl spoke quickly. "This roof is just tar paper—just roofing paper laid over boards. It was the quickest and easiest stuff we could pack in here to make a roof out of. And the gravel blows down from the canyon rim, way overhead. It makes an awful racket sometimes. On account of this shack having no ceiling, we get all the sound."

The storm was slowly passing. In spite of the fact that the wind still roared down from the mountains and swooped and billowed through the deep gash of the canyon, it was evident that the main fury of the storm was already over. The rain flurries had long since ceased and the flaring flashes of the lightning no longer ripped the darkness. It had been long since even the faintest rumble of distant thunder had echoed about the mountain peaks. The storm, all but the wind, had drifted away, and with it also the night. For already the gloom outside, as frequent glances through the ragged hole in the wall told Kent, was lightening. Morning was not so far off. Daylight would come slower here in the canyon depths than elsewhere, he realized. But it was coming.

And the knowledge that dawn was on the way set Kent sharply to worrying. Again he returned to his former thought that perhaps it would be better to make an attempt to get away under cover of the dark. And again, after reflection, he abandoned the idea. It was impossible now. The bonfire, which was still blazing brightly among the rocks in the narrow section of the canyon, rendered it futile to hope that they could get through that narrow neck without being observed. And with that chance gone there was nothing to be gained by leaving the house. The shanty, with its low wall base of solid adobe, offered at least a fairly strong position for defense—and they now had plenty of arms and a fair amount of ammunition. It would be the wisest plan to remain in the house, Kent decided. Had he been alone he might have been tempted to abandon it and stake his chances on playing a game of stalking and sniping with the two ruffians outside. As it was, however, there was the girl to consider. He did not dare to expose her to such a risk.

"There's, nothing to do but to wait, Rodney," as though she had interpreted his thoughts and read the reason for his long silence, the girl spoke abruptly. "We might as well stay here and see what they're up to. We're two to two now—so it isn't such awful odds. But they've got us at a big disadvantage and there's no sense in playing into their hands by getting impatient and letting them make targets of us. There's still some canned food here in the house—and there's lots of flour. The bucket of water that I brought from the spring yesterday evening is still almost full. We can stand a siege for a while.... Want some more biscuits?"

"No, thanks, I'm just about through." He checked her movement as she pushed the package towards him.

"I guess I am too—and I feel better. I'm glad we ate. I knew we needed something. It's—It's hard to fight if you're cold and weak and—and miserable." She spoke with a brave effort at calmness, but her voice at the end broke and she moved hastily to thrust aside the empty beef can and to place the bottle of brandy, the cups and the remainder of the biscuits to one side in a safe place. Kent knew that again the thought of the cold, still form of her father on the earth floor just a few feet from them had come to her with crushing chill.

"They're still keeping their fire going," he spoke quickly to distract her mind. "They must have lots of wood."

"Yes, there's a juniper clump right close there," she said as she moved her head to glance out through the hole. "No, there's no danger that they'll let that fire go out. They're not going to take any chances on our getting away."

She crouched down again close beside him, so close that he could feel the faint, strangely thrilling pulsations of her body and the soft, thuddy beating of her heart. The wind tore around the house with an eerie yell and once more a crashing spatter of gravel rushed across the roof. The girl gave a little shiver.

"It's—it's a queer place this, Rodney," she said huskily. "A queer, spooky place sometimes. A person's mind plays him strange tricks here sometimes—or maybe it isn't tricks. I don't know. I—I never took *toloache*—like father did. But I've had queer fancies and feelings since I've been living here. These desert solitudes can teach you a lot."

"Why did your dad take *toloache*?" Given the first real opportunity he had had to clear up a matter that had worried him, Kent put the question bluntly.

"He wanted to find the treasure," she answered simply. "That's the only reason. It wasn't for his health—but I didn't dare to tell you that at first."

"Did it help him?" Kent asked curiously.

"You ought to know," she answered quietly. "You saw him tonight. You heard what he said."

"Y—es," Kent said slowly. "And I guess that wasn't the first time I'd seen him." Briefly he told her of his weird experience on the old trail.

"Yes, that must have been father," she agreed. "That poisonous stuff did give him some sort of uncanny power—just like the old Indian who told him of it claimed. It was a *toloache* vision of father's that was responsible for my trip to San Diego. He said that there was something very important to be sold in a bookstore. He didn't just know what it was or where. He hurried me off there and told me to buy all the papers when I got there and read all the 'for sale' ads. That's why I learned about that sale of relics."

"I—I wondered how you'd learned about that—away out here," Kent said, uneasily conscious that there was something more uncanny to the whole business than he cared to admit. "And Chink Halloran saw you pass his shack and tipped Hesfor off? They must have shadowed you in San Diego."

"Yes," she said. "Chink Halloran has been keeping tab on us for a long while. Oh—oh, I wish that gravel rattling would stop. It's worse tonight than I've ever heard it. I—I guess my nerves are on edge."

But Kent was thinking. "Marie," he said slowly, "just what did your dad mean—the things he said tonight to Hesfor, just before he started shooting? He said something about being chained to a rock...accused Hesfor of having left him to die in this canyon...It—it didn't make sense."

"It did—and it didn't, Rodney—depending on the things you believe," the girl spoke slowly, in a low, tense whisper. "Do you know the whole story of the Hesfor robbery?"

"Only the published accounts I've read. They're rather sketchy, I'll admit."

"Yes, they're very vague and general, most of them," she said. "Did you know that Judge Banniston's body was never found?"

"Y—es," Kent admitted. "I did read something about that. The account said that when Hesfor held up the stage singlehanded, near Vallecitos, he took the strong-box, the principal contents of which was the judge's fortune. He also took the judge prisoner. The last that was ever seen of Judge Banniston was as Hesfor rode away into the desert, taking him along as a prisoner lashed in the saddle of a led horse. Hesfor had taken the precaution to kill all the coach-horses before riding off, so pursuit was impossible. Judge Banniston was never seen again, so of course it was a certainty that Hesfor had eventually murdered him. Hesfor had an especial grudge against Banniston. Or at least that's what the account I read said."

"Yes," she said, all that's correct, as far as it goes. Wolf Hesfor did have an especial grudge against my great-grandfather because in his capacity as judge he had sentenced a villain named Blarnsdel, Hesfor's pet crony, to be hanged. That's why Wolf Hesfor took my great-grandfather away with him as a prisoner instead of killing him at the time of the hold-up. He wanted an especial vengeance."

"Then what became of Judge Banniston?" As the girl fell silent a moment, listening to the gusty roaring of the wind, Kent spoke tensely. "What really did become of him?—Do you know?"

"Yes," she said quietly, "I do know. Hesfor brought him here to this canyon, to this very spot. It was in this canyon Judge Banniston died—died a dreadful death of thirst, chained helpless to a rock, while that fiend Hesfor mocked him. And it was here in this canyon somewhere that Hesfor afterwards concealed the treasure."

"But—but no one has ever suspected such a thing," Kent gasped, remembering all at once with a chill, uncanny feeling the scatter of whitened human bones which he had seen on his first visit to the canyon, two years ago. "How do you know all this?"

"Principally from father."

"*Toloache?*" Kent asked quickly.

"*Toloache* helped," she admitted quietly. "But *toloache* was just the medium—the drug that worked on his nervous system and enabled him to break down the barriers to a past memory. At that it only worked imperfectly. He couldn't recall everything—only as through a disconnected dream. He could never get things clearly. That's why we haven't succeeded yet in locating the exact place where the treasure was hidden!"

"But Marie," his startled mind already fastening on the substance of the uncanny things which the girl undoubtedly believed implicitly, Kent spoke incredulously, "that *toloache* weed is only a drug—and a deadly one at that. It's like any other drug—opium, hashish—any of those vision-producing drugs. The stuff a person imagines while under their influence is just dream stuff, nothing more."

"In some cases," she said. "But there are times when you know— deep down inside of you—whether a thing is true or not. Rodney, this is one of those cases. I know—perhaps because I am of the same blood—but I *know* that the things father got through *toloache* were true."

"And you mean you believe that—that your father...?"

"Was the reborn spirit of my great-grandfather, old Judge John J. Banniston," she cut in quickly, finishing the sentence for him. "Rodney, I know that that was so. I've always felt it—and since I've come here to live I've become certain of it. Besides, I've studied the old Judge's picture hundreds of times—we've got in here in this trunk somewhere. There's no possibility of mistake. My father was the very image of him."

❦

CHAPTER 22

A New Peril

"**B**ut Marie," staggered by the weird notion but forced almost to belief by the girl's deadly earnestness and the recollection of the things he himself had seen and heard that night, Kent spoke seriously. "You told me a little while back that Jeff Crossman and your father were doubles. That was an accidental resemblance. Your dad's resemblance to the Judge might be the same."

"Rodney, there's no such thing as accident. Father's resemblance to Jeff Crossman was no accident. It was just another link in the chain of proof. Father always said that Jeff Crossman was Wayne Banniston."

"Wayne Banniston?" Kent repeated the name, puzzled. "Who was he?"

"Judge Banniston's twin brother," the girl answered. "He was a gem expert. He was murdered in China just a little while before the Judge was killed."

"But you *can't* believe that?" Held silent a moment by a particularly violent swirl of wind and gravel upon the flimsy roof, Kent spoke protestingly. "The name—Crossman isn't Banniston. And besides…."

"It isn't necessary for a kindred spirit to come back in the same family or under the same name, Rodney," she interrupted. "Haven't you *ever* met people that you felt you already knew?"

"Sometimes," he admitted, a bit bewilderedly. "But this…Good God! Did Jeff think that too?"

"He never knew," she said quietly. "He was a materialist, when it came to stuff he couldn't prove in black and white—just as Wayne used to be, according to the evidence of old letters. So father never dared to tell him. But the moment Jeff wrote asking to lease the ranch father had a hunch. Father asked him to come to Berkeley, and when he'd met him he felt certain. The resemblance was startling. The only difference between Judge Banniston and Wayne had been a mole that Wayne had on the back of his neck. Father invented some pretext and got a chance to look at the back of Jeff's neck. Jeff had the mole.… That was proof enough. And then when you come to think of it, it was significant that Jeff should have wanted so badly to lease this run-down place. With money it could be made as good a ranch as ever it was. But Jeff had no money—and said so. Father leased him the ranch for a merely nominal sum—and over the heads of far better offers."

And—and that was all of the family—the original family, I mean?" Kent said amazedly. "Judge Banniston must have had a son."

"Yes—one son—a worthless character who was in San Francisco presumably studying for the law," she answered. "He was my grandfather. That was all the original Banniston family. Wayne never married and Judge Banniston's wife was dead. The property—the ranch, there wasn't much cash, Hesfor got away with that—came to my grandfather, Morgan Banniston. He let the ranch run down till it became practically worthless. When he died it was about the only thing that he left to father, but father always hung on to it tenaciously. Father was his only child and his wife had died. My mother died years ago. And now father's gone…I—I'm the last of the Bannistons." Her voice caught in a quick, strangling sob.

"But there couldn't have been such an awful lot of cash after all, Marie—the stuff that Hesfor got, I mean," Kent spoke quickly to change her thoughts. "Gold and silver coin have considerable weight. If it had been so awful much Hesfor couldn't have carried it away single-handed."

"It wasn't in gold altogether," she said. "It was largely in gems. Rubies, diamonds and emeralds. I told you Wayne Banniston was a gem expert. He'd purchased them for the Judge. The Judge had been changing his money into jewels as fast as he accumulated it. They were easier to store and hide. He kept all his wealth on the ranch. He didn't believe in banks. At the time of the robbery he was moving to San Francisco with the idea of spending most of the rest of his life there to be near his son. That's why he was taking the fortune with him."

"And that's what Hesfor got," Kent said reflectively. "And that's what you and your father came here to find."

"Yes," she said simply. "Father's health—quite apart from that *toloache* stuff—was very poor. He had to give up his profession and we came down to absolute poverty. He was worrying himself to death about the possibility of his dying and leaving me destitute. And I was worried about him. If we only had money I felt sure his life could be prolonged with proper care and medical skill. So I wanted the treasure as badly as he—but for his sake. That's why we came here…And—and that's why we've come to this. Oh, it's awful!…It seems as though there's a curse against anyone that hunts that treasure. Poor, poor father…Oh, why did I ever let him come here!"

"Hush, hush, Marie, you've got to keep up your heart," quickly, in an effort to calm the breaking nerves which another dry little sob betrayed, Kent slipped a comforting arm around her. "Your dad wouldn't want you to break down. I guess all the Bannistons have been good, gritty fighters. Keep up your heart."

"Yes," she said huskily, "I'm going to. But oh, Rodney, it's hard."

Again, for a space, silence fell between them, the girl fighting bravely to control her grief and Kent lost in a dizzy whirl of amazed speculations. More than ever, now that the girl's explanation had laid a definite plan to everything, the eerie, uncanny feeling, which from the beginning of the whole affair had been steadily increasing, took possession of his mind. Yet, despite its fantastic seeming, he was forced to admit that there was nothing so startlingly illogical about the matter. The understanding of the world on the mystery of life and death had been broadening a bit, during the last few years, he reflected. The notion of reincarnation was not so scoffed as it had once been. After all, there was no telling. What if what the girl believed should actually be true—that the actual individuals who had been involved in those tragic happenings of the past had returned under a decree of some mysterious law to replay and complete the grim drama? It seemed weirdly fantastic, but could if be true? He did not know, but almost he was inclined to believe it. As the girl had said there was an atmosphere in the grim desolation and wildness of these desert solitudes which made easy the acceptance of strange things. And if he should accept it—if indeed the girl's conviction was correct—what then? What was to be the end of this grim play of Fate, the first acts of which had all been staged amidst tragedy and death? What would the end be?

The wind was slackening. The rustling noises upon the steep, flimsy roof of boards and tar paper had ceased. It was still dark outside, but the gloom was thinning appreciably and the air that whistled in gusts through the hole in the wall was chill with the bleak touch of coming dawn. The thin coldness of it seemed to penetrate through Kent like the touch of an icy hand, bringing with it all at once a strange sense of fear and unutterable despondency. The girl seemed to feel it too, for close against him he felt a tremulous shiver pass through her body—a shiver that was of a sudden changed to a violent, terrified jerk as abruptly, with a wild, startled cry, she clutched his arm:

"*Fire!* Rodney!" she gasped. "*Fire!*…My God!…they've fired the roof!"

∽

CHAPTER 23

A Furnace of Flame

And even as the girl cried out, Kent saw that she spoke truly. For almost at the same instant his eyes, too, had caught the sudden burst of flaming pin-points which, like rows of myriad stars, seemed to leap out all at once along the cracks of the roof boards overhead. And with the sudden blaze of them came the gusting odor of flames and smoke and burning leaves and roofing felt. All too late Kent realized in a flash what the majority of those clatterings and rustlings of supposed gravel had been. It had been the stealthy tossing of dry branches and grass upon the steep roof. And with equal stealth the whole mass had seemingly been fired in a dozen places. All at once a raging furnace of flame was roaring along the whole windward side of the roof. The roof-paper was shriveling like parchment. Even as he glimpsed them the tiny pin-points of fire widened to gaping cracks that sucked in shooting tongues of flame and choking spurts of smoke and sparks.

"Here!—here!...this way!" Galvanizing all at once into frantic energy as though her mind had leaped to a sudden inspiration, the girl caught at Kent's arm. "Quick!...Here!—Father's bed. Help me shove it aside."

Already she was dragging at the heavy, home-made bunk of juniper logs, tugging and pulling it from the wall. Without pausing to question, but well enough aware of the deadly, unfightable peril which every instant flamed hotter above their heads, Kent leaped to her aid. All at once it seemed the darkness of the cabin's interior had changed to a glow of dull red light through which yellow, sooty smoke poured in choking clouds. With a heaving tug, aiding the girl's straining muscles, Kent wrenched the heavy blanket-littered bunk from the wall and toppled it across the floor.

"Here—help me," gasping the words in the sudden choking smoke-swirls, the girl was on her knees on the floor, tugging at a rusty' iron ring set on one edge of a square of heavy planking. "It's the hatch of the old cellar. We never used it. But now...."

With a sudden creaking jerk, yielding to their combined strength, the square hatch-cover heaved open and tumbled backwards on the earthen floor. Out of the black, timber-framed opening thus suddenly revealed came a gust of dry, stale air, followed by a cold, eddying draught.

"There's a ladder here," the girl panted, gesturing downwards. "Quick!...Oh—we'll need the flashlight." She sprang away, darting to the corner where she had left it.

"You get down—down under cover—" With a bound Kent was at her side. "I'll bring that! You get down that ladder. They'll be shooting soon. Come on! I'll take these things."

And barely had he spoken when, as if to justify his words, the report of a rifle broke dully above the blurring roar of the fire. A random-fired bullet whizzed through the shack walls—a shot which, as Kent hastily caught up the flashlight, the rifle and the extra ammunition, was followed by another and another. In a spirit of pure fiendishness the two villains outside were firing random bullets into the flaming shack.

"Oh, the book—the book—we'll take that too!" With a gasp of sudden remembrance, reckless both of the rain of blazing fragments that was now pouring from between the shriveling roof planks and of the deadly hum of the wild-fired bullets, the girl sprang to the trunk and flung back the lid. "We'll take the book. I think there's some of the clue in it. And I won't chance their getting it." In the red light of the smoke-dulled flames she clawed frantically through the tumbled books.

"Hurry—hurry!" smoke-blinded and gasping in the stifling heat from the roaring inferno above, Kent snatched at her arm. "Quick!—for God's sake...The roof'll fall any minute. Never mind the book. Quick! Quick!"

"I've got it!...I've got it!" With a choking gasp she staggered back, clutching the tattered little Bible in her hand. "Come on!"

And indeed it was high time. Already the flimsy, sun-dried rafters were blazing furiously and the twisting, flaming roof-boards above them were falling through into the room in great fire-spurting sections. Even as Kent sprang to the hatchway and half lifted, half helped the gasping girl on to the top of the heavy ladder that led downward, a big section of the roof in the far end of the cabin tumbled inward with a deafening crash and a volcano of blinding sparks. And barely had he swung himself into the opening, scrambling downward in the wake of the descending girl and dragging the heavy hatch-cover back into place behind him, than a deafening roar and a thudding concussion on the heavy trap-door that he had just shut down above his head told him that the remainder of the room had fallen in. Smoke spurted down from above in acrid, choking jets. The cracks in the heavy planks of the hatchway were outlined suddenly in lines of flame. With startled horror, as his descending feet checked abruptly upon the earthen floor, Kent realized all at once that they had but staved off one ghastly death only to doom themselves to another and a worse one. In the light of the electric torch which the girl had switched on he saw that the cellar was merely a deep, earth-walled pit with no egress. When the dry planks of the hatchway overhead burned through, the fiery debris above would pour down upon them in a flaming cascade. They were caught like rats in a hopeless, hideous trap.

South's watercolor of a view of the Vallecito Badlands from the top of Ghost Mountain

CHAPTER 24

Prisoners of the Pit

But even as the crushing realization that they were doomed clutched Kent like a hand of ice, his heart leaped to rekindled hope. *There was a draught!* Faintly, drawn towards the cracks in the hatch planks by the suction of the fire above, a faint air was stirring in the cellar. A draught!…Kent remembered now that he had noticed it when first the cellar trap had been wrenched back.

"The outlet!…there must be an outlet here somewhere!" In breathless question he caught the girl's arm. "There must be a tunnel out of here some place."

"There isn't." Dulled all at once by a sudden exhaustion that had succeeded her frenzy of activity, she shook her head hopelessly. "There's no way out of this cellar. That's why I didn't mention it before as a chance of getting away. I—I don't know why I had the sudden panicky notion for us to bolt down here. The idea just seemed to come to me like a flash and I acted on it. I—I'm sorry…Now we're trapped. When that hatch burns through we'll be—we'll…."

"But there *is*—there is an opening somewhere!" Almost fiercely Kent broke in upon her halting words. "There's a faint draught some place. Feel it?" His hand tightened tensely on her arm.

Trembling and white-faced in the glow of the flashlight, she shook her head. "No," she said, "I can't feel it, Rodney. There's no opening here. You see, this was an old, ruined cellar that was in the foundation of this old shack when we came to rebuild it. We cleaned it out and fixed it up—though we never used it. There was an opening once—a big hole that the storms had washed in one side and that opened into that deep ravine full of cat's-claw that runs along the side of the house. But father and I blocked that up—walled it up extra secure with rocks and with adobe bricks. We didn't want anyone sneaking into the cabin by some underground way."

"Where?—Where?—Which side was that on?" Hope that had wilted at the girl's first denial flamed again in Kent's heart. "Quick!—Which is the side?" Snatching the electric torch from her hand he swept its beams feverishly over the interior of the pit.

"Here—down here in this corner." Almost listlessly, numbed seemingly by the sudden sense of terror and hopelessness that had fallen upon her, she pointed. "But it's no use, Rodney…We set all the adobes solid in mud and chinked all the cracks with mud plaster. And there's piled rocks outside."

"This is where the draught comes from, all right." Scarcely listening to what the girl was saying, Kent had leaped to the side wall and was scanning it frantically by the light of the close-held flash. "Yes—and here's a little hole—that's where it comes in. Your wall's not so safe after all. The gophers have been working around it. See here!" He pointed excitedly to a small, black-mouthed opening in the corner, below which was a little mound of sand: "Here—you hold the light."

Feverishly he set to work. His idea had been correct. The gophers and the little burrowing animals of the desert mountains had been working on the wall, and it was clear that their unnoticed labors had already been spread over a considerable period of time. It was not the almost stone-hard adobes that they had attacked, but they had worked around the end of the wall, where the close-set bricks abutted upon the stony earth in the corner of the pit. The earth here, in several places, was soft and crumbly from their industrious burrowing.

But in spite of all this, Kent was forced speedily to realize that the girl's belief that egress that way was impossible was well founded. She had spoken truly when she had said that they had closed the old opening with extra precautions. They had indeed made a good job of it. How thick they had built the wall or how great a quantity of rocks they had piled on the outside of it he did not—for fear of adding to his growing hopelessness—dare to ask. But the bricks on the inside were close set and so well chinked and plastered that they presented a surface much harder than the sides of the pit. He could dislodge the end ones only with the greatest difficulty. Digging furiously, using the rifle both as crowbar and shovel, he was sickeningly aware of steadily dwindling hope. In the light of the electric torch that the girl held, the excavation upon which he toiled seemed to enlarge only with heart-numbing slowness. The pile of dirt and shattered adobe fragments at his feet were sickeningly small, despite his best efforts. Moreover his digging operations had plugged the tiny passage. The hope-arousing air current no longer entered from the outer world. The draught had stopped.

And the grim pit that held them trapped was growing hotter. The leaping flames of the crumbling shack, which overhead had become the roaring funeral pyre of the two bodies stretched upon its floor, were eating swiftly at the cellar hatchway. The cracks in the heavy planks were widening fast. Glowing sparks were already sifting down through them. Hot, heavy smoke was settling into the cellar in ever-growing volume. It would be only a few more moments now, Kent realized, and death would plunge down upon them in a ghastly, flaming flood. In a dripping lather of perspiration and with a heart cold with icy fear, he dug frantically on.

And then, all of a sudden, his furiously-driven rifle muzzle seemed to plunge into emptiness. Almost to the butt the weapon drove forward through suddenly-crumbled earth into unresistant space. With a life-giving rush, through the narrow opening, poured all at once the cool, fresh outer air—air that was fragrant with the smell of green branches and wet rocks.

"We're through! We're through!" With a hoarse, breathless gasp Kent voiced his joyful relief. "Just a bit—just a bit more an'…we can…crawl…."

His words choked away in smoke and in the panting fury of his own efforts. For indeed there was little time to be lost. One glance as he had straightened for an instant had told him that. The trap-door above their heads was warping and sagging in under the weight of the flaming debris piled upon it. Flames were spurting through the wide, gaping cracks of the burning planks and already a sift of red-hot coals was dropping into the pit. In that one frantic glance through the smoke-filled air he saw by the ruddy glow of the flash that the white-faced girl had shifted her position. In a desperate effort to escape the trickling cascade of embers from overhead she had pressed close to the pit side, almost within sweep of his furiously-digging arms. A few more fleeting seconds at most and the overhead trap would collapse.

"A'right!…Go 'head!" Gasping, almost inarticulate as he clawed out a final litter of gravel and smashed adobe chips from the narrow opening; Kent dashed the sand and sweat from his eyes and gestured frantically to the waiting girl. "Go on! Quick!…Get through there!" Fiercely, as she hesitated, he caught her arm and pushed her towards the narrow opening. "I'll be right after. G'wan!…Quick!"

A clatter of burning fragments which of a sudden pitched through a widened crack above helped emphasize his words. The girl hesitated no longer. Thrusting the flashlight into his hand, but still gripping the little black book to which she had clung tenaciously, she thrust her head and shoulders into the narrow opening and with a clawing, squirming struggle vanished through into the outer gloom.

Thrusting the rifle, six-shooters and ammunition ahead of him, Kent followed hard on her heels. The hole was narrow enough and the girl's difficult exit had held a warning. But there was no time now to attempt to widen it. For, even as he thrust his arms and head into the opening, the cellar trap gave way. Into the pit, billowing out a sudden withering blast of heat as it plunged, fell a flaming avalanche of burning timbers.

and fragments from the furnace above.

And the hole into which he had wedged was *too narrow*. Sickeningly, his whole body swept all at once with an icy chill, despite the blistering burst of heat, Kent realized that. He was jammed tight. His arms were through and his head. The cool damp wind of the canyon fanned upon his face and close by striking savagely against his clawing hands as he gripped at wet slippery rocks in an effort to pull himself through, were the whipping branches of cat's-claws. *But he was jammed fast.* The cool wind was upon his face, but his feet and the lower portions of his legs were already burning and blistering in the waves of scorching heat that billowed into the short tunnel. Jammed and trapped, in a dreadful natural torture trap, his feet were as tight held to the flaming blasts as those of any hapless victim of the Spanish Inquisition.

"Rodney!…Oh, Rodney!…Pull!—Pull on this!" Frantic, her face white and terror-stricken in the dancing, ruddy glow that beat down into the ravine from the flaming ruins of the shack on its edge, the girl dragged to his reach a stout branch of one of the near-by thorn bushes. "Pull on this," she panted, as reckless of torn fingers she wrenched aside the thorns and thrust the limb into his hand. "It's that rock that's holding you. You pull—I'll pry with the rifle and…."

Her panted words choked—choked away all at once in a breathless gasping cry as, checking in mid-motion as she stooped to lever at the pinning boulder, she swung round to confront a dark shadow that had of a sudden risen up out of the thorn thicket almost at her elbow. "*Rodney!*" she screamed, "Rodney!…It's…."

But Kent heard no more. For on that instant, blurring both the sound of her wild cry and his glimpse of the dark, hulking shape that had of a sudden wound arms about her struggling figure, something hard and violent crashed upon his head. For the second time in that short span of peril-fevered hours—but this time with more utter completeness—his senses swam out into soundless blackness.

CHAPTER 25

Taunted

"**S**o yer wakin' up, Mister Buttinsky—huh? 'Bout time yer was."

To Kent the thick, coarse voice, breaking in through the dizzy mists of blackness, seemed to beat upon his throbbing brain with the brutality of hammer blows. Dazedly he opened his eyes—opened them weakly to a sudden consciousness of a hot, blinding glare of sunshine.

"A long time comin'-to, wasn't yer. I reckon he did give yer a pretty good sock on th' head. But he figgered yer had it comin' fer' what yer give him th' other night."

Painfully, his head throbbing as though a pounding trip-hammer were imprisoned inside it, and his blinking eyes dazzled by the blinding glare of the sun, Kent twisted to look at the speaker. He was dully aware too of a queer constriction about his body and also that his ribs and shoulders were sore, as though they had been scrubbed with a wire brush. He tried to sit up, but the effort was a failure and he sank back weakly. There was sand under his clutching fingers. He was stretched prone, he realized, upon some sandy surface.

"No, yer ain't goin' t' feel like goin' t' no Sunday school picnics yet a bit." Wolf Hesfor emitted a malignant chuckle. "We damn near skint yer alive, I reckon, haulin' yer through that hole. If it hadn't been fer me, though, I reckon yer would ha' been left there t' get th' feet cooked off o' yer—my pardner here don't like yer none too good. But I'm soft-hearted, I am…Haw haw!"

Kent's throbbing eyes were clearing. Close to him, standing to-gether and seeming to tower over him as he lay stretched at their feet on the sand, were Wolf Hesfor and the bullet-headed thug. Both of them, notwithstanding Wolf Hesfor's grim jocosity, were regarding him with deadly, malignant triumph.

"Well, I reckon we hadn't oughter be too hard on yer—kinda too bad comin' a botherin' o' yer like this." Again, with thick gloating sarcasm Hesfor spoke. "But seein' as th' gal was kind enough t' bring along this here book with her—t' sorta help out with that there bunch o' poetry you was a packin' around—we thought you'd kinda like t' know that we're a startin' out t' dig up that bunch o' dough that you an' all th' rest has been so interested in. Haw haw!"

With a struggle and a violent effort Kent clawed himself up to a sitting position. Hesfor's mention of the book and the instant sight of the tattered little volume in the outlaw's ham-like hand had acted like an electric shock on his blurred brain—bringing back the thought of Marie in a cold, agonizing rush of recollection and fear. Where was she? What had happened to her? What had these two devils done with her? Wildly, his whole body shaking all at once with a sick, icy terror, his dizzy eyes swept about him.

"Haw haw!—jest of a sudden discovered that th' gal ain't here, huh?" Guessing correctly at the reason for his sudden frantic alarm, Wolf Hesfor spoke brutally. "No, she ain't settin' nowheres near yer. She's cooped up good an' safe in th' old' mine tunnel yonder. We're keepin' her as what they calls th' 'piece de resistance' fer after we collects th' dough we're a goin' t' dig up. She ain't hurt *yet*, Mister Buttinsky. Yer can amuse yerself a hollerin' back an' forrard t' her whilst we're gone. She ain't outa earshot."

"'Ell, yes, keep up 'er 'art," the bullet-headed thug spoke up for the first time. "We wants 'er in a good temper when we gets back." With an evil, revolting snicker he licked his coarse, sensual lips.

"Haw haw!...listen t' that, will yer!" Hesfor emitted a thick, explosive laugh. "Well, come on. Let's be goin'. We got work t' do."

He turned on his heel. But on the instant, and with a grin, as though suddenly recollecting some overlooked piece of pleasantry, turned back. "Thought mebbe you'd like t' take a look, Buttinsky," he chuckled, stooping and thrusting suddenly towards Kent's face the tattered little Bible. "See here—pretty picture, ain't it?" He flipped open the worn cover and jabbed a stubby forefinger. "See!—pretty good drawin' o' a hand...even if my ole grandfather did make it. Got it pretty good, didn't he? Particular as he must ha' done it from memory while he was in th' pen. Take a good look at it, Buttinsky, fer that's th' closest yer ever goin' t' get t' seein' where the stuff is buried. But I thought mebbe it'd make yer feel better t' know how you an' th' gal has helped us out in findin' it.... I think yer need some encouragement. I'm soft-hearted, I am...Haw haw!"

He closed the book with one snap of his huge, heavy hand and with another gloating, throaty chuckle, swung about and accompanied by his scowling, bullet-headed companion, tramped away across the sun-blazed floor of the canyon.

South's pencil sketch of a cave or mine

CHAPTER 26

Padlock and Chain

A ching in every bone, his half-raised body propped up by his arms, Kent watched the departing ruffians. Without even troubling to give him a backward glance they tramped across the bottom of the canyon, and pausing for a moment near the fire-blackened ruins of the shack to gather up a pick and a couple of shovels which they had evidently placed there previously, they vanished among the clutter of giant boulders on the far side of the gorge. Well enough Kent knew where they were going. From the point where they had disappeared among the tumbled rocks a steep but easily-climbable incline led up to the isolated height near the canyon's rim, upon which stood the ominous Dead Man's Hand rock. For the grim natural freak, though seemingly set upon the south rim of the canyon, was not so in reality. Between it and the actual brink of the gorge stretched another and a narrower chasm, the south cliff of which, like all the cliffs which here marked the borders of the canyon proper, was unscalable. Though rising from a tiny plateau that was level with the canyon rim, Dead Man's Hand was located upon a sort of precipitous island that towered upward from the floor of the gorge. Three sides of this isolated bulk were as sheer as the canyon sides themselves, but on the east side the cliffs had broken down into a long, steep slope thickly grown with catclaw. It was up this slope, hidden from sight by the screening bushes, but their ascent still traceable by the faint sounds of rolling stones and voices, that Hesfor and his companion were now making their way.

Kent, however, wasted little time in listening to the steadily-dwindling sounds that came each moment more faintly from across the gorge. His senses were still partly blurred and he felt deathly sick.

But in the short time that had elapsed since consciousness had first returned to him, his brain had cleared and his strength had come back in a marked degree. It had been indeed a terrific blow that had been dealt him on the head, he realized, and coming so soon after the shock of his other fall, it had all but made an end of him. By only the narrowest of margins had his skull escaped fracture. But it *had* escaped. Throbbing and hammering though his head was he could judge the pain well enough to know that it was something that would pass with time. Even the blinding glare of the sun, the presence of which still somewhat bewildered him, seemed to be aiding the throbbing pain somewhat.

"Marie!…Marie!…Where are you, Marie?" Huskily, not waiting to clear up the still dully puzzling riddle of his own whereabouts, but his mind clutched eagerly to the fact that Hesfor had said that the girl was within earshot, Kent sent the call through a parched, dry throat. "Where are you, Marie?

Can you hear me?"

"I'm here, Rodney—here in the old mine tunnel," faintly, muffled, as though drifting through some intervening barrier, the girl's voice came with the hollow sound of an echo. "Oh, Rodney, are you badly hurt?"

"Not near so bad as I might have been," with sudden new heart as though the sound of her voice had been an actual stimulant, Kent called back the answer. "I'm all right except for a headache. But you— how are you?"

"They haven't hurt me, Rodney. All they did was to tie me up until it got daylight. Then they shut me in here. Oh, Rodney, you lay so limp and so helpless after they dragged you out of that hole…I was certain they'd killed you. Are you sure you're not badly injured?"

"No, I'm not hurt bad. Nothing I won't get over quick enough."

"Oh, thank God for that. Where are you, Rodney? I can't see you through any of these cracks. Just where are you?"

"I don't know exactly. Oh yes, wait a bit—" Heartened and strengthened by the glad knowledge that the girl was still alive and well, Kent forced his swimming brain and eyes to take in his immediate surroundings. "I'm out here in a sandy patch in the bed of the canyon—near a tall shaft of rock that sticks up out of the sand."

"Oh—then that's why I can't see you—you're too far to one side. I can't see you through these door cracks. Can you move, Rodney? Have they got you bound?"

"N-no—I guess I'm not tied," for the first time the fact that his arms and legs were free dawned upon Kent. "No, they don't seem to have tied me. Oh yes, they have too." Aware all at once of some hampering impediment as he essayed to get to his feet and again conscious of the queer constriction about his body that he had noticed before, he corrected himself. "I guess they have got me tied after all. They've got a chain around me some way…Got me tethered to this rock."

"*What?*—what's that?" with a sudden terrified sharpness that startled even Kent's throbbing brain the girl's voice came in a gasp. "What's that you're saying?"

"Got me chained," Kent repeated, investigating as he spoke. "Long heavy chain. They've cinched one end round my waist and fastened it with a padlock. The other's passed around this shaft of rock and padlocked too. I've got about a seven-foot stretch of chain between me and the rock. I'm tethered out." In a chill of consternation, the shock of the ominous discovery scattering the last blurring mists from his eyes and mind, he stared at the stout, heavy links and tested them with a wrenching pull.

"Rodney—listen to me," despite its muffled distance the girl's voice was vibrant with a strained, tense note. "You listen to me and do what I tell you. *Get back in the shade.* If you're not in it already, get back in it quick—the shade of the rock, I mean. There's not much of it, but you've got to keep yourself in all of it that there is—especially your head. Follow that shadow as it moves with the sun. Keep in it. You've *got* to. You don't know how hot that little patch of sand gets in the daytime when the sun gets to beating down on it. It must be ten o'clock or more now and the heat will keep mounting right along. You've got to keep in all the shade you can get. And listen, Rodney, you better stop calling to me too—unless there's something vitally important. That—that will save you a bit. You don't want to get your throat dry. Put a little pebble or something in your mouth and suck on that. That'll help a bit too. Rodney, you've got to…Can you hear me, Rodney?"

"Yes—yes, I can hear you." Startled and sobered, not alone by the grim realization that had of a sudden rushed upon him, but also by the girl's tense, terror-strained voice, Kent softly called the answer. "All right, Marie, I'll watch out and do all that. But don't you worry. It's not going to get that bad—not yet awhile. But you keep up your heart anyway."

"We've both got to keep up our hearts," she called back. "Where did Hesfor and that other brute go?…To hunt for the treasure?"

"Yes."

"Then that means that we'll be left alone for a little while at least. Oh, Rodney, do please try and shelter yourself."

"I will," he promised soberly.

"Please—for my sake. And now you'd better stop talking. You'll only get yourself thirsty that much the quicker. Don't worry about me.

I'm all right. And—and I'm going to pray, Rodney. Maybe—maybe some help will come."

"Sure it will," he answered. "We'll get out of this alright somehow, Marie. Don't you lose heart."

But in his own heart, in the silence that fell between them he knew that he had no hope in his optimistic words. The sun, blazing out of the cloudless desert sky, was beating mercilessly down into the steep-walled canyon. The stretching spread of white, glaring sand that lay around him seemed to his awakened imagination to be becoming swiftly hotter and already his dry throat and lips were acutely conscious of the need of a drink. Far overhead, a tiny ominous black speck against the turquoise blue, a buzzard wheeled. In his heart Kent knew well enough that for the girl as for himself all hope was dead.

South's pencil sketch entitled "Rock"

ℭ∂

CHAPTER 27

Hopeless

It was only for a few moments, however, that Kent allowed himself
to be crushed beneath the black weight of despair which, with the
complete clearing of his mind and vision, had descended upon him.

He was still deathly sick and weak. But somehow the knowledge
that Marie was alive and, so far unharmed, was within call, had done
more than anything else to call up a fierce will to live and to fight. The
appalling realization of what inevitably awaited the girl at the hands of
the two merciless ruffians was a dreadful goad to his throbbing brain.
By sheer savage force of will he dragged back keen clarity to his mind
and slow-returning strength to his aching limbs.

And first, in a swift survey, he took in clearly his own position and
immediate surroundings. Situated a little distance up from the site of
the cabin—the fire-blackened ruins of which he could see clearly—the
wide, irregular patch of white sand was near the base of the north
cliff of the canyon. It was not an unbroken stretch of sand for, besides
the tall, shaft-like rock to which he had been tethered, several more
widely-separated boulders, some of them of considerable size, broke
the sun-blazed white surface. All of these rocks however lay in line with
his own—a line roughly paralleling the base of the canyon cliff and at
a considerable distance from it. And though the nearest of them was
quite close to him it was still far beyond the length of his tether chain.
He could neither reach it nor, from its position, would he ever gain the
slightest particle of shade from it. Far from being of any protection,
Kent saw at once that this big rock would be more of a menace. Like
the sheer side of the canyon it would act as a reflector of the burning
sun and render his position all the hotter.

Nor did a careful examination of the manner in which he was secured add to his hopes. The chain was a stout one. Even with a good file it would have taken him a long time to cut through the heavy links. The padlocks with which both ends of it were secured were of the rugged old-fashioned sort that would have defied anything save an assault with a heavy hammer and chisel. There was no hope either of worming his body through the encircling loop of the chain. It had been cinched around him so tight as to be painful. And the other end was equally securely fastened around the rock. With a circumference at its base of not much more than that of a very large barrel, the pillar-like rock to which he was secured bulged considerably in its upper portion. There was therefore no chance of raising the loop of chain and slipping it off the top—a maneuver which, even if it had not been for the difference in dimensions, would have been impossible, for the rocky shaft was all of fourteen feet high. Glass-smooth from the wear of centuries of sand-charged wind storms, it was absolutely unclimbable.

Reasonably convinced that as far as human precautions went his captors had made a thorough job of securing him, Kent turned his attention to a careful study of the location of the girl's prison. As his first half-stunned view of it had told him, it was at a point obliquely across from him. There—a rough patch upon the base of the sun-seared north cliff of the canyon—a heavy door built of roughly-hewn juniper logs hunched grey and brown in the sunshine. It was from between the cracks of this massive barrier that the girl's voice had come.

Wedged back in the narrow strip of shade cast by his rock and already, in spite of himself, beginning to be acutely conscious that water would be a grateful relief for his dry, aching throat, Kent studied this hulking door with close attention. He remembered now that it marked the position where, on his previous visit to the canyon, he had seen the mouth of the ancient mine tunnel. The mouth of the tunnel had then been no more than a gaping black hole. It was evident enough that the door was something recent—the work doubtless of Marie's father. Probably, Kent reflected, Professor Banniston and his daughter, when they had first moved into this canyon, had built this door and used the old tunnel for living and storage quarters.

And they had made an excellent job of it—too excellent. Scanning now the massive barrier and the stout and thorough manner in which it was fitted against the face of the rock cliff, Kent's heart sank. Those logs—those massive, improvised iron hinges—that bulky door-fastening secured with a huge padlock bigger even than those which held his own chain—would have defied almost a battering ram. To the weak strength of a girl it offered an utterly impassable barrier. The short tunnel was driven into rock. It had no other outlet. Marie, like himself, was a prisoner beyond hope of escape.

South's pencil sketch of a rock cave

CHAPTER 28

The Shadow of Dead Man's Hand

A long time, his mind frantically racing, Kent sat hunched in the narrow line of shade, striving desperately to think a way out of what he knew well was an utterly hopeless situation. Goaded by the dreadful knowledge of what must inevitably be the fate of the helpless girl he could not bear to accept the bitter decree of Fate that had delivered them so absolutely into the hands of Wolf Hesfor and his villainous partner. There *must* be some way out, he told himself desperately. There must be! For Marie's sake he *must* find a way. Somehow—no matter by what means or cost—she must be saved.

And yet, only too chillingly even as his anguished mind wrestled with the hopeless problem, he realized that he was only beating off temporarily the facing of dreadful facts.

From this steel web of merciless circumstances there was no escape. His own position was hopeless. Without tools—without even so much as a stone within reach which would serve as a hammer—he had no chance in the world of breaking his own bonds. Frantic tugging and wrenching at his chain had demonstrated that it was utterly beyond any power of his to break—and a search through his pockets revealed that everything in them had been removed. A bit of wire, a nail, a penknife—anything, had he had it—would at least have given him some glimmer of hope, however faint, of picking the heavy padlocks. But he had nothing. To wrench and claw at them with bare hands and teeth like a crazed animal would get him nowhere.

And the girl's prison was equally hope shattering. Sitting there staring at the hulking square of rough timbers that formed the bar to her freedom Kent felt his heart sink slowly into the utter depths of despair. He knew well enough that the fact that the girl's life and his own had been spared thus far was due only to cold-blooded precaution on Hesfor's part—to the notion that they might still know something vitally necessary to the locating of the hidden wealth. The moment, however, that the two ruffians had the treasure in their hands the girl's doom and his own would be instantly sealed. It was a black prospect. One that held out not even the faintest shadow of hope.

And all the while the sun, mounting slowly in the hard, bright vault of the sky, was growing hotter. Perhaps, Kent told himself desperately, it was just imagination—a grim, terrible imagination growing out of the realization that it was to this very rock, in the centre of this very patch of glaring sand, that almost three-quarters of a century ago the original Wolf Hesfor had chained his helpless victim to die. But it *did* seem hot—terribly hot. The sand, the rocks, the face of the cliff opposite all seemed to be working on the principle of a reflector oven. Heat waves seemed to gather and beat around the grim shaft of stone to which his chain held him. Here, far back in those dim, fled years of the past Judge Banniston had died, mocked and taunted by the merciless scoundrel who had robbed him. Undoubtedly, Kent reflected, the whitened bleached bones that even as late as two years ago had been the sport of wind and sun and sand, had been those of the unfortunate judge. Was it the ruling of fate, Kent wondered chillily, that his own whitening bones should here, through the years to come, carry on the memory of that grim drama of the past?

Tortured by these and by a host of other ghastly fancies, but most of all by the dreadful fear that grew from his realization of the fate that was in store for Marie, Kent followed with steadily changing position the slow movement of the narrow strip of shade as it altered place with the motion of the sun. He no longer disguised from himself the fact that he was thirsty nor that he was suffering from the airless, stifling heat that seemed for some natural cause to concentrate directly upon him. He was suffering, but he knew that his present discomfort would be as nothing to what would follow if he got no water nor relief. Today would not end him. But tomorrow very well might. And—and always there was the thought of the imprisoned girl. Only God himself could tell what horrors might happen *before* tomorrow.

In a mental agony, almost insane and fighting now to keep his mind from dwelling on the inevitable, Kent crouched helpless, staring out across the shimmering waves of rising heat at the sere brown cliffs opposite. Following the girl's advice he had slipped into his mouth a small, smooth pebble that he had raked from the sand at the foot of the rock. It helped a little seeming in a measure to keep his mouth moist and to prevent the utter drying of his throat. And he tried to keep his mind off of the mounting heat and the thought of water.

Silence had settled upon the canyon—the vast and utter silence of the desert. No call of bird, no stir of wind. Long, long since, distance-swallowed, the last faint sounds of voices and movements from across the canyon had ceased. Wolf Hesfor and his partner were doubtless diligently ferreting out the hiding-place of the treasure, Kent reflected—digging around in the little cave among the catclaw that he remembered having once seen there. But they were too far off for any sound of their activities to reach his ears. Nor could he see anything of them. Many times, moving around and scanning with hand-shaded eyes the rocky height near the south rim of the canyon, he searched for some sign of them. But the pair, hidden by the clutter of big boulders and tangle of bushes and catclaw that crested the height, were invisible. Dreadful and grim, its outlines stark and ominous against the sun glare, the weird Dead Man's Hand rock bulked sinister against the sky. Its lean finger-like pinnacles seemed to lean clutching above the canyon, like the menacing claws of Death. But of Wolf Hesfor and the bullet-headed thug who had gone with him the hushed solitude betrayed no sign.

The hours passed on, slowly and grimly. Occasionally, softly, Kent called across to the girl and she answered. But this was only at rare intervals and always she cautioned him against the risk of expending even that much energy. There was little to be said. A sort of grim lethargy had fastened upon Kent and, from the sound of the girl's voice, he judged that the same hopelessness had settled upon her also. The sun had long since passed the zenith and was traveling westward. The heat was not yet abating, but long shadows were reaching from the rocks. Across the white width of the glaring sand patch a long lean point of gloom was slowly creeping. Twisting his head a little Kent saw that it fell from the index finger of the great stone hand. Like clutching talons the shadows of the fingers of Dead Man's Hand were reaching down into the gorge. Dully, but with an odd sense of sudden foreboding, he watched the slow movement of the great shadowy finger as it crept across the sand in the direction of the north cliff of the canyon. The white glaring sand grains, as the shade of the pointed band of gloom blotted across them, turned a dull, ashy grey. In the path of the sinister, shadowy talon a bunch of beavertail cactus flaunted a glory of orchid-like blossoms. One moment they were a blaze of pink-scarlet fire, like wondrous artificial blooms cunningly fashioned from crêpe paper. The next, as the shadow fell across them, their glory had dimmed, choked and throttled to a dull, struggling tint beneath the sullen band of shade.

And watching, Kent of a sudden started—started violently, as though someone had struck him. Trembling of a sudden in every limb,

he leaned forward, hands out-thrust against the hot sand as, supporting his half-reclining body he stared with wide, startled eyes at the
patch of shadowed blossoms. Out of a darkness—from somewhere as
from out of a great depth—the scrawled lines upon that old, yellowed
sheet of paper seemed to leap back to his mind in letters of fire….

> *"Flowers on the cactus. Bones on the sand.*
> *Gold in the reach of the dead man's hand.*
>
> *Black in the shadows. White in the sun.*
> *Death stands guard with a dead man's gun.*
>
> *Over the catclaw. Under the cave.*
> *When you find it, fool, you'll have found your grave."*

Staring, trembling, feeling for an instant as though his heart had
stopped and that his parched throat had so constricted as to stop his
breathing, Kent stared at the moving shadow finger. He swallowed
hard. "Flowers on the cactus"—God!…Was—was it possible that
in one revealing flash, from somewhere out of the infinite, the true
meaning of those cryptic lines had leaped to him? Good God!…Was it
possible that after all…?

Quivering, his whole body atremble all at once with wild hope and
excitement, his eyes darted about him. Like a vast, ghostly hand the
weird, ominous shadow of the grim rock had reached down into the
canyon bed. Not only the index finger, but the shadows of all the other
fingers also were already upon the sand, spreading on either side of
him, stretching out across the canyon floor and also moving slowly
sideways from west to east as the sun traveled westward and declined.
The bulky blotting shadow of the hand itself was following the fingers.
Dark and sinister, but welcome all at once in its cooling shade, it crept
across the shaft of rock to which Kent was chained and seemed to
hover there. The biting, stifling heat of the sun was gone.

Weak with a wild excitement that for the moment seemed to rob
him of the power of movement, Kent crouched, staring as though
fascinated. Hope had flamed in him, a wild throbbing hope that sent
the blood galloping through his veins in a sudden pounding surge of
mingled hope and terror. God! if this were true!…If this were only
true—this thing—this wild notion that had flashed to his brain! Why,
if it were true it might mean that…that after all he could….

He checked his racing mind. The leaping, dawning hope was too
unnerving in the possibilities that it held out. Racked and unstrung by
hours of torturing fears he could not yet bear to allow himself to accept

the staggering, almost miraculous chance of escape that it might hold. He could not bear to face the idea. It might only be a wild fantasy of the imagination…It might fail—it might be after all but a grim jest of fate, the dispelling of which would be utterly crushing. The very thought of it now set him in a damp sweat of terror. Trembling, fighting now to control his pounding heart and quivering nerves, he swallowed hard. "Marie," he called huskily; "Marie! Oh Marie! Quick! Listen!…"

But even as he called, his heart went suddenly cold. For all at once there fell sharply upon his ears the sound of footsteps and voices. From around the corner of the clump of rocks—emerging into view so abruptly and so close at hand that he had no chance to call another word to the listening girl—came Wolf Hesfor and his evil-faced partner. Their rifles were slung across their backs, their hands were empty and their faces were savagely grim. It needed but one glance to tell Kent that they had failed in their search—and in the same glimpse he read also their present deadly purpose.

South's watercolor of a Mojave yucca—Yucca shidigera

∽

CHAPTER 29

Kent Makes a Bargain

"**W**ell, Mister Buttinsky, so yer think yer fooled us, huh?" In a voice hoarse with deadly rage, as he halted almost within arm's reach of Kent, Wolf Hesfor snarled the words. "Yer knowed right well there was more t' that there clue than what was writ in th' book an' on th' paper, didn't yer? Yer been apattin' yerself on th' back knowin' that we been a diggin' round th' hull blasted day on a fool's errand, huh!...Well, yer joke's over. Yer been a holdin' somethin' back what yer knows. But now yer goin' t' spill it—an' spill it quick! See this?" With a savage jerk he suddenly whipped out a long, evil-bladed sheath-knife from his belt and took a threatening step closer. "See this here knife?...Well, c'mon now, damn yer!...Talk up!...Where's that bunch a' loot buried?

Out with it quick or I'll cut th' livin' lights outa yer." Glaring-eyed and with fury-working face he hunched menacingly forward.

"Aw 'ell, Wolf—there's a quicker way than that." With a thick snicker, reading correctly the glint of stubborn defiance which had leaped to Kent's eyes at the threat, the bullet-headed thug spoke up. "Wye waste time on 'im? Bring out th' skirt an' put 'er through 'er paces. She prob'ly knows all 'e does an' even if she don't, seein' 'er dance will make 'im talk farst 'nough."

"She *doesn't* know," with a sharp drawn breath, fear-chilled at the light that had flamed across Hesfor's face at the monstrous suggestion, Kent snapped the words. "She doesn't *know* where the treasure's hidden. But *I* do. And I'll give you the information—at a price."

"Th' hell yer will!" The sudden greedy expression that lit Hesfor's brutal features was mixed with contempt. "Th' hell yer will. We ain't makin' no bargains with yer. We don't hafta. Spill that dope quick—or we'll bring out th' gal."

"Listen here, Wolf," forcing a steady voice despite the cold fear which the outlaw's words sent through his pounding heart, Kent spoke calmly. "Listen to sense. I've *got* to bargain. It's the one chance that the girl and I have. You know that as well as I do. You want the money—we want our lives. If I tell you where it is just off-hand you'll go get it and then kill us both off. But if I refuse to tell you and you kill us off in an attempt to make us tell, you'll be out of luck because, without the information I've got, you wouldn't find that cache of treasure in a million years. So it's worth bargaining for on our part. Unless I have sense enough to strike a bargain with you beforehand, you'll kill us just as dead, whether I tell you or don't tell you. I know that. So I can be just as stubborn as you can. Kill us both if you want to, but unless you agree to give us our lives and our freedom in return for the information I'll let the secret die with us. The girl doesn't know because she hasn't had a chance to find out. But I *do* know. And unless you agree to the exchange—our lives and liberty for the treasure—I'll never tell you a word. No matter how you torture me."

"Aw bull—let's get out th' skirt." With a bestial impatience which could scarce wait till Kent had ceased speaking, the bullet-headed thug pulled at Hesfor's arm. "Th' 'ell with wot 'e says. We c'an get…."

"Shut yer trap!" With a savage snarl, his face alight now with a glint of cunning, Hesfor shook his partner off. "Shut up an' stan' still. I'm a doin' th' thinkin' fer this outfit, so hold' yer jaw." He turned and stood glowering down a moment into Kent's face as though appraising the depth of the sullen, savage stubbornness he read there. "Yer reckon yer *do* know jest where that there stuff is buried?" he demanded.

"Yes," Kent said coolly, "I do."

"A'right then, I'll go yer." Apparently satisfied by his scrutiny that Kent was capable at a pinch of being stubborn enough to carry the secret to the grave with him in spite of physical sufferings, the outlaw spoke gruffly. "Give us th' dope an' if it's c'rrect an' we find th' stuff, we'll turn yer both loose an' let yer go safe."

"Set us free first," Kent insisted.

"Th' hell I will!" Sudden suspicion flared in Hesfor's face. "Think I'm a fool—give yer a chance t' work some monkey tricks? I've give yer me word, ain't I? We'll turn yer both loose a'terwards—providin' we finds th' stuff. That's fair 'nough, ain't it?" His eyes flickered with a gleam of crafty cunning.

"All right," apparently convinced of his captor's good faith. Kent nodded briskly. "Then go get the girl an' bring her over here."

"Hell, no!" Again Hesfor bristled. "She stays where she is too. Watcher want her fer?"

"All right, suit yourself," Kent shrugged. "Only if you really want to know where the treasure is you'll have to bring her. She knows landmarks in this canyon that I'll have to ask her to point out. Are you afraid she'll hurt you?" His lip twitched scornfully.

"G'wan, bring her out." Sullenly Hesfor produced a string with three padlock keys attached, thrust it into the bullet-headed man's hand and propelled him with a shove in the direction of the mine tunnel door. "Bring her here—an' don't claw her none with yer clumsy mitts." He turned again to Kent. "What else d'yer want?" he snarled.

"That old Bible and the sheet of paper."

"Huh—so's yer can rip 'em up, I s'ppose?"

"You can hold them yourself—out of my reach if you want to—just so I can see them," Kent said patiently. "What time is it?"

"Purty nigh three o'clock, I reckon." The outlaw fished out a battered silver watch. "Yeh-ten minutes of."

"All right," with a quick nod and a flashed warning glance to the white-faced, startled-looking girl who, accompanied by Hesfor's villainous partner, had now come across the sand and halted near him, Kent swept his eyes up and down the canyon. "All right. Then show me that paper."

South's pencil sketch entitled "jackrabbit"

15

∽

CHAPTER 30

The Unraveled Clue

"Here's yer paper." Scowling, plainly impatient and suspicious, Hesfor extracted the yellow, now crumpled sheet from his shirt pocket. "Y'can look at it from where yer are. I ain't gonna give it t' yer." He straightened the sheet a bit and held it before Kent's eyes— but just out of all possibility of his reach.

"That's plenty good enough," Kent said coolly. Apparently studying the lines, but in reality sparring for time while his brain raced feverishly, he scanned the sheet in silence for a few seconds. Then he turned to the girl.

"Marie," he said evenly, "I'm making a bargain with Wolf here. He hasn't had any luck hunting that cache of treasure and, as I've figured out just where it really is, I've promised to tell him in return for his giving us our lives and freedom. But I want your consent first. It's your treasure." Desperately, with his eyes, he tried to flash to her a warning and some hint of the things in his mind that he dared not speak.

"It's no more my treasure than yours, Rodney." In a strained but level voice, plainly enough doing her best to puzzle out the meaning in his eyes and to play up to his lead, the girl spoke. "We're both in this together. What is mine is yours too now. Whatever bargain you make I'll stand by."

"Even if Wolf don't!...ha ha…." The bullet-headed man emitted a cackling chuckle. "Anyways, y'carn't 'elp yerself an'…."

"Shut yer damn trap, yer blasted fool!" With a flash of white fury Hesfor wheeled on his companion. "Another pipe outa you an' I'll bust yer addled head…G'wan now, feller!" he swung back impatiently to Kent.

"Well, I'll tell you, Hesfor," deliberately to give his whirling brain some chance to figure ahead of his words, Kent spoke slowly. "These verses that your grandfather wrote aren't just plain directions. They carry a meaning that's got to be figured out. Some of the things he wrote are just bunk evidently—just stuff to scare folks away from hunting the treasure. But some of the lines really mean something— and that's what I've figured out."

"Spit it out! Spit it out, an' be quick about it," the outlaw growled irritably.

"Well, there's the first line," Kent went on imperturbably. "It says: 'Flowers on the cactus. Bones on the sand.'…There's your first hint. Just look around you. See that bunch of beavertail cactus over there? It's got flowers on it, hasn't it? And see those *bisnagas* over there—and over there? They've all got flowers on them. What does that mean except that it fixes the time of the year. The cactus only flowers at a certain season, doesn't it?"

"Sure—but what th' hell's that got t' do with it?" Hesfor's sullen face had lighted with a gleam of interest, but he was frankly still impatient and suspicious.

"It's got everything to do with it. Now there were some bones lying here once—on this sand. The bones most probably of the man your grandfather chained here to die. They lay hereabouts somewhere." He turned to the girl. "Do you remember seeing any bones here, Marie?" he asked. "Some scattered human bones that lay as I remember somewhere right near the base of that other big rock over there?" His eyes tried desperately to flash a message to her.

"Yes, there were some bones," the girl said slowly. "They were in a little scatter right at the side of this rock." She gestured back of her, indicating the bulk of the big rock that stood nearest to the one to which Kent was chained. "We buried them."

"Then I want you to go over there and stand right on the spot, as near as you can remember, where the bones originally lay," Kent directed. His heart, now that the girl's words had told him that she had read his hints aright, was pounding with relief and mounting hope.

"Hell, what's all this monkey business gotta do with th' loot?" Hesfor growled savagely. "I never heard tell o' no bones here."

"Then that's something you slipped up on," Kent retorted. "They *were* here, because I saw them myself when I was here about two years ago."

"I think yer lyin'," Hesfor snarled. "An' it don't sound straight. If they was th' bones o' th' old geezer what my granddad tethered out here, they'd ha' been lyin' at the base o' *this* rock… th' one here what you're hitched to." He made an irritable gesture.

"Your good old granddad shifted them—he purposely shifted the body of the man he murdered," Kent shot back. "He was figuring out his plan of laying the bearings for the treasure…Go on over there, Marie," he continued as, deterred by the menacing movement of the bullet-headed thug and by Hesfor's glowering disapproval, the girl still hesitated.

"A'right…let her go over there. Whatever this fool says. She can't do no harm," Hesfor snarled reluctantly. "What's she got t' do with it, anyways?"

"Everything," Kent snapped. He was watching the girl. "Is that the exact spot, Marie? It seems to me it was just a bit back and closer to the rock."

"Maybe it was. Yes, I think you're right." Uncertainly, then with decision as she read his eyes, the girl shifted her place. "Yes, it was here." She stood erect, waiting.

"Then you stand right there and keep standing there till I tell you to move," Kent said. "And now, Wolf," he turned again to the sullenly suspicious outlaw, "see where her shadow falls—the direction, I mean?"

"Hell!" Sudden excitement leaped into the hulking ruffian's face. "Yer mean that…?"

"No, no—not so fast!" With a gesture Kent checked the big man's words and half begun movement. "There's more to the clue than just that. What does the rest of the verse say? 'Gold in the reach of the dead man's hand.' And the other parts of the poem, the only parts that mean anything: 'Black in the shadows, white in the sun.' And farther on—the first line of the last verse: 'Over the catclaw. Under the cave.'…That's what it says. Now, Wolf, show me that old Bible—quick!"

CHAPTER 31

"Death Stands Guard..."

"**H**ere...Here y'are!" Gripped now by a sudden strange excitement, an excitement which had communicated itself to the bullet-headed man who, leaving the side of the girl, had come hurrying across to listen, Hesfor produced the tattered little volume from his shirt and jerked it open at the crude drawing of the hand. "Where is it? Where's th' stuff? Quick, damn yer—quick!"

"This is a drawing of a hand, Wolf," Kent went on calmly, ignoring utterly the others' mounting frenzy of excitement. "It is a hand with numbers over the fingers. You showed me that before you went hunting up in that little cave at the base of the hand rock which was a false lead, as it was intended to be. But these numbers over the fingers of the hand...See!—there are several of them, one over each of the four fingers. But we don't need to take notice of more than one—the number over the first finger. Your good old granddad put the others in just out of natural cussedness—or maybe to help out with his pretty picture. Anyway, they don't matter much. But the first finger—the number over the tip of the first finger is three. That stands for three o'clock— for three o'clock in the afternoon during the season of each year when the cactus is in bloom—when the sun will be in a certain position in the sky and the shadows of objects will fall in certain definite places.

"Wolf, look across the canyon. See that old dead catclaw, low down on the cliff, just a bit to the right of the door of the old tunnel? See the mouth of that shallow hole or cave a distance above it? And see that round white rock that looks something like a death's head just about midway down, between the two of them? In other words, 'Over the cat-claw, under the cave.' *There's your treasure, Wolf.* It's three o'clock now, and you see that the shadow of the first finger of Dead Man's Hand is upon that rock right now and the shadow has made the color of the rock seem to change from a sun-glared white to a blackish tint. Gold, Wolf, *there's* your gold! 'Gold in the reach of the Dead Man's Hand.'... Pry out that boulder, Wolf, and you've got it!..."

"Gawd!...Gawd A'mighty!" The words were a fevered gasp of re-alization and excitement—a choking, almost bestial greed-thick cry that broke explosively from Hesfor's thick lips, and with which the babbling, incoherent shout of his bullet-headed partner blended and blurred. "*Gawd!* Gawd A'mighty!"

With tigerish bounds, wheeling and plunging away almost before Kent could finish speaking, the pair were sprinting across the narrow span of yards which separated them from the mouth of the ancient tunnel and from the finger-shadowed rock that leered grimly, low down on the canyon wall. From the base of the cliff a narrow, ledge-like incline—narrow and difficult, but enough to give precarious foothold—led up to a point just below the ominous death head boul-der, which, as though it were the stone plug of some hole in the rock, projected almost half its thickness from the face of the cliff. And it was towards this little ledge-like incline that Hesfor and his companion were racing.

"Th' skirt! Watcher gonna do 'bout th' skirt?" as he ran, panting, the bullet-headed thug gasped the question dubiously.

"Th' hell with her!" Hesfor flung a backward glance over his shoul-der. "She can't let him loose. You got the keys in yer pocket, aint' yer?" Without pausing in his stride he shook a wild fist at the girl. "Y'stay where y'are, sister," he yelled. "If yer moves a foot I'll blow yer light out, see!" He shook savagely the rifle which, as he ran, he had unslung from his shoulder.

"Wolf!...Wolf!—the bargain!" Kent yelled. "You promised to let us loose! You promised...."

"Shut up, yer fool!" With a savage bellow that seemed to hurl back redoubled from the face of the beetling cliff the outlaw's derisive yell cut him short. "Watcher think I am—a born ijjit? Let yer loose?...Yer crazy! I ain't *never* gonna let yer loose. I'm gonna bump off th' both o' yer—an' have some fun with the gal first. Watcher think I'm...Here, feller, here"—panting, without even waiting to finish his shouted words, he broke off to bark directions to his partner—"Not that side. Get th' other side, an' get a holt on that corner...Lemme see if I can pry her some with th' gun-barrel."

Kent's heart had checked. The ruffianly pair who had scrambled up the narrow, broken ledge like maniacs were now clawing savagely at the projecting stone which, roughly round, almost eighteen inches in diameter, and marked with gruesomely suggestive natural hollows and dark blotches, seemed to leer from the cliff like some grinning skull. Panting and tugging—the bullet-headed thug on one side dragging with all his strength while Wolf Hesfor on the other levered in a crevice with his rifle-barrel—the pair were working desperately, while struggling at the same time to maintain their footing upon the narrow, crumbling ledge.

"This here's th' place!…This here's th' place right 'nough!" In a pant of breathless excitement Wolf Hesfor gasped the words. "They're a bit o' rusted wire a runnin' back inta this crack. C'mon now, feller. All t'gether!…She's a movin'! She's a movin'!…Now once more!…Now! Both t'gether!…Cmon! We'll…."

"Behind the rock, Marie!…*Get b'hind the rock!*" With a sudden frantic shout that blotted the outlaw's panting words Kent screamed the warning. "*B'hind the rock!* G'behind!…*Quick!* The cliff…."

Thunder rolled across the world—thunder in a stunning blast which, even as the girl leaped frantically to shelter behind the huge boulder beside which she stood, drove out across the canyon in a shattering avalanche of roaring sound. In one blurred glimpse—one light-swift glance as, flinging madly round on his chain, he, too, sought cowering shelter behind, his rocky pillar—it seemed to Kent that he saw the whole face of the canyon cliff sway forward and leap towards him.

Then the world seemed to slip from its fastenings. The sun went out in a roaring, crashing inferno of darkness and dust; of heaving earth and of falling, thundering stones.

CHAPTER 32

"What's Mine Is Yours"

"**M**arie!…Marie!…Where are you, Marie!" Staggering to his feet, his lungs choked and his eyes half blinded by the billowing clouds of rock dust that drove and eddied about him, Kent shouted the words hoarsely. "Where are you?…Where are you?" He heaved frenziedly upon his chain.

"Here!…Here!…"—in a breathless gasp, but clear enough to Kent's straining ears, the answer leaped back through the eddying dust. "I'm all right. I'm coming!"

And even as he heard the words he saw her figure loom up suddenly through the red, swirling haze as she came scrambling towards him across the tumbled heaps of new-fallen rock fragments. Abruptly, however, she stopped, and with a sharp, startled cry dropped to her knees, her hands fumbling at something which lay in a little hollow. A moment later she sprang to her feet.

"The keys—the keys," she gasped. "I've got the keys!…That man—Hesfor's partner—he's lying here dead…I got them from his pocket!…Oh, Rodney! Oh, God!…What has happened?…Oh, what has happened?…Oh, please…."

Already, panting, gasping excited words that were almost incoherent, she was fumbling at the padlock which held the chain about his waist. An instant later the key grated rustily. The lock jerked open and the loosened chain fell with a dull clinking thud to the ground. Kent staggered free.

"Oh, Rodney, what happened? What happened? The rocks…the whole side of the canyon…."

"The blast—it was the blast." Dust-choked, breathless and suddenly almost as unnerved and incoherent as she was, Kent gasped the words: "It was the powder cache…hid back in that cave…That was the warning—'Death stands guard with a dead man's gun.' The part of the poem that Wolf and his partner overlooked. It all came to me…came to me in a flash as I sat here watching the shadow…just before Wolf and the other man came back. Good God!…what a blast!…It must have been planted by an expert…The whole side of the cliff's fallen. Where's Wolf? He must be buried here under these rocks somewhere."

Breathlessly, in the grip of a tense excitement, he led the way out over the heaped confusion of violently hurled rock masses towards the new, raw face of the canyon wall. The dust was settling and the sun, cutting down once more with increasing brightness through the swiftly dispersing haze of explosion scattered particles, was illumining the ragged piles and ridges of debris with a hot, all-revealing light. The girl checked her scrambling steps all at once with an exclamation, and stooping caught up a curious, shattered object of wood and metal.

"It's an old-fashioned pistol—or what's left of it." Answering her unspoken question as she held it towards him, Kent took it from her fingers and examined it. "It's one that evidently used to belong to your great-grandfather. See here"—he pointed to an engraved J.J.B. still dimly visible on a section of the twisted brass-work. "Well, that clears up the final link of proof. That old poem was a literal statement of facts."

"I—I don't understand," white-faced and wide-eyed the girl was staring. "Oh, Rodney, I—I don't understand yet just what happened."

"It was a devilish and clever scheme, Marie," Kent spoke slowly, "and one that could only have been worked out by a clever and utterly villainous brain such as the original Wolf Hesfor must have had. This old pistol here is the 'dead man's gun'—your great-grandfather's gun. This is the gun that 'Death'—that skull-faced rock-stood guard over the treasure with. There was a big cache of explosives stored back in that deep natural hole, the entrance of which the skull-faced boulder closed and Hesfor had fixed some arrangement by which this old pistol, loaded and cocked, would be discharged and set off the blast whenever the skull rock was dragged out of its place by treasure-hunters. He probably had a wire or a raw-hide thong that led from the boulder to the pistol trigger. And he probably also had some means by which he could trip the trap and render it harmless in case he himself should wish to open up the cave. Didn't you hear Wolf yell something about a bit of rusted wire that was wedged in the crack at the edge of the stone?"

"But the powder—the explosive?" Her face alight with startled realization, the girl breathed the question. "Where did Hesfor get all that?"

"That must have been the property of the old miner who was the original settler in this canyon," Kent answered. "Hesfor probably murdered him to begin with."

The girl was breathing hard. Her eyes, restless and awestruck, were traveling over the heaped masses of newly shattered rock which lay along the foot of the cliff. "However did you figure it out in advance, Rodney?" she breathed. "You must have had it all figured out. You gambled on that. You turned that whole scheme to suit your purpose and save our lives—nothing else could have done it. How did you figure it out?"

"I don't know," he said soberly. "It seemed to come to me. I was watching the shadow of the finger of Dead Man's Hand travel over the cactus flowers. Then, all of a sudden, out of somewhere beyond me, almost as though someone had told me, the whole meaning of the poem leaped into my mind. I felt sure I was right. I couldn't be quite certain, of course…But I had to gamble on it. It gave me a pretty bad time with the fear that after all I might be mistaken. And with the other fear that, even if I wasn't, that perhaps—after all these years—something might have gone wrong with the trap and it mightn't work…You see, I had to bank on the explosion getting rid of Wolf and his partner."

"But where did I come in?" she asked, suddenly remembering. "You had them bring me out of the tunnel to tell you the place where the bones originally lay. And you know that wasn't the place where they were at all. And then my shadow on the sand—what had that to do with it?"

"Nothing," he said, "nothing at all. That was sheer bunk and bluff. I had to get you out here somewhere, and somewhere where you could have a reasonable chance of springing to shelter. Look where the mine tunnel used to be."

She looked, gasped and suddenly whitened. "Oh," she faltered, "so that was…."

"Sure," Kent nodded. "The powder was planted just close to that tunnel, and I saw that naturally when it went off it would blow the tunnel in. It's possible that the old miner drove that tunnel in the first place with the sole idea of finding out how the rock formation of the cliff went. He had it figured pretty carefully, because otherwise that blast wouldn't have done so much destruction. As it is, the whole face of the cliff came down."

She drew closer to him and slipped her hand into his. He felt the sudden warm pressure of her fingers—a pressure that was tight and tense and spoke more eloquently than any words could have done. Then, as suddenly, she withdrew her hand and her eyes roved swiftly over the wreckage of broken stone. "I wonder," she said slowly, "I wonder what happened to Wolf Hesfor. He must have been killed."

"He was killed all right," Kent said. "He and the other man were right in front of the blast. It was just a freak that flung that bullet-headed thug's body out where you found it. Wolf was probably blown to pieces. Come, let's look."

But their scrambling search was of short duration. A scant dozen paces and, rounding the corner of a monstrous section of solid rock that had plunged downward from the rim of the canyon above, Kent stopped dead—staring startled. Halted, stunned in his tracks.

"Wolf!...So—so that's what happened to him!" It was the girl who cried out. Her voice coming in a terrified gasp as her eyes, leaping ahead, glimpsed the grim hand—a single hand with outstretched clutching fingers which, stiff and claw-like, projected from below the lower edge of the towering, titan block of stone.

"Yes—that's what happened to Wolf," Kent said. He spoke slowly, his eyes fastened to the ground. But it was not at the grim hand of the dead and, rock-tombed outlaw that he was looking. He was looking at something else. Staring, almost incredulous, he moved forward slowly, stooping over...staring...His lips moved in a whisper, an almost inaudible whisper that seemed to come not from himself but from somewhere far, far away in the deep silence of the canyon solitudes. "Gold!" he breathed. "Gold!...'Gold in the reach of the dead man's hand'... God!...Merciful God, Marie! Look!...Look here!"

But already, her eyes fastened suddenly upon the thing that had held his own, the girl was at his side, her hands tight-gripped upon his arm as she leaned forward with him, staring—staring in stunned unbelief at the massive iron cash-box which, with partly opened lid, lay upon the litter of smashed rock chips, spilling its content of gold coins, and flashing scatter of gems mockingly about the dead clutching fingers. Staring, her voice came in a hoarse, dry whisper that was as breathless as Kent's own had been. "The treasure!" she breathed. "The treasure! Old Judge Banniston's treasure!...Oh, oh, Rodney!...We've found it!"

"Yes, we've found it!" Huskily, but pulling himself together as though the girl's voice had broken the weird spell that for a moment had gripped him, Kent spoke. "Yes, Marie, there's your treasure. The blast must have hurled the old iron box, out of the cave. It struck here against the rocks and burst the lock. But I don't think there's much spilled out of it that we won't be able to find. You're rich, Marie...rich at last! Look! Look at these gems!...Why, each one of them's worth a fortune. Look!—and look here!..." Swiftly, methodically he began to collect the scattered coins and sun-flashing stones and restore them to the battered iron strong-box.

"Not my treasure, Rodney—*our* treasure." Huskily, her voice suddenly tremulous as she dropped all at once on her knees beside him, the girl spoke: "Why, Rodney, how could you say such a thing? You—you know what I said—what I said when you were bargaining with Hesfor. What's mine is yours. Oh, oh, Rodney, did—didn't you think I meant it?"

"But—but girlie," stammering, confused, overwhelmed all at once by the light he read in her eyes, he reached his arms towards her. "You—you can't...It's not fair...I—I don't want any of—of ...."

"And—and I don't want it either, Rodney." With a choking, impulsive little cry that checked his stammering words she pushed aside his hand, scattering carelessly a sparkle of gems upon the ground. "I—I don't want the stuff—not without you. After what we've been through together I—I...Oh, Rodney, I don't want this stuff—not alone...It can stay here. If—if that's what it amounts to...."

"And I don't want it either, Marie, but I *do* want you." His voice was suddenly husky and tender as with sudden, controllable impulse he caught her in his arms and drew her face down against his cheek. "I do want you, Marie...I've wanted you from the first time I saw you. And—and now...."

They were the centre of a scatter of jewels. Locked in each other's arms, half kneeling, half sitting in the midst of a sunlit sparkle of gems and gold coins which they had forgotten utterly, they were conscious only of the pressure of each other's lips, of the glad, tumultuous throbbing of each other's hearts. A tiny stir of breeze came stealing down the canyon and rustled through the branches of the junipers far up along the cliff edge. Somewhere away up among the sunlit rocks a lone desert bird broke the silence with a faint whistling note of song. With a sudden glad intake of breath that was almost a sob of joy the girl raised her head and with a swift motion dashed the welling tears of gladness from her eyes.

"And so it's settled, Rodney," she breathed softly. "It's all...all settled...And I'm going to have my cattle ranch and everything, just like I've always dreamed. And we'll rebuild the old ranch house, the one the old Judge used to live in. And we'll stock the range and—and we'll change the name of the old ranch once more. We'll get away from that Robbery Range stuff and get back to the old Robles Ranch idea. You know, 'robles'—the Spanish word for oaks? It was originally named after the oaks that grow along the foot-hill canyons of the high sierras—away over on the south boundary of the ranch. But now we won't call it Robles Ranch either. We'll just call it The Triple R."

"The Triple R? What's that stand for, sweetheart?" He smiled at her whimsically.

"Foolish." She drew his head down to hers and kissed him. "It stands for 'Rodney's Robles Ranch.' It's just a wonderful name, and don't you ever forget it."

Once more, as he gathered her into his arms, her lips met his hungrily. And once more, as the warm stir of the breeze rustled again through the junipers, the lone, far bird woke the silence with a tiny trill of song.

THE END

South's watercolor of a bird and a nest

MARSHAL SOUTH RIDES AGAIN

Interior Photographs & Illustrations – Credits

Photographs and drawing by Marshal South were provided by the Jeri Botts estate, Christopher Cornette, Diana Lindsay, Marsha Rasmussen (Marshal South's granddaughter), Rider South (Marshal South's son), and the State Library of South Australia. Period photos are from the archives of Anza-Borrego Desert State Park and are used with permission of California State Parks.

Jeri Botts Estate: xiv (photo), 51 (South photo), 125 (South oil painting), 178 (photo), 250 (photo), 293 (South watercolor), 308 (South watercolor)

California State Parks: xxi (bottom, photo), 16 (photo), 157 (photo), 205 (photo)

Christopher Cornette Collection, Julian Historical Society: 37 (South pencil sketch), 55 (South pencil sketch), 285 (South pencil sketch), 196 (South pencil sketch)

Diana Lindsay: xxiii (photo), 6 (photo), 44 (photo of Crocker painting now privately owned), 92 (photos of South jewelry with estate of Jeri Botts), 131 (South oil painting), 255 (photo)

Marsha Rasmussen: xvii (photos), xviii (top, photo)

Rider South: iv (photo), vii (photos), xii (photos), xiii (cover photos), xvi (photo), xviii (bottom, Crocker oil painting), xix (original covers), xxi (top, South photo), xxiv (South linoleum blockprint), 2 (original book cover), 100 (South watercolor), 104 (South pencil sketch), 110 (South linoleum blockprint), 117 (South pencil sketch), 148 (South oil painting), 209 (South ink sketch), 217 (South watercolor), 225 (pencil sketch), 274 (South watercolor), 281 (South pencil sketch), 288 (South pencil sketch)

State Library of South Australia: xvi (South self-sketch)

Marshal South
and the Ghost Mountain Chronicles:
An Experiment in Primitive Living
The Complete Collection of His Writings
from *Desert Magazine*

Edited and foreword by Diana Lindsay
Introduction by Rider and Lucile South
ISBN: 9780932653666
336 pages, softcover, retail $21.95
Date of publication: 2005

For 17 years, from 1930 to 1947, poet, artist, and author Marshal South and his family lived on Ghost Mountain—a remote, waterless, windswept mountain-top in Blair Valley on the western edge of the Colorado Desert, now part of the Anza-Borrego Desert State Park. Over a period of nine of those years, South chronicled his family's contro-versial primitive and natural lifestyle through monthly articles written for *Desert Magazine*. His articles were the reality entertainment of the day—a sort of early version of Survivor with thousands of readers awaiting the next installment.

South wrote with lyric quality, painting word pictures that only a poet or artist could. He wrote with passion about the desert, its beauty and natural history, the desert's healthful qualities, its silence and beauty, and he praised its early inhabitants and their lifestyle. He advocated a return to simplicity and a close relationship with nature.

Now for the first time the real story of Marshal South is fully explored and revealed in this captivating story that separates myth from facts.

Published by:
SUNBELT PUBLICATIONS
1256 Fayette Street
El Cajon, CA 92020
619-258-4911
www.sunbeltbooks.com

SUNBELT'S DESERT BOOKSHELF

Recommendations for readers of *Marshal South Rides Again*

About Sunbelt Publications

Incorporated in 1988, with roots in publishing since 1973, Sunbelt Publications produces and distributes natural science and outdoor guidebooks, regional histories and pictorials, and stories that celebrate the land and its people. Sunbelt books help to discover and conserve the natural, historical, and cultural heritage of unique regions on the frontiers of adventure and learning. Our books guide readers into distinctive communities and special places, both natural and man-made.

Visit us online to see all of our regional books
www.sunbeltbooks.com